To Destroy Jerusalem

By Howard Kaplan

Also by Howard Kaplan

The Spy's Gamble
The Damascus Cover
Bullets of Palestine
The Chopin Express

ISBN: 978-1723912351

IN MEMORY OF MY NUMEROUS FAMILY MEMBERS KILLED IN THE HOLOCAUST

CHAPTER 1

May 3

In Memorial Sloan Kettering Cancer Center in Manhattan, a tall, skinny, freckled twenty-three-year-old strode down a basement corridor fingering the stiletto in his pocket. A little after 6:00 p.m., the fluorescent-bathed corridors were empty and his tennis shoes squeaked on the floor. He had been here the night before, spotted the short brunette, and watched her walk past him on her way to the elevators while he stood around the corner by the emergency exit door. He had wanted to grab her then but there was some white coat nearby and he had bolted.

Heart sounding in his ears, he approached the emergency exit, twisted the knob with a damp hand, shoved the heavy fire door open and tensed. No alarms sounded. He darted into the stale, concrete, high-ceilinged stairwell and leaned back against the wall. His eyes flicked one flight up to the emergency way out to 72nd Street. An alarm would blare as he barreled through that door, but by then it would not matter. He hit his head back against the wall, the small thumps echoing in the quiet. The tension was so tight he had to pound it out. He removed the stiletto and peered through the crack in the door at the corridor. He ran the sharp blade across his wrist repeatedly in fascination, feeling the tickle of the steel, but did not draw blood.

In her office, Joan Reynolds tied her dark hair in a small ponytail off her neck before venturing into the unseasonable heat outside. She had worked at Sloan Kettering for three years, since graduating with a medical physics masters from Georgia Tech in 1988. She thrilled at calibrating the linear accelerator that produced radioactive photons that destroyed cancerous tissue. Joan had come to Manhattan to prove to herself that she was fine on her own, without her wealthy Atlanta parents hovering over her every move, and in the last few months was finally feeling confident.

Sitting behind her desk, she slipped off her black pumps, pulled her sneakers from the plastic D'Agostino's bag and laced them on for the walk to the subway. She had a date tonight with Steve Terrell, her sculptor boyfriend. In her mind she sorted through the possible outfits she might wear. She was leaning toward her short red skirt with a red and white checked blouse, obviously no pantyhose and white flats. She had battled away ten pounds earlier that year in her frustrating struggle with junk food. Now, at five foot three, one hundred fourteen pounds and with generous breasts, she knew she looked fabulous. She pictured Steve working in his torn jeans and clay-splattered sweatshirt and bounced happily to her feet.

Joan took a small key from her pocket, unlocked the top drawer of her file cabinet and grabbed her purse. She slung it over her shoulder, extinguished the lights, and headed into the basement corridor.

The skinny youth heard footfalls in the quiet from around the corner, the direction of her office. He quickly slapped the stiletto into his left hand, wiped his right hand on his jeans and felt a sweat bead at the base of his hair. "She better not scream," he mumbled between trembling breaths.

To Joan's disappointment, she only saw Steve two nights a week because of his schedule at the Metropolitan Cafe in the Village, where he carried trendy plates. Struggling for five years, he had sold only a few pieces and sometimes she wanted to wrap her arms around him to heal his hurt. Tonight they were heading for Cuban food at some funky place he wanted to show her near the East River. This was the best relationship she had ever been in. He knew what he was feeling, expressed it, and encouraged her to open up more, which was hard for her, but she felt terrific when she finally unleashed inadequacies.

She heard footsteps behind her. She started to turn and terror raced through her as a man's hand clamped over her mouth and his other hand grabbed around her waist and tugged her backward. She screamed soundlessly against the muzzle, clawed, bit the inside of his hand. He squeezed so hard she thought her jaw would shatter and, her whole body shaking, she stopped fighting as he dragged her into the stairwell. The door to the corridor shut with a heavy click.

He dropped her hard on the concrete on her back, his fingers gone from her mouth. Stiletto in hand, he pressed the blade against the skin at her throat and straddled her on both knees. "Just don't scream," he said, wild eyes inches from her face, breath foul.

Terror reached every part of her. "Please don't."

His free hand ripped the front of her blouse; the buttons popped off and the material tore. Crying, she tried to squirm away. He roughly pushed her bra and breast, riveting her to the ground, pulled the bra up and sliced the material between the cups. He fondled one bare breast with calloused fingers as his other hand stuck the point back to her throat. She felt it pushing into her skin and choked. Teats glistened down her cheeks. She squeezed her eyes shut and slowly spread her legs.

"Just don't kill me," she said.

"Shut up_and you'll live."

He touched the other breast, then moved down to her legs, the blade coming away from her throat. He threw up her skirt.

She felt a rough hand on the inside of her thighs. He would kill her afterward, she just knew it. Abruptly, she kneed him in his groin with all her strength. A surprised grunt of pain escaped him. She kicked her left leg up hard at his right arm, caught the wrist and sent the stiletto flying up the steps. She screamed wildly, the sound reverberating, and scratched at his face, feeling blood under her nails and then the pain as he slapped her face hard.

She punched him directly in his eye. He jumped off her and

grabbed her purse from the landing, then he ran up the stairs, retrieved the stiletto. She tried to get up to run but couldn't, screamed and he hesitated and dashed for the door. In a daze, she watched him reach the emergency exit, and then he was through it. An alarm reverberated in the high closed space, going through her, and she lay there, still, not believing that he was gone. She squeezed her eyes.

What felt like an eternity passed. No one came. Finally, she pulled herself into a sitting position and wrapped her arms around her legs and folded her head on her knees. The clanging alarm echoed in her ears.

Anger began to rise slowly, then ballooned inside her at the crime and this city and women's helplessness. Since she was not hurt and he would be far away now, she decided her first priority was to hurry home and cancel her credit cards. She wiped her cheeks with the back of her hand. She only had twenty dollars in cash in her purse, nothing else of value, but she was goddamn not going to let him run up charges on her cards even if she wouldn't have to pay them.

Joan struggled to her feet, tried to cover her chest with the torn blouse. Shaking, she headed defiantly back into the corridor. She had a sweater in her office, several subway tokens in her desk, and the super could let her into her place.

An hour later, Joan took a cab alone from her apartment to the police station to file a report. Steve was not home so she had left a rambling message on his machine. While the taxi alternately raced and slowed in traffic, she trembled, her fingers laced on one knee. She felt his hand on the inside of her thighs. Suddenly, she felt like she had to throw up, so wound the window farther down and let the warm air strike her.

The officer who took Joan's complaint told her that since she had neither been raped nor injured there was really little they could do. She flashed furious.

Back at her apartment, Steve was waiting on the stoop. They sat on the sofa and he held both her small hands in his. She looked up at his deep, piercing, blue eyes, confident and concerned but it didn't help. "I'm supposed to take a shower now to wash him off me. I've seen all the TV movies." Her voice was loud. "He could have killed me cause I kicked him. What if I'd been wrong?"

"You weren't. You were terrific."

She nodded, then tears sprang to her eyes. "I'd like someone to strangle that asshole."

They ate delivered Chinese, though Joan mostly brushed her food around her plate. She showered then they watched *Key Largo*, her head on his thigh, her legs pulled up near her body. She had faith he would become a success and could be happy even if he never broke through.

He watched her more than the film. Twice in recent years he had been with women who loved him, but after a while drifted away. Painfully, he knew if he was having shows in the major galleries both of them would have stayed.

A little before 10:00 p.m. the phone rang and she bolted up as if it had been a shot. The police officer on the other end informed her that a purse with her library card in it had been discovered on the floor of a diner on 110th street. The money, driver's license and credit cards were missing but other personal effects, her keys and the empty wallet, had been found. They immediately took a cab to the precinct station on 86th Street. After signing paperwork and retrieving her belongings, they returned to her apartment.

Joan was exhausted so they slipped into bed. It was too hot for blankets and she was grateful to lie under the sheet with her back against him and his arms around her. She felt vulnerable and frightened and angry and lucky all together. In the silence, she felt Steve kiss the back of her neck and draw her closer which helped.

Long afterwards, with her pillow hugged to her breasts, Joan sensed the rhythm of his chest against her skin as he slept. Restless, she thought about getting some Sara Lee banana cake from the freezer and eating the icing off it. She closed her eyes, felt that blade at her throat, and jumped. Steve continued to snore. She wanted to wake him, knew he would not mind, but decided not to. She pushed her head into the pillow and tears rolled down her face. She looked frequently at the digital clock, her last sighting 3:12 before she drifted off.

Earlier that evening on 72nd Street, Kenneth Khalidi of Dearborn, Michigan, sat behind the wheel of a rented Chevrolet, its rear license plate obscured with mud. A second man, Palestinian Abu Uthman, was in the passenger seat and held a Walther PPK below the sweater on his lap. As they waited, motor idling, Khalidi, a new assistant professor of physics at UCLA, was amazed he felt none of his normal nervousness now that there was real danger. He glanced at the veteran Palestinian fighter beside him. He did not need him, could execute this on his own.

The skinny, freckled youth emerged running from the side of the hospital, an alarm following him. In seconds he was inside the back seat.

"Floor the motherfucker," the kid said as he slammed the door.

Khalidi carefully eased away from the curb and drove uptown, where he had earlier that week made the young man's acquaintance on a basketball court on 98th Street. As Khalidi drove at precisely the speed limit, the freckled boy ransacked the purse to determine whether it held more than the thousand dollars cash he had been offered to swipe it.

Watching him in the rearview mirror, Khalidi was concerned about the identifying scratches on his face but said, "I would appreciate if you would please hand my associate the purse."

The youth bent forward over the seat, purse in one hand, credit cards in the other fanned like a poker play. He noticed the Arab's slim hands on the wheel: no rings, some cheap watch. He had seen the other Arab for the first time on the drive down and he was obviously the muscle.

"Hey, you want these cards? Nothing motherfucking else here."

"Please hand me the purse and the wallet, with the cards," Khalidi said quietly.

The kid dropped the purse and the cards onto the muscle's lap.

"Thank you."

Khalidi slowed to catch a red light. Stopped at the signal, he ran his long fingers through the wallet and found a New York City

Public Library card in it. It read Joan Reynolds and gave her address. He nodded with pleasure. Then he looked at the kid's scratches in the rearview. "Please tell me what happened."

"No sweat. It was the chick in the picture you laid on me. Just like yesterday. Only she was alone. I dragged her into the stairwell, touched her a bit like you said. Tits felt real smooth, like a baby's ass."

"I instructed you to be careful with her. Did you in any way hurt her?"

"Nah."

As the light changed, Khalidi pulled across the traffic to the right curb and stopped. He felt inside the purse for a moment, then reached in his shirt pocket, withdrew eight hundred-dollar bills and handed them toward the rear, where they were immediately snatched from his fingers. Khalidi had given him two in advance.

The kid could not figure these fucking Arabs out. Maybe they just had more money than God. He leaned over the seat again toward the driver. "Hey, why so many Franklins for a purse that don't have dick in it?"

"I do not believe that is any of your concern." Khalidi's voice had risen.

"All right, all right, don't climb out of your pants. Listen, you got anything else coming down I can tell you where to find me." The money had disappeared.

"Thank you. I do not believe your services will be required again. I trust this is a convenient place to leave you?"

"This whole place's a sewer. Where don't matter shit." He climbed out, then turned and saluted them as he walked up the street.

Khalidi checked the traffic carefully before he pulled out. He would cut up the credit cards and dispose of them later. He had not wanted the youth arrested using them and recounting his story. He drove toward a key duplicating shop he knew not far from Columbia University.

Before dawn in Jerusalem, wearing only his pants while exhaustedly dragging a blade across his whiskers, Shai Shaham glanced up in the mirror. He saw Tami, his younger wife by twenty-two years, staring at him when she thought he was not looking, worry bright in her eyes. She was dropping weight, and it was as if the pounds flew off her and onto him. He had indications of Palestinian terrorists readying to blow up American servicemen in Frankfurt in retaliation for the Gulf War and was off again on the 8:00 a.m. flight.

"I'm going to lose weight soon, absolutely," he told her with enthusiasm, without looking back from the mirror as he stroked the blade rapidly.

She neared, her voice just above a whisper. "Well, you won't need a new pair of tennis shoes since you've used yours so little."

Six months ago his doctor had dispatched Shai to a cardiologist at Hadassah Hospital, who, after his examination, threatened to not treat Shai unless he began to take better care of himself.

Shaken, the following morning Shai had started out early, drove to Mount Scopus and fast-walked for an hour around the Jerusalem hills and through the Arab village of Sheikh Jarrah. He had friends there, which only worried Tami more with the Palestinians knifing lone men in the city, or more recently four women at a bus stop. "They're here, we're here, neither of us are going away and we have to find a way to live together," he told her which to her surprise had calmed her. She realized it was the hope. Shai kept up his early morning strides for two weeks, until an agent missing in France sent him hustling to Paris. He had left the tennis shoes behind in his closet and had not laced them on since.

The taxi honked in the darkness outside. As he stood clutching his battered bag, he felt the intermittent pain fizzle in his chest but he allowed it no voice on his face.

"I'll watch myself, promise."

"For lunch why not have a yogurt. You know how long those Russians live."

He forced a smile, was very concerned about her.

She looked away, could near bear the exhaustion on his face. Every moment he was out there she was terrified he would either drive himself into heart failure or be caught by a bullet, as he had some years before in Rome just before they were married. The Palestinian Ramzy Awwad had saved his life there. She had tried to mask how frantic she was these last months, did not want that burden on him too, and was upset she was not controlling herself better now.

"While you're gone, I'm going to start taking a night class," she said, forcing cheer into her tone. "The conflict through Arabic and Israeli fiction. To see how the Palestinians feel." She brought her eyes to him. "We're going to be reading some of Ramzy's stories, in English."

"Terrific. Just don't tell Carmon, or he'll have me in the Teheran marketplace—selling Israeli flags."

She circled both arms around her husband, hugged him, and he felt her thick, dark hair wonderfully in his face. Tami worked as Meir Carmon's girl Friday, which was how they had met. The Service high prelate, who had vaulted to his position late in life, had inherited Shai the way a belated groom is saddled with unruly stepchildren. Carmon could not bear Shai's "coddling" the Palestinians and his friendship with the likes of their terrorist-writer Ramzy Awwad, but Shai's record was too impressive for Carmon to dislodge him on mere loathing.

The weariness weighed on Shai as he stood at the entrance to their apartment holding her, his case heavy in his hand. He inhaled the unwashed fragrance of her neck and, his face hidden from her, squeezed his eyes shut and kissed and tasted her skin. Then he hurried outside to extract himself from emotions he could not step into now.

As soon as his taxi was out of sight, Tami flipped on all the lights then switched on everything that made noise: the mixer, dishwasher, television, stereo, a fan. Not knowing what to do with herself, she headed into the bathroom and turned on her hair dryer too and left it running on the sink. Twisting her hair tightly, in the cacophony she sat on the living room floor.

Descending the mountains in the cold taxi, the pines like an army of sentinels in the dark, Shai dozed restlessly, the taste of Tami still on his lips. He dreamed they were under the blankets, the children they did not have bouncing on the bed to wake them late on a sun-swept morning. Then Tami's face dissolved into his first wife Sarit's, who'd been infertile when he so wanted children. As the taxi burst free of the mountains and accelerated between the flat kibbutz fields, he awoke abruptly, feeling guilty about her death.

In the darkness, he watched the small, green cotton plants flash by the window. After his near-fatal shooting in Rome and the serious heart rumblings, if he died soon he did not want Tami saddled with a small infant, or infants, in a society with so many single women due to interminable war death. Without children, she would stand a far better chance to find someone, and she would, the way he had discovered her after Sarit's terrible accident.

It amazed Shai how quickly his view of life had changed with his deteriorating health. When he had married Tami, the future had seemed far lengthier than the past. Now, he was with difficulty moving toward the decision to divorce her and free her for a life with a younger, healthier man, one who would sleep beside her more than occasionally and offer the family she needed. A heavy sadness rolled over him and he sank back into the seat beneath it.

Physically Shai was very strong, and despite his height and considerable girth, he eased agilely through the crowds in the departure terminal. He wore a solid blue shirt he'd yanked off a New York discount rack, and inexpensive pants of an approximately khaki color he'd bought in a hurry, which was the only way he moved. On the outer cliff of middle age, his thinning brown hair had crept back from his creased forehead and was shot through with gray. His face was anything but handsome, with a nose too large and small, irrepressibly blue eyes that more often than not were veined from avoidance of sleep. "I heard that ninety percent of people die in bed, so I spend as little time there as possible," he often said. Those concerned about his health, which was everybody, were little amused.

Winging toward Frankfurt, Shai inhaled the airplane meal and, trying to rise from his deepening melancholy, listened to a suite for flute and jazz piano full bore. The only jealousy Shai knew was for what these musicians could improvise.

His spirits lifted, he prowled the aisles and struck up conversation with a young sabra couple, who were prospering in Berlin in plumbing. Where earlier he would have mounted passionate argument for their return to Israel, he asked if they were involved with the Jewish community there. Plagued by this relentless war, Israelis were moving abroad in droves, and he wanted them to survive as Jews. After two generations the Israeliness would wane and their children assimilate if not connected to the Jewish people where they were and Israelis abroad were clannish. He edged in with the same folksy, friendly chatter that was the hallmark of his interrogations, tapes of which Carmon's predecessor, The Colonel, had instituted into their training programs. Carmon had replaced them with lectures by psychologists, but the tapes could still be checked out by trainees and veterans if requested.

Soon, Shai tiredly removed a blanket from the overhead compartment, dropped down in his seat and looked out the small window at the Greek Islands below in the glistening sea. Shai pulled the thin blanket around him. Eager to arrive, he closed his eyes to try and rest but his mind would not stop. A stewardess rolled a cart in the aisle and the man beside Shai ordered two tiny bottles of red wine, said it always helped him sleep. Shai smiled, but beneath it remembered how three decades ago at the Hebrew University, after an American girlfriend had returned to the States from her year abroad, he had spent the following year drunk on cheap cognac. Shai was not known to take half measures, and after emerging from that interminable stupor, he had not on a single occasion since had even a glass of wine. At religious ceremonies he had grape juice. He ordered a Coke, then thinking of Tami, quickly switched to sparkling water.

Khalidi had a gun in his pocket as he walked down the Memorial Sloan Kettering basement corridor beside Abu Uthman. With the 8:00 p.m. moon bathing the hot sidewalk outside, Khalidi had quickly and uncomfortably pushed the small weapon into his white doctor's jacket, which had been provided by his companion along with stethoscopes. "The weapons are only for emergencies," Abu Uthman had warned in soft Arabic.

Khalidi had nodded then continued in silence, but just before the main entrance he turned to Abu Uthman. "Though your presence is not necessary here I want to thank you for helping me."

With copies of Joan Reynolds's keys in his pocket, Khalidi led Abu Uthman toward the lower level. Radiation therapy departments always stretched across hospital basements, hugging the earth as a shield. There should be no one in the hot lab. What time to attempt the break-in had been of paramount consideration to Khalidi. Only on the rarest occasions would a hospital perform radiation therapy at night. Khalidi did not want to enter too late, however, when an unusual face might be remembered.

Khalidi carried a doctor's black medical bag containing a heavy boron and lead pig to store the Californium-252 he required. He felt incredibly fortunate his life had changed so completely, and feared not that he might be killed, but only that with failure he would be swept back to his former existence.

He had walked through the corridor during the day, passed by Joan's office twice before he found her at her desk, then had photographed her from across the street with a telephoto lens. He hoped the purse had been returned to her but even if it had not and she had reported the loss of the keys to the radiation safety officer, it was virtually assured they had not replaced the hot lab safe or the door lock. The isotopes utilized in medicine were weak and of no value to anyone outside the hospital. The safe was secured only for radiation safety purposes—all the more reason the attack in the stairwell would deflect attention from her keys.

He had learned at the UCLA biomedical library that only four research hospitals in the world experimented with a neutron source, specifically Californium-252: Fox Chase Cancer Center in Philadelphia, MD Anderson Cancer Center in Houston, Churchill Hospital in England, and Memorial Sloan Kettering. He had selected Sloan Kettering for the break-in because as a doctoral student at Columbia University he had done research here, knew the exact location of the hot lab, and would not have to waste time searching for it.

Silently, Khalidi led Abu Uthman around the corner. The door to the Block Cutting Lab, like many they had seen in the radiation therapy unit, bore a plastic plaque with a small white rectangle inside a red circle, like the warning sign of wrong way entrance onto a freeway, and red lettering that read: AUTHORIZED PERSONNEL ONLY. He listened. There were no sounds inside and no light beneath the door. Both men slipped on rubber gloves. Abu Uthman, who had once narrowly survived an aerial assault on a Palestinian base east of Sidon and bore a scar across his cheek, slipped his fingers around the gun in his coat.

Khalidi inserted a key in the locked door and opened it. The two men stepped in and in the darkness Khalidi eased the door closed. Out of the openness of the corridor and in his work environment, Khalidi felt more confident. Abu Uthman produced a thin flashlight from his jacket pocket and the beam danced around the room and alighted on a pile of Styrofoam blocks on the long narrow cutting saw, then jumped to a counter and sink with the melting alloy dispenser that looked like a large, fat coffee pot. Molds were cut from the Styrofoam and the heavy liquid alloy poured in to form the precise shape to place against the body and block the organs the physician did not want irradiated.

Khalidi guided Abu Uthman's beam toward a wood door beyond the dispenser and relief dropped through him as he saw the yellow sign with bold magenta lettering that read: CAUTION, RADIOACTIVE MATERIALS.

"There?" Abu Uthman asked in Arabic.

"Yes, precisely."

Abu Uthman brought the thin beam to the knob. Khalidi fingered the two simple Schlage keys, slipped the first in the lock and twisted. Nothing. He tried the second, turned it and the door moved. They stepped into a small, dark room. Across from them stretched a counter, almost like in a kitchen, with wood cabinets above and below it. Abu Uthman's light stopped on another yellow, magenta-lettered sign cautioning radioactive material behind it. Several pairs of large, foot-long forceps had sloppily been left beside the small safe.

Khalidi crossed quickly to where the sign was taped to a two-foot high lead block. He switched on a lamp with a round tube bulb and it flickered for a second with a buzz and then flooded the small room. Khalidi pulled the long metal arm of the lamp and, his hand shaking, pointed it at the map taped to the wood cabinet above the counter that gave the location and color codes of the sources in the safe drawers. He wiped his hand on his white coat. The map indicated that Californium-252 was stored in the lower left of the four drawers, with a green dot atop the vial. The map pointed users quickly to the location of each source to minimize exposure. Since neutron sources were cumbersome to handle and a nightmare in terms of radiation safety, few research centers had experimented with placing them in tissue or cavities for attacking tumors. Gamma-producing isotopes were cheaper, equally effective and posed far less hazard to the handler.

Khalidi pulled the fluorescent light down to illuminate the safe, pushed the key in and opened it.

At the same time, on the second-floor oncology ward Dr. Robert Geller, a radiation oncologist, walked into his patient's room with Joan Reynolds. Joan was pushing a cart with a heavy lead pig on it.

"Hello, Mrs. Markstein," Dr. Geller said with a smile to the middle-aged woman in the bed. "This is my physicist, Joan Reynolds. Joan's going to remove the cesium sources then I'm going to get the applicator right out of you."

Under mild sedation, Mrs. Markstein nodded.

Seventy-two hours before in the operating theater, Joan had placed the five, two-centimeter cesium sources into the applicator. Then, Geller had inserted the long tube-like Fletcher-Suit loading applicator into the patient's uterus and packed it tightly in place with gauze.

Geller had had a parent-teacher conference at his younger daughter Lindsay's school earlier in the evening and had timed the implant removal so he would not have to miss it. Geller drew back the bedding and, as Joan approached Mrs. Markstein, sat in the chair beside her. "I know this has been uncomfortable, but everything went extremely well."

The room was specially shielded with lead in the walls, floor and ceiling. Joan pulled the source holder from the tube and placed the cesium inside the heavy pig and closed the lid.

Geller rose and looked at Joan. He knew about the attack in the stairwell and had been hesitant to ask her to stay. "Thanks for staying late."

She nodded. She was still not sleeping well and Steve was coming over late after the restaurant every night. "I'm better if I'm busy."

Geller smiled.

Normally Joan replaced the radioactive sources in the hot lab immediately, then returned to do the exiting room survey. But she did not want to go down there alone. "I'll just do the room survey now. "

"Sure."

Joan pushed the cart into the hall to remove all radiation from the room. As Geller unpacked the gauze around the long tubes, Joan unhooked a probe attached by a coiled telephone-like cord to the Geiger counter. She began surveying the area to guarantee no sources had been left either inside the patient or the room. She saw tiny fluctuations on the lowest scale.

"Everything's fine," she said. "No readings above background." She filled out a form indicating the room was clean, signed it and set it on Geller's chair.

Mrs. Markstein gave a small cry of pain. He had the applicator out now. "Great, Joan. Thanks again."

Joan headed outside. Though the empty hallway had never bothered her before, now it seemed frighteningly quiet. She remembered that hand on her mouth. She could feel it dragging her into the stairwell. She leaned back against the wall, crossed one foot over the other. She was furious that he had made her afraid to go into her hot lab, thought about defiantly going downstairs alone. She waited for Geller.

Some minutes later he came out. Geller saw the fear in her face, her tight posture, and approached.

"Will you walk me to the hot lab?" she said.

"Of course. I should have thought of it myself. And then I'm going to put you in a cab. The fare's on me."

She did not like others taking care of her. "You don't have to do that."

"No, but it will make me feel better. Let's go."

Khalidi stood in front of the small steel safe calmed by the precise work. Often nervousness ran through him like a river, especially when he was not occupied, and was why he had stomach problems. There was an open gap as a work area between the safe and the lead shield near him. He had already placed the boron and lead pig and small glass vial with inert isotopes in the work area. Khalidi looked through thick, yellow, leaded glass.

He unscrewed the top of the cylinder. The Californium-252 was probably not used much, and a typical medical physicist only checked the decay of their sources once every six months. It would likely be quite a while before anyone noticed the Californium-252 missing.

Using forceps, Khalidi grasped the handle on the lower left drawer. He required only a gram. The glass vials were dropped in holes with only the color coded caps protruding. In the back row he immediately saw the green dot. Khalidi lifted the vial with the forceps and brought it toward him and near the leaded glass shield.

He turned the small glass vial in the forceps' jaws. Californium-252 had a half-life of only 2.6 years and he had to be certain he had a batch that would remain hot for another six weeks. The date confirmed that he did. He shook it and dozens of the sources, which looked like tiny lead-colored seeds, jumped in the vial.

"You have what you need?" Abu Uthman asked nervously. He preferred danger he could see.

"Yes, it is exactly as I thought."

Khalidi lowered the vial beside the pig. Using forceps in both hands, he held the vial with one pair of forceps and expertly peeled the green dot from the cap with the other. He set the vial into the waiting pig. With forceps still in both hands, he fastened the green dot to the vial of inert seeds he had brought. He had hoped to be able to switch caps, but he could see the vials were of slightly different size. Khalidi replaced the slightly smaller vial in the space and looked through the glass again. He did not think it would be noticed.

Then he heard a sound—the outer corridor door opening and voices, a man's and a woman's, loud in the silence. Fear bolted through him.

Joan wheeled the cart with the heavy pig into the Block Cutting Lab. "So tell me already." She flipped on the light. "What'd the teacher say about Lindsay?"

"It was just an unbelievable conference," Geller said. "The teacher said she's a pleasure to have in the class, a leader, well liked, that's she's progressed beautifully in her reading, and that all her skills are above where they're supposed to be for a first grader. She said she didn't like to use the word, but Lindsay's the perfect_child to have in a class. I feel foolish repeating this, but here I am."

"I was that kind of first grader too. If she's anything like me, you have some surprises coming when she's around fourteen and suddenly hates being perfect." Joan slipped the key in the hot lab door and thought about how she wanted to have children soon, but still work full time. With Steve's schedule, it would be easier.

Inside, Joan was surprised the light was on, and then shocked to see two white-coated physicians she did not recognize and who looked foreign. One was pushing the safe door closed with forceps. Joan knew everybody in the hospital who was authorized to use the safe.

"Who the hell are you?"

Khalidi recognized her and panicked. Then he remembered she had not seen him before and fought to calm himself. "I am a doctoral student at Columbia," Khalidi said, his accent authentically mid-western. "I'm doing an experiment upstairs, placing iridium in rats. Dr. Bernard Forsyth gave me a key." He used the name of the head of the department he had seen on a doorway. Khalidi brought his eyes noticeably to Joan's body badge that registered radiation. "I presume you are one of the medical physicists?"

"That's right, and he didn't say anything to me about it and there was no memo."

"Well that must be annoying."

"You bet it is."

Geller was silent. This was yet another Sloan Kettering bureaucratic snafu and he was anxious to hurry home.

Khalidi forced a smile as he closed the safe, thinking rapidly. He could get away with the Californium-252 but they could identify him. Once it was determined Dr. Forsyth had not authorized him to remove anything she would search the drawers. They would tie the missing Californium-252 to Mediterranean types, and the authorities would raise Arabs as the most likely possibility.

"I want your names," Joan said.

Abu Uthman was quiet. His heavy accent would betray him. Khalidi lifted the heavy pig and placed it in his black bag on the floor, the old nervousness running through him. "My name is Barry Calivari and this is Armondo Bonasera."

Khalidi closed the bag with his left hand and forced his right into his coat pocket, grasped the gun handle fiercely. Why did they have to come now? He did not want to kill them, but the Americans would alert the Israelis who would plummet onto his trail like hawks. His legs felt weak. If he did not kill them, his whole plan might be over before it started. Khalidi pulled out the pistol and pointed it.

"*Kuss ommak,*" Abu Uthman swore.

Geller was near the door. Khalidi aimed the gun at him but, his hand shaking, could not pull the trigger. Geller ran and Abu Uthman fired twice, hitting him in the head and mid-back, the force propelling him forward to the ground, blood flooding the floor. Joan ran for the door. Khalidi pulled off two rapid shots, both slamming hard into her chest. She crumpled, blood leaking from her.

"Outside," Abu Uthman said.

They moved quickly into the Block Cutting Room. The corridor door was closed. Abu Uthman opened it slightly, peeked out. It was clear. He replaced his gun in his coat and motioned Khalidi to do the same. Khalidi followed, dazed, as if this was happening to someone else and he was watching it.

As they entered the hallway and saw no one, Abu Uthman headed for the emergency door, preferring an alarm to being noticed walking through the hospital.

They came out directly into the swelter of 72nd Street, Khalidi carrying the heavy medical bag. Alarm clanging behind them, they walked hurriedly up the vacant sidewalk to where their car was parked. The driver behind the wheel started the motor. A taxi passed them on the street, music blaring through open windows. As they climbed into the rented Chevrolet, which jerked away from the curb, Abu Uthman looked from the back seat to see if anyone on the sidewalk was watching. The street was dark and empty, bathed only in puddles of light from the lamps.

As the car sped around the corner, Khalidi leaned back in the front seat. His face was burning and each breath caught in his chest. This was for a great cause, for freedom for his people. He looked down. The nervousness tugged at him.

Abu Uthman said, “You were right about killing them. When they discover the missing Californium, now the authorities will not know who took it. They will not be able to tie it to you, or any Palestinians.”

CHAPTER 2

May 11

Under the glare below heavy white clouds that filled the Manhattan sky, the humidity soaked Shai's shirt as he barreled down University Place. Shai arrived early in the square, concrete park that occupied a city block. Sounds of steel drums rose from an Afro-American trio. A mumbling woman fed a flock of pigeons. A vender hawked hot dogs. Joggers, some with earphones, panted along the sidewalk periphery of the park. A smile spread across Shai's face. He loved the mayhem of New York, the cramming of so much optimism into so small a space. America looked to the future. In the Middle East, past entitlement threatened to bury the present.

Shai's smile widened further as he saw Paul McEnnerney emerge from the heart of the park. Paul rode the always-bucking CIA Middle East desk. Mid-thirties, tall, with stylish short blond hair and smooth skin that hid a half dozen years, McEnnerney wore white linen pants, loafers, and a white linen, short sleeve shirt. Vuarnet sunglasses shielded his eyes. Americans believed image was everything, but Shai knew image was preposterous. Besides, he could be any persona the role required.

Shai affected a grave air as McEnnerney approached. "I haven't received an invitation yet," he said.

Though Shai regularly greeted him this way, McEnnerney still laughed. "I suspect it's connected to the fact there's no wedding."

"I was hoping it was the Israeli mail. What happened, you break up with somebody again?"

"The regular. Passion, Illusions, then finally they see that I'm a boy in a man's skin." McEnnerney smiled. "Then again I don't much try and hide it."

Shai was an older brother figure to McEnnerney, who had one very insecure and correspondingly self-righteous younger sister. McEnnerney boasted to colleagues but confided in Shai.

Shai frowned disappointed, though he liked that McEnnerney lived without self-deception. Shai threw his large arm around Paul's shoulder. "So how are you, McEnnerney?"

"No complaints. Most people spend their days actually working."

They began to walk through the grassless park. Leafy trees sprouted alongside the blacktop walkways, which were spotted everywhere from the flapping and cooing pigeons.

"Everybody's talking about Frankfurt," McEnnerney said. "You've made yourself some new buddies in DC."

His people had had the assassins under lock and key; all Shai had done was some sweeping up. "Unlike a lot of people, we Israelis can always use more friends."

"It's official today, on the record," McEnnerney said.

Shai nodded and unconsciously picked up his pace.

"We have bad news and worse news."

"The usual." Shai sighed, more to himself than McEnnerney.

"Memorial Sloan Kettering here in Manhattan. Five days ago. A physician and a medical physicist are working late. They go to return some very innocuous isotopes they've removed from a patient. Apparently the woman was attacked in the stairwell three days before and presumably doesn't want to venture to the basement alone at that hour. Outside the safe with the isotopes, they're shot, two slugs each. Both with Walter PPKs but different weapons, if you're interested."

"I'm always interested."

"Here's the deal. A janitor calls the emergency room. The doctor's DOA but the woman is rushed into surgery and miraculously makes it, which is how we know what we know."

"The janitor saw nothing I presume."

"You want two witnesses?"

"Actually, I'm surprised we have one." Shai stopped across from the swings, hinges squealing as children rose above the blacktop. He pocketed his hands. "There's nothing very powerful used in radiation therapy."

"No, there isn't," McEnnerney said, wondering how he knew that. "The safe was locked. At first glance, looks like nothing's missing. Then, at our urging, the head medical physicist takes a closer peek."

Shai gazed away, a greater distance in his eyes. "Something was taken."

"That's why you're here."

Shai watched a middle-aged man in a suit and tie who looked like a lunching banker eat a flawless banana while he ransacked a wire trash can and lifted empty bottles into an upscale Balducci's market bag. Shai could not grasp whether the man was eccentrically rich or dashingly poor. The breadth of America; he loved it. Shai returned his attention to McEnnerney and waited.

"Californium two-fifty-two," McEnnerney said. "They took a miniscule amount, a little more than a gram. It's a neutron source."

"The chapter and verse on that?"

McEnnerney had three-quarters expected him to know. "The medical physicist at Sloan Kettering went over it with me and then I double-checked with our boys. A neutron source is radioactive but it has few possible uses. Certain neutron sources could contaminate a region, a car or a house and do some death. If you had a neutron source and, say, stuck it in someone's chair, over a period of time they would die and nothing would show on the autopsy. It would look like death by aplastic anemia. So I thought, maybe we're looking at somebody who wants to plan a fancy killing and not get caught."

"For about two seconds you did."

"A bit more, actually, but not much. The problem is the neutrons expelled from Californium don't penetrate far enough, so it wouldn't work. You'd have to stick it in the person and that would be telling. Nobody needed the Californium for medical purposes because it's not used that way now, outside of research. For the few things they could use it for, if they wanted to use it for them, which they wouldn't, they could get cobalt easily and for next to nothing in Mexico, and a lot of it, not just a gram."

"What special trouble does that leave us with?"

"Only one thing and you're really not going to like it," McEnnerney said.

"I already don't."

McEnnerney pulled off his sunglasses. "A neutron source is a necessary and vital component in triggering a nuclear explosion. If you implode plutonium, you get a critical mass but nothing goes until you bombard it with neutrons to initiate the chain reaction. A gram of Californium, they tell me, will do the job nicely on a bomb that could take out a good-sized city."

Shai said nothing. No change of expression on his face. He watched the children swinging back and forth for a long moment. A flick of pain lanced through his heart but he hardly noticed it. He turned to McEnnerney and said, "You don't know who took it."

"It's not that bad, it's just almost that bad. We're lucky the woman survived. You can talk to her. Name's Joan Reynolds. She's devastated about the doctor's death. Just out of intensive care. Eager to help is an understatement. She's some chick." He smiled. "Unfortunately she's taken. When I have time I'll look into how seriously."

Shai smiled and waited for McEnnerney to continue.

"Two men, dark-skinned," McEnnerney obliged. "From their looks, she thought southern Italian, Greek or Arab. She said they gave Italian names so we know that's out. The man at the safe spoke English with a Midwestern accent. The one who killed the doctor didn't speak at all, except an angry word or two in a foreign language just after the English speaker pointed his gun. That's how it got to me. Seems we can cross off the Chechens."

"Why?"

"That's the beautiful part. This you will like. She said he used a foreign word that was something like couscous. Cous something. Said it was like he swore it."

A smile touched Shai's lips. Kuss ommak—fuck your mother. A common Arabic curse which of course McEnnerney knew.

"I want to talk to her right away."

He started to guide Shai back to where he had garaged the vehicle on East 9th Street. "A white, freckle-faced youth pulled the attempted rape in the hospital stairwell a few days before. Got her purse with the safe key. Joan insisted the police bring mug books to the hospital. Went through all of them, her boyfriend holding the pages up for her. Zilch on the Arabs and Mister Freckles. You want to see the hot lab while we're there?"

Shai said nothing, eyes straight ahead as they strode up University Place. McEnnerney had experienced Shai not answering him, often. By trial he learned Shai remained unaffected by repeating the question. McEnnerney knew Shai heard but chose not to answer while ruminating on something he considered more important.

Beyond the thickly graffitied metal walls of a sidewalk newsstand, a plywood table was piled with inexpensive wool sweaters. A woman wearing a turquoise and beige pullover checked her reflection in the window of a supermarket.

Nearing, Shai looked toward her and spoke enthusiastically. "Looks terrific on you."

She turned. "You really think so?"

"I'd take it, absolutely." With the high prices in Israel he liked shopping abroad for Tami.

"Obviously, the neutron source is the minor chord," McEnnerney said as soon as they were away from the crowd. "If they can get their hands on some plutonium we could all be in for a very nasty weenie roast."

Shai kept walking, remained silent. McEnnerney contently matched his stride and silence. As they started down the ramp to the garage, Shai turned to him. "So what is it? Iraqis after Washington, Palestinians after Tel Aviv? Saudi Arabia after all the Shiites? What?"

Since it was not a question, Paul said, "On our greedy little planet, buying plutonium's not going to be *that* hard."

"We have to find where they got it, or are planning to get it. That's the trail."

"You have any idea where to start?" McEnnerney asked.

Shai stormed toward the car.

CHAPTER 3

The Previous March

Kenneth Khalidi sat on the floor sharing a meal with family he had never met before in his cousins' house in the village of Beita in what they called Occupied Palestine. Uncomfortable with strangers, which included his undergraduate students, he said little as the men talked among themselves about the coming almond harvest in the Arabic dialect that was identical to the one he had grown up with in Detroit. He knew this was the fourth year of the Palestinian *intifada*. Commonly translated as "uprising," the word literally meant "flooding," as in people flooding to the cause. Khalidi was always precise, and focusing on exactness quieted the anxiety that so often upsettingly coursed through him, like now. Though never part of the cause, he knew the details of its 1987 genesis: a racing Israeli army truck had slammed into a Palestinian car in the Jabalia refugee camp and killed four camp residents. A popular swell rose like a tidal wave after an earthquake—a general strike, an economic boycott of Israeli products, a refusal to work in their settlements, to pay taxes, to keep the blue West Bank delineating Israeli license plates on their cars, graffiti, stone and Molotov cocktail throwing. Khalid experienced it all from a distance, like watching the sun set, but he was aware that he felt nearly everything that way.

The day before, they had picked him up near Damascus Gate in East Jerusalem and driven through the low hills. Twenty kilometers south of Nablus, the dusty Toyota turned off onto a narrow one-lane ribbon of granite that wound up a mountain to the village of six thousand surrounded by stone terraced olive and almond groves. Mounds of piled rocks rose periodically beside the climbing road and his cousins proudly informed him that earlier Beita had declared itself a liberated village, and nine times had shut the single road in. He had sat in the back seat examining the landscape with eager interest, puzzled at their pride as the Israelis could easily clear the road.

Khalidi had nearly been fired and had fled here between winter and spring quarters, as far from Los Angeles as he could imagine. Reed-slim with black hair slicked down and every strand in immaculate place, he had a quiet face that at first glance broadcast innocence. But more observant eyes saw the testimony of long loneliness: the premature web of lines on his temple, the slack mouth, the anxiety in the moist, red-veined eyes that most attributed to the long hours of his entry-level academic position.

Because Kenneth was family, they sat on thin mattresses on the stone floor of the sleeping room and not in the formal *diwan*, with its couches and chairs around the perimeter. The arched stone walls of the sleeping room were blue and a fan dropped from the high, white ceiling. It turned rapidly, lifting the single sheets of newspaper on the floor. A tall china cabinet rose against one wall.

From the separate kitchen across the high-walled courtyard, the women entered in long embroidered dresses carrying small plates of olives, eggplant and pine nuts. A round metal tray piled with a mountain of couscous soaked with gravy and topped with chicken quarters was set before them. Each man ate off the section of the platter nearest him. When Khalidi had first seen this yesterday he had abhorred the thought of placing his spoon into the same food, as there were no individual plates. He had hardly eaten, tasting just a narrow section in front of him and, to his dismay, clearly displeasing the women. Now, not wanting to hurt their feelings and hungry and happy from laboring with them in the almond groves, Khalidi pushed his spoon carefully into the wet *maftoul*. He did not allow the gravy to drip onto the newspaper the way the others did and he brought the full spoon to his mouth. The juicy grains tasted delicious.

The outside door in the courtyard flung open and someone ran up the stairs, shouting wildly. A young cousin appeared at the door, breathing hard.

"Settlers," he said between panting. "At the springs. Children, guards. We threw rocks. Taisir Daoud told them to leave. In Hebrew. Their guard shot him in the stomach. Then he shot Mussa Saleh in the head. Killed him! They're bringing Taisir. And the Israeli kids."

"I'll get an ambulance." One of the men ran.

Hundreds of shouting voices rose from beyond the house. The men burst outside, leaving Khalidi alone. He moved into the courtyard, heard the chanting nearing, saw the women hurry through the small door in the wall after the men. Frightened, he stood motionless for a long moment, then climbed the stairs to the flat concrete roof for a better view. Almonds lay loose everywhere, drying.

Below, people crowded noisily into the small, rocky, dirt crossroads as more charged up from the rest of the village. He watched as hordes of young, shouting Palestinians descended the narrow path to his left from the village's eastern spring.

A tinny, electrically amplified voice erupted from the mosque behind him. "Village of Howwar," the voice bounded over the terraced hills toward the village at the highway. There were no telephones in Beita. "Phone Nablus. We need ambulances. Village of Howwar..."

The Palestinians boys and young men filled the crossroads. Khalidi realized they had circled the fifteen or so Israeli children and two armed guards, who were still pointing their weapons as the crush of the crowd propelled them forward. The Jewish children were so young; some looked under ten years old. The girls were all in long, blue denim skirts and long sleeve blouses. They looked terrified, and some seemed hurt. Blood trickled from a small boy's ear below his skullcap. Khalidi's heart went out to these children. Why do they have to come here, Khalidi thought, confused, though the answer had been explained to him yesterday in the car. The settlers were saying, it is our country, we will go where we want.

The crowd's momentum stopped at the level clearing. People flowed to the spot from everywhere in the village, scampered atop walls, roofs, covered the hills like ants. The circle closest to the Israelis were teenagers and young men raising clenched fists, shouting rhythmically, "PLO, Israel no. PLO, Israel no." The chanting pushed the circle tighter and tighter. Khalidi was scared, wanted it to stop. One skull-capped Israeli brandished his rifle defiantly. The other held his toward the dirt, tried to shelter the children with his body.

Then, from the hill to Khalidi's left in front of the stone building that housed the olive press, a woman—the sister of the boy slain at the springs, he learned later—threw a large rock at the Israelis. It struck the guard with the raised rifle in the head. He spun, blood dripping down his face, and fired his M16. A villager cried out and grabbed his leg, the crack of the shot echoing through the hills.

The Israeli spun again, fired wildly—into a Jewish girl's head. Blood poured down her face and she slumped to the dirt, the crowd abruptly silent. A villager grabbed the Israeli from behind in a viselike grip, their bodies close. The Israeli thrust his M16 under the villager's neck and fired. The bullet went straight up and out his head in a geyser of blood. In a noisy frenzy, young men pounced on the Israeli, pounded his head with stones. The other Israeli dropped his weapon, fell to the earth and started mouth-to-mouth resuscitation on the Israeli girl. Khalidi could see from his crazed reaction that she was dead. A young boy grabbed the first Israeli's M16 and smashed it against a rock over and over until the rifle butt shattered.

Dizzy in the relentless sun, Khalidi grabbed onto the railing. A car honked hard and approached from down village, the small SEAT Malaga parting the crowd. Young Palestinian men, a half dozen to a body, quickly lifted the villager shot in the leg, the Jewish girl's limp corpse, and the boy wounded in the stomach who had been carried from the springs. When they were in the car, people pushed back in all directions to allow the Malaga to turn around in the small space. Khalidi assumed they would meet the ambulance on the main road. The

Israeli guard was face down in the dirt unmoving, his head bloodied.

Village elders bustled the Jewish children and the other guard down the road and into a house three homes from where he stood to protect them. Khalidi looked at the pools of blood in the dirt and felt nauseous. He forced himself downstairs back into the relative coolness of the house and sat alone on the floor.

Two hours later helicopters descended frighteningly loud. In anticipation, the younger men and boys had fled for nearby villages and the caves in the hills. In the house with the women and two of his older male cousins, Khalidi sat at the window biting a fingernail and watched wave after wave of the thundering birds drop and hover. Uniformed soldiers jumped out as the helicopters danced a few feet off the ground. The soldiers evacuated the Jewish children and two guards. To Khalidi's surprise, the first guard had survived the pummeling to his head and had been carried to the house with the children. Soon hundreds of jeeps, armored personnel carriers, and trucks bearing more troops labored up the winding asphalt strip from the main Ramallah-Nablus Road. Two trucks hauled in artillery pieces. The pounding helicopters landed troops on the crests of the surrounding hills and sealed off the village. More helicopters dropped leaflets on nearby villages warning that anyone who sheltered boys from Beita risked his home being blown up.

Inside the house, Khalidi sank back from the window in shock. They must have brought in several thousand soldiers. He bent his head, his hands moist. Troops were trotting noisily through the streets going house to house. Soon, a half dozen soldiers burst into their courtyard, then into the house, rifles pointed.

"We want the settlers' guns," one with a bar on his shoulder said in Arabic.

Khalidi stood, approached him. "The Jewish guard shot the girl, accidentally. I witnessed it."

"We want the guns," the lieutenant said. "If we learn they're here, this house will be demolished."

"They're not here," a woman said.

"All men between the ages of fourteen and sixty to the

schoolyard," the lieutenant ordered. "Now."

Outside, men were being led down the dusty road toward the school in the valley near the entrance to Beita. Khalidi walked, watching his feet. How could they not listen? He had told them precisely what happened. The road faced the southern valley and the nearby village of Lower Beita on the ravine floor, its single pencil-thin minaret thrusting above the low homes. In all directions the stone terraced olive groves covered the rolling hills, the silvery leaves shimmering in the brightness.

A Palestinian whispered as they walked that Israeli radio reported the ultraorthodox Jewish children said an Arab on a rooftop with a Kalashnikov had shot the girl. Khalidi absorbed that news and then slowly, as if one too many sacks had been heaved on a laden cart, smashing it, rage crashed inside him. It was as if a wave of fury abruptly rose up and flowed through every pore. He was livid at the monstrous injustice here, and at UCLA. With no outlet, he continued to walk, hands clenched at his side.

Twenty minutes later they reached the school and he joined the hundreds of men sitting on the ground inside the immense soccer field, hands ordered around their knees. He sat, inched beside his cousin. Word spread that the boy who had broken the Israeli's gun had been hauled away, and that one of the young leaders of the village, Issam Abdul Said, had been shot and killed in the hills when he disobeyed an order to stop running. Khalidi hacked a channel in the ground with his foot.

They sat for hours with armed soldiers patrolling the periphery. The sun gradually sank behind the hills, silhouetting them in yellow-orange. A little after seven o'clock, Khalidi heard and then felt an explosion. He looked up toward the village, and in the darkness saw a flash and then the earth shook as a house went up and then dropped back to earth. It was followed by a second flash and rumble and then a third, a fourth, fifth, sixth—each raising the anger inside him like a growing drumbeat. Then, as he watched the top of the hill, his cousins' house rose then splattered into pieces. The night fell silent and the dust spread in the darkness. All the lights in the village winked out. One of the demolitions must have toppled the power lines. Khalidi was so furious he was trembling despite the warm evening.

He turned to his cousin, despair in his whisper. "Your home."

Tears rose in his cousin's eyes but he said nothing.

Around him, Khalidi watched the men cower and look down. He felt a familiar feeling but vastly amplified—powerlessness.

"This cannot continue," he said to his cousin.

"We fight them with our stones and gasoline bottles," his cousin said, eyes down.

"It is not enough. You must do more."

"It's impossible. If we shoot they'll come with their tanks."

"You have to find a way to defeat them," Khalidi said, too loudly.

His head still down, his cousin whispered, "Shut up. There is no other way. Look at them." He glanced at Khalidi. "You don't understand. You're an outsider with an American passport."

Khalidi felt as if he had been slapped across the face. Here, now, he longed to be part of them but he knew he was not. He watched the Israeli soldiers on the tops of the mountains, others still moving through the village. He crossed his arms tightly against his chest and looked down like the others, his face hot. There had to be a way to stop them.

Ten days later, the afternoon before Khalidi flew home he shuffled through Jaffa Gate into the Old City of Jerusalem, the almost ever-present anxiety wearing him out. His life was not so bad and he did not understand why he was always so nervous. He was at the beginning of his career and it was expected that he would be working very hard. In addition to his teaching and departmental responsibilities, he sat on five senior professors' dissertation committees—met with their students, pulled data for them, helped run their statistics, solved computer problems. It was all right that the full professors garnered all the credit for their progress. That was how the system functioned and eventually he would be in their place and do the same. He was glad to have landed a tenure track position at a prestigious institution like UCLA.

Still, he had not been sleeping well in his Hollywood apartment, often woke between three and four a.m. and was then up for hours before drifting off. He had overslept several times and was late to teaching his class. Once he had forgotten to bring his lecture notes and badly stumbled through an improvisation; he hated the rare occasions when he was disorganized. He wished he could dress without showering first to save time when he was late. Then that blowhard Professor McCarry insisted Khalidi take on supervising yet an additional student, one of his, in acoustics and cryogenics. When he protested that low temperature physics was not his field, McCarry had the audacity to say he was doing Khalidi a favor by helping him catch up in the area. Khalidi told him he did not have time and not to dump students outside his field on him. The Dean summoned him in and told him he better get professional help for his obvious personal problems lest he lose his tenure track position.

Tears rose in Khalidi's eyes now as he recalled leaving his office and running to the inverted fountain, reaching into the descending waters and splashing his hot face. He had imagined such a different life when he came to Los Angeles—that he would finally not be so alone. As his breathing had slowed, he turned and sat on the edge of the fountain. He could not go home for spring break and let his father see him like this. His father owned a small grocery store in the heavily Arab émigré suburb of Dearborn, Michigan. Then an idea struck him. His father was always badgering him to visit their relatives on the West Bank but he had not been much interested. He had to get far away from UCLA, however, so he'd come here. In the afternoon Jerusalem heat, Khalidi wore a blue T-shirt with a yellow UCLA in bold letters and his jogging shoes; his cousins did not want him mistaken for an Israeli and stabbed. Khalidi passed the sleek stone tower of David's Citadel without looking up. His mind turned to the destruction of his family's house, apparently for the crime of being so near the shootings. Sixty members of the village had been arrested and six expelled to Lebanon.

As hatred rose in him, it calmed his anxiety. Map in hand, Khalidi descended into the eerily empty covered and cooler Arab souq. Each shop was shuttered. The cry of the *intifada* was scrawled everywhere over the walls and metal shutters like a wild growth, then, at the soldiers' orders, painted over with broad strokes. His cousins had told him that since the *intifada* all commerce in the Territories ceased daily at noon.

Under an arched ceiling Khalidi walked through the dark marketplace, his feet squeaking softly on the worn stone steps. Tormented about Beita, he was frightened too about what faced him at UCLA. But he felt he should see as much as he could while he was here. Down the incline in the center of each step, an old man led a donkey laden with green bananas over the stones. From around a corner, a small boy darted in front of him.

"Mister, you want to visit my father's shop? Here." He pointed at a shuttered store. "I take you around the back. We have special prices because we are closed."

"No. I am sorry," Khalidi said. He wanted to be left alone.

"Just look, please. We have many nice things. Very big discount. No charge for looking."

"No!" Khalidi hurried away, down The Street of the Christians and past more shuttered shops, kept running. A cat gnawing at chicken bones scampered away with a hiss.

At home, he jogged each evening around the UCLA perimeter to snap the tension. He felt terrible now, like he was a violin and somebody was tightening the strings mercilessly. He had memorized the route on the map. He made a right and stopped, hardly exerted, at the entrance to the Church of the Holy Sepulchre. Three armed Israeli soldiers outside the entrance looked but said nothing.

Khalidi entered, walked past the cushion recess of the doorkeepers and into the Rotunda. The huge church was completely empty. Khalidi stood in the middle of the circular area and stared up at the magnificent dome. Light streamed through high windows on one side and crossed in a diagonal shaft that struck the other wall. He continued straight into the Chapel of the Angel. A Greek Orthodox priest in dark robes turned from the stone set in marble in the center of the room. A filigreed cross hung from a deep chain below his white beard shot through with black hairs.

"Welcome. You are a Christian?" the priest asked.

Khalidi shook his head no and the priest's wrinkled face evidenced no disappointment. The priest said, "This stone is said to be the one which closed the door of the sepulchre. Matthew tells us that an angel descended from heaven, rolled the stone from the door and sat upon it. The angel had the women tell his disciples that Christ is risen from the dead." The priest pointed toward a low door. "The sepulchre's there. You can see the stone shelf on which Jesus's body lay."

His robes lifted as he walked back toward the Rotunda. Unclear about how much of it to believe, Khalidi bent and moved through the door into a small crypt hewn from stone. The room was musky. A rectangle of polished marble covered the shelf. Khalidi stared, did not know what he was searching for.

Ten minutes later he walked quickly back through the Rotunda, so anxious he was afraid he might scream in the high, echoing space. He ran outside. Following his map, he hurried the short distance through the empty marketplace and down the Street of the Chain. Nearing him a young boy carried a tray laden with plates of lamb and rice, the smell wonderful. Khalidi already missed eating with his cousins off the communal tray.

He abruptly emerged into bright sunshine, his eyes hurting. Before him, two middle-aged armed soldiers sat on chairs in the shade going through the purse of a Jewish woman, her head covered with a scarf. They were obviously searching for bombs. He approached and they impatiently waved him on. Past them, he stopped at the edge of the enormous white stone plaza, the sun glinting everywhere. Before him towered the Western Wall, tiers of massive limestone blocks. Ahead to his left, black-coated Jews bobbed on the men's side; a smaller number of women stood at the base of their smaller section to the right.

Above the wall on the temple plateau rose the enormous golden dome of the Mosque of Omar. Beside it rested the smaller silver-domed Al-Aqsa Mosque. They were staggeringly beautiful. Khalidi crossed the plaza and mounted the enclosed wooden path that wound up the height of the Wall. More soldiers stood at the entrance to the Temple

Mount, searching bags. He continued onto the plaza, where Arab East Jerusalem police patrolled in dark uniforms.

The octagonal, gold-dome mosque to his left, almost directly above the Wall, was exquisite. Slabs of marble and multi-colored but predominantly blue mosaics covered the high facades. The rock from where Muslims believed Mohammad had ascended to heaven was inside. He stopped, looked from the gold dome to the silver dome, back to the gold dome.

Khalidi thought about the soldiers behind him searching for bombs and an idea came to him and he was abruptly happy, as if standing in the eye of a hurricane. It was ridiculous. It was too wild of a notion. He approached. There were spouts for the faithful to wash their hands and feet before entering. Octagonal steps descended around the mosque leading to the four entranceways.

The day after the killings in Beita the Israeli army had bulldozed two olive groves near the highway, claiming security needs. He had been enraged then, but now he felt peaceful. The most the Israelis and Americans talked about was returning some of the land to the Jordanians, who his cousins assured him were more brutal than the Jews. No Palestinian state. The Israelis have peace on their lips when speaking to the West, he thought. Here they rush more settlements into our hills.

He turned and stared back toward the stone Old City. His thoughts were grander but no crazier than what he had witnessed in terms of brutal force in Beita. He had the technical knowledge. He could assemble a nuclear bomb in this city and demand the Israelis withdraw from the West Bank and East Jerusalem…or he would detonate it. He would threaten to turn the center of the planet's religious consciousness into rubble. The Christian world would go insane at the danger to The Holy Sepulchre, the Via Dolorosa, the Stations of the Cross, and would mount excruciating pressure on Israel to capitulate. Khalidi felt hot all over, his breath tight in his chest. If the Israelis refused to retreat from the Territories, they would deserve his exploding the bomb.

The Mosque of Omar was the third holiest site in Islam. Look what had happened when Salman Rushdie wrote one novel. He was overwhelmed with images of the entire Muslim world rising up to blame Israel, the chanting in the streets, the mobilization. The Americans would be alone, would not take on eight hundred million Muslims for three million recalcitrant Israelis. Whatever its arsenal, Israel would not survive wave after wave of the *jihad.* And afterward, the Palestinians would have all the land. He would only need fifteen pounds of plutonium to destroy all of Jerusalem, and he had a notion of how to obtain it.

First, he needed to have a look at the Tel Aviv marina; he had an idea how he could get the plutonium into the country.

CHAPTER 4

May 22

Seated on an Amsterdam tram, Shai leaned his head against the cool pole. Closing his eyes, he attempted to let his thoughts quiet with the sliding of the car but they leapt to the worry that he still had no lead to the Arabs' identity, the reason he had flown here to meet Ramzy Awwad. He believed the stories Ramzy formed meticulously in his head while constantly moving—because either the Israelis or the hard-line Palestinians were impatient to kill him—then set down in a single outpouring in near final form relieved the pressure of his repeated failures on behalf of his people.

As the tram jerked to a halt in front of the Central Station, Shai's forehead remained against the metal bar. He slowly forced his eyes open, heaved an audible sigh and was up. Once moving, he hurried down the steps, though his legs and feet hurt him. Electric wires sparked overhead as the tram eased away. Shai glared at the watch imbedded in his thick wrist hairs as if he could will its acceleration. He was twenty minutes early for their meeting in back of the station. More worn out than hungry, he walked toward a nearby herring stand.

The light changed and in front of the Victoria Hotel a pack of bicycles swarmed into the intersection. Shai dipped the gutted herring into a bowl of diced onions and ate rapidly without tasting it. At the same time, he eased his gaze in both directions, saw nothing suspicious, so he continued toward the harbor. In Jerusalem, Meir Carmon had pointed one of his ubiquitous burning Swiss Muratti cigarettes at him and ordered Shai to take a team to babysit his backside should Ramzy suddenly decide to demand a reckoning for his brethren killed continually in the Territories. Shai had stood quickly. Absolutely, he would bring the men in from Paris, then once in Europe neglected to assemble them. Ramzy was his friend, his symbol in this conflict that the enemy could be reached.

Three years ago during the Lebanon War, Shai had captured Ramzy, a high-ranking PLO operative, in Lebanon and had held him in their massive tent Ansar Prison just north of the Israeli border. Without Shai knowing at the time, Carmon's predecessor, The Colonel, from his seaside exile had pulled the strings of friends inside the service to have Ramzy freed in the hope he and Shai would pool their contacts in the hunt for the murderous and elusive Abu Nidal. Shai had driven Ramzy into the Lebanese hills, asked the simmering Ramzy to meet him in Europe, then left. Ramzy had shown up. Eventually, together in Rome they had Abu Nidal trapped. Then a shot from an unseen car slammed into Shai's chest. Ramzy had rushed him to the hospital and sacrificed eliminating the cornered extremist, who had been killing Ramzy's men across Europe in retaliation for Ramzy's retreat from the quest to destroy Israel. Their friendship had solidified.

Shai bustled toward the wide channel with the Shell Oil Company offices rising across the water. Ramzy Awwad was standing alone on the far end of the sidewalk. A burst of excitement ran through Shai at seeing his friend.

Unlike the front of the Central Station, little traffic flowed on the narrow street here at the channel. The sparse trees along the sidewalk had slim trunks too narrow for anyone to hide behind. The quay was empty. As Shai increased his rolling gait, he watched Ramzy wait with characteristic stillness. He wore a blousy cotton shirt with large pockets, pleated cotton slacks and canvas shoes—was the kind of man who could wear anything well. Though he had lost weight, his curly hair was full and dark, marred by only a splash of gray at the ears. Yet the crevices at his eyes and the etched lines down his cheeks betrayed a vulnerability that, along with his natural good looks, Shai was certain would have lured women like a meteor rushing to earth if Ramzy had desired it. They were also the lines of a man who no longer held illusions. He was three years Shai's junior.

As Shai approached, to his surprise Ramzy was pulling hard on a cigarette, his cheeks hollowing further. Shai knew he had quit smoking several years before.

"I would ask you how you are, but I think I know," Shai said. "I'm glad to see you."

"And should I be glad to see you?"

"I hope so. You have any good news at all? How's Dalal?" Ramzy's wife still worked in the refugee camp school outside Damascus where Ramzy had taught and earlier had planned to live his life.

"I haven't seen her in a long time."

"I'm sorry. Maybe you should. You look lousy by the way."

A flicker of a smile touched Ramzy's lips then was gone.

"Shall we stroll?" Shai said.

Ramzy began to walk, and moving along the channel, Shai had to rein in his pace to match Ramzy's soundless steps.

"How's the writing?" Shai asked. "I haven't seen a story in a while. Did I miss something?"

"No." Ramzy pitched his cigarette in the water. "What do you want?"

"Not to talk about the situation. I have sympathy for what's happening to your people. You know that." Violence on both sides had soared since the Gulf War.

"Sympathy. Well, I'm definitely happy to hear that."

Shai knew Ramzy had risen with hope at the onset of the *intifada,* only to deflate as possible progress toward a Palestinian state fell through his fingers like sand. Shai believed that if he were a Palestinian youth in a teeming West Bank camp he would detest them and throw stones himself. But Shai knew well, too, the place inside his body where fear of them turned into hard anger. The Israelis had sat in sealed rooms during the Scud attacks wearing gas masks, watched the Palestinians on Jordanian TV screaming bomb them, gas them. After each launch the Israelis ran to the phones to find out where it fell, on what neighborhood, on what block, who was safe, who was not. The gas masks had propelled their collective unconscious back to Auschwitz.

"So I've got bad news," Shai said.

Ramzy lit another cigarette, exhaled smoke as he talked. "Why else would you be here."

"I'll give it to you without wrapping it. We have evidence of Arabs stealing components to assemble a nuclear bomb."

Ramzy showed no reaction. A low, sleek, glass-enclosed boat packed with camera-clicking tourists sliced through the water and Ramzy followed it, wondered what secrets each tourist hid inside himself. He held too many secrets from Dalal, once believed he never would.

He turned back to Shai, his vast eyes hard, charcoal pupils blended into his irises. "And here I thought you were only going to ask for help silencing the stone throwers, so your soldiers wouldn't have to endure murdering them. I read your press, how hard it is for them to shoot young boys. Or are they getting used to it? Tell me, Shai, would you say it's becoming easier for them over time?" The color of his face deepened. "I'm interested. I want to understand it."

Shai stopped walking. He greatly agreed with Ramzy, but saying so would be perceived as calculating. "Sixteen days ago two Arabs stole a gram of Californium-252 from a New York research hospital. It's enough to trigger a bomb large enough to blow up Washington or Tel Aviv. It's the only use."

"Actually, I never much cared for Tel Aviv. Sloppy planning, congested, dirty. When I used to walk through the empty dunes there as a boy, the coastline was extraordinary."

"How about the Arabs in adjacent Jaffa?" Shai's voice rose. "You eager to see them obliterated too?"

Ramzy pulled hard on his cigarette, the paper crackling. He

blew the smoke over his head. Shai waited, said nothing, silence his second home.

Finally Ramzy said, "In New York, which Arabs?"

"We don't know."

"May I ask what you do know?"

"We know they'll need someone highly qualified to assemble it but it's feasible. To destroy a good-size city all they'd need is twelve to fifteen pounds of plutonium. With high explosives wrapped around it, the whole thing might weigh fifty pounds. They could trigger it any one of a dozen ways. Plutonium emits little radioactivity once it's machined. It could be handled safely without protective equipment."

"Really? I'm surprised to hear that."

"We're checking scientists with known sympathies for the Arab cause," Shai said. "We've considered the possibility of this kind of thing happening. But with Pakistan, India, and Russia crumbling now, getting their hands on some plutonium might be too easy." He ran over the details of New York, then added, "We can't find a whisper about the bomb anywhere. I believe we're dealing with people not previously known to us."

Ramzy said nothing for a moment. "That will make them harder to find."

Shai nodded.

"You have no idea whether they want something or plan to just detonate?"

"None. Even if they're holding us hostage for whatever, something could easily go wrong, even an accident, and then . . ."

Ramzy turned to him, his hand wavering slightly as he brought the cigarette toward his lips. He'd had nothing but coffee all day. He lowered the burning cigarette to his side. "So you want me to help you stop it. Because of friendship? Because you believe I'm rational?"

"Ramzy, this is a nuclear bomb! If an Israeli city goes up, those in power, they'll act this time. Decisively. There will be nothing left to stop them."

"So, I should help to stop *you* from destroying my people."

Shai thought about the irony and had nothing to say to disagree with Ramzy's feelings, which he shared.

Ramzy took a long drag of his cigarette then dropped it on the ground and rubbed the glow with his toe. His head came up slowly. "It seems we better stop this."

Shai felt the tiredness it seemed he was always trying to outrun these days, but smiled. "Let's go get a cup of coffee. You're wearing me out."

Ramzy smiled, his face softening. "There's a place in Vondelpark with a nice view."

They began walking back in the direction of Dam Square. A gull wheeled overhead.

"I should have arranged to see you without a crisis. I get wrapped up in the right now."

Ramzy felt genuine affection for the Israeli who had shown him so much about the previously faceless enemy. Ramzy's famous novel *Men in the Darkness* took the Arab people to task for not giving the Palestinian cause more than lip service. "I've missed you, Shai. I mean, who could live without constant chaos?"

"Actually I can see it, old age, sitting on the beach in Netanya, playing chess, telling children stories about magicians and dragons instead of raids and reprisals."

"Yes." Ramzy laughed. "That's exactly how I picture you."

"You should. I'll be there one day." He pointed a finger at him. "You'll see."

"I doubt that I will," Ramzy said. He fell quiet again. Though he did not believe he would succeed in helping his people, he continued steadfast in that effort. He fueled himself with the belief that his stories of their plight would outlive him, and that his battle with gun and pen for an equitable solution would serve as a role model.

They continued in front of the station without talking, and then Ramzy said, "I'll want to take this up in Tunis first, see if anyone's heard anything that hasn't reached me. Outside the Middle East, London's become the center of Arab activity, as you know. I have a few contacts there."

"In other words, you know everybody who's up to anything in

the city."

"I have some ideas where to make inquiries."

"People I bet I'd like to know about."

"Then if I still come up empty handed I'll try America directly. Your witness from Sloan Kettering said our Arab spoke English with a Midwestern accent. I'll try the Detroit-Dearborn area too." Arab émigrés had formed a sizeable community around auto industry jobs.

"Thanks, Ramzy," Shai said, then added a friendly admonishment, "When this is over, take a vacation with Dalal. You hear? All the problems with us will still be there a few weeks later. You can count on that."

Ramzy said nothing, and it struck Shai as an afterthought that he could have been speaking about what he needed.

As the El Al 747 streaked along the sunset toward Tel Aviv, Shai hoped that either through Ramzy or one of his own outstretched tentacles, they would grasp onto a lead. Jerusalem had contacted allied intelligence services to lower an ear to all known Arab cells around the globe for any nuclear noise. The Egyptian Mukhabarat was terrified of nuclear terrorism and had agreed to liaison with the Arab capitals, including Damascus.

Before dinner, Shai declined the flight attendant's offer of alcohol easily as he always did, for he could manage nothing in moderation. Not in the field, not in friendship and not in love and frustratingly not at the dinner table.

There were no lights anywhere in the darkness outside, save for the small blinking on the tip of the wing. He reached out, slowly shut the shade and listened to the familiar purr of the engines, comforting, like Tami's breathing beside him in bed. He pulled the small blanket higher around him and closed his eyes to snatch some sleep. But he did not doze off, and a long time later as the plane descended, tossing in his thoughts, he heard the flaps whine down and under him the landing gear rumbled then locked with a thud. He was scared that he had no road to who was assembling this bomb, or to where they had or would get the plutonium.

Shai's battered blue Renault was waiting at the airport like a sleeping loyal pup. Approaching the stone city below the crest of the mountains, he was so tired he had to rivet himself to stay awake, focus on the hundreds of thousands of lives that depended on him so he better not bolt off a cliff. Beyond the rocky Valley of the Cross and the walled monastery, he drove into his suburb of Bakaa, small cars parked everywhere diagonally up on the sidewalk. Luckily he found a spot below his building and bumped up over the curb. He looked up at his apartment. Lights shone from the bedroom. Abruptly he backed up, bounced down into the street and sped off.

An hour later, parked atop Mount Scopus, he sat gazing down at the dark rolling desert he so loved. Tami's parents were concentration camp survivors who always found fault with her, an unconscious attempt to drive achievement that would protect her, but in fact sapped her self-assurance. Tami's cupboards always brimmed with excess food and she would not take a walk anywhere, no matter how short, without her ID card, afraid if anything happened that authorities would not be able to identify her. Since the age of twelve she had been taught to search for breast lumps. He had not known all this when they married, but he loved her more for her frailty.

He squeezed the steering wheel. Neighbors mentioned that when he was away she was often up in the middle of the night baking. He knew he had to decide about freeing her soon, that no decision was the worst choice. She would blossom in a safer environment. He felt himself shaking inside. So desperately tired that he could hardly keep his eyes open, he drove home.

CHAPTER 5

May 27

Hal M. Bundy sat on the beige leather sofa in his living room in San Diego watching the Padres on television. At bat in the top of the ninth, bases loaded, the Padres' three million dollar bonus baby slapped into a quick double play, ending the game. Bundy shook his head, flicked the remote control and blackened the huge screen.

From the glass table he picked up a small book, *The Soon To Be Revealed Antichrist*, the cover of the shrouded instrument of Satan illuminated by glaring spotlights. It told that the rapture of the Church could happen any day, quoting Paul the Apostle from first Thessalonians which he turned to in his Bible: *"'For the Lord himself shall descend from heaven with a shout, with the voice of the archangel and the dead in Christ shall rise first. Then we which are alive and remain shall be caught up together with them in the clouds to meet the Lord in the air. And we will forever be with the Lord."*

Bundy leaned back contemplating the promise. His hair was platinum blond, clipped short, moustache the same color, eyes blue-gray, his body muscled from fiercely competitive racquetball. He had stayed in top shape since volunteering for a second Marine tour in Vietnam more than twenty years before, though he and Mary had already had a small daughter. Mary had accepted the Lord into her life too now and she was at a women's Bible study group. He rather enjoyed the quiet away from her chattering. He reread the passage from Thessalonians, felt certain the Believers would be snatched up into the clouds *before* the horrible reign of the Antichrist. The Lord would not have them suffer that.

The phone rang. Bundy set the small book down like a tent. A familiar hello_bellowed over the line and a warm feeling reached through Bundy. It was George Craven, a vet too, and his AA sponsor, who had introduced him first to the program and then to Jesus as his personal savior. Bundy had not downed a drink in twelve years but George still checked in every few months, which meant a lot to him. They were both rabid baseball fans and had actually met at a Padres game.

"Hey, George, you watch the game?" Bundy asked.

"No, actually I forgot about it."

"Good thing. What a disaster. They hit into double plays in the fifth, eighth and ninth." Bundy laughed. "Tell me, are you absolutely certain Jesus wants me to love these guys?"

"I hear Jesus is a football fan. You sound great."

"Everything's A-OK here."

The doorbell rang.

"George, there's someone here. Let me get back to you."

"No need. I'm going to bed early anyway." Craven could tell immediately by the sound of the voice whether someone was drinking, and he had already had a long evening on the phone with a man on his second bottle who had been fleeced in a real estate scam.

"Thanks buddy." Bundy hung up. Kenneth Khalidi from UCLA had phoned a little while before, happened to be in San Diego and had asked to stop over. He had worked with the young physicist several times machining difficult specifications for him in his shop, which he had started in a garage and now boasted twenty-seven employees. It was common to go outside the university machine shop, especially for the high precision work he specialized in.

Outside, Khalidi waited for Bundy to answer. There was no

way to mask the melting and segment casting of the plutonium as some other project since the process was extremely radioactive and there were not many machinists capable of the work. In his windbreaker pocket Khalidi felt the .22-caliber Beretta with suppressor he had purchased in Culver City. He did not know if he could really shoot Bundy and anybody else in the house to prevent the authorities being alerted if, after he detailed his plan, Bundy balked. He had phoned at the last moment rather than make an appointment so nobody would know he was here, and he had parked around the corner.

The door swung open.

"Come right in, young fellow," Bundy said and clapped Khalidi on the back as he entered the narrow foyer lined with ferns and small indoor palms.

"Thank you very much for seeing me on such short notice."

"Nonsense. You're always welcome here." Bundy stretched out his arm. "Let's have that jacket."

"No, thank you. I would prefer to wear it."

"All right. Suit yourself, son. Come, we'll have some coffee and see what you have in mind."

As they entered the living room, Bundy noticed Khalidi had not brought any drawings. Often scientists described what they needed without a clue to how it would look and he figured out a way to make it.

Bundy sat ramrod straight on the sofa beside Khalidi. "So, how are you?"

Khalidi thought about how in a few days he would be flying to Brazil with Amal Tawil for the plutonium. Though he did not dare believe anything would happen between them, but unbelievably they would be together. She had taken his survey physics class and wrote for the radical campus *La Gente.*

"I feel very good."

"Now that's what I like to hear. Everybody complains too much. I say they're soft, don't know what tough is."

Khalidi again remembered the anger in Bundy's eyes when he talked about his proselytizing in Israel, the treacherous Israelis and how since 1967 the Jews had poured ten billion dollars into an infrastructure in the Occupied Territories to oppress Christian and Muslim Arabs while red-blooded Americans subsidized their country with foreign aid.

Khalidi was not sure how to approach this. "Excuse me, but if I may ask you, you told me that when you traveled to proselytize in Israel that you did not succeed."

"God works in unseen ways, son." Bundy stood. "Now, how about that coffee? It's decaf."

"Yes, that would be very nice, thank you."

"I'll bring some fruit." Bundy patted his hard stomach. "No cookies or cake allowed in my temple."

In the spacious, white-tiled kitchen, as he prepared the tray Bundy thought with disappointment about his trip to the Holy Land. After his experience in the Asian theater when only a nominal Christian, he had planned to spirit Bibles into someplace like godless Red China. However, it had struck him that Bibles were already finding their way there and he could contribute far more by bringing His word to the Holy Land.

He had rented a car in Tel Aviv, drove around the country and picked up young hitchhikers, working the conversation around to a discussion of Jesus while taking them where they needed to go. After three weeks he compiled a list of twenty-one seemingly interested people who gave him their contact information. He invited them to a gala dinner at the Jerusalem Hilton, had a film rented to show afterward. Only two showed up. Very upset, he had returned home and in a brief moment of stupidity almost started drinking again. After Nam, each night he had downed a large water glass of 80 proof Akadama plum wine, which soon moved to two tall glasses. Then the Lord had placed George Craven in a seat next to him at a day game where he had been swigging too many beers, and George had invited him and Mary over for an improvised supper immediately afterwards. His life changed. Jesus filled the deep vacuum inside him, and with the alcohol gone, business boomed.

Bundy brought a tray into the living room, poured the coffee, added nonfat milk to both without asking. "To answer your question,

Kenneth, God has his own agenda. I don't fail in what I set my mind to. For some reason He didn't want me to succeed. He may have been testing my faith." Bundy gave a sharp nod. "If so, I passed with flying colors. Not an iota of conviction shaken despite the stiff-necked Jews. Strengthened, if anything, against adversity."

The nervous fear drummed in Khalidi's ears. There was no alternative but to come out with it. "Two months ago I visited Palestine. What I saw…"

"I know, son. It's rough."

"The Palestinians must have a state of their own. They must."

"I sympathize with you. They too are God's children."

Khalidi abruptly stood. He did not know why he believed Bundy would help. He wanted to hurry from the room but he held himself in place. "If the Jews could be forced to relinquish their occupation over us, would you assist us?"

"I follow my beliefs to the end. I'll fight for freedom anywhere on the globe."

Khalidi placed his hand on the gun in his pocket. He had the Californium-252. This time he knew he could fire if he had to. The state was at stake. "If there was an operation and a machinist was required to complete some dangerous work that could be accomplished here in San Diego, I am asking if you would consider taking the risk."

Bundy set his cup down. "Stop pussyfooting around, boy. What's this about?"

Khalidi held the gun tightly. "I plan to smuggle a nuclear bomb into Jerusalem and threaten to explode it if the Israelis refuse to grant the Palestinians a state. I believe I can obtain plutonium oxide. I require someone to fashion the plutonium into a perfect sphere."

Bundy gave a low whistle, stood, crossed the room to the sliding glass door and looked out at the large, lit hotel on Coronado Island. Emotion gathered in his throat. To his surprise, he thought about his rough-and-tumble father, a World War II sergeant highly decorated for bravery at the Battle of the Bulge who had died when Bundy was a boy and never saw what he had accomplished. When he was a child, his father had spent every night by the radio drinking, and Hal was ashamed that after Vietnam he had done the same thing.

He turned. He had grown increasingly restless in recent years. It could not be a mere coincidence that Khalidi was here.

"Now, son, what if the Jews don't withdraw? Would you blow the thing, in Jerusalem? Obviously you realize I couldn't be any party to that."

"They will withdraw. They will have no alternative. I am certain of it."

Bundy said nothing for a long moment, saw that Khalidi was right. He felt the same way he had when he watched the early fighting in Vietnam on television, the urge to be part of it, to show he was a cut above. "I can do far more than cast the sphere," he said. "I can be invaluable inside Israel. They watch Arabs. What their security won't be suspicious of is a whitey like me. I'll be able to move everywhere freely."

Khalidi looked at him in disbelief, removed his damp hand from around the gun. He was stunned. "You are willing to do this?"

"Let me tell you, this is not something I'd say if I didn't mean it."

"Thank you," Khalidi whispered. On every front it was piecing together. "Then I want to tell you the rest. We are going to assemble two bombs."

The night of May 28 in the Grande Ca' d'Oro Hotel in Sao Paulo, Brazil, Khalidi sat unmoving in the dark on the large bed. He had been eating dinner with Joaquim Vargas downstairs, then more than an hour ago had feigned painful turista and insisted that Vargas finish the meal, which was already charged to Khalidi's room. He had claimed the reason for the vacation was a small inheritance from a deceased uncle. Vargas was a senior chemist and the accounting officer in the refining plant that separated the various elemental materials from the by-products of the Sao Paulo nuclear reactor.

Earlier, in the middle of their meal, Amal Tawil had made her entrance. Her black, off-the-shoulder evening gown flared at the hips, stopped well above her knees and wrapped tightly around her fantastic figure, revealing a trace of cleavage. She wore black lace stockings, tall heels to boost her short height, and a strand of pearls around her bare upper body. Her black hair was freshly blow-dried and swayed at her ears as she walked alone to the table beside them that Khalidi had tipped the maître d' to reserve for her. Khalidi had seen Vargas staring at her repeatedly as they ate and it was hard for him to keep his eyes from her himself.

From the bed, Khalidi looked out at the lights of the high-rises on Ninth of July Avenue. Beyond them the plateau city sprawled in all directions to the foot of ringing mountains. There was no reason to sit in the dark but he preferred it, as he felt nervous and worried that the scheme would fail. The shootings in Sloan Kettering still unnerved him. He had gone for the neutron source first because he had believed it would be the easiest to achieve.

He remembered when he had approached Amal. The Arabs had no special interest newspaper at UCLA and she wrote articles about the Zionists arming Central American dictators for *La Gente,* the Chicano-Latino campus paper. She had taken his Physics 10 class, which fulfilled the science requirement for humanities majors, in the fall. When she bothered to attend, she invariably sat in the back row with her longhaired Chicano boyfriend, Geraldo, the editor-in-chief of *La Gente,* their hands always all over each other. It had taken him fifteen minutes with the phone in his lap before he could lift the receiver and actually dial her number.

They had sat on a bench in UCLA's sculpture garden. Amal wore shorts and a sports bra that exposed her bare midriff. Her sandals were in her pack on the ground. He had talked around the subject, about her writings, and then finally had asked quite bluntly if she was merely playing revolutionary while she was young or if she was serious.

She crossed one leg over the other and her bare toes stretched only inches from him. "Look," she said, "I don't know what kind of game you're playing. If this is some kind of come-on, you get a D. Just lame."

"No, it's nothing like that. " His voice was tight. Her lips were pouty and her bare legs so close. He did not want to tell her about

Jerusalem, fearing she would be horrified at the risk to the Arab population and the mosques there. "Please. You must understand what I'm saying. I can bring Israel to her knees."

"Yeah? What can you do?"

"I can kidnap Tel Aviv." He told her his plan, only telling her that he would put the bomb in Tel Aviv.

She laughed. "You've never done anything for the cause and now you want to build us a very big bomb?"

"This is what I can do." His voice was hard. "This is what I am doing now."

"This is out of control." She sat back, held one hand in the other. "Can you get plutonium?"

"I believe so. That is where I thought you might help."

"Me? How?"

He was silent for a long moment. "I'm sorry to have to ask you to do this. You would have to go to bed with somebody. His wife is very Catholic."

She laughed. "That's all, fuck some guy?"

The exterior door of Amal's adjoining hotel room opened jarring Khalidi back and he jumped inside. If Vargas was not with her she would have knocked on his door.

Khalidi stared at the adjoining door, which was unlocked from her side. Light suddenly appeared under it. Vargas had been finishing his doctorate in nuclear chemistry at Columbia University when Khalidi started the physics PhD program there. Vargas had already been married with two small children then, and as a handsome, Latin teaching assistant he bedded fabulous undergraduates while terrified his wife would find out and take his children away.

Khalidi walked to the window and gazed out, but his eyes did not look beyond his own mind, where he pictured Vargas with his hands, his mouth all over Amal. He heard the sound of bodies sinking on the bed. He gripped the windowsill. Maybe a minute crawled by.

He turned, crossed the room and picked up the camera with the motor film advance. He sank back on the edge of the bed and listened, heard a male moan through the door. He looked down and waited for her signal.

He held the camera tightly with both hands as Vargas's sounds grew louder. A loud "oh" erupted from him through the thin door and Khalidi abruptly stood again, though the signal would come from her. For a long time there was nothing, then he heard springs sag.

Khalidi felt each second singly, like the ticking before an explosion, was gripping the camera so tightly he suddenly was afraid he would break it. He heard a high-pitched gasp from Amal, then wild sounds escaped her throat. *She is acting,* he told himself.

She had laughed at him when he told her the signal but had agreed.

"Yes," she said loudly. "Oh yes, yes."

He twisted the doorknob and managed somehow to silently open the door. The lights still on, she was naked on her back as he sprawled in the opposite direction, his face between her legs, her hand on him, pulling. Khalidi stood there, paralyzed. Amal nodded vigorously.

He abruptly looked through the viewfinder, focused. Both of them sharpened in the frame and it struck him that they actually looked handsome together. Quickly he squeezed the shutter. The pictures fired off like bullets. He kept the shutter depressed, the clicking loud. Vargas turned drunkenly, confusion on his face, and then his features tightened. He swore in Portuguese.

Khalidi stepped back, continued shooting. Vargas lunged at him but Khalidi sidestepped quickly and Vargas fell heavily on the floor. Khalidi was taller, younger, in good shape from jogging and sober, the camera a weapon that he could swing.

"I do not intend to hurt you," Khalidi said. "Please do not attempt that again."

Vargas looked up helplessly from the floor. "Why?"

Khalidi turned to Amal, who was sitting on her knees on the bed. Her breasts were large and brown with dark aureoles. She was even more magnificent naked than he had imagined. He was suddenly hard, and mortified, in the midst of a mission. He brought the camera down to hide it.

"Please go into my room and get dressed," he said.

She hopped off the bed and crossed to the closet with no more self-consciousness than if she has been strolling around UCLA. She pulled a red robe from it, draped it around herself and headed into Khalidi's room. She did not close the doors.

Khalidi turned to Vargas, who was rummaging for his clothes. His bare back to Khalidi, Vargas stuck his dark legs through his underwear. Then he put his pants on and turned, breathing hard.

"You bastard, you know what my wife will do if she sees those."

"Yes, in fact I do."

"What the hell do you want?"

"I am going to have to ask you to deliver forty pounds of plutonium."

Khalidi heard the sound of the shower from his room. Good, she was washing him off her.

"I can't get it," Vargas said. "This was all for nothing." He forced on his shirt, stuffed it into his pants, swept his long hair back, reached for his socks and shoes.

Khalidi waited until he was finished. The elemental by-products of the Sao Paulo nuclear reactor came out on filters as fine uranium, plutonium and other "hot" powders, then were bagged and sealed. For safety, Khalidi knew the process was entirely accomplished by robotics. Fortunately, unlike some of the other by-products the plutonium was not that dangerous to handle as long as one kept the quantities separated to prevent them from spontaneously exploding. After being bagged, the "hot" powders were taken to shielded storage areas to "cool." An additional by-product of the process was harmless lead oxide powder.

"Who do you sell your lead oxide to?" Khalidi asked as Vargas began to tie his shoes.

"Why do you care? Car battery plants mostly."

"I am going to create a fictitious car battery company in Los Angeles. You will sell them bags of lead oxide. Only you are going to ship the plutonium oxide in its place. You'll arrange that the bags of lead oxide you send to the storage area are not assayed."

Vargas stopped, glared at him, said nothing. He saw it could be done.

"For that you will receive all the photographs, negatives and a substantial monetary payment," Khalidi went on.

Vargas' head came up. He rubbed his moustache, could smell the bitch's juices on his hairs. "How much money?"

"A hundred thousand dollars, in cash."

The sound of the shower stopped. Vargas stared through the open doors. "Where the hell'd you find her?"

Khalidi's voice was suddenly taut. "Please leave her out of this."

"Leave her out of this? You're the one holding that camera."

"I will bring the pictures to your office tomorrow." He would find some rental photography lab and develop them himself.

Vargas stood. "I want two hundred thousand dollars and it may take time to set up, a couple of weeks. I'm not going to get caught. I'll have to wait for the right moment and cover the paperwork."

"A couple of weeks will be acceptable, but I will pay you only a hundred thousand dollars."

He glared at Khalidi with a hatred that penetrated. "All right," Vargas said. Then he left, slamming the door behind him.

Elation jumped through Khalidi. As he hurried into his room, Amal came out of the bathroom, a large white towel around her dark body. Her short hair was wet and stringy.

"I am sorry, excuse me," he said, stopping. "I will get your clothes."

"Wait! What did he say?"

"He agreed."

She brought both hands together in front of her mouth, bit the tips of her forefingers. "We really did it."

A large smile came to him and he nodded.

She moved toward him, reached both bare arms up and circled them around his neck and kissed him. It was so unexpected he did not respond. Her touch was light, barely perceptible. His mouth parted slightly and he tasted the wine on her, which he liked. He was aware that his hands remained awkwardly at his sides. Slowly, he reached his arms around her, felt the wetness on her back and the warmth of her skin from the shower. She kissed him harder, almost hungrily it seemed to him. Her hand reached in front of her and the towel dropped between them.

He took one breast in his hand, the nipple erect in his long fingers. He squeezed and a small sound rose in her throat and she wrapped both arms around him. He kissed her deeply and she led him to the bed.

He sat on the edge and she knelt beside him on her knees and released the buttons on his shirt. She drew the shirt from him and ran her small hands through the curls of hair on his chest. He untied his shoes, pulled them and his socks off, then stood and climbed out of his pants, leaving the underwear. A smile swept her face and she pulled the elastic on the white jockey shorts and drew them to his ankles.

"We're going to have to get you some boxers," she said.

He liked the sound of "we" and stepped quickly from the jockeys.

She slid back farther on the bed. "Vargas was for a reason. I want you to know I don't do this with just anyone." She laughed. "Mostly."

He said nothing, had not slept with a woman in almost two years. Then it had been with a skinny lab tech who made no sounds and, feeling more alone with her, after several months he had ended it. He joined her on the bed but then remained still, afraid this would somehow be taken from him. He looked at her body, and after a moment, his fingers tentatively touched her cheek. She turned her head and kissed them. Still, he hesitated. She smiled and encouragingly lifted a breast toward him. His tongue rolled on the erect nipple while a hand rested on her waist. Small noises escaped her throat and her fingers slipped through his hair grabbing his skull in a tight grip. Her whole body began to move and come alive.

He kissed her neck, her ear, her shoulder and his tongue swept her smooth skin from her breasts to her ear as his hands felt her body. She nibbled at his neck and shoulder, and with her bare feet moving on his legs sensation ran everywhere through him.

She dropped on her back and he ran his fingers under her buttocks and she slowly drew her legs apart. His hand found its way there. The hairs were still wet from the shower and the inside was very wet and she arched. He searched up through the mound of hair with a single finger through the folds and her knees came up, parted and she dug her toes in the bedspread. He massaged gently. She rocked with his motion, rising as he moved his finger faster and faster. She let out a guttural noise and dug her nails into his shoulder and he loved the small pain. Not wanting to wait any longer, he descended gently to her.

He felt her body stiffen for an instant, then relax as they were together. He pushed his hands through the wet hair at the sides of her head, kissing her, moved and sounds came rhythmically from her. Silent, he altered the movement and she lifted her legs high in the air vertically, drawing him in deeper. They were moving together, building, building, then she tightened with a loud rasping inhale, wrapped her legs around him and shuddered in soft pulls against him. He continued soundlessly for an eternity of seconds before he sagged, feeling more wonderful than he ever had in his life. He fell against her neck breathing hard and felt her warm skin against his. Still together, he circled his arms around her. They lay there unmoving for a long time.

"How are you going to get the plutonium into Israel?" she asked after a moment, breaking the quiet.

Pride flowed through him, the nervousness gone, but more from the plan than the sex. "Under an Israeli yacht. They vacation on Cyprus then return to Tel Aviv. I watched one dock at their marina. The Israeli customs agents only search the boat. Seawater will not harm the plutonium and it will not require shielding. If I attach a fifteen pound sphere to the bottom of one of these yachts on Cyprus, nobody onboard will notice the weight."

"All you'll have to do is have a frogman go into the marina and get it."

"Yes, precisely."

She stretched both arms back over her head. "Wow."

He started to ease out of her and she quickly threw her arms around him. "No moving."

He felt her muscles tighten, relax, tighten. He could not believe this, how happy he was. He filled with scenes of their living together, later, pictured a family. Then his face turned stone serious as he thought about her and Geraldo. He placed a hand on her shoulder and she stopped.

"No lies," he said.

She seemed puzzled. "All right."

"This need not continue beyond here. I want it to, and if it does, that is what I ask. You do as you wish, but no lies."

"Got it," she said and glowed, feeling even closer to him. She did not lie. Well, did not like to, and she hated having to keep stories straight. "I don't know where this is going, but all cards will be face up. Every hand."

He was thrilled. Geraldo's writings were nothing and she would see he was the better man. He felt himself harden. A smile lit her face and he grinned too. He grabbed her buttocks and began to move against her.

CHAPTER 6

June 20

Shai's first break in the case came unexpectedly from South Africa, which was fitting as he had been roaming the halls like a bull elephant in search of a watering hole. At Ben-Gurion Airport, Shai waited eagerly on the humid tarmac as, engines whining, the large South African Airways 747 taxied to a halt. For security reasons, no planes were permitted near the terminal and there were no jetways at the airport. A wind carrying the odor of fuel kicked dust along the ground. In Europe, while parked at jetways El Al planes always ran their engines, ready for abrupt escape. Shai watched as the ground crew pushed two ramps against the flank of the plane and the passengers headed down to the tarmac and continued past the Uzi-toting soldiers to the waiting buses.

Jan Voerward emerged. He was facing the final ascent to fifty years old, which he would not hoof with grace. Despite the South African sun and beaches, his was a pale face accustomed to desks and files without clear character, eager to receive and implement orders, one that took pride in duty rather than initiative. A face blemished by the raised veins on his nose from too frequent tipping of a bottle.

Wearing a lightweight seersucker suit and carrying a garment bag, Voerward took a folded white handkerchief and patted the sweat off his brow. Shai approached, burying his dislike of Voerward the way he entombed unpleasant memories, and reached out his hand.

"Welcome, Jan."

Voerward shook it. "Beastly sticky here, don't you think."

"I suppose so. Let's get you someplace more comfortable." Shai led him away from the waiting buses to a small jeep. Shai hated their close relations with Pretoria but they had few enough friends as it was. They climbed in and the soldier behind the wheel sped toward the terminal.

"Let me have your passport," Shai said above the noise of the jeep and Voerward handed it to him.

None of the buses had arrived and the terminal was empty. Within minutes they piled into his blue Renault.

Voerward glared at the torn seat. "Carmon bloody economizing?"

"My car, I'm afraid. Not to worry." He smiled. "It almost always makes it up the hills. We have you in the King David."

"I should think so."

Shai wanted to put him up in a closet. The car's weak air conditioner blasted full force, which still left sweat dripping down the folds of Voerward's face, though he had laid his jacket over his lap.

Voerward chatted about Mandela, the wife, who he claimed had actually killed that *kaffir* kid, and what a balls-up letting Nelson out of prison of all things was just now.

"What have you got?" Shai asked, glancing at him, unwilling to wait for the formal presentation in Jerusalem.

"Something I should think you'll be rather keen on," Voerward said. "A man approached the security officer in one of our embassies with rather an interesting offer. Cautiously, you see. I presume you're aware that our nuclear reactors are essentially useless for anything but bloody electricity."

Shai nodded. In the mid-1970s when gold crescendoed to near $800 an ounce, riding the crest of that wave South Africa had enormous global purchasing clout. Many nations were willing to turn a blind eye to apartheid and sell them anything that wasn't nailed down too tightly. The South Africans glimpsed the future and were trying to buy big before the embargoes hit. On principal, both the American and British governments decided against selling nuclear technology to South Africa, but seeing Krugerrands in their beer steins the West Germans rushed in but salvaged some conscience by dumping old 1960s technology reactors on Pretoria instead of the new breed. Pretoria discovered to their dismay, rather late, that the low concentration of plutonium produced in the old-style reactor's waste could not be successfully separated from the other waste products to yield weapons-grade plutonium.

Shai tapped the steering wheel as he drove along a field of green cotton bushes shooting out yellow blooms. "So somebody wanted to sell you plutonium. Not a bad idea. If I wanted to unload some, who better to approach? You've got money. And if I cared, all you might blow up is the tip of nowhere."

"Yes, some might look at it that way, mightn't they. We rather see ourselves as the center of the universe. Then I suppose everybody does."

"They do around here." Shai laughed.

Voerward removed his handkerchief and swiped at the beads on his forehead. His hair was full and thick, but entirely gray. "We're suspicious of walk-ins of course, so we question the lad. What's the deal? Why the offer now? That line. He tells us he was forced into it not terribly long ago by a stitch of blackmail, though he won't discuss what. The subsequent reports on him I've read suggest he's the randy sort. Not terribly successful. Not terribly moral. Not terribly anything, really. You getting the picture?"

"In rainbows of color."

"Yes, good. Then let's toil on. He tells us he got paid a sizable sum—and again he won't divulge the particulars—above and beyond the blackmail. He confesses that he went through it rather rapidly. Clever chap that he is, he had a little chat with himself and figured out a way to put his grubby hands on more. Rather eager about it too, so the file indicates."

"He didn't by any chance rush to tell you who he gave the plutonium to?"

"Alas, no. We pushed him as hard as we dared on that. Didn't want to queer the whole thing of course, not with your concerns foremost in our minds. I must confess too, there was some debate back home over whether to buy plutonium from him first and tell you people later, but then with whatever wogs are now running around with a bomb for however long we of course wanted to alert you immediately."

"His name," Shai said, figuring the Afrikaners had already bought enough plutonium elsewhere. "I trust you can share it with me."

"I didn't do that yet? Bloody sorry. Wish I could claim it's the time change but we're in the same zone, now aren't we. Vargas. Joaquim Vargas of Sao Paulo. I have our complete file in my bag for your perusal." Voerward shot a glance at him. "If your people haven't already lifted it on the plane and copied it."

Shai sidestepped. "Do you know when he delivered?"

"We can guess. He bought a new BMW in Sao Paulo on June four, paid cash."

With blackmail, it was more likely they paid him a small part in advance and the balance on delivery. Likely he bought the BMW with the lion's share paid on delivery. Shai leaned forward as he drove, as if he could urge the car faster. He had a sense now of their timing and whatever they were launching was soon. A plan was bursting to the fore and he ached to assemble his team. With a bit of luck it would be his plutonium. How much pilfered plutonium could be running around at the moment anyway? Rather than answer that he chose to believe he was finally at the mouth of a trail.

They approached Sha'ar Hagai, the Gate of the Valley, which marked the abrupt winding ascent from the flat fields through the rocky hills and pines to Jerusalem and Shai pushed the accelerator. "Maybe we ought to be getting there already."

Voerward nodded. "Don't suppose I can blame you for the rush. Going out on a flight to Zurich first thing tomorrow myself. Best to be safe and out of here, don't you agree? This isn't my battlefield."

"No, it's not," Shai agreed with sufficient politeness to pass as friendship.

In UCLA's sculpture garden, Khalidi waited in front of the Theater Arts building, had come to north campus to surprise Amal after her acting class. He still wore his coat and tie and felt dampness beneath the white shirt he'd precisely ironed himself. He had another shirt in his office and would change as soon as he could. A dozen iron and bronze sculptures rose from grass mounds, with concrete footpaths shaded by pines and redwoods snaking between them. It was amazingly different than the concrete science quad, which he felt was what a college campus should look like.

He heard a small group of students exiting MacGowan, turned, and his emotions plummeted through him like a lead weight. Laughing, Amal was walking next to that sloppily dressed Geraldo Chavez.

After two days vacation in Rio de Janeiro, she had thrown her arms around him in the shower and said, "This is out of control. I'm definitely breaking up with Geraldo." A week after they returned she told him she had ended it. He had wanted to ask her to move in immediately but did not, feared her saying no. He would proceed slowly. He was on his way to Jerusalem after all, and once he had erected the Palestinian state they would be together.

Amal saw him, said something to Geraldo, then approached with short, brisk steps. She was wearing shorts and a loose T-shirt that said: LIFE'S A BEACH.

"Hey, great surprise. I'm starved. Let's get pizza."

He wanted to ask about Geraldo but did not. "If it is all right, I want to go to my office first to change my shirt."

"Cool. Lose the jacket and tie. Kenneth, it's summer."

"I was teaching."

She rolled her eyes.

All the way to the physics building she chattered about the scene she had just performed. She did not mention she had acted it with Geraldo. As Khalidi listened, with his other mind he repeated to himself that she had left Geraldo immediately and come with him. Men must have wanted her her whole life, he thought. He wondered what it was like to occupy such a beautiful body, if people confused the person with the package. He had read in his research on women that beautiful, shy women were perceived as cold not just by men, but to his surprise even more so by women.

Entering his office, he switched on the harsh lights.

"No lies," she said, closing the door. "I'm still attracted to Geraldo."

He gave a small nod, knowing his hurt showed. "I saw. "

"Kenneth, I just don't know if I'm ready to be serious with *anyone*. I feel you want to be. That's maybe why I don't see you as much as I'd like." She saw his face sag further. "Look, I don't know what I feel exactly. But I'm way happy when we're together. It's great."

He looked at her for a long moment. He loved not just the wrapping he told himself but the person—her freedom, dashing places without plans. She took him for a merry-go-round ride in Santa Monica, and then she abruptly wanted to go fishing off the end of the pier so he had rented two poles.

"If you are happy when we are together, that is enough," he said. "There is no hurry for anything."

"Really, that's great. Really? You sure?"

"Yes," he said, though he was not certain he believed it. He did not know what he would do if she left him for Geraldo.

"That's so sweet. Thanks." Happiness filled her voice.

He nodded, opened the desk drawer and lifted out a folded white shirt. He knew he did not make her laugh the way Geraldo did. Graduate applications for admission to the department that he was supposed to review rose from the corner of the desk. He had drawn that drudgework committee too and would begin his careful summaries of them after they had eaten. He removed his jacket, modestly turned his back to her and pulled his tie loose.

Amal dropped her pack on the floor. She found his shyness appealing, especially after the way Geraldo and all the others like him usually wanted to talk to her for about two minutes before jumping her. Still, the intense way Geraldo talked and locked his gaze with hers when they did a scene together completely flipped her switch. Kenneth often averted his eyes when she looked right at him. She had not expected to still have these feeling for Geraldo, especially since she had decided to be with Kenneth. What he was doing thrilled her, was far more than all Geraldo's pot and talk, and *she* was part of it.

"Is the first plutonium sphere on its way to Cyprus yet?" she asked.

He finished tucking in his shirt and turned. "It will be placed under the Israeli yacht in three days."

"Wow." She neared. "How's it getting there?"

He thought again about her laughing with Geraldo, stared at the pile of graduate applications, and spoke with intensity. "A London shipping magnate. Sabri Barakat. It was loaded on one of his freighters in San Diego." Abruptly, he slapped at the applications and sent them spinning over the floor. "We'll have pizza later."

Stepping on the papers, he locked the door, approached her and lifted the T-shirt over her head, revealing unleashed breasts. He slipped his fingers inside the waist of her shorts and underwear and drew them down. Surprised and very excited, she stepped out of them. He undressed quickly and tossed his clothes onto the chair.

He kissed her hard with his lips, tongue, teeth. His hands reached around to her rear and as he lifted her she clasped her fingers around his neck and kicked off her sandals. She happily gripped her legs around him, loving this no lies business, that she could tell him everything. He carried her easily, leaned her against the bookshelves, and moved up against her hard, smashing the books and matching her excited intakes of breath with his own newly discovered deep noises, not caring who heard.

Sara Stein stood at a window in the Jerusalem apartment of a vacationing professor that Shai had acquired somehow for the briefing. Recruited several years before by Shai himself, her American parents had hauled the red haired, copper-flecked, green-eyed Sara from New Jersey to ultraorthodox Kiryat Arba above Hebron and attempted to shroud her teenage inquisitiveness with long clothes. In class, with the Bible and the Midrash exegesis open on her desk, she read Wonder

Woman comic books on her lap. Her confidence shaken by relentless disapproval, after the army she had drifted into the Bohemian Nachlaot quarter of Jerusalem. She adored staying up late, smoking, drinking and talking to struggling painters and writers, and anyone else wandering in who volunteered more doubts than answers. And if they wanted to stare at her long, shapely legs in the shorts she liked to wear with a sweatshirt even in winter, she could appreciate that artistic sensibility too. She was out of the family home but her psyche was not and she slept with none of them. Then she fell fabulously in love with an older man of thirty-five, who taught her wonders that had not been even hinted at by any members of the Justice League of America. When it was over she cried for three days, then thought: who's next?

"This flies all over me," Sara said about selling plutonium, since Shai was not yet talking. She offered to snare Vargas with sex, adding it would take her and Cilla about one hour max to tie Vargas naked to bed posts.

Seated on the sofa, reserved and always appropriate, the tall, Liverpool born Cilia Phillips, her blond hair bluntly cut at the chin and fifteen years Sara's senior, wished she had indulged her youth like Sara rather than marrying and bearing children so young, it all crashing in the divorce. She had married her husband both because he had asked and because she had felt it was expected of her.

Cilia reached for her cigarettes and suppressed a smile. "I'm not too keen on popping into bed with Vargas, actually."

"Come on, we'd be snug as a bug in a rug, the three of us," Sara said with a laugh. "It'd be great fun."

"Smashing fun for Vargas, you mean."

Sunk in an upholstered chair waiting for the last member of the team to arrive, Shai laughed. The simple truth, he offered finally, was that their quarry could be hung full clothed by his ankles with the threat to his freedom, readily available in this instance. Shai winked at Sara and told the two women that he had commandeered them to utilize traits other than their bodies.

"But it's always good to have a few marv bods around just in case," Sara added, and no one was known ever to have disagreed about that.

A knock sounded on the door. Their South African, who could affect an impeccable British drone, had arrived. Shai was up immediately, the door open, pumping Hirsh Schiff's hand and asking about the last leg of his journey from London. The product of a staunch Zionist upbringing in Johannesburg, Hirsh had packed his bags at sixteen and flown home to a place he'd never been, to Israel. Short, with jet-black hair, rugged and handsomely compact, he was a veteran of both wars at home, running networks in Beirut and Tripoli, and in the mid-1980s, comfortable in Africa, had been instrumental in smuggling hordes of Ethiopian Jews to Sudan, and from there to Israel via Europe.

Shai disregarded psychology as much as possible, preferring the textual experience of the rabbis, and, consciously or not, drew scarred loners under his wing as long as they had reasonably sound centers. As a young army officer, Hirsh had commanded the counterattack on the northern Israeli border school at Ma'alot when Nayef Hawatmeh's flavor of Palestinian murderers had seized ninety teenagers and demanded the release of twenty-three Palestinians in their prisons. When negotiations broke down the terrorists began slaughtering the children. Hirsh's security forces rushed the school, and in the firefight, the toll was twenty-one teenagers dead. For months afterward Hirsh hardly spoke, and began in his silence what would blossom into a talent for charcoal sketches on paper. These later greatly occupied him during the interminable waiting of his profession, and also served to recreate faces where the pointing of a camera would have been awkward. Though women located his bed without much difficulty, he did not form intimate relationships with them.

Shai liked his teams to coalesce in the hearth of home before he launched them. In this case they would have to gel quickly as they had flights and separate connections to Sao Paulo that evening.

From the now-augmented Pretoria file, Shai detailed everything they had on Vargas. Time, which he was never on the best of terms with, always either too early or too late, was breathing hotly down his neck. If Vargas had passed the plutonium, the bomb could be anywhere. As Shai talked, Hirsh did an affectionately irreverent sketch of him, hands under his bulging stomach to hold it up as he walked, sweat flying from his brow. Shai stopped in mid-sentence, pointed and declared he would tape it to his refrigerator as a reminder and everybody smiled.

After tea and insipid cookies that only Shai ate, he unfolded the whole of it and the theft of the neutron source. Sara burst out that it was ridiculous, that Palestinians could never sneak such a thing into the country. For the first time in anyone present's memory, Shai blew up, shouting that there were legions of extremely able Palestinians. One might mention the remarkable minds behind the *intifada*_and the printing presses they could still not find if a citing was necessary. He did not want any stone left unturned, and he would countenance no underestimation of their cousins in this land.

He calmed quickly and began to clean up the debris of their cups and cookies. He smiled at Sara and said the only exclusive women's work he believed in was honey traps. Sara smiled back, saying she was sure with Shai's good looks he could handle it if Vargas swung that way. The team broke up in laughter, ending a difficult moment.

In the apartment they spoke only English to accustom themselves to doing so in South America, intending Vargas not gather he was being burned by Israelis. Everywhere people seemed eager to betray their country or themselves, as long as it was not to the Jews. Fortunately, Israel had native speakers in about every language worth suborning anyone from.

After the women departed to assemble their foreign purchased wardrobes, Hirsh remained alone in the kitchen intent over the stove, monitoring the heat under a brass *ibrik* with a long, hollow handle he had found above the refrigerator.

"I suspect you didn't have time to unpack," Shai said.

Hirsh did not turn to face him. "No." He had been in Baghdad recruiting disgruntled army officers, who believed they were merely unburdening to the British for a handsome fee.

"Make mine with two sugars." Shai smiled. "You've inspired

me to cut down."

Hirsh nodded. The coffee boiled and at exactly the right instant he lifted the pot and poured the thick Turkish coffee into two short, handleless glasses with spoons, to prevent them from cracking. He added the sugars to each, stirred and passed a hot glass to Shai by the thumb and forefinger.

Shai waited for the mud of grounds to settle. "Sorry to pull you out so abruptly. I needed the accent, among other things."

"Fine."

"You haven't been back much recently, have you?"

"We're out tonight. I'm not here."

"If you're home too long, you don't want to leave." Shai made it a statement, not a question.

Hirsh downed his coffee, said nothing.

"I'm the opposite," Shai said. "Restless if I'm here too long."

Hirsh turned to him. "Don't envy anyone who loves you."

Shai said nothing and his eyes became distant as he drank his coffee.

"We'll find it," Hirsh said roughly.

Shai was silent for a long time before he spoke. "That's what we always say, don't we." A depression was rolling over him like a wave, seizing him, pulling him down beneath the water. "The Six-Day War, Entebbe made us believe we could do anything. We can't, any more than the Americans can. The Gulf War was the fluke. They'll have more Vietnams. That's what we and the Americans have in common, Hirsh, we both march with our eyes closed. We think building settlements on the mountaintops is bringing us back to our pioneering days but we're ignoring the Palestinian villages below those mountains, and eventually it will explode." Shai did not know why he was talking like this, why he was despondent now that he was finally on the trail. It was not like him.

"That's the politicians' problem," Hirsh said. "Mine is finding the fucking bomb."

Shai fought his way back up, took a long drink of the coffee. He changed tact. "You work with Sara before?"

"Once, in Beirut with Schulmann."

"What'd you think?"

"Too headstrong. Knows she's good. Took her a while to see that, it seems but she's there."

"Smart?"

"Very."

"Pretty enough for, well, whatever?"

"Obviously." Irritation came through Hirsh's voice. He hated when Shai ran this way, when only he could see the finish line.

Some of the bounce was back in Shai. "Spend some of your free time with her. How shall I put it? Delve a bit. I'll want your opinion about possibilities." He was moving and already halfway to the door.

"What the hell you talking about?" Hirsh swore at the departing figure, who slammed the door behind him. He had no clue what Shai wanted. He was getting more like the potty old Colonel all the time. He'd probably start muttering to roses soon too. Hirsh lifted the glass of coffee and despite himself, he smiled.

Back in his office, Shai put in a call to Switzerland to have Ramzy contact him. The response came an hour later that Ramzy had disappeared into the Arab world and could not be reached, which Shai knew was his modus operandi. Abu Nidal and the other extremists were a greater threat to Ramzy in Arab countries that sheltered them than they were in Europe. Shai left a message for Ramzy to phone when he could, eager to learn what he had uncovered on his end. The road to everyone involved with the bomb would have many branches and Ramzy had reach around the globe Israel did not.

In Arab East Jerusalem, Samir walked along Suleiman Street with a slight limp, an infirmity from birth. A student at Birzeit University near Ramallah, he served as a member of the grassroots Council on Health Education for the Occupied Territories. On June 3 they had set up National Health Day, where health committees provided extensive medical tests and services to their people free of charge. He knew a great number of the doctors and dentists in the West Bank, and had been sent on a mission he did not understand but would obey without hesitation. He was supposed to collect fifteen lead dental aprons from a variety of dentists and deliver them tonight to a vacant lot in Tulkarm at the westernmost tip of the West Bank, not far from Tel Aviv. A note had been delivered by a teenage runner, addressed to him personally and signed 'The Voice of the People.' He was happy to help in any way needed.

Across the wide street to Samir's left towered the limestone walls of the Old City. Every shop to his right was shut. Across the metal doors and stone facades painted strokes blotted over the *intifada's* cry for freedom. In every town, village and refugee camp each new communiqué's provisions crawled across houses, shops and walls. Printed every two to three weeks, the communiqués announced cultural symposia, general strike and total boycott days of the civil administration, a day for renaming institutions and schools with Palestinian names, as well as a day to celebrate the authority of the people by striking at those remaining outside the people's will.

Samir disagreed as did most of his friends with murdering, mutilating and hanging in public the bodies of those among them who collaborated with the enemy. Some had been blackmailed, some in desperate financial hardship. He loved all his people and wanted none of them harmed by anyone. Samir limped past head-covered village women from Nahalin, Hussan, Battir—the villages recognized by the distinctive colorful embroidery on their long dresses—who sat cross-legged on the sidewalk selling fruits and vegetables from plastic cartons. With the shops closed at noon every day everywhere through the West Bank and Gaza, the Unified Command showed the Israelis and the world that they controlled the population. Today the shops had not opened at all. On Sunday and Monday Israeli soldiers had killed six people; two in the Balata refugee camp near Nablus, one in Ramallah, one in Khan Yunis, and two more in the Bureij Camp in Gaza. A three-day commercial strike had immediately been declared. Unlike a general strike, transportation was not halted and a row of seven-passenger Mercedes service taxis lined up across the street waiting for passengers for Ramallah.

Under the Schmidt's Girls College across from Damascus

Gate, Samir waited at a red light as people bustled in all directions in the heat. A young Palestinian in cheap Western clothing with leather basketball high-tops approached him flashing a wad of currency held with a rubber band. "Shekel, dinar," he sang out. "Shekel, dinar." Samir shook his head, and as the light changed, he crossed toward the building that held the dental office that was his destination. The Jordanian dinar was still used along with the Israeli shekel in the West Bank, the Jordanian-held land having fallen to the Israelis in the calamity of the 1967 war.

He stepped through the paper and debris from the fruit, vegetable, and spice sellers squatted here. The pleasant scent of rosemary, basil and za'atar swept up to him from the overflowing boxes. Men stood behind carts piled with peaches and green apples. A few young Americans, or Europeans, bearing backpacks trudged through the crowd of both Western and traditionally dressed Arabs, apparently heading to one of the nearby hostels, which were cheaper than on the Israeli side.

An old, shriveled, toothless woman, her palm outstretched, stood in front of a row of closed shops also with painted over writing. Despite devastating economic loss the strike had become a part of daily life, for month after month his people adhered to the self-imposed curfew with collective will, sharing hardships while they developed communal resources. They had ceased acquiescing, ripped away the camouflaging layers of public harmony, bared their desires and regained their self-esteem.

Just after the newspaper stand, Samir entered a three-story stone building, the high-ceilinged entranceway substantially cooler that the bright, dry heat outside. A merchant had different flowers in buckets under the stairwell and colorful spools of sewing threads hung from the wall. Samir climbed up the whitewashed stairwell through the sweet scent of the flowers toward Dr. Souheil Masri's office. Medical and dental offices were exempt from the commercial strike.

The entrance room was jammed, people all waiting quietly, some reading newspapers. In the corner, an old woman in a long black dress, her hair covered with a worn purple scarf, bounced a child on her lap. Samir limped toward the receptionist, a thin, elderly keffiyehed man with a moustache who tossed green worry beads in one hand.

"I must see Dr. Masri," Samir said.

The man clutched his beads and motioned toward the people in the waiting room. "Sit," he said, then shrugged. "Maybe an hour, maybe more."

Samir paid him no attention and walked through the doorless passageway into the offices. The receptionist burst up from his chair with surprising agility for his age and hurried after him shouting threats.

Dr. Masri, middle-aged with thick glasses, appeared from one of the treatment rooms. He spoke quickly to the trailing receptionist, who retreated like a chastened dog. Samir approached and they kissed on both cheeks.

"What now?" Masri asked good-naturedly. "I suppose you have plans for me to work through half the night again."

Samir smiled. Everywhere his people eagerly helped each other. "This time it's easy. I only need a few minutes."

"Easy, only minutes. I am very happy and I'm sure my wife will be very happy, and our children." He playfully boxed Samir's head. "I'm about to start an extraction. What?"

Samir motioned him toward a corner of the corridor, then spoke quietly. "The thin aprons you put over the body when you do x-rays."

"Yes, the lead cling shields."

"I want as many as you can give me."

"I have two, if you include an old one with the plastic torn. If you need more, I can order you some from a dental supply company in Tel Aviv. Unfortunately, there's no other place to get them."

"No, don't order any. Not for me, and no replacement ones for yourself until I tell you. I need both." His instructions had been explicit on this matter.

"Samir, what for?"

Samir said nothing, looked down.

Masri stared at him for a moment. In this time of clandestine committees and mass arrests of their people, one did not ask questions.

He knew Samir worked tirelessly providing health care, especially for the small villages and refugee camps. "Wait here," he said. Masri went into an office, came out with a lead apron, then walked to a storage room at the end of the hail, rummaged inside and pulled out another one. He returned and handed Samir the cling shields, rounded at the top to fit around the neck and cover the shoulders, and long enough to stretch over the tops of the legs.

"How soon will I get them back?"

"I don't know. Soon," he said, though he did not know.

Outside, Samir carried the lead aprons to where he had parked his car around the corner in front of the closed marketplace. Across the sun-drenched street in the dirt lot, dozens of service taxis waited to race passengers up and down the West Bank and Gaza. He opened the trunk and piled the lead shields in on top of the eight he had already retrieved in Hebron and Bethlehem. He would get the last five from Nablus, where he lived.

Samir drove north toward his parents' home. He had been instructed to deliver the lead aprons exactly at 10:00 p.m. The road threaded through the mountain plateau dotted with low Arab homes with Eiffel Tower-shaped antennas on the roofs. The shops along the two-lane main road to Nablus were all eerily shut, with the ever-present, multi-colored, blotted-over script growing on their facades. Frequently, huge orange cans advertising Club Cola sat atop the roofs of shut businesses. The Palestinians boycotted Coca-Cola and its subsidiary Sprite, sold inside Israel. Recently, a Palestinian with a British passport had begun manufacturing Club Cola in the West Bank, and though it tasted awful, the Palestinians guzzled it like it was nectar from the Gods.

North of Ramallah, a truck heading toward him from the opposite lane flashed Samir and all the other blue license plated cars as he passed them, the signal for an Israeli military checkpoint up ahead. Israeli and settlers cars all had yellow license plates to identify them to the military—ironically also pinpointing the Jews for the stone hurling youngsters. Samir thought quickly. As a lone driver in a passenger car, he likely would be waved through. He could probably bypass this checkpoint, but he could not avoid all of them on the way to Nablus. They shifted locations daily and there were not always side roads to circumvent them.

Furious at the Zionists controlling his land, Samir quickly pulled off the road to the right, and in the lack of traffic typical since the *intifada* as people stayed home rather than face the delaying checkpoints, he turned around. Three kilometers back he pulled off on a dirt road that led north through the Kalandia refugee camp. There was a military outpost on the hill overlooking the camp but he had never seen a roadblock inside it.

Spraying dust, he rolled up the windows and drove on the narrow road with the jumble of one-story cinderblock houses pressed against each other on both sides of him, many with corrugated iron roofs held down with boulders. Without air conditioning, the heat was stifling inside the small Toyota. Dirt lanes wove between the huts, where laundry flapped from washing lines and occasional tomato plants and corn stocks pushed up through the dirt beside the homes. Two or three times he saw small illegal flags with the red, green, and black Palestinian colors fluttering from the electrical wires. The young boys weighted them with stones and tossed them up. The soldiers often grabbed random boys and forced them to climb the poles to retrieve them, and there had been several electrocutions.

Samir's Toyota burst back up onto the main Ramallah-Nablus Road and he quickly rolled the window down letting in welcome fresh air. The bright sun bounded off the mountains. A half hour later, nearing Nablus the sparse traffic suddenly slowed—a roadblock, with no way around it. Samir stopped behind a service taxi. On the side of the road, khaki canvas supported by four poles shaded a desk and several soldiers seated there. A thick pile of computer paper with names either of the wanted list or the delinquent tax list sat on the desk. Usually they harassed taxis and buses, particularly the drivers, checking their identification cards against the list to see if they had paid their taxes, which early in the *intifada* the Palestinians had substantially ceased doing. If a soldier matched the identification card number to someone on the wanted list, he called out, "Bingo." The legions of "bingos," young men pursued by the authorities, darted from house to house or hid in the caves in the hills, rarely daring to sleep in the same place two nights running.

Several lines of large rocks stretched three quarters of the way across both lanes of the highway, and cars, when motioned forward, had to weave slowly between them. Traffic was stopped in both directions. Two rifle-toting soldiers who looked no more than eighteen or nineteen stood in the center of the two-lane road.

A yellow plated car came up from behind them, swung out to the left of the row of idling blue license plated cars, and drove through the checkpoint without stopping. Samir felt the humiliation of waiting here hot on his face.

One soldier beckoned the car in front of the service taxi forward. The driver approached slowly and stopped. The soldier asked him several questions through the rolled down window and then waved him on. Fortunately there were no cars waiting in the other direction and the soldier motioned for the service taxi. As the heavy car crawled forward, the soldier pointed to the edge of the road and down several times.

Samir swore to himself. There would be further delay. The large diesel Mercedes, its motor loud stopped where it had been told to. The soldier approached, said something, and the driver switched off his engine. The driver turned around and Samir could see that only the men inside pulled out the orange plastic covers of West Bank identity cards. When they were gathered the driver handed them to the soldier who took them to the older soldiers sitting at the desk under the khaki flap and one started flipping through the computer paper. Samir looked down, not wanting to draw attention to himself. Another yellow plated car wound through the roadblock from the other direction and passed him.

Ten minutes elapsed, fifteen. Samir looked up. The soldiers either had found someone or were taking their time. He could not tell from the activity around the table. So far no one had been ordered out of the Mercedes. Finally, a soldier carried the orange holders to the driver and motioned him on. The Mercedes wove through the rock barriers as people inside the car passed back the identity cards.

The soldier looked in the other direction. There were still no cars heading south, so he motioned Samir forward. Trying to ease the hatred from his face, Samir carefully stopped beside the soldier. Suddenly he was afraid they would find the lead aprons, confiscate them, arrest him. He tried to calm himself. They looked for fear.

The peach fuzz faced soldier bent to the window, asked in Hebrew, "Where are you going?"

"Shechem," Samir answered with the occupier's Biblical name for his city.

"You live there?"

"Yes "

"Where are you coming from?"

"Jerusalem."

He pointed to the side of the road for Samir to pull over. Panicked, Samir drove slowly then stopped. The soldier must have sensed his panic.

The soldier came over, looked into the empty back seat. "Your identification card."

Samir handed the orange plastic through the window to him. The soldier flipped it open and took a brief look. "Get out of the car, please."

They must have known. They knew everything, he thought miserably as he climbed out.

"Open the trunk," the soldier said.

Samir saw that it was over. He would be in prison for six months, a year, if not more. The certainty that he was caught brought defiance and he inserted the key hard, tugged up the trunk.

The soldier looked at the lead aprons covered with plastic, pushed his rifle muzzle into the edge and lifted several. He called over another soldier, who trotted near, and the first soldier bent into the trunk and searched through the aprons with his hands now. Finding nothing under them, he turned to Samir.

"What are these?"

He was already known to their computers as a member of the

Health Committee. "They are dental x-ray aprons," Samir said, his voice shaking. He hated himself for his cowardice and not answering firmly. "Some dentists are coming tomorrow to x-ray teeth in Yatsid and Burqa," he said, naming two remote villages north of Nablus.

The soldier looked at him for a long moment, then handed him back his papers. "Go on."

Relief flooded through Samir and he quickly shut the trunk then carefully drove forward. Samir collected the other five required aprons and, nervous, spent the rest of the day in his parents' house without leaving it.

Though it was only a thirty-kilometer descent from Nablus toward the coast to Tulkarm, Samir left his parents' home at 9:15 in the event he was delayed at another roadblock. As he drove down from the cool heights, he felt more excitement now than nervousness. Five kilometers after the village of Anabta, he was waved through the single military roadblock he encountered. Past it and more relaxed, he wondered again what the lead aprons were for but knew he would never mention them to anyone. He raced down the final descent into Tulkarm, headlights stabbing the night, the air warm and sticky. Across the flat dark fields he could see the Jewish lights of Netanya at the ocean, a mere sixteen kilometers away.

He drove into the large town of fifty thousand, another twenty-five thousand swelling the adjacent refugee camp. A full moon brightened the empty streets. He circled the traffic roundabout at the top of the market street and slowed in front of the Al-Madina Pharmacy. Small palm trees ran down the divider of the street, which descended in the direction of the ocean. He peered down it. A single light in front of the Orient Hotel threw out a semicircle in the darkness illuminating signs on the shops beside the hotel for TIME CIGARETTES and CRYSTAL SODA. He did not know why someone did not rip down the signs for the Israeli products. So close to the Green Line—before the *intifada,* on Saturdays more Israelis had shopped here than Arabs.

He drove past the Dar al-Yateem home for orphans and deprived children, a large three-story stone building with tall pines rising above the swings, basketball court and other play areas. He checked his watch, was fifteen minutes early. He continued toward the vacant lot at the top of the street where he had been told to wait, pulled in and shut off the motor. He sat there for a while a little frightened in the dark quiet, then switched on the ignition and turned on Al-Quds Radio, which broadcast nonstop about the *intifada* from somewhere in Syria.

Tired from the excitement, he rested his head back against the seat. The radio was screaming that they had to fight the Zionist oppressors. Samir did not like its hard-line, anti-Arafat position, but the station was still theirs, the voice of the uprising. To his utter amazement, they knew everything that happened in the Occupied Territories. Once he himself had watched soldiers ordering young boys and girls to paint over strike communiques on a school wall in el-Bireh and moments later it was broadcast on Al-Quds. It was wonderful.

Suddenly someone stuck his head through the driver's window and Samir almost jumped in the seat. All he could see was the eyes, nose and mouth in the openings through the wrapped keffiyeh. Samir had not heard him approach.

"Samir, thank you for coming. You have them in the trunk?"

Samir climbed out. "Yes, I'll open it."

The man, dressed in blue jeans and sandals, followed him as Samir limped towards the rear of the car.

"You have taken a big risk," the man said. "It is appreciated, as is the work you do on the health committee."

"It is a small thing."

"It is not. There is nothing more important than caring for the sick."

His hand shaking, Samir had trouble in the dark fitting his key into the slot. The man flicked a lighter, brought it near and illuminated the area with a dancing flame. Then he touched Samir's arm gently to calm him.

Samir pushed the key in, turned it and lifted. The man reached in and hauled out all the dental aprons together.

"Wait ten minutes, then go home. Know you have done as

much as the bravest fighter."

He walked away carrying the cling shields and disappeared around a corner.

Shai sat alone in the small office Carmon had cleared for him, strewn now with the carnage of files and Styrofoam coffee cups, the computer relegated to the floor. It was after 5:00 p.m. and he was unraveling cigarettes and building the tobacco into a mound on top of a file. He inhaled the seductive scent and swept the remaining cigarettes and the pile into the trashcan. He had stayed behind while the team winged to Sao Paulo, hoping for word about the plutonium. Again depression tugged at him, a heaviness he sensed had started somewhere in fear and moved to sadness. He dropped back in his chair, removed his half-moon reading glasses and rubbed his eyes with both fists. He was aware his breathing was labored though he was sitting.

The wind rattled the open window. He looked up, assured himself that he would feel better once in the field. He stood. Everywhere he had worries—a nuclear physicist had warned him that even the most sophisticated ionization detection equipment could not penetrate lead.

The doctor had told him his pre-diabetic condition, in addition to a weakened heart, would be helped with the shedding of both weight and stress. How could he slash stress with the array of enemies out there? When the initial shock had passed, he decided to carry on as before, with the recognition that the burden of retirement, for him, would be greater. He believed too that there were no guarantees in life—he might abandon the field and even more quickly go in a car crash, as his first wife had. So he chose to accept the inevitability of his death as fact, but stubbornly believed it would not be soon.

Shai drank the last bit of cold, sweet coffee from a Styrofoam cup, extinguished the light and shuffled tiredly through the empty corridors to the elevator. His dentist, Pia, whom he had talked into emigrating from Sweden, had called him this afternoon and harangued him, as he had not had his teeth cleaned in over two years. She refused to take a no and he was giving her a half hour now. He did not at all suspect that Pia had an entirely different reason for insisting to see him.

On Cyprus, Motti Burg, his wife Adina and their guests, a couple from Petah Tikva, climbed aboard DEBRA'S JUDGMENT, talking and laughing. The forty-six foot Gulfstar motorsailer, had been sailed several years before from Florida to its new home in Tel Aviv, where Motti had purchased it. The four Israelis had driven into the hills to a small Greek village restaurant Motti knew with a view of the vast sea. Since no one in the restaurant spoke English, the owner had led them into the small kitchen and lifted the lids on the various simmering metal pots. Motti had eaten an incredibly tender lamb stew with fresh mushrooms and green beans and they had stayed late drinking a second bottle of Pella.

"Did I need this vacation," Adina said, leaning affectionately against her husband's chest as they stood on deck, the stars glittering in the blackness.

"Sorry I've been working so much. Stupid really. Who on their deathbed says, 'Wish I'd worked more.'"

She turned and kissed his neck. "It's a shame we only have two more days here."

At 5:00 a.m. the phone screamed. Shai stumbled up, not remembering where he was, then realized he was home and snatched at the receiver. He listened.

"Finally," he said to Cilla. "I'm on my way."

Her head in the pillow, Tami brushed strands of hair from her taut face. She forced herself up and leaned back against the headboard.

He cradled the receiver.

"Vargas bit," he said. "It looks like our plutonium."

"Thank God." She jumped out of bed. "You want something to eat before you go?"

"No." The guilt was assaulting him again. He went to the closet, then turned. "Tami, maybe when this is over I can do something about my health."

"Maybe you can do something about it starting right now," she said. “So we don’t lose you in the middle of this.”

He grabbed his packed bag, kissed her softly on the lips, but as he left said nothing, his mind on Brazil.

CHAPTER 7

June 23

Shai looked out the window as the plane headed inland from the sea and then over the sugar cane fields toward Sao Paulo. The timing of Vargas's recent plutonium sale gave him hope that he was climbing the right mountain.

The enormous city sat atop a high plateau of crystalline rock that rose from the coast. Descending, they burst over the dense working class and industrial areas in the north, and then headed over the city center where crowded skyscrapers pushed up through trapped brown air, an unholy alliance of humid mist and industrial pollution. Shai looked away from the window; to him, foreign cities were all similar fields of battle.

It was early Saturday morning, and after clearing airport formalities, Shai took a taxi along the wide Avenue Adolfo Pinheiro. According to prearranged instructions, he had the driver turn off and deposit him two blocks from the safe house in the residential southwestern district that had been rented in a rush for them by a member of the substantial Jewish community here. After the alcohol-fueled Chevrolet disappeared back toward the city center leaving a faintly sweet odor in its wake, Shai walked down the street, glad to move after all the sitting. He had had to wait half the day in Madrid for the overnight connection.

From the safe house window, Sara spotted Shai charging up the walkway, ignoring the pain shooting from his feet up the back of both legs. When she rushed and happily opened the door, he hurried past her, saying, "Let me see the photos," before his battered bag hit the floor.

She retreated behind the couch where Cilia and Hirsh sat. Cilia gracefully put out her cigarette, reached into her purse and handed him the curling black and white photographs she had developed herself moments before phoning him. "They're Sara's talented efforts," she said.

Still standing, Shai rifled through the photographs like someone pressed into examining someone else's family pictures, though they all knew that was simply the way he worked—fast and with apparent disinterest. He finished then turned to Sara, who had dropped heavily onto the arm of the sofa, her shapely legs dangling.

"The snaps are marv," Shai said with raised eyebrows.

A small smile crawled, then jumped up her lips. "Aren't they," she said, laughing.

Shai turned to Hirsh, who had flashed a pack of authentic-looking South African papers at Vargas provided by Carmon's forgers, mostly older men trained in Europe's ghettos and the struggle against the British, who were currently educating a few younger graduates of the Israeli mafia in Netanya.

"The quality of the tapes?" Shai asked.

Hirsh glared at him.

"You don't hear like that on a call from Jerusalem to Tel Aviv," Sara chimed in.

"When are you seeing him again?" Shai asked.

"Tonight," Hirsh said. "He's expecting a down payment. Bloody bastard's coming to the hotel at seven."

"Fine. We'll make it a party. Let's all be there." He glanced at each of them. "Good job. I want to hear the tapes, then I want to see the nuclear facility, where he lives, the hotel." This is where I belong, he might have added, but instead said, "Hirsh, with me in the hotel room. You lovely ladies in the lobby to watch Vargas's backside."

Cilia suddenly seemed uncomfortable. "Shall I ring Carmon? He's been phoning all morning."

He looked at her, could see the pain beneath the reserve, but she always held herself together. "Pretend you forgot his number for now." Shai turned to Sara. "Care to cart an old man around a bit?"

She bounded to her feet, her hair swaying at her shoulders. "What else do I live for?"

At 6:00 p.m., Shai and Hirsh ate in the Othon Palace Hotel dining room. Vargas was due upstairs in half an hour. Shai had ordered them beef empanadas, sweet potatoes and a mountain of fried plantains. The waiters carried skewers of meat and pushed off hunks directly onto diner's plates. No stranger to beef from the African savannas, Hirsh had finished quickly, while Shai was only beginning his second round of everything from the platters, as well as more filet mignon and morcilla sausage.

Hirsh spoke in a fierce whisper. "You're going to kill yourself before others manage it for you."

Shai smiled. "The assessment psychologist told me I'm suffering from a death wish. It's total bullshit." His smile was gone. "I'm actually afraid I'm going to fail just when it matters most."

"Worrying is helpful, up to a point. " Hirsh ate quietly and then said, "It's not that we need you. Everybody's replaceable. But too many people will miss you. Especially me."

Shai looked at the anguish in Hirsh's small eyes and, a little shaken, set his knife and fork down.

Hirsh said, "That's a start. When this is over, you don't keep it up I'm going to bloody beat your face in. And not only once."

"Okay." Shai took out his wallet and left cash on the table.

Upstairs, the desk had been pulled out from against the wall and Shai sat behind it facing the corridor. Sara's photographs rose in a pile face down in front of him. Hirsh stood leaning against the wall near the door, a Browning automatic pistol he'd lifted from the Israeli consulate in a shoulder holster beneath the inexpensive sports jacket he wore with elegance.

The phone chirped and Shai moved quickly toward the bed and snatched the receiver. At Shai's loud, recognizable hello, Cilla said, "On his way, quite alone."

Shai nodded and returned the receiver. Hirsh unlocked the door and backed away from it, every muscle tensed. Shai laced both hands in front of him on the table.

Soon they heard fast footfalls in the corridor followed by rapping on the wood and Hirsh called out with his guttural South African accent that the door was open. Vargas burst in enthusiastically carrying a leather briefcase. Middle-aged and unfairly handsome Shai would joke later, Vargas had a full mountain of hair and a mustached face that projected a boyish cockiness.

As Vargas entered Hirsh locked and chained the door, then eased forward and slipped the briefcase from Vargas's fingers, lay it on the bed and snapped it open. It was empty; he was coming to collect.

"Who's this?" Vargas demanded of Hirsh, pointing at Shai.

Hirsh did not answer. Instead, he moved toward Vargas and roughly began to pat him down. Vargas shoved his hands away.

"I would really let him finish," Shai said.

Vargas froze for an instant, not resisting Hirsh's hands, then spun toward Shai, deducing correctly who was the authority in the room.

Shai observed him—the tanned skin, the expensive black-faced Movado watch. Shai said, "Please sit." He motioned toward the chair across from him.

"Why should I?"

Shai spread the photographs out facedown then, like a casino dealer, neatly flipped them over, the faces all suddenly showing. "Please indulge me. I have something I think you'd like to see."

Vargas did not move. With a stubby forefinger, Shai pushed each one closer to Vargas, who stepped forward and glared down, still standing defiantly.

"So you have pictures of me with that man. Who cares?"

Shai removed a small tape recorder from the drawer. He depressed PLAY and Vargas heard his own voice from his discussions with the South African in Dom Pedro Park. They were concluding a deal for him to sell Pretoria plutonium. Shai watched Vargas's face fall and the defiance go out of his eyes as if a light switch inside his head had been turned off.

"Do have a seat," Shai said. "As you see, we have a number of matters to discuss."

Vargas dropped into the chair and his arms lifelessly flopped into his lap, his whole body sagging like a ragdoll.

"You're American?"

Shai did not answer the question. "Senior Vargas, as you realize, you have a considerable problem. My interest is not in seeing you imprisoned. If that were the case you would be speaking to the authorities at this moment instead of us. I must assure you, however, failure to cooperate fully will without doubt produce that appointment with the police we have for the moment put off."

As Shai spoke he watched Vargas sit higher, his dark eyes brighten somewhat as he pushed his fingers through his hair. "If you want money, you've caught a mackerel not a whale."

You mean a shark, Hirsh thought with fury, wanting to literally drown him in the tub.

"Money?" Shai dismissed the notion with his arm. "You're absolutely right, if we wanted money we should have done our homework and found a whale, as you call it. But let me assure you that we *have* done our homework."

"Who are you?"

Shai began to build a bridge Vargas could cross. "I can tell you I'm American and my esteemed colleague was born in South Africa, though he lives in the States now," Shai added for further clarification.

Given some solid ground to tread on, Vargas stood and swept the photographs onto the floor with a slap, as if reproaching a woman. "You have nothing on me. I was the one trying to entrap you." Like a car having negotiated a dangerous curve and heading down, he was picking up speed. "Foreign agents have entered our peaceful country, attempting to purchase dangerous material. I felt it my duty to entrap them, fearing if I turned them away they would find some other country, some less patriotic worker to bribe with their Krugerrands. It was my obligation as a citizen to learn more about who they are. That is of course why I came here and I told my wife so. She is my witness."

Shai clapped his hands together repeatedly as if he had just attended a virtuoso performance of the London Philharmonic. "Bravo," he said, then turned toward Hirsh. "That was good, wasn't it? Just the right amount of indignation."

Hirsh spoke with quiet menace. "Under other circumstances, I might have been bloody worried."

Vargas charged for the door. As Hirsh glided in front of him Vargas launched a vicious fist. Hirsh parried it with a side block, grasped his wrist, twisted it sharply behind his back and rammed Vargas's face into the wall. Blood dripped from Vargas's nose, staining the wallpaper, and pain stung his whole face.

Fucking sell plutonium, Hirsh thought, and smashed his nose into the wall again.

Vargas screamed.

"Oh, Joaquim, Joaquim," Shai said, uncomfortable with the violence but appreciating its efficacy. "You see, we of course considered the possibility, and it was a good one, that you might play the patriot, especially given your Latin temperament." Shai came out from behind the desk, bent and retrieved the photographs, then returned to his seat and shuffled them, indicating that he held all the cards. "But, Joaquim, unfortunately you confessed to my friend here that you already sold enriched plutonium oxide not more than a few weeks ago. We have it quite clearly on tape as I remember it, but we can play it back if you'd like to check my memory. We have plenty of time."

Hirsh released his grip. Vargas did not remove his head from the wall.

"You could, I suppose," Shai went on, "claim that too was a lie, part of the effort to entrap us, but there'd be an investigation. It would all come out, the plutonium oxide missing from the storage area."

Vargas's eyes closed. He said nothing. A drop of blood rolled down the wallpaper.

"And here right on this very tape you've confessed to selling it. Then you buy an new BMW for cash. Black convertible, isn't it?" Shai started to collect the photographs. "Very sloppy really, I'm sorry to say."

A moan issued from Vargas's mouth, partially muffled by the wall.

"Selwyn," Shai said, addressing Hirsh by his cover name. "Why don't you get our guest some tissue from the bathroom and maybe some water." Shai spoke a little louder toward Vargas, but with endless warmth. "Unless Joaquim would like something a bit stronger. Vodka and grapefruit juice I understand is his favorite. What do they call that, I can never remember."

"A greyhound," Hirsh said.

"Ah yes, a greyhound. How do they name drinks anyway, I wonder." Again the sweep of his paw. "Never mind. Please, Joaquim, have a seat. We'll order you a nice greyhound. This is a wonderful hotel. Nobody takes all-day siestas here. It should be up in a flash. Or would you prefer water?"

Vargas wiped his nose with the back of his hand and stared at the blood in fear. To Shai, he appeared a man who had never faced his essential mortality, who saw life as big problems and small opportunities, the opposite of Shai's essential view. Suddenly sharp pain jabbed through Shai's chest.

"Water," Vargas said hoarsely.

Shai's hands sank into his lap. The pain reached through his left arm. His mouth was dry. He was frightened.

Hirsh was heading into the bathroom. "Water for me too," Shai managed.

The tap ran, then Hirsh emerged and set a paper cup and bunched toilet paper on the desk opposite Shai, noticed he looked pale. He placed a second cup in front of Shai. The pain began to subside. Shai wiped a damp hand on his leg, reached slowly for the water and sipped some.

Vargas moved toward the desk, his legs unsteady. Still

standing, he lifted the toilet paper, wiped his nose and drank some water. Finally, he dropped into the chair and brushed at his nose again with the bloodied tissue.

Shai downed the water, crumpled the paper cup in his hand below the desk and gripped it there. "I want you to know we are quite reasonable people," he said. "If our business is concluded to our satisfaction, we will disappear and you shall never hear from us again. It will be like a bad dream you keep to yourself, which is what we all do with actual bad dreams."

Vargas touched his nose and flinched. He looked at his fingers; no blood had come away on them. "What do you want?" He stared down at his hands.

"It's quite simple. We want to know all the times you've sold plutonium. No omissions." He did not want to emphasize the Arab purchaser. From the top desk drawer Shai removed a yellow legal pad to take notes, giving the impression the session was not being recorded—it was, via a second cassette player in a slightly open desk drawer.

Pen poised against the paper, Shai's eyes were on the pad and his voice came out matter-of-factly. "When did you first sell nuclear material from the Sao Paulo reprocessing center?"

Vargas looked down at his hands, said nothing. Hirsh leaned back against the wall. There was always one last barrier, the type of pride that would not suffer blackmail, that would endure prison over surrender. Vargas remained silent.

Feeling stronger, Shai dropped the paper cup on the floor, placed his pen on the desk and spoke softly. "There is no need for a scandal, for anything in your life to be disrupted. You enjoy the ladies, well that's none of our concern. By the way, I can see why they flock to you. As for me, well, I'm lucky to have one good one, so I hang on to her for dear life."

There was a long silence. Shai simply sat.

"Only once," Vargas finally said.

Shai waited with a complete patience he knew nowhere else in his life.

"I was blackmailed," Vargas said, eyes on his hands.

"By whom?"

Vargas squeezed the pile of toilet paper, shredding now in his grasp, kept his eyes riveted to it. Vargas looked up, shouted, "How do I know you won't do something to me if I tell you?"

"If we were interested in punishing you, this would be a prison interrogation. You could be questioned far more brutally there, I assure you. But nobody seems to be able to keep a secret. There would be reporters, publicity we'd rather avoid, a public panic. All we want is that plutonium out of circulation."

Vargas threw the fragments of toilet paper to the ground. Why should he protect him? He was the blackmailer. He exhaled. "Kenneth Khalidi." And it was done. His voice came out stronger now. "He teaches at UCLA. Physics."

Khalidi. Palestinian. Shai's plutonium. Shai picked up his pen, wrote Khalidi and UCLA superfluously on the pad. "How much did you sell him?" he asked without looking up.

"About a hundred pounds of powder. He could reduce that into about thirty pounds of metal."

Enough for two bombs Shai realized, fresh fear plunging through him. Shai wrote again, the numbers 100 and 30. "Did he say what he intends to do with the material?"

"Build a bomb, wouldn't you think?" Vargas said, laughing nervously.

"Well, yes." Shai put the pen down. "The target was really what I was after."

"He didn't say, would not answer when I asked. So I dropped it."

"Who contacted you for him?"

"He flew here supposedly on his way to Rio for a vacation. He called me himself. We went to graduate school together."

"Where was the plutonium shipped?"

"To an address in Los Angeles, by boat. I don't remember it. I have it at my office."

"No problem. Let's move on to your meeting with my

colleague here." Shai retrieved his pen. "Oh, before I forget. The blackmail, how did that play exactly?"

"I've told you everything you need to know," he said loudly. "It doesn't matter."

Shai steepled his fingers together. "Actually it does, I'm afraid. We tidy it all up, then everything returns to how it was. You go back to work. Speed around the mountain in that marvelous car of yours. But there can be no loose ends. None."

Vargas rubbed his hands on his shirt to brush the shreds of toilet paper from them. He reached out and sipped from the cup of water. "It was a woman." He spit out the word, set the water down. "You want to know where too?"

Shai preserved his silence.

Vargas exhaled heavily. "All right. All right. The Grande Ca' d'Oro. He...he took pictures of us. I'm a family man, you see." Vargas beseeched the interrogator for understanding. "She caught me once, took the children away."

The pen was back in Shai's hand. "The woman's name?"

Vargas wanted to pick up the water, throw it in the fat man's face. He closed his eyes for a moment. "She said it was Theresa. I don't know if it was her real name or not."

Shai was about to ask for a description when a thought struck him. "Where have you put the pictures?"

Vargas reached out again for the cup of water, sipped some, said nothing.

Shai again remained silent.

"In my office. They're in my office, damn you."

Vargas had seemed to him the type who would hold on to the photographs from vanity, maybe even to show them around later, omitting their provenance. "When did this occur, in the hotel?"

"I don't know. The end of May sometime."

Shai was wondering if he could get a name from the hotel registration but it would be tough. "Do you remember the room number?"

"It was on the seventh floor somewhere. That's all I know,"

Vargas shouted. "I was concerned about other matters at the time."

"Yes, well I can certainly appreciate that. Now," Shai said, placing his pen on the desk. "Does your wife know about any of this? Where you are now?"

Vargas gave him a look.

"I take it that means she does not. Fine. You're going to phone her now. Tell her an emergency's come up at the reactor in Brasilia. Don't alarm her, but tell her you're going to be out of town for a while, that you'll phone her again soon."

Vargas sank back in the chair.

"Now, I want to remind you that if we find you've omitted any other sale or sales, the authorities will have everything we have on you within an hour. I want to give you the opportunity to think again, in the event something may accidentally have slipped your mind. We will fully understand if you suddenly remember something."

"Once," Vargas said. "I sold it once."

"I suggest you consider that enough for a lifetime."

In the rental car, when Hirsh sat down beside Vargas in the rear seat, the explosive fury was so hard in his eyes that for a moment Shai was concerned he might lose control and snap Vargas's neck. Sara drove, with Shai beside her.

Hirsh and Shai flanked Vargas through the reprocessing plant security to retrieve the photos and the Acme Battery shipment address—South Robertson Boulevard in Los Angeles—and the shipping documents. The plutonium should have arrived there eleven days ago. Shai was excited, had not expected to be so close behind it.

Sara and Cilia sped Vargas to the safe house while Hirsh headed to the airport to purchase tickets. Shai did not know how long he would hold Vargas, but did not want him tipping off Khalidi. He could always have Vargas call the plant with some excuse for his absence. He would play that one as it came.

Shai finally felt momentum building and optimism rose in his stomach. As an additional bit of luck, on Saturdays a VARIG flight departed from Sao Paulo at 11:45 p.m., boarded additional passengers in Rio, and, with the time difference, arrived in Los Angeles at 7:15

a.m. Sunday morning. They could make tonight's flight.

Shai took a taxi to the Israeli Consulate on the Rua Luis Coelho and phoned Carmon on a secure line. After listening to him threaten about the lack of communication, Shai ordered spotters on Khalidi in Los Angeles. Carmon snapped to Shai that *your* terrorist Ramzy phoned an hour before and was waiting for Shai's call, had left a number in London. Wouldn't goddamn talk to anybody else.

Shai dropped down on the edge of the desk and waited with anticipation as the scrambled line was put through. Ramzy finally came on the phone and told him he had drawn a blank in Tunis, which corroborated Shai's theory of this being an independent operation. Ramzy continued, his voice rising with enthusiasm. There were indications an Arab shipping magnate in London had agreed to move the plutonium into the Middle East by freighter. Ramzy was near it. Shai absorbed the good news without allowing himself too much further excitement and gave Ramzy the number of the Israeli consulate in Los Angeles where Ramzy could reach him. The route of the plutonium was crucial because there was no way to know if Khalidi was still in Los Angeles, and even if they captured the physicist, it was vital to stop the dangerous plutonium from entering Israel.

After he hung up, Shai arranged for consulate security to assume the babysitting of Vargas so Sara and Cilia could mop up their presence here and then join him in Los Angeles the following day.

As Sara drove Shai to the airport, Shai sat distractedly silent, drumming his fingers on the open window ledge. Sara asked if he thought Khalidi was still in Los Angeles and Shai seemed not to hear her. Frustrated at his silence, she drove faster.

As she slammed the brakes at the airport curb and they lurched forward, Shai grabbed the canvas bag at his feet and, his other hand on the doorknob, turned to Sara. "When this is over, we deliver Vargas to the authorities on a platter ready to be cooked."

Before Sara had time to voice her approval, Shai hurried toward the airport entrance, the car door maddeningly left open for her to close.

In his Hollywood apartment, Khalidi sat on his sofa and stared at the dark television screen. He told himself that he should switch on the evening news and use his time productively. He picked up a geode from his coffee table and stood, fingering the blue crystals inside the stone. Abruptly, he threw the geode. It crashed noisily into the television and glass splattered the carpet.

He felt no better. Amal had gone camping in the High Sierras with the staff of *La Gente,* with Geraldo.

"I had this relationship," she had explained to him as they sat in a Chinese restaurant on Westwood Boulevard. Nervously, she drained her wine glass, while he had hardly touched his. "It seemed so good for so long, then it was gone, just like that. I owe it to him and to myself to find out what I feel."

"It would be best if you made a decision one way or the other about him," he said.

He should have taken a stand, told her not to go. He felt the anger hot on his face at his timidity. It was not fair. He had waited so long for a relationship like this. He walked into the bedroom, sat on the edge of the bed. Maybe he should just drive up to where they were and confront them. Tell her that he loved her.

He felt alone and nervous. He looked around his sparsely furnished bedroom, computer on a desk in the corner. Before he had been so accustomed to solitude. Now it saddened him, made him sentimental. He found himself thinking about his older sister in Dearborn and her two daughters. He pictured the younger one, the five-year-old with straight black hair who looked so much like his sister, and like him. When he visited, after opening the presents she always said, "Uncle Kenny, want to come to my room and play?" Then she let him pick the board game because he was the guest. She was growing up without him. He wanted to phone her now, talk to her, feel that connection to family. But it was too late; she would be asleep. And often when he called, she would not come to the phone anyway, transfixed before the television. Before Amal, he had been worrying he might remain alone all his life.

A sudden tapping on the bedroom glass that faced the courtyard jarred him and a voice spoke through the open window: "Kenneth, what was that sound? I heard an awful noise. Is something the matter? What are you doing in there?" It was the short, overweight Mrs. Gates, the widowed manager who lived in the apartment next door.

He did not answer her.

More tapping on the glass. "Kenneth, I know you're in there. I heard you. Answer me. What was that noise?"

He rose and went to the window, did not part the drapes. "It is nothing, Mrs. Gates. I knocked my television off the stand. I was moving it."

"Be more careful next time."

He heard her waddling steps move away. He stood and, not knowing what to do now, sat at his desk. He removed a blank sheet of paper from a drawer, took a pen and began to write a love letter to Amal. He would leave it with her roommate for Amal to read on her return. Emotions welled and he wrote quickly—told her how magnificent everything they did had been, how he had not fully realized how unhappy his life was before he met her, how beautiful she was, how he understood she had to explore all her feelings. And then he wrote that he loved her. He set the pen down, felt a wonderful release. She could not fail to be moved by the intensity and honesty of his feelings.

He reread the letter and panicked. He sounded so adolescent. She was sleeping with Geraldo this weekend. She would think him a weak, lovesick fool. He tore the paper into small pieces, carried them into the bathroom and flushed them down the toilet. He looked up, saw himself in the bathroom mirror, the moist glassiness of his eyes, the red veins. "This should be over," he shouted at the mirror and grabbed onto the sink. He was two weeks away from achieving a Palestinian state, had been certain this nervousness would cease with the plan in motion. He turned away. Why was everything always so difficult for him?

He padded back into the bedroom, dropped heavily on the bed and turned onto his stomach. She would not be back for three days. He did not feel like going anywhere, doing anything.

In the darkness off Cyprus, two Palestinians were lowered in a dinghy into the Mediterranean from London shipping magnate Sabri Barakat's freighter, which was churning through the sea on its way to the Suez Canal. One wore a frogman's gear with air tank on his back, the other only a bathing suit in the warm night. The frogman held an underwater compass with a luminous dial. As the dinghy dropped into the water with a soft splash, the Palestinian in the swimming suit immediately paddled through the darkness toward the faraway lights that marked the 140-mile long island. Behind them, the freighter was swallowed up by the blackness.

The Palestinians had to be careful. Local residents often complained that Hebrew radio transmissions from yachts in the area were so powerful they blocked out the BBC World Service. They paddled toward shore, and an hour later, the coastline at Larnaca bobbed in close view. The frogman picked up the walkie-talkie and pressed the button. "Where are you? We want to go fishing," he said in Greek, the text memorized, the accent not good but not immediately recognizable either. "I'm coming now," the response cackled back in perfectly accented Greek. Palestinians had been on the island for many years.

The frogman pulled the mask over his face, sat on the dinghy railing and rolled back into the water with a splash; it felt pleasurably cool. He cleared the mask and reached a hand up. His companion handed him a net with a heavy, greenish sphere and a small strip of identical metal. They had followed orders, had not asked what the sphere was. The second Palestinian rowed the dinghy north. He would sink the boat on the far side of Larnaca and swim ashore. Papers to fly to Morocco awaited him in Nicosia.

With a swift kick the frogman descended through the blackness, his parcel, light in the water, trailing behind him. The net should already have been attached to the hull of DEBRA'S JUDGMENT while the Israelis were away eating. He swam with determination. He could feel a straight course, did not need the compass. At twenty, he hardly felt his muscles as he drew his arms through the water in harmony with the flutter of his fins.

Forty minutes later he reached the rock wall of the marina.

Guessing the entrance was to his left, he swam along the boulders and soon saw the movement of a diver treading in place holding a small light.

He approached and the waiting diver extinguished the beacon and headed into the marina. The Palestinian dragging the plutonium followed. The two frogmen approached the left extension of the docks. There was a small danger their bubbles might be seen on the surface. They swam under one, two, three hulls, and then the guide swam up close to the fourth hull. The frogman with the plutonium saw a net hanging in the water under the hull, kicked, reached the hull and placed his parcels up into it. The two turned and swam back toward the marina entrance, hoping their bubbles had not been detected.

Soon out in open sea, several feet under the surface they dug through the water. Finally the Cyprus-based Palestinian grabbed his compadre's shoulder and motioned him up. They burst through the surface, near the shore but out of sight of the marina. Still not speaking, each released the remaining air from his tank in a loud whoosh. The guide held both tanks while the frogman from the ship struggled out of his wet suit. He wore a bathing suit underneath. They tied their equipment to their tanks and let them sink then they swam for shore.

The Palestinian who had brought the plutonium knew the yacht would certainly dock in Israel during the daytime. Their diver in Jaffa would retrieve it as soon as it was dark. It would not have to sit under the boat in their marina for more than half a day.

On the substantially empty 747, Hirsh stood and opened the overhead compartment in search of a blanket and small pillow. Engines roaring, the plane had reached thirty-two thousand feet and begun to follow the curvature of the earth toward Los Angeles. Hirsh looked across the empty aisles. Shai had said he was going to stretch out in the back on four seats, but Hirsh saw him now, plastic glass of soda in his hand, in thought as he leaned against an abandoned drink cart. He approached, had to get Shai to sleep.

"What the hell's bothering you?" Hirsh said. "Besides that it went so well."

Shai looked at him. "This blackmail feels amateurish."

"It was. So?"

"Professionals move in predictable patterns, amateurs follow impulses that are harder to track."

"And if Khalidi moves with total amateurish illogic he might circumvent us."

Shai nodded.

"Will you get some fucking sleep," Hirsh said. "You're going to keep me up all night too with this."

Shai sipped his sofa. "Sleep. Good idea. Yes. We should, both of us."

Hirsh started to leave then stopped. "By the way, I went for a ride this morning with Sara. She drives like a maniac."

Shai smiled. "I've had the experience."

"What did you bloody want me to look for there?"

"Oh, that? Nothing. Best to forget it."

Hirsh gave up. "I'm going to sleep." He headed off.

Back in his seat, Shai finished the soda in one pull. Her whole life, Sara's parents had slapped her with disapproval and her father, on occasion, with an actual back of his hand. Both she and Hirsh had built high walls so no one could reach in and hurt them, and each now found the barrier too tall for them to climb out themselves. If they could pull the other over, each would thrive, as well as understand when either dropped back down behind their barrier. And they would produce gorgeous, spirited children. It was a short step from them to thoughts about Tami, which made Shai even more restless and he chewed on the small ice cubes from the plastic cup. At the prospect of losing her fear echoed inside him.

Shai opened the *Herald-Tribune.* He was a voracious reader, loved esoteric details, but now he followed an article without realizing what he'd read. He strode to the bathroom. On the way back he picked up a magazine, which he then pushed in the pouch in front of him unopened. He dropped back in the seat, shut his eyes. He wondered who this Khalidi was, what terrified him, and if thwarted would he blow the bomb? His mind still racing, he leaned forward, reached with difficulty into his pants pocket and removed a small plastic bag closed with a rubber band. He looked up, did not want Hirsh to see him. So keyed up, afraid he might not sleep, he removed one of the small, white pentagonal pills and slipped it under his tongue, where it dissolved. He knew from experience the grogginess would be mostly gone when he left the plane.

Shai pulled up the arms of the chairs on both sides of him and fastened the seatbelt loosely around his middle so the flight attendant would not wake him in any turbulence. He stretched out, drew a small blanket under the seatbelt and around his shoulders. He closed his eyes, felt the tiredness like a sinking weight as he pressed into the thin cushions. Despite the pill, thoughts battered him like a storm against a loosening pier. Shai flipped restlessly onto his back in the small space and the blanket slipped partially off his body.

Maybe he was wrong. Maybe he should come in. Maybe it was all giant egotism. He felt tightness in his throat and realized suddenly that it was fear. What was he afraid of? Others changed their lives when faced with reality, and no one was indispensable. The army frequently rotated chiefs-of-staff. He pulled up the blanket. Even if he came in, because of his precarious health it would not alter the decision he had to make about freeing Tami. He would suffer the same heart condition at home. He banged his body back against the seats.

After awhile, he was so nervously exhausted he unfastened the belt and paced the aisle. Coming back down it, he saw Hirsh snoring, curled peacefully in two seats, his dark hair and pillow against the bulkhead. He stopped, stood there for a long time watching him, and thought about how wonderfully the second and third generation of young Israelis had turned out much to their pioneering parents' surprise. Shai returned to his seat and, greatly comforted with that assurance, finally slept.

CHAPTER 8

June 24

Shai arrived in Los Angeles sufficiently rested, the slight grogginess from the pill overwhelmed by breakfast and a half dozen small cups of coffee. After clearing airport formalities, the consulate confirmed that Khalidi's apartment had been under surveillance since last night. Shai pounded onto the street a little after 8:30. It was already warm and he removed his coat.

He met Hirsh on the sidewalk and almost immediately a green Oldsmobile Delta stopped in front of them. Shai took the front seat and Hirsh the back. The driver, Aryeh, known as Andy in Washington, DC, where he sometimes labored on his doctorate in computer programming at George Washington University, darted back into the traffic circling the lower level of thc airport. He had been able to arrive here in the early hours of the morning along with two agents from New York. Surveillance teams would be descending from Europe and Tel Aviv all morning.

"What have you got?" Shai asked.

"The warehouse where they shipped it is completely empty. Khalidi's apartment is listed in the phone book and surveillance got there a little after 9:00 p.m. We verified it with the directory outside the building. We didn't want to try a wrong number call and risk alerting him."

"He inside?"

"No sign of him yet this early."

The large car burst up the ramp onto the wide 405 freeway and headed north. The traffic was light.

"What about where Khalidi lives?" Shai needed Khalidi to lead him to the plutonium and wanted a lengthy look at his apartment while he was out.

"Hollywood, low rent district. It's a two-story building, sixteen units. The bad news is all the apartments open outside into a courtyard. No back doors. In that kind of place a lot of people don't work or have part-time jobs. The good news is the building's owner is Jewish."

After a moment Shai said, "Take the ten freeway east and get off at the first exit. You're going to drop me in Cheviot Hills, then I want you to get everything you can on the building's owner. In the meantime, if Khalidi comes out stick to him."

"Got it."

Soon they were driving through winding streets of large houses with manicured lawns, hedges, roses and colorful small impatiens in the heavily Jewish Cheviot Hills. Volvo station wagons, Cadillacs, Mercedes-Benzes, Lincolns and Acuras slept in driveways. Shai thought about the Tlingit natives of southeastern Alaska of ten thousand years ago. They erected poles outside their homes, the taller and more decorative the higher the owner's status, exactly like these cars. The need to look important was widespread, Shai thought, though he felt no desire for recognition himself. Shai directed his driver through the maze of streets, down a hill then left on Krim Drive. Shai had Aryeh stop short of the end of the cul-de-sac, hopped out, left the door open and hurried up the stone steps to the large but modest two-story house.

Shai rang the doorbell. Sam Wolf, an East European, fit-looking man of seventy opened the door. Bald, with a hedge of dark hair, his face brightened and Shai bear-hugged the small man.

"You should have called. I'd have taken you to the club for

breakfast," Sam said, referring to Brentwood Country Club, his golf club. "Doesn't matter. We can still go. I'll have coffee."

"No time." Shai turned and waved the Oldsmobile away then turned back. "I need your help."

"Then come in already."

Four years before, they had met in Auschwitz-Birkenau. The size of the camp, along with the incongruous beauty of the birch groves and ashes fed lilies rising lushly from the ponds, had sucked the breath from Shai. He had met Sam with his grown son and daughter in an open field near the still-standing garment disinfection station. Sam, his children and a guide were standing in the grass beside a mound of hundreds of blackened spoons remaining from the sorting of valuables.

"My family's here." Sam burst out crying and waving his hand across the camp. Tears trekked down Shai's face too and they hugged and wept together. The sole survivor of his family of seven, he had left Poland alone two years before Hitler goose-stepped in. After the war, Sam met a gorgeous Hungarian Jewess, a graduate of Auschwitz's distinct pedagogy, and they were quickly married, though it turned out they had little else in common.

Sam's adult children stood apart to the side, his daughter crying. Shai sensed the distance between all three of them. As a child in the anti-Semitic Polish countryside, the basic experience of Sam's youth had been powerlessness. It was mere chance whether he survived or not. Survivors like Sam regained power, or the illusion of power, by controlling everything in their reach, a recipe for success in business but not at home. When Sam complained to Shai about his son's low salary as a high school English teacher, as well as calling his son disrespectful, Shai saw that Sam's need for security and control robbed him of the relationship with the boy they both desperately needed. A building contractor, Sam had a crew of eight, and doling out cash bonuses to shoulder responsibility, he arrived four days a week on the golf course by 1:00 p.m. Shai had said that he toiled for the Israeli Foreign Office and Sam had not, after an initial barrage of questions Shai sidestepped, pressed the matter.

Sam led Shai into the backyard, where with a kiss on her cheek he said hello to the attractive, blond Anne. The yard sat on a cliff overlooking an elementary school and had a long view of endless flat homes broken only by the spiked buildings of downtown in the far eastern haze. Anne excitedly gave Shai a tour of her many varieties of flowers that sprouted in a riot of color, then showed him the vegetables growing in a corner. Shai did not mind the delay, for he felt what it meant to an Auschwitz survivor to nurture life. Shai sensed sadly that Sam and Anne lived separate lives and had never seen affection between them. She had declined the trip to Auschwitz—crying, she said she'd already been there.

Finally, Sam turned to his wife and said, "Why don't you call Sharon and Josh and see what they're doing tonight. Maybe they'll bring the kids to the club for dinner."

"All right. Shai will join us?"

"I'll try," he said. Shai felt the golf club was less status for Sam, but rather replacement of the extended family that had been snuffed out. Shai hoped and believed that Sam's children would escape the camp legacy by wholeheartedly supporting and praising their children.

Anne smiled and headed into the house to phone her daughter.

"So you want me to show you the video of our trip to Hawaii or are you going to tell me why you're here?"

"You know anyone in the insect extermination business?"

"Sure, Irving Miller. He's a member of the club. A little cheap with charity. What do you need?"

"Some trucks and equipment, for a day."

"Simple. We'll call him now." Sam looked at the Israeli's sagged face with its deepened lines. "Something the matter?"

Shai shook his head. "Just tired. I'm locating the Jewish owner of an apartment building in Hollywood. I'd like you to come out with me to see him, as an introduction."

"Easy too. If I don't know him, maybe I'll know somebody who does. Is it a big outfit?"

"I don't know. Let's find Miller and maybe by then I'll know."

Miller was not at home but they reached him on his car phone. Sam made the pitch and Miller's voice came back over the sound of traffic. "You want trucks to help Israel, I got trucks. No charge. How many ya need?"

Within a half hour, Shai learned that the owner of Khalidi's building was a wealthy developer named Jonathan Aronfield, who lived in tony Bel-Air. Sam did not know him. He phoned three large developers without success, racked his brains, then called his buddy Frank Sinclair. Also an ardent Zionist, Sinclair had founded the giant Sinclair Paint Company and moved in higher-end, non-Jewish philanthropic circles where Sam felt uncomfortable. Sinclair had pushed Sam, despite his success still a shtetl Jew, into something he never would have considered on his own—joining the Brentwood Country Club.

"Sure, I know him," Sinclair boomed across the line despite recent stomach surgery. "Bright guy. Extremely wealthy. Not married. I don't think he's too interested in Israel. More the type for auctions at Sotheby's and flying to Hong Kong than riding a cable car up Masada. Gives a lot to Cedars-Sinai."

Sinclair called Aronfield, who agreed to see them, and Sam drove Shai to Aronfield's immense home in the Bel-Air hills. On the way, at Sam's prodding they talked Middle East politics, a subject on Shai's mind so much he hated to discuss it.

As they walked toward the front door, Sam said, "I don't know why Israel won't negotiate with the PLO. We've had worse enemies."

Shai looked at the short man. "I think that's the problem."

Pain filled Sam's eyes. "I tell you, we're brought on this earth to suffer."

Shai put a hand gently on Sam's shoulder and squeezed. Shai had told him that his son was fabulous, but Sam only repeated that he could have been a lawyer.

Aronfield was tall, handsome, of indeterminate age, with tiny X's at his scalp beneath his wavy hair, from the transplants. They moved through an elegant living room with what Shai recognized in the display behind glass as lovely Ming Dynasty Chinese bondeshine porcelain, and into a small library. Aronfield wore jeans and a plain button-down shirt.

Seemed an original sort, Shai thought; too many Americans blew about in the tyranny of the latest trend. Two art magazines lay open on the coffee table next to a half full cup of tea.

Shai felt it would be adversely patronizing to remark on his recognizing and admiring the bondeshine porcelain, so he launched directly and almost straightforwardly into his interest in a tenant at Aronfield's building on Bernendo Street that there was certainty of his involvement in terrorist activity. Shai requested keys to all the apartments in the building, as they were going to pose as exterminators.

Aronfield leaned forward with interest, wanted to know what the tenant was suspected of. Chemical warfare against Israel, Shai responded, not terribly far from the truth. Aronfield talked about his CNN addiction during the Gulf War, told them how emotional he had been watching Israelis go to work with gas masks. He would help. Outside, they followed his beige Ferrari to a high-rise on the corner of Wilshire and Westwood boulevards.

At Shai's prompting, over the phone Aronfield asked the manager, Mrs. Gates, about each of the tenants. At Khalidi, she said she had talked to him through the window the night before, but often he did not come to the door or answer his phone. He was a loner, a little bit less recently as he had this very pretty young girlfriend she was actually surprised would be interested in him.

In the meantime, Shai's spotters waited for Khalidi to leave his apartment. A check determined his car was in his stall. The spraying would require everyone to leave the building for three hours. Shai relished the opportunity to study Khalidi up close when he knocked on his door. The manager had seen Khalidi the night before so he was not yet on his way to the Middle East. They should be able to follow him then snatch his whole operation in one coordinated swoop. Still, Shai remained cautious.

DEBRA'S JUDGMENT sliced through the Mediterranean, sails full in the stiff wind. Below deck, Motti tossed dice into the new mother-of-pearl inlaid olive wood backgammon set he had bought recently while on reserve duty in Hebron. Their friends from Petah Tikva played opposite him as a team while Adina had the wheel.

"It's so peaceful here," the woman said. "I can hear the quiet." She picked up the dice and rolled a double four. "See, everything goes right."

Motti stood. "Roll for me. I want to bring Adina some coffee."

"Now that's my idea of a husband," the woman said, and jabbed hers with an elbow. "All be brings me are his orders for dinner."

The husband ignored her. "When will we be in Tel Aviv?"

"If this wind holds, in two and a half days."

By 7:00 a.m. the following morning, Khalidi had not been sighted and Shai knew something was wrong. The phone machine picking up the wrong number call did not help. The manager said he often was inside for days. In Israel's long-established safe house, an apartment in Venice Beach where the comings and goings of people were not much noted, Shai hardly touched his breakfast and did not look up on the two occasions Hirsh attempted to speak to him. Hirsh was worried about him, and angry that he was worrying.

"You want to starve yourself, it won't exactly kill you," Hirsh said finally. "Just tell me so I don't waste the food. Or maybe next time you want to see a bloody menu?"

Shai's head inched up. A smile came to his lips and he pointed a fork. "Just don't start with any of that cereal that tastes like twigs and is reputed to be healthy." Then he skewered a wedge of potato and began to eat.

A little after 8:00 a.m., a small van with the logo of a mouse standing on its hind legs, its hands trembling in the air, pulled up to the building on Berendo just south of Sunset Boulevard. The lettering read: CRITTERS GET THE JITTERS WHEN MILLER COMES NEAR. Khalidi's car was still there, and Shai reminded himself in L.A. people drove to get a loaf of bread. He jumped out of the passenger seat into the already hot, smoggy air. Hirsh, Aryeh and Shai, all wearing overalls with Miller's frightened mouse on their shirt pockets, lifted exterminator tanks to their backs. Hirsh took Aronfield's photocopied announcements about the spraying, and Shai carried a small, hidden walkie-talkie for communication with the spotters, in case Khalidi chose to return while they were tossing his place.

The street was wide and sun-swept, with towering thin palms lining both sidewalks. Not indigenous to Southern California, they were grown in spring-fed Colorado mountain ravines. Everything needed to be brought in here, even the water and Shai found it all an impressive achievement. He moved up the cement walkway, approached the meshed iron gate, pushed the button beside number eleven and immediately heard Mrs. Gates's voice cackle, "Who is it?"

"Miller Termite."

The gate buzzed. Shai pushed it open and the others followed. A white stairway rose immediately to their left. Shai headed upstairs while Hirsh and Aryeh slipped the notices under each door. Shai returned with a fist of keys from the manager and he and Hirsh headed to the far end of the second floor while Aryeh began on the ground floor. Shai did not want any tenants mentioning to Khalidi that they had bounded first to his mid-floor apartment.

The tenants in the corner unit were already out. Spraying insecticide inside the apartment, Shai felt like a racehorse bridled at the gate. He tasted the harsh chemical through his mask and wondered for the thousandth time who this Khalidi was. He saw a roach scamper along the kitchen linoleum and sprayed in its direction, halting it in a quick dance of death. Then he busied himself intently on the task of spraying, thorough by both habit and temperament.

Ten minutes later, Shai and Hirsh stood outside Khalidi's apartment. Shai knocked on the door. "Exterminators," Hirsh called out, and the truth of the depiction was not lost on either of them as Hirsh reached into his jacket pocket and fingered the pistol there.

No answer.

Shai slipped the key in the bolt lock first, turned it, but the bolt was not closed. On a chance, Shai tried the knob with his hand but it did not turn, so he used the key. He pushed the door open and stepped inside, Hirsh at his heels.

What Shai saw smashed into him like a blow to the stomach.

"Fuck," Hirsh said, closing the door behind him.

Less experienced eyes might have seen a burglary—drawers gaping open, the belongings scattered on the floor. Amateur, dope-driven thieves traveling light might pass on the small AIWA stereo mini-components, which would spark suspicion carried through the street, especially by minorities. But no criminal would have abandoned the Canon camera sitting on the coffee table or the small telephoto lens on the floor beneath it. Khalidi had left in a great hurry and he had abandoned his car, which could be traced.

Shai stormed down the small hallway. The bedroom was in similar disarray. A suitcase sat on the floor below a closet, hangers littering the carpet. The computer was still on, the empty A> command an electronic green.

Hirsh entered, stared at the room for a long moment. "Doesn't exactly look like he went on holiday."

Shai said nothing. His heart beating fast, he lifted the suitcase on the floor, and as expected, there was nothing in it. Shai gazed up at the empty top shelf of the closet and tried to gauge if there could have been one or two additional suitcases there. He lifted the suitcase from the floor, slid it up and determined there was enough space for only one additional bag.

"The landlady talked to him Saturday night. Vargas couldn't have tipped him off," Hirsh said. "We had him already."

Shai said nothing, his face pale.

Hirsh went to the computer, threw aside some books. "Who warned him?" He stopped abruptly, turned to Shai. "Was somebody watching Vargas we didn't see?"

"We'll have to try and find out," Shai said.

Hirsh angrily ransacked the desk for disks but found none. The computer was a double floppy system with no hard drive he could attempt to retrieve off of, even if it had been erased.

"Go through all this," Shai said. "And do leave everything exactly as it is, just in case somebody returns." He resumed his fingering through drawers. "We'll do his office later." If nothing else, Shai wanted to absorb a sense of this person. Like a social scientist who studied a culture's garbage with a view to the character of those who dumped it, there was much to be learned about Khalidi from what he had abandoned: preference in clothes, how much alcohol was around, what magazines he read, who wrote him, what he hid that he did not want visitors to see.

Soon, Shai summoned Hirsh into the kitchen that he had been picking apart to no avail. "You continue here," Shai said, "and make sure you and Aryeh finish spraying all the apartments."

"Where you going?"

Shai left the apartment without answering.

Shai walked up to Sunset where he had parked his car, stood on the sidewalk and, fists clenched, stared up at the brown Hollywood hills, the disappointment at missing Khalidi by so short a time hard in his stomach. Realizing he was holding his breath, he let go and stepped quickly into the car. He drove several blocks until he spotted a phone booth outside an El Pollo Loco fast-food restaurant. He made a call to the consulate, told them what he wanted, and said he would phone again in twenty minutes. He entered the restaurant, where dozens of halved chickens sizzled on a grill above gas flames, and changed his clothes in the bathroom.

Shai pushed his bulky frame back in the car, drove west on Sunset. Fifteen minutes was enough. At a gas station pay phone he quickly punched the buttons. When the voice came on the line, they had what he wanted. The head of UCLA's Israel Action Committee, a young woman named Camille Edry, had a summer job toiling at her father's law firm in Century City and was expecting someone from the consulate within the half hour.

Twenty minutes later, Shai pulled his car into the small parking lot in front of the twin Century City towers that allowed eight minutes free, then charged a ransom for anything beyond that. As he stepped from his car, a man in a business suit screeched his Jaguar to a halt, burst out and brushed past him, shoes clicking on the cement, a Federal Express envelope in his hand. Shai knew people needed the illusion of the importance of their work to invest so much in it, and he slowed his pace. With the humble part of his nature he wondered again if there really were younger men who could do this as well or better, if he was clutching an illusion *he* required. He stopped himself. Maybe he could just get on with finding the bomb.

In the law firm waiting room, a young woman emerged through a door, her brown hair bouncing. She wore a dark business suit with a red scarf loose around her neck.

"Hi," she said, approaching. "I'm Camille."

He was up from the sofa, stretched out his hand and took her firm grip. "Hello. You have a minute? Can I buy you a cup of coffee?"

"Sure on the minute. Let's skip the coffee."

She crossed the lobby and pushed the elevator button, which lit. Downstairs, as they moved through glass doors into a bright plaza with nobody around them, Camille turned to him.

"All I do here is drink coffee. What's up?"

He removed a small photograph from his wallet, a head and bare shoulders shot of a young woman. He had snipped the rest of the photograph away, and Vargas's bare stomach in the background looked like a square. He handed it to Camille and she looked at it.

"Amal Tawil. So what?"

It was that easy. Shai smiled. This happened about never. "What can you tell me about her?"

"You read her junk in *La Gente?"*

"No. Apparently I've missed the opportunity."

"Israel and Central America. High decibel bullshit, ninety percent of it. I could get behind solid criticism. The Jewish paper wrote a tough piece on Israeli training guards for Columbian drug smugglers. From the Palestinians and their cheerleaders never a word of any wrongdoing on their part. They just blow it. It's easy to be sympathetic to their cause, until you have to deal with them directly. Well a lot them. The minority extremes on both sides make the situation intractable."

He rather knew the feeling. "You have any idea where I might find Amal?"

"You could call *La Gente* and give them some bull. She and the *La Gente*_editor were an item last I heard. Geraldo Chavez. Or check the student directory." She gave him a look. "I could ask around, but I somehow think you can manage it on your own."

"Yes, I suppose I can. Thanks." Shai pocketed the photograph. "I hope you're not going to waste yourself in law school."

"Law school? Who's more boring than lawyers? I'm here for the summer to not get disowned. They already want to lynch me cause I want to go to Rabbinic school."

Shai laughed. The obsession with money must come from so much wealth everywhere here. "They'll get used to the idea. I suspect they're not going to have a choice."

On the safe house sofa, Sara removed her hairclip, releasing her wavy red hair into her face. She shifted her skirt to remove a wrinkle and crossed her legs. Cilia sat beside her, smoking. Sprawled on the chair across the living room, Hirsh looked at Sara's legs, which seemed even longer and lovelier below her short skirt. Noticing his staring, she thrust the hair away from her face.

"Take a picture, it lasts longer," Sara said.

"But it's not three-dimensional."

"Well, it won't walk away either."

Sara stood and headed toward the kitchen for a glass of water. She had been surprised that Hirsh asked to take a drive with her in Sao Paulo, had waited for what he wanted, but all he did was chat. She wondered if he was interested in her; he seemed sort of hesitant with women he wasn't treating as dessert. Still, she found him good-looking, incredibly confident, and while she hated that her looks intimidated most men, she felt sure he wasn't. She found herself smiling.

Shai came through the door, slammed it and collapsed on the sofa beside Cilla. He seemed pale to her. She quickly set her cigarette in the ashtray groove and turned to him. "We miss something in Sao Paulo? Somebody alert Khalidi when Vargas didn't turn up at home?"

"I don't know," Shai snapped.

Cilia reached down for her cigarette and drew the lipstick stained filter to her lips, puzzled. It was unlike Shai to bark at that kind of question. She wondered what else was bothering him.

Shai had a sense, more a feeling than a logical conclusion, of how Khalidi had gotten onto them. He pushed the thought away and quickly unwound the particulars for the assault on Amal. Then Sara phoned Amal's number with Shai hunched next to her, ear to the receiver. The brief surveillance outside her building had not sighted her. He was worried she had fled with Khalidi.

A female voice answered. "Hello?"

"Amal?"

"No, she's camping in the Sierras."

"I have an important message for her. Do you know when she'll be back?"

"Tomorrow. Probably late afternoon or early evening, depending if they stop."

"Cool. Should I try her at this number or Geraldo's?"

"I don't know. Here, probably. You want to leave a message for her?"

"I'll be out all day tomorrow," Sara said, pushing frustration in his voice. "Just tell her Victoria called and I'll call back."

"Sure."

Sara thanked her and hung up. Shai rubbed his face with both hands.

"She'll be home tomorrow," Sara informed the others.

"Go with them to Khalidi's office," Shai said to Hirsh. "And try and see to it they don't get caught."

Hirsh glared at him, was about to snarl back, then left without responding.

Cilia drew one leg over the other and tugged helplessly on her cigarette. He was so tense she feared he was about to burst internally. She wished she had the courage to get him to unburden himself to her, but she just didn't know how. Seducing a man was so much easier than befriending one. She stood. "I'm going to make some coffee. Fancy some?"

Shai was already lifting the receiver and shook his head no as he dialed. He was transferred to another extension and the starter at the Brentwood Country Club informed him that Sam Wolf was indeed on the course.

Shai drove up the coast the short distance to his club. The

starter explained that "Big Sam" should be on the eighth or ninth hole and called a cart and caddie to take his guest out. As Shai rode on the electric cart past the artificial lake and through the gorgeous grass and trees, he thought with the first pleasure he had felt all day how far "Big Sam" had come from a small town in Poland and the incineration of his family. They found him at the eighth hole green standing over his ball, feet planted intently. He wore a peaked blue cap to protect his bald crown from the sun. As Shai approached on foot, Sam looked up at him.

"Do I at least have time to sink it?"

"Sure."

Sam stroked the ball, which bounded across the green and continued way past the hole to the right. "You made me nervous," he called to Shai as he walked toward the ball. Despite his outward success, in his gut he was a shtetel Jew without the self-assurance to ever admit fault. He tapped in, told his foursome he had to go, and arranged with his caddy to take his clubs. He and Shai walked across the grass toward the clubhouse. A warm breeze off the ocean two miles away rustled through the trees.

"Problems with Miller?"

"No."

"So?"

"I need a storage area. Someplace that isn't used very much that I can take over for a number of weeks, or longer."

"Okay, let me think." He walked quickly despite his size and Shai actually had to hurry to catch up. "Maybe my son-in-law, Josh. He owns an office furniture store, an okay business. He has an overstock warehouse somewhere in Culver City. I've never been there but it might do. Let's go see him and find out. What else?"

"Air-conditioning units and humidifiers."

Sam looked up at the Israeli as they walked. "Okay, this time I have to ask. What for?"

"To create humidity in the warehouse," Shai said.

"Put humidity into a warehouse. You're *meshuganah* you know that?"

"Not too many people would argue with you about that."

"Okay, we'll get you humidifiers."

"I'll need a few other things too."

"Oy. Let's hear."

Josh's warehouse turned out to be perfect, and as he had a second warehouse, he was willing to let Shai use it indefinitely. When Josh drove them into the large Culver City industrial park, because of the lack of privacy Shai almost told him to turn around. The complex housed storage for twenty or thirty companies in a half dozen, twenty-five-foot-high buildings. But Josh quickly pulled his gray Mercedes off the main road and down a corner driveway, with the side of a building to his right. The first ramp led to ORB FIXTURES. JOSH 'S BUSINESS INTERIORS occupied the second half of the building, which dead ended at an open concrete channel that carried drainage to the ocean. Inside, the news was even better.

A little after six o' clock Shai returned to the warehouse, where several small vans and workers' trucks were now parked. He hustled up the ramp. The large, high-ceilinged area was filled with desks turned on their ends to conserve space and chairs covered with plastic. Ahead of him, two men were laboring on the large air conditioning and humidifier units on the warehouse floor. To Shai's left, steel stairs led to a second-floor office raised above the ground to allow storage beneath it. Shai had expected to have to erect an entire room. Rows of lamps had filled it. Shai climbed the stairs toward the sounds of pounding and hammering and opened the door.

No lamps had been left inside the long, narrow, single room with suspended tile ceiling, sprinklers, fluorescent lights and a window near the doorway looking down at the warehouse floor. A dozen Israelis were hauling up a partition to divide the office and hammering thick padding around the square walls at the far end. Having fled Israel for reasons ranging from comfort to freedom from war, which Shai understood, construction was his countrymen's typical occupation in the San Fernando Valley, and they were adept at it.

That same afternoon, Hal M. Bundy of San Diego landed at Ben-Gurion Airport and drove his rental car to Jerusalem's King David Hotel. His boredom gone, he relished being back in battle.

Outside, he studied his map then sped to Gilo, one of the modern suburbs built after 1967 that encircled and effectively united Jerusalem. There in the southern hills, Reverend Wayne Littell of the Pentecostal Church of Philadelphia invited him into his apartment with a broad grin. Littell ran a Christ Assembly organization that met at the YMCA. Designed by the same architect who built the Empire State Building, its 152-foot bell tower was an icon of the city, coincidentally located across the street from the King David. In Jerusalem for seven years, the Israeli Ministry of the Interior had repeatedly renewed Littell's temporary resident status, tolerating his proselytizing in exchange for the political support from the groups of Pentecostal tourists he pulled to the country from the American northeast. Littell found it frustrating that the Israelis embraced Evangelical support but dismissed the true Christian prophesy that Israel had to be strong and rule the land as a precursor for Christ's return. They truly were a stiff-necked people. Bundy had met Littell on his original trip to Israel and, after his own failure, occasionally sent him small contributions, admiring his perseverance if not the man himself.

Bundy sat on the balcony in the surprisingly cool night, excitedly looking across the hills toward the lights of Arab Bethlehem. *A land without a people for a people with a land,* the Zionists had proclaimed in the late 19th and early 20th centuries. Bundy chuckled, as the land had not been exactly empty, but it had been an effective slogan. The arrogant Israelis did not know the phrase had been conceived by Christian Restorationists. The Scottish Reverend Alexander Keith, had penned the concept in his 1844 book *The Land of Israel According to the Covenant with Abraham, with Isaac and with Jacob.* The Jews' return as prerequisite for His Second Coming had long been on Christian minds.

Littell carried out a tray with two frosty glasses of iced coffee, served in the Israeli style with vanilla ice cream instead of ice cubes. He eased the tray down on the small table between them. He was a short, fat man with long brown hair and a certain nimbleness.

"Spectacular view up here," Bundy said. "You can absolutely feel that He walked these hills."

Littell nodded vigorously, sat, and spoke in a confiding ministerial bellow. "My dear boy, it's marvelous to see you. I told Sally as soon as you phoned. By the by, she's leading a women's Bible study group at the Y and will join us just the minute she finishes. Anyway, as I said, I was telling Sally we just don't see enough of Hal Bundy in the Holy Land. What a treat that you're finally upon us. So tell me what you've been doing, every morsel of it. You look absolutely wonderful, ten years younger than your age. I mean it. Ten years, if a day. How's that beautiful wife of yours?" He could not quite remember her name, so he lifted one of the iced coffees toward his mouth and his pink tongue darted out and swept some of the froth from alongside the ice cream then disappeared back into its cavern with a smack.

"Mary."

"Yes, Mary." Littell laughed. "Now how could I possibly forget that name? Anyway, let me warn you. I've had a lot of dealings with these Jewish anti-missionary groups since you were here." Littell held his glass between his fleshy thighs gently like a child. "They're relentless. They send spies to my classes. I never know who to trust. It's ghastly. The Jehovah's Witnesses in Israel had a huge seminar event scheduled in a sports stadium, Ra'anana, in the heart of the country. This anti-missionary organization, Hand To The Brothers, got the municipality to cancel it. They lied, said the Jehovah's Witnesses were busing in innocent Jews for a mass baptism. The city's excuse for canceling the event was that it would hurt the feelings of the community."

Bundy reached for his drink and sipped some of the cold coffee, which tasted good. "It's a good sign. They're afraid of His Word." Though he had no appetite, he supposed because of the time change, he was dehydrated from the long flight and the dryness of Jerusalem. "These anti-missionary groups are unimportant," Bundy said.

"Yes, well I suppose so in the larger scheme of things. Then so is a mosquito, but when it's sucking your blood it's goldarn irritating."

Bundy set his glass down. "You still have good contacts with the Christian Arabs?"

Drained glass wedged between his legs, Littell dove into the ice cream with a spoon. "Yes, yes. Of course. We can't neglect the faithful while we pursue the heathens." He ate some ice cream then motioned with his spoon toward the hills. "Right in Beit Jala. See, over there." He pointed again.

Bundy swiveled slightly on the wood chair and saw a nearby mountaintop that overlooked Jerusalem from the south. "Yes."

"There's a school up there, uses an ex-Jordanian army base. The little Arabs play in the concrete trenches and everything, practice shooting with stick guns the way the Jordanians used to fire at the city. It's simply the way here. I dare say, one accustoms himself to it. I must take you up to see them. They're really darn cute. Anyway, I rent a classroom there one night a week. I have Christian Arabs flocking in from Beit Jala, Bethlehem, Beit Sahour—a half dozen neighboring villages. Thursday you'll come. Mark it on your calendar, I insist. To see them read Scripture will bring tears to your eyes. These people are hungry for His word, more so now in these trying times for them." Littell clanked his spoon down into his glass. "There's so much to do here, but alas funds are always, well, a problem."

"It would be a privilege to provide money," Bundy said. "I've been fortunate in the area of funds."

Littell swept his spoon in a horizontal swing. "Not now. You're tired, you just came in. Ah, it's a pleasure to have someone like you just to talk to. You can't imagine what it's like here, monitoring your every word. Sometimes I fall asleep at nine o' clock right in front of the television, exhausted from it all." His tongue came out and cleaned the moist edges of his little mouth, then his lips turned into a self-satisfied smile. "Actually, it's like being a spy for God." He placed his glass on the table. "But enough about me and my travails. We'll have plenty of time to discuss money later. What about you? You haven't told me a thing. How's your business? Your church?"

Bundy leaned forward. "I'm here to help the Palestinians."

Littell sat up excitedly. "Do tell all. Are you staying in the Holy

Land for a while? Please tell me the answer's yes."

"This is a short trip but I shall be coming back in ten days. Actually, I'd like your help."

Littell bobbed his small head. "Anything you need. You surely know that. Just say the word, and if it's in my power, the deed's done."

"I understand some Palestinians have weapons."

"Yes, yes I'm sure that's the case. I had one student, an orderly from the Makassed Hospital in East Jerusalem. He'd served five years for possession of a handgun."

Bundy stood. Someone might overhear from a neighboring balcony. "Why don't we go inside."

"Sure. Whatever you wish."

They headed through the open sliding glass door, leaving the glasses and tray behind. Bundy pushed the door shut. The apartment had new teak furniture, Bibles and other religious books on the shelves, but no crosses or other overt signs of Littell's Christianity on the walls that might put off Jewish visitors.

"I require a gun, here, in Israel," Bundy said. Guns could not be purchased over the counter in Israel and applications for any legal weapons had to be cleared through the Ministry of Interior. "Pistol or revolver, doesn't matter. I want you to get it for me from one of your Palestinian students. It's for the *intifada.* If it costs, money is not an obstacle."

Littell backed up, shaking his head, spoke loudly. "Hal, I don't know. The risk. I could go to prison. I don't know who to trust. There are these anti-missionary people everywhere. What do you need it for? It's too dangerous."

"Ask the student who spent time in prison. They know you're not in the Israeli's pocket. One handgun. Even you can get it in ten days if you pay the price." Bundy removed his wallet, withdrew a blank check from the folds and held it out to Littell. "This is for your work. I'll fill it in right now. Five thousand dollars. You spend what you have to for the gun and keep the rest."

Bundy removed a pen from his pocket, set the check on top of the television and began writing. Littell said nothing more. Bundy signed his name with a tight flourish and handed the check toward Littell. For a brief moment it dangled from his fingertips.

"I can try," Littell said, grabbing the check from him.

CHAPTER 9

June 26

As the horizon lightened, the Mediterranean was rippled and deep blue, white churning with a gentle sound beside the hull of DEBRA'S JUDGMENT. Motti stood behind the wheel barefoot, wearing shorts and a T-shirt. His body was bronzed, his hair blended through with gray. He listened to the flapping of the sails and through a squall line watched the yellow ball of the sun peek above the water. A small frown pulled at his face.

His wife came up from below deck and saw his expression. "Anything the matter?"

He kissed her on the forehead. "Not really. She's handling a touch sluggish."

"I hadn't noticed. Probably barnacles. Everybody picks them up around Cyprus."

"That's what I've been thinking. I'll put her up in dry dock the instant we get in. I want to take Avraham out as soon as I can so we can have a meeting about the Holon project without his beeper going off a million times."

She leaned her body against him, felt the goose bumps on his tanned skin, and as his arm circled around her, she nuzzled even closer. It had been a perfect vacation on the slow moving Greek side of the island, where buses often stopped for passengers anywhere they hailed them. She was not looking forward to returning to the noisy rush of Tel Aviv, but at least they still had a full morning of gorgeous sailing before they docked.

As the Wednesday morning sun rose over the Mediterranean, it was a little after 7:00 p.m. Tuesday evening in Los Angeles. The phone screamed in the Venice safe house and Shai snatched the receiver. "She just arrived," the voice said. "Went up alone."

He breathed relief. "Let me know if she leaves."

After a camping trip, the odds were she would want to shower and rest. "Victoria" could not call immediately for fear of arousing suspicion. "Twenty minutes," Shai said to Cilla and Sara, before they baited her. Hirsh was out addressing the surveillance.

Sara strode to the sink.

Shai went to the window and leaned his head against the glass, stared down on Rose Avenue. Finally, Amal was back. Now, where was the plutonium? Khalidi? He heard water running from the kitchen behind him.

From the sofa, Cilia watched Shai. Worried, she lit a cigarette and thought back to how surprised she had been when he plucked her from the Zionist Youth Federation office in London. She was the quiet type who dressed down, never complained, and whom nobody much noticed. Well, until she got over her shyness with someone new, then she was pure passion. With two sons, she had still been in the shock, guilt and terror of leaving a husband she had really never loved.

Cilia slowly rubbed her cigarette out and watched Shai, bent forward against the window. She wanted to help him but dared not intrude. *Do it, he needs you, you silly cow*, she told herself. Five minutes ago they were in danger of the whole operation going tits up. Still she did not move. Finally, she forced herself up and approached Shai's back. She had never seen him so alone. "Can we have a chat?" she asked.

He turned, looked at her affectionately and nodded. They moved toward one of the two back bedrooms, sat side by side on the large bed, neither of them speaking for a long moment.

She wanted to ask what was troubling him beyond the obvious danger, but instead folded her hands in her lap and looked at them. "You know, my life was frightful when you found me. I was in such a state. Why were you ever keen on me?"

"It was a hunch." He shifted on the bed and faced her more fully. "I haven't liked that I've taken you from your boys so much."

Her head came up and she looked at him. "It's awful to admit, but you see, their father is really much better with them. I fret and hold them too close and really being their mum is not enough for me." The phone rang in the living room and she reached out and held his hand. "Don't ask me why now, maybe it's this frightful bomb, but I just wanted to thank you for believing in me, when I didn't."

He squeezed her hand, suspected she was saying this for him not her. She must have sensed his isolation. In the living room, Sara picked up the receiver and Shai looked up and headed slowly in.

Cilia lit a cigarette, and her hand wavering, she brought it to her mouth. Sometimes she wondered if she had made a mistake, no matter how good she was out here.

Cilia heard Sara's worried voice. "Somebody's watching Amal. At least two teams. Arabs. One just relieved the other."

In the living room, Shai grabbed the phone. "Tell me," he spoke into it.

Cilia rose, walked to the doorjamb. Shai listened, then he gave orders for the surveillance and hung up. Standing the whole time, he made a series of calls, rousting people, putting them on the street, propelling workers back to the warehouse.

When he was finished, he said, "We wait a little while now to see what we have. But we still go tonight."

Cilia dropped in the armchair. "Who are the bodyguards?"

Shai looked away and said nothing.

Periodically the phone rang with reports. Shai paced with the phone as he spoke. A little after 9:00 p.m., with the warehouse near ready and Amal still home, he gave the order then hung up and handed the phone to Sara on the couch. “Okay, Vicki.”

Sara looked at the piece of paper on the coffee table and pushed the buttons. Shai lowered himself beside her and leaned toward the receiver. After three rings a woman’s voice answered tiredly.

“Amal?” Sara asked

A yawn. “Uh-huh.”

“My name’s Victoria.” Sara lowered her voice. “Kenneth Khalidi gave me a message for you. I tried to reach you yesterday. It’s important.”

“What?” Amal asked.

“He said not to speak over the phone. Can you meet me?”

Shai held his breath.

“Where?” Amal said.

“There’s a car wash on Pico and Beverly Glen. I’ll be in a red Honda Accord in the lot. Twenty minutes.”

“He’s all right, isn’t he?” Amal spoke with urgency.

“Perfectly, but he needs your help. In twenty.”

Sara hung up and punched Shai in the shoulder.

Alone in the Honda Accord, Sara sped into the empty parking lot, her headlights striking the dark car wash facade as she went up the driveway. She spun the car around, tires squealing, cut the motor and waited. She rather liked going up against another woman; men were too easy. Across the street rose a large Spanish-style church with arches and a red tile roof, surrounded by grass and palm trees. Soon an old Datsun drove into the car wash and stopped. Sara’s windows were up despite the warm evening and she held both hands high on the steering wheel. Shai wanted Amal to come to her. Amal turned off her engine, extinguishing her beams. Seconds later she opened her door and approached. Amal wore black stretch jeans and a tight, white T-shirt that showed off her small waist. Marv figure, Sara thought for such a short girl.

Before Amal could head toward the driver’s side, Sara leaned across the seat and opened the passenger door. Amal ducked in the car and closed the door.

"We can't talk here," Sara said. "We'll pick your car up later." She twisted the ignition and raced down the drive and turned left along a large park.

"Where's Kenneth?" Amal asked, locking her door and winding on the seat belt. She had reached his phone machine.

"He's fine, had to leave in a hurry. There's a problem with Vargas in Sao Paulo. He wants more money. He's suddenly threatening to expose everything."

"He's out of his tree. He'll go to jail. Who are you?"

"Vargas seems to believe he can blackmail Kenneth."

Approaching Motor Avenue across from 20th Century Fox Studios, the light was turning yellow. Sara slowed though she normally would have burst through. At the light, she glanced up in the rearview mirror. A blue Dodge with two Arabs in it pulled directly behind her.

"What does Kenneth want me to do? Who are you?"

"Not to worry. We're not together that way. I like them older," she said, not terribly far from the truth. "Daddy thing, kinda, more about feeling protected than my actual one."

Sara looked in the mirror again. Cars roared up on three sides of the Dodge, and men were out, brandishing handguns, one of them Hirsh. She watched him in the rearview as he fiercely and fluidly smashed the glass on the passenger window with the butt, showering the Arabs. Amal spun to the sound. Two more cars slammed to a halt at the sides of the Honda. Their rear doors flew open. Two men yanked open the Honda's back doors, jumped in and Sara hit the accelerator, turned right.

"What the fuck?" Despite the car moving, Amal had her seatbelt off, groping for the small ring handle in the panel. Shai had chosen the Honda because of the difficulty in quick exit. From behind, Amal felt strong hands around her neck.

"If there's no one there, drive into the park's lot," the man said in Hebrew.

"I'll look," Sara answered in the same language.

"*Israelis.*" Defiance filled Amal's tone. Had she been a professional, she would have wondered why they were revealing themselves.

Aryeh removed a syringe from his inside coat pocket, pulled the cap from the needle and spoke in English. "Amal, you've been quite the subject of conversation in Tel Aviv in recent days. Some people there are most eager to meet you."

"You can't do this, " she said, voice shaking.

He drew her left arm back between the bucket seats, and when she resisted, the other Israeli tightened his grip on her throat. "This won't hurt. You'll sleep for a long time and wake up groggy, that's all."

Fear reached every part of her. She was afraid she would lose her bladder and pressed one foot hard on the floor to stop it. She felt the sharp needle. "No," she screamed. A hand clasped around her mouth. Her head was warm. The traffic was spinning. She was nauseous. Then the hand around her mouth was gone and she felt herself falling forward through space.

Aryeh reached out, caught her and pulled her body back into the seat.

On Fifteenth Street in Santa Monica, two cars and an unmarked van drove into the street where Aryeh had earlier tailed the two Arabs, recently relieved from their surveillance of Amal. Shai suspected Amal had not known they were there. The residential street was quiet at the late hour, the houses dark but with streetlights bright. Shai needed everyone in the house taken before they could report that Amal had disappeared. If surveillance on Vargas had tipped Khalidi, Shai would sweep everybody up this time before that could happen again. Though he knew he was so down because of another possibility of how Khalidi had been alerted.

Hirsh and another Israeli exited the car several doors from the dark target house. It was maybe fifty years old, Spanish style with a red tile roof, one-story and appeared to be two bedrooms. Farther down the block three more Israelis approached from the other direction. One carried a black sledgehammer wrapped in a jacket. They had waited until all the lights had gone out in the house forty-five minutes earlier. The Israelis wore rubber-soled shoes, dark clothes and light jackets over their muffled pistols. The van remained parked across the street with four additional men with Uzi machine guns, if needed.

Drapes were drawn across the leaded glass living room window. The Israelis slipped down the driveway to a low, wood gate that was padlocked. Silently, they pulled themselves over it, the last handing the sledgehammer over before he vaulted the fence. A cinderblock wall blocked all view to the neighbor's house—the safe house probably chosen for the privacy—and the first three agents continued along the dark kitchen to a side door and waited there. Beyond there was a bedroom with large windows, mini-blinds closed and dark. The fifth man continued soundlessly past the bedroom and around it to the small backyard. He saw that a sliding glass door led to the second bedroom. There were no lights behind the closed drapes. He crouched and waited in the tall grass, pistol leveled at the glass with both hands.

Hirsh's knees were weak. Assaults always reminded him of his rush on the school in Ma'alot—the screaming children, the blood—and a nervous fear slid through him for the agents who would burst in behind him. His mouth was sticky. With a hard headshake, he shook off the thoughts. In the event the neighbors heard, they had to be in and out fast. Hirsh pointed to the agent with the sledgehammer, who raised it high and, with a tremendous swing, noisily shattered the knob and lock. Hirsh shoved the door open with his shoulder and continued in. Three agents burst in behind him, flashlights on, and were into the kitchen. One ran through a small hall to the left into the first bedroom, his flashlight piercing the dark. An Arab there was fumbling for his gun on a nightstand. "Don't or I'll shoot," the Israeli shouted in Arabic and the Arab froze and dropped back against a pillow and raised his hands.

Hirsh was in the second bedroom. The Arab in bed there fired in the darkness at the doorframe, the shot ricocheting splinters off the wood. Hirsh dove to the ground firing. Two muffled shots hit the Arab in the chest and he cried out as he fell forward. At the sound of the firing, the third Israeli raced back from the empty living room, but as Hirsh came up off the floor and flicked on the light, he breathed relief. The man with the sledgehammer, who had remained in the hall, his pistol out, went to the front door, opened it and waved the van to pull into the driveway. He saw lights go on next door and he ran back in and told them to hurry.

A syringe appeared and the Arab prisoner was injected. Like Amal, he fell unconscious after a few seconds. Hirsh and another Israeli scoured the house rapidly and grabbed loose papers. They quickly carried both the dead man and the unconscious man into the van, then all three cars sped toward the warehouse in Culver City. As Hirsh sat in the passenger seat, his breathing tight in his throat, he looked at his hands gripped together and released them.

Nauseous, Amal woke slowly. A headache pounded behind her shut eyes, which felt sticky. She tried to lift an arm to wipe the inside corner but her limbs were too heavy and she could not move. She tasted metal in her mouth. And then she remembered. Fear scattered through her and she wondered where she was. She forced open her eyes. The bright lights hurt and she shut them again, the nausea like waves.

She was naked on a cot. She rolled onto her side and felt like she was going to vomit. It was hot and humid in the cell and she heard the heavy rumbling of buses or trucks outside and high-pitched honking that sounded far different than the deeper American car horns. She bit the ends of her fingers. She felt like she had been sleeping a long time. She realized she must be in Tel Aviv.

A door opened across from her and a heavyset man and tall woman with short blond hair entered. The woman was carrying a tray with orange juice and a paper plate with some olives, hummus and a diced cucumber and tomato salad. The man handed her a long, blue, cotton jellabiya. A manila envelope remained in his hand. Amal slowly struggled into a sitting position. The queasiness was worse as she sat, and she fell back against the warm wall.

"I thought you'd be comfortable in this," Shai said.

She reached for the traditional Arab garment, slipped it somehow over her head, drew it down over her buttocks and legs. She tried to button it to remove the exposure of her breasts but could not manage the coordination and her hands fell.

Cilia had the urge to button it for her but she restrained herself. It was past midnight. "I know it's frightfully unsettling," she said with genuine warmth, "so I thought you'd like to have a go at breakfast." She set the tray down on the floor and Amal, thirsty but not hungry, made no move for it.

Shai turned to Cilia and spoke in Hebrew. "Why don't you leave us alone to talk."

Cilia responded in Hebrew. "Fine. Let me bring a chair so you'll be comfortable."

"Thanks."

As Cilia left, Shai stood over Amal. "Please, some orange juice. I asked them to bring you fresh squeezed instead of processed. And you needn't worry, it's not drugged. We could simply inject you if we . . . well, as you know." He added hurriedly, "But we hope that unpleasantness is over."

Her voice came out hoarse. "I want to speak to the American Embassy. This is kidnapping."

"Of course it's kidnapping," Shai said. "We do it all the time. Fortunately for us, El Al flies direct to Los Angeles now. Your car was left in front of a noisy bar, the San Francisco Saloon they tell me it's called. See how this plays. You left to meet a friend. The police eventually are called by your roommate, find your car. They assume you maybe drank a little too much, went home with some stranger and then. . . Look at all the movies about what happens to beautiful women in those situations. They'll continue to look for you for a while, I suppose. And as for the American Embassy, I really can't see any reason to trouble them while you're our guest."

Cilia entered with a chair, set it down beside Shai and left. Shai sat. "Would you like to use the facilities before we begin? I'd be happy to leave." He glanced at the bucket in the corner. "I must apologize for them, but then we're not in the Grande Ca' d'Oro in Sao Paulo, are we?"

She shrank back against the wall.

He retrieved half a dozen photographs from the manila folder and handed them to her. She took the pictures, saw herself naked with

Vargas. Her face collapsed and the photos tumbled from her fingers. Shaking, she reached down and picked up the paper cup of orange juice and, steadying it with both hands, sipped some. It tasted good with the stickiness in her mouth. Exhausted, she drank more.

"Now, you met Kenneth Khalidi at UCLA, took Physics 10 from him last fall. Is that correct?" They had found copies of Khalidi's grade rosters in his office but little else. They had discovered the same photographs in a file labeled AMAL, along with clippings of her articles from *La Gente*. Shai guessed she meant something to him.

Amal looked into the cup, terror running through her. How could they know so much?

"Come, Amal, you received a B minus in the course. How was he, by the way, as a professor I mean?"

"He was great," she said, though he had been methodical and a bit boring.

Good, she had answered. He wanted to keep her talking. "I don't care much for Sao Paulo myself, too big and congested. What'd you think?"

She drew the thin blanket from the corner, slowly balled it over her stomach. "I liked Rio better."

"Rio, now that's a spot. Couldn't agree more. You make it to the Copacabana beach? What a bay—green water, white sand, those mountains."

"We had dinner there, overlooking the water," she said. Her voice was quiet.

"I'm sure it was lovely. Grande Ca' d'Oro Hotel's pretty elegant itself. The photographs were taken there by Khalidi and used to blackmail Joaquim Vargas for plutonium oxide." He crossed one leg casually over the other. "How did Khalidi feel after his success?"

She said nothing.

"Was he exuberant? You two go out on the town and celebrate? You seemed to have nailed Vargas, just like that." He snapped his fingers. "I mean how was it, really?"

She wrapped her arms tightly around the blanket and herself.

"I would have been excited, I tell you. Genuinely." He leaned forward. “How was it for you?”

“You mean did I mind Vargas sticking his tongue inside me? So what?”

“You ever been here before, have any friends here, seen Jerusalem?”

“No.”

“If you’d like, we can arrange a tour. Take you through the souq, to the Dome of the Rock.” A smile lit his face. “I love it up there. The mosque’s really magnificent, no matter which God you pray to.”

She stared at the overweight Israeli with the receding hairline, the infectious smile and those warm, blue eyes. Walking through Jerusalem would be a dream come true. Then she yanked herself back. “I’d like to see Jerusalem—as the capital of the Palestinian State.”

“You mean, assuming it doesn’t go up in a nuclear fireball. What does Khalidi intend to do with the bomb? Destroy Jerusalem?”

“No. Not Jerusalem.”

“Tel Aviv then.”

She released her grip on the blanket, looked down at the photographs. She basically had already told him if it wasn’t Jerusalem. Her head came up. They knew about the bomb already. It did not matter if they knew why. “He’s going to threaten to blow up Tel Aviv if you don’t end your illegal occupation of the West Bank. If you won’t...all this will die.”

Shai leaned forward. “Let me tell you, Amal, we don’t give in to blackmail. If we do this time, someone will come back next year with another bomb and threaten to blow it if we don’t *all* go to Los Angeles. If that’s the case, we may as well let Tel Aviv go up now.” His voice hardened. “Then let me tell you what happens. We use our own nuclear bombs, of which we have a considerable pile, and we take out everything from Amman to Baghdad. The West Bank and Gaza.” He snapped his fingers. “We can clear those of Arabs like that. *That’s* what you and Khalidi will achieve.”

Her fingers tightened around the blanket again. The light was very bright. The nausea came back, the tiredness, the drugs all tugged at her, swallowing her. She listened to the rumble of the traffic outside.

She wanted to scream. It couldn't happen like that. The Israelis would give in. After Lebanon they had traded, she couldn't remember exactly, but thousands of Palestinian prisoners for a few of their own. But she realized that had really cost them little. Her head remained down.

"Listen, Amal. We've known about the bomb, the way we knew about you. We debated what to do about nuclear extortion. The decision came down. These are Holocaust survivors in power. They'd rather destroy the entire Arab world than go passively again. You understand *never again?* What that means?"

She was twisting the blanket between her hands, staring down at it. What if the Israelis were really willing to take everything out?

He spoke gently. "Amal, there's something else."

She stopped and her eyes came up.

"Amal, if this bomb gets through to Tel Aviv, when we find it, and we will find it, that likely will be enough to encourage those in power to transfer all the Palestinians east. I don't want to see that, Amal, but you and Khalidi will be giving them the excuse they need to do it. You think the world will blame us? Not when we unveil this bomb, assisted by the Palestinians among us."

Her face drained of color. Exhausted tears moistened her eyes.

"I have sympathy for your cause, Amal. A lot of Israelis do. We know Khalidi was in Beita in March. I'm sure he told you what happened. An injustice was committed there, no question. Maybe the government felt they had to appease the settlers by blowing up some houses and uprooting olive groves. Jews uprooting olive groves. I detest it. There's a Beita Committee here, Amal. Dozens of Jews go to the village every few weeks and help them rebuild, redress the wrongs." He was proud of the Beita Committee.

His voice abruptly rose. "There anything on the Palestinian side like that? You know what the Palestinians did in Amman during the Gulf War? Manufactured replicas of the Scuds to wear as jewelry, cigarette lighters, candles on birthday cakes. The protracted struggle brings the worst in people to the fore, on both sides." He remained silent for a long moment and then said, "You can stop this disaster falling on your people, Amal. You and maybe only you."

She was biting her fingernails.

"There will be a solution in time," he said. "If Khalidi's stopped. If there's a Middle East left."

She clasped her hands together, looked at the Israeli, so close to her. "Your people don't care. They've shown us they can live with the *intifada*," she screamed. "That's been their response to us. Kenneth is our response to you."

Shai sagged inside. He had been close but she had turned the momentum. He scratched the back of his head, the signal for those watching from the camera above one of the ceiling tiles.

Cilia came through the door. "There's a call for you."

Shai rose, looked at Amal. "Excuse me."

He turned and left the room while Cilia neared, looked down at the untouched food. "I see you weren't terribly hungry. That's understandable." Cilia eased down on the edge of the cot. "He really is a gentle man, about the best we have. You're really quite fortunate." This time she reached over to the jellabiya and fastened Amal's buttons. "You don't mind, do you?"

Amal shook her head.

"Good." She finished the last button. "Better, isn't it." Cilia bent, retrieved the tray and stood. "Just tell him if you're hungry and I'll bring you something to eat straightaway."

"Thank you," Amal said, wishing this woman would not leave yet.

Cilia smiled, turned on long legs, strode across the small cell and opened the door to the next room. A wall rose immediately beyond the door and Amal could see nothing beyond it as the door shut.

Cilia walked through the room where two Uzi-toting guards waited, exited and clamored down the steel stairs to the command post on the warehouse floor. Underneath the stairs, an agent monitored the tapes of Tel Aviv. Several other agents stood around and Shai sat at one of the desks, hunched forward, staring at the monitor. Across the warehouse on the far side of the stacked furniture rose the partitions and padding thrown up earlier, where the three Arabs were being interrogated.

"I thought it would come," Shai said.

"It was good for a first run," Cilia said, nearing. "You'll manage it soon."

"You were terrific with her."

"Couldn't help myself, actually. She's only a child. How long before you have another go?"

"Don't know. I'll watch the monitor."

"I'll get sandwiches." Cilia walked away.

Hirsh approached from across the warehouse. Shai had left the interrogations of the Arab guards to those proficient in physical force, something he could never manage. The two who had been taken from the car behind Sara and Amal had been blindfolded but not knocked out, so Hirsh had had them for a while.

"They're talking their heads off," Hirsh said. "It's because they don't know anything."

Shai was on his feet, barreling at him, stopped inches from the smaller man. "You want to tell me they flew here on their own? There's no time for what you can't do. I have to know who sent them." He was shouting. "You hear me?"

Hirsh glared at him. Maybe he was getting old. "You want me to squeeze orange juice from radishes? Get me Moses's staff. There's worse news."

"By all means, don't keep me in suspense."

"The one I killed in the safe house, Abu Jihad they appropriately call him. He was the leader, the one in contact with the outside. All three of them said so independently, including the two I took *before* they knew he was dead. He was the only one who knew who sent them."

"Go back and make sure," Shai said loudly.

Furious, Hirsh spun around and walked back toward the interrogation. Halfway there he picked up his pace. Maybe he could squeeze orange juice from radishes for him.

Against the wall, lighting a cigarette to occupy her concern, Cilia wondered if it was the bomb or something else that was squeezing him so tightly. She had never seen him lose his temper before.

Shai turned toward the monitor and watched Amal huddled against the wall like a frightened animal. He sat, placed his elbows on the desk and massaged his temples. He closed his eyes to rest, then opened them, afraid he might miss some signal on her face. Amal had brought her knees to her chest, was leaning back against the wall and gazing at the ceiling. Her eyes were glazed.

There was a glass with yellow pencils on the desk. Shai reached for one, held it in his hands, then abruptly broke it in half and smashed it down before him. He grabbed another, snapped it, flattened it against the desk, then he halved another and another.

Watching him, Cilia pulled hard on her cigarette.

Shai watched Amal chewing fiercely on a fingernail. He would not have to wait long.

At the same time, 10:45 a.m. in Israel, DEBRA'S JUDGMENT neared Israeli coastal waters. Motti picked up the microphone and, following standard security procedure, contacted the navy. When a response came, he identified himself and his call number.

"That you, Motti?" cackled over the line. "Shimon Burg here. Over."

Motti frequently sailed outside Israeli territorial waters on day excursions and he knew a lot of the coast patrol. "Who else? Over."

"Motti, we're going to board you when you're a few hundred meters out. Over."

"What for? All right. Over." Probably another damn terrorist alert, Motti thought, hanging up the microphone. The navy had no reason after all this time to suddenly suspect him of smuggling.

He sailed toward Tel Aviv and in the distance the high-rise hotels lining the beach came into view. A patrol vessel cut through the water toward him and Motti released his sails until the boat was floating. The navy cutter bobbed up alongside them and three Uzi-toting patrolmen and Shimon bounded the short distance onto the large motorsailer. Adina came up from below with the couple from Petah Tikva.

"What's the problem?" Motti asked Shimon.

"Nothing. Routine check," Shimon answered as two of the men went below, Uzi's ready.

"Right. I'm out here a couple times a month and you've never boarded me before but this one's routine."

"You see anything suspicious on Cyprus or on the way?"

"No. What are you looking for?"

"The usual."

Quickly the two men came up from below.

"It's okay," the young soldier said. They were searching for Palestinians who might have taken the crew hostage to smuggle nuclear material into Israel.

"Fine." Shimon turned to Motti. "Sorry to disturb you."

Within seconds they were gone, though Motti noticed the navy cutter with its Gabriel missiles stayed in visual contact as he headed for the marina. They were making certain no one interfered with him. He wondered what the hell was going on. Motti shrugged and his thoughts turned to his own problems. He wanted the boat on dry dock the minute they came in so he could take Avraham out tomorrow and trap him at the sea until they closed the Holon deal.

Soon, Motti maneuvered through the opening in the rock breakwater then eased her into her slip below the tall Moriah Hotel. About three hundred boats moored here. As he came in, Motti already felt himself accelerating to Tel Aviv's rhythm. He jumped onto the wood dock, tied her off, then called back to Adina on deck. "I'll be right back."

He hurried along the dock to the marina entrance that housed the police, customs inspection, and marina offices. Just before them stood a wood hut. Motti entered the hut and saw Ibrahim, an Arab of middle age who wore a black and white keffiyeh, sitting on a straw stool hand repairing a hole in a fishing net.

"Ibrahim, I need DEBRA'S JUDGMENT put up in dry dock right away. She's dragging a little. I think I picked up some barnacles. Can you clean her off so I can take her out tomorrow afternoon?"

Ibrahim set his net down. "I'll get the boys, Mister Burg. We'll have it out of the water as soon as we can."

Motti liked the old man a lot. "Thank you, Ibrahim. I appreciate it."

Shai moved through the door in the partition. Amal's head jerked up from where she sat against the wall nervously digging at the cuticles on one hand. He sank down on the cot beside her, crowded her and remained silent. He looked at her hands. One was bleeding around two nails. She drew the hand under her.

"We have a problem," he said. "Jerusalem wants to move you to far less pleasant surroundings and employ, well...force."

She moved back into the corner, fear and exhaustion in her eyes.

"Nobody can withstand the combination of pain and the new drugs. Everybody gives in. Hardened fighters with years of training. It's the drugs really, well, along with the pain."

She turned away from him, the blanket in her hands again.

"Amal, I'm worried." His voice was gentle. "Tell me about Kenneth. We have him as someone introverted, who's come out for his big moment. That essentially correct?"

She gave a small nod.

"When we don't give in, with all his frustration, all his hopes and dreams, everything he's done, maybe even to impress you, all destroyed, if he gets the bomb in and we refuse to capitulate, can you assure me that he won't blow it? Are you so completely certain that you'll risk millions of Arab lives on your decision?"

The exhaustion pulled at her, tugging her beneath it. She had not considered that they might not capitulate. She saw mushroom clouds rising over Arab capitals, spreading across the sky. She was desperately tired, scared to the edge of shrieking. "The Palestinians deserve a homeland."

"They do," he said, meaning it. "And the Israelis cannot keep occupying almost two million people without choking on them. We know it. I think deep down even the hard-liners know it. A solution will have to be found. Amal, I understand what Khalidi's trying to do, his sentiments. I even understand the frustration. But his way will lead not to a state for your people but to incalculable death." He stood, walked to the other side of the room, then turned back. "We have over two hundred nuclear weapons. Do you realize what that means?"

Tears rolled down her cheeks. A long silence, then she whispered, "You have to give in."

He came near, leaned both hands on the iron edge of the cot. "If Khalidi wanted people from our prisons, yes we would give in. But not this. There's no chance we'll capitulate on this."

She was crying quietly. She held on to the blanket, was so tired she couldn't think. How had this happened to her? She thought of Geraldo and wished she had stayed with him.

"Amal, all we want is this bomb. We have no interest in holding you. You played a very small role and the truth is you pose no danger to us in the future. We'll return you to where we picked you up in your life."

She looked down, dug at her bleeding finger again.

"Where did Kenneth go?" he asked.

She thrust the injured hand down and began to wrap the blanket around it.

"When did you last see him?"

She stopped the movement. "Thursday. Before I went camping. We saw a movie, *Dances with Wolves*."

"Did he say he would be leaving on Saturday?"

A whisper. "No."

"Who's helping him, Amal?"

Silence.

"He's very smart but he still would need assistance. Who put up the money? Some rich American?"

She looked at the small bucket in the corner, had refused to use it but needed to. She did not know if it was day or night. The lights were very bright, the tiredness pulled at her. Fear went through her again. She glanced at the ceiling, bit what was left of her fingernails.

He remained silent.

She wrapped the blanket tighter around her arm. Her hand hurt.

He sat beside her, but this time not crowding her. He wanted her to feel her way out was near. He said nothing.

She looked down. "Ramzy Awwad." It was barely audible, her lips framing the name with little voice." She'd gotten carried away. This was too big. Her head came up slowly to look at the man near who seemed like a father type to her. "Ramzy Awwad's helping him."

Shai showed no reaction. He had known it. But still, to actually hear it knifed into him, then deflated him like air escaping a balloon. He lowered himself onto the chair opposite her. "How did they meet?"

"Ramzy gave this talk at UCLA. He spoke with such feeling. Kenneth had been thinking about it ever since he got back from visiting his relatives. Listening to Ramzy made him decide to do it. Kenneth told him his plan. He hooked Kenneth up with someone in London. He owns some shipping business. Ships to move the plutonium."

"Who?"

"Some guy, Sabri Barakat."

Shai's expression feigned skepticism. "Ramzy worked this out with you and Kenneth?"

"Ramzy thinks I only know about Sao Paulo. Told Kenneth not to tell me more. Kenneth swore he didn't. But I kept asking him." Her voice lowered. "He wants us to be more than we are."

"How are they getting the plutonium into Israel?"

"They're bringing it in from Cyprus."

"How?"

She dropped against the wall, banged her head back against it. "Kenneth found the way. On the bottom of an Israeli yacht. He said they wouldn't notice the weight. Somebody'll dive for it when the boat's in Tel Aviv."

Fresh fear shot through him. The simplicity of the inexperienced—it would work. "Which yacht?"

"He didn't say."

"Who's helping him in Israel?"

"I don't know. Ramzy arranged it." Tears welled again. She knocked her head back against the wall several times. "Please, that's all I know. I have to sleep."

"Where's Kenneth now?"

The tears spilled over her lids. "I don't know."

"How's he getting into Israel? He told you."

"He *didn't.* I'm telling you everything."

"He wanted you to know. It was a terrific idea, like the smuggling of the plutonium. He said you shouldn't tell, no matter what else you divulged. What was the plan?"

"I don't know," she said hysterically. Her whole body shook in convulsions of crying. "I told you. I told you, that's the truth. I don't know."

"Where's Kenneth?"

She grasped her knees. *"I don't know.* Oh, God. How did this happen." She started screaming.

Shai reached both large arms around her and pulled her to his chest. She cried there as he soothed her as if he was her father and a guy has crushed her heart. After a moment, when she had quieted, he lay her down on the narrow mattress and drew the blanket over her. They could not allow her to alert Barakat and there was a chance Khalidi might try and contact her. They would have to hold her indefinitely.

Downstairs in front of the monitor, Cilla and Hirsh stood by the desk and watched Shai coming down the steel staircase. They had seen and heard Amal.

Cilia watched the way Shai shuffled head down, grabbed onto the railing for support. "He knew," she said to Hirsh. "That's what's been killing him."

Hirsh lived with his own burden and suddenly felt even closer to Shai. Shai approached and said nothing. He lifted the phone and dialed the thirteen digits to Carmon's private line. As he waited for the connection to complete, he turned to the two agents.

"I told Ramzy we were on our way to Los Angeles. That's why he alerted Khalidi."

The camouflaged Bell helicopter bore down from the Jerusalem mountains toward the coast. Its heavy rotors beat loudly in Meir Carmon's ears as he sat beside the pilot and stared at the sprawling stucco buildings of Tel Aviv coming toward them. *On the bottom of an Israeli yacht,* he repeated to himself, tightening manicured fingers around a pack of Muratti cigarettes. Wiry, with a full head of gray hair, Carmon wore his signature Savile Row suit tieless with a starched white shirt. A cleft dug into his chin, his face otherwise indistinctive.

The pilot asked, "You want me to land on the beach in front of the Sheraton?"

"No, I want you to land in the ocean. Then I'm going to walk in on the water."

The helicopter dropped toward the line of luxury hotels. Beyond them the Mediterranean stretched to the horizon like slate. Like a stone finger, a short distance down the coast rose the lighthouse at the ancient port of Jaffa. The port, first mentioned in the Book of Jonah, had been used for seven thousand years. Carmon thought how the world did not grasp the depth of his peoples' connection to this land.

A check of records determined that only one yacht, DEBRA'S JUDGMENT, had returned from Cyprus in the last two weeks. It had docked an hour and a half earlier, their first big break. The plutonium would still be in place. The terrorists would not risk removing it in daylight when Israel's ever-vigilant population was far more likely to spot a lone Arab diver entering or returning from the sea with a parcel. The navy was due to have had frogmen in the water ten minutes ago. They would follow whoever retrieved it. He wanted everybody involved, especially since Vargas had sold Khalidi enough plutonium for two fucking bombs.

The sun's rays beat ruthlessly despite the Bell's tinted glass. The helicopter crossed low and noisily over the hotels and the cafes along the beachfront strand, the sea blue-green and frothy near the rock breakwater. The Bell hovered and people on the beach slowly moved away. Military maneuvers were routine here. Carmon gripped the dashboard in front of him; he hated these small, enclosed machines. The helicopter descended over the emptying beach, spraying sand. It had to be a diver, for the marina was both too well secured and directly in the sight of two or three high-rise hotels.

Carmon felt the skis touch down and immediately his seat belt was off. "Go back to the Ministry of Defense. Quickly." He opened the door, sand kicking up in his face, the sound of the rotors deafening. Carmon jumped down and ran under the fierce attack of the sand and the noise toward the hotel. The helicopter lifted i, spraying even more sand painfully into Carmon's face, despite his ducking as he ran.

As the helicopter burst over the hotel, Carmon stopped and swatted at his hair to brush the sand from it, the warm salt breeze full in his nostrils. Unrelated to his operation, a lone female soldier began unbuttoning a beige air force uniform, removed her skirt and blouse revealing a brightly colored bathing suit beneath, and ran happily toward the sea. He hurried across the sand to the rear entrance to the Sheraton, pulled the glass door of the hotel, and maddeningly had to release it and wait to be buzzed through. A hotel guard was stationed to keep non-paying Israelis from using the changing rooms.

The small rear lobby was empty. He pushed the elevator button, and though it lit, he fiercely pushed it again. He rode it to the twentieth floor. In room 2067, a half dozen uniformed and non-uniformed men fell quiet at his entrance. A walkie-talkie on the bed emitted no sounds. Carmon slammed the door behind him.

"All right, give it to me."

A civilian clothed man from the Internal Service, whose name Carmon could not remember though he had earlier worked for him in the External Service for years, spoke evenly.

"They must have had some reason to risk removing it in daylight. The net's still on the bottom of the hull. We ordered a sea watch along the entire coastline in the event the frogman's not out of the water. Roadblocks are pulling into place all over the coast."

Carmon's pack of cigarettes dropped from his hand. The plutonium was inside Israel.

In Independence Park in the heart of Jerusalem, two Arabs in checkered keffiyehs continued digging a pit beside the rose bushes. The first, Omar, was tall and broad, with massive muscles and a soft, face that would not sprout a beard. Tariq, who was in London, had instructed him to bury the plutonium here in a public park far from Arab East

Jerusalem, which might become cordoned off. He had brought his cousin along without telling him what this was about.

A high mound of the rocky, red-brown earth rose beside the hole. This secluded spot could not be seen from Agron Street, which ran down a hill along the park toward the old no-man's-land before Jaffa Gate and the Old City. It was being renovated now that the Jews controlled all of Jerusalem. The tall tower of the Plaza Hotel, just outside the park in the other direction, was visible through the trees. They continued to dig. Two Jews sweating in this kind of work would have aroused more suspicion. Omar had been driven up the highway to Jerusalem, then they stopped well short of the normal police presence at the entrance to the city. With the sphere in a pack on his back, Omar had hiked alone the short distance through the hills to Givat Shaul Street inside the city, where his cousin had been waiting in a yellow-plated car from East Jerusalem rather than a blue-plated West Bank vehicle. He shook his head at the yellow plates in East Jerusalem, a futile Israeli game to show the city was undivided. Omar dreamed of a time when all this would be over, the fighting, the roadblocks, the fear that at any moment in the middle of the night their soldiers could burst into any home.

Satisfied at the depth, Omar's cousin lowered himself into the pit. Omar suddenly saw a young couple, the man in a soldier's uniform, walking toward them. Frightened, Omar froze for a moment, then forced himself to pick up the irrigation pipes they had placed beside the hole. The couple passed without even glancing their way. *Arabs were invisible to them*, he thought. With his hands, Omar dug through the dirt at the edge of the pit, uncovered and removed the sphere. It was not heavy and he lowered it to his cousin. He went to the dirt on the other side of the pit, reached into it and pulled out the dental aprons he had buried there in the event anyone wandered near. He had kept them in his uncle's garage in Tulkarm after taking them from Samir's trunk, and now handed them down to his cousin, three at a time.

At the bottom of the pit, Omar's cousin completely surrounded the plutonium sphere with layer after layer of lead shielding as he had been instructed. When that was accomplished, he reached up a hand

and Omar pulled him out easily. Sweating in the hot afternoon, moisture pleasantly filled the folds in Omar's stomach. They rapidly shoveled the dirt until the hole was covered. As Omar replaced the carefully removed sections of grass on the top, his cousin stamped them down. Then they shoveled the excess dirt along the edge between the nearby roses.

At the same time, another Palestinian, in the small park at the top of the hill in Old Jaffa, stood above a much smaller hole beside an aging palm tree spouting dead fronds that had not yet fallen. A stone plaza crowned the hill and he viewed the long Tel Aviv coastline to the north. Shortly before, he had watched a helicopter descend on the beach. Around him, Rain Birds played on the bright green grass, broken by smaller palms and tall pines. He heard the thud of church bells pounding out the hour from the nearby bell tower. Down the hill toward the ocean, at one end of the broad, stone promenade lined with restaurants and shops stood the peeling yellow and red St. Peter's Church, which overlooked the sea.

The Palestinian dropped a very small sheet of heavy greenish metal in the hole then quickly covered it over with dirt. He scuffed the spot under the tree with his shoe then took his shovel and headed down the wet grass.

In the Tel Aviv marina, Ibrahim lifted another net, began patiently repairing it and thought, *they think we should be so grateful for their kindness, that they pay us for doing their dirty work.* DEBRA'S JUDGMENT was of great importance to the *intifada,* though he did not know how. He had informed the youth who had come to him originally, his face covered by a red keffiyeh, of Motti Burg's departure for Cyprus. He had been instructed to alert them to DEBRA'S JUDGMENT's return. After Motti had returned to his boat, Ibrahim had picked up the phone.

When the voice had answered, Ibrahim said, "She's docked."

"Good."

"They want me to put her up in dry dock right away. The

owner's insistent. Does that matter?"

"Delay it for two hours. Will that create a problem?"

"No. They expect Arabs to be lazy. I'll wait until then."

He smiled now and rose to gather the boys to lift the boat into dry dock.

"Do you want me to ride with you?" Hirsh said to Shai as Shai climbed into the red Honda outside the warehouse. He had just received word from Carmon that the plutonium had been removed from DEBRA'S JUDGMENT.

"No."

The interrogators were mopping up with the three Arabs while Amal slept, it seemed peacefully. Ramzy had phoned the day before, enthusiastic about a lead in tracking the plutonium along a sea route. Shai yanked the car door closed. Ramzy would report his discovery of the route soon—now that the plutonium was in Israel.

Shai started the motor and drove out of the industrial area. His complexion was ashen, his lips trembling. He made no effort to wipe away the tears rolling down his cheeks as he gripped the steering wheel, his knuckles white. Carmon and not a few others warned that he could never trust Ramzy. He had argued vehemently with them but they had been right. He took a turn fast, tires loud. Wasn't sure where he was, didn't care. The hatred he did not feel for Amal, he could not now feel for Ramzy either. He longed for the simplicity of hate, for its force, its energy. What he felt now was a kind of opposite. He was emptied and desolate. Shai gripped the steering wheel tighter. He had no purpose now to be out here beyond stopping and killing the other side.

Shai had called the contact number for Ramzy in Switzerland and requested a meeting in Europe.

In London, Ramzy approached the Apollo Theatre on Shaftsbury Avenue, cigarette dangling from his lips, feeling little excitement at the safe arrival of the plutonium. The production of *A Madhouse in Goa* should already be deep into the third act. A ticket had been left for Tariq, his contact from the West Bank, at his Charing Cross hotel.

Ramzy slowly put out his cigarette on the sidewalk, did not like the raw taste in his mouth, nor that he was smoking so much. He was worried about the risk of assembling a nuclear weapon inside Israel.

At a break of laughter, a female student ushered him to his aisle seat, where he greeted the young Palestinian to his left with a silent handshake. Ramzy leaned back, the tension taut inside him. He needed Tariq to clear the path for smuggling Khalidi into Israel. As Ramzy watched the rest of the act, Tariq bobbed his head in awe, constantly looking around the theater; it was clear he could not follow the words. Though Ramzy did not know the play, he quickly became absorbed in the conflict between the wacky, itinerant Mississippi widow and a naive homosexual meeting in a Corfu inn. He laughed at the Tennessee Williams-esque lines and some of the strain eased from him.

As the heavy red curtain closed, Ramzy turned to Tariq and nodded. Outside in the streetlights, Ramzy saw the tall, pencil-thin Tariq had a pitted complexion and an ardent step. They walked silently the short distance to the corner, turned left and headed into the honky-tonk Soho, where two dark-skinned men speaking Arabic would arouse no attention. Tariq had been chosen by friends in Ramallah close to Ramzy and was unknown to the Israelis. Tariq gawked in all directions as they walked.

"How are your accommodations?" Ramzy lit a cigarette and handed the pack to Tariq, who eagerly took one of the Rothmans and Ramzy gave him his matches.

"Wonderful. It's… so huge. Everything. I've never been farther than Amman before."

Ramzy remembered how exuberant and wide-eyed he had been at his arrival in England to attend Manchester University, had actually been pickpocketed in Piccadilly his first week. For a moment, he wished he were the Ramzy who could be pickpocketed. Across the narrow street, a skinny woman with long brown hair, a pale face and severe red lipstick danced lethargically to music from a tinny speaker at a bar entrance. A sign over her head read: MALE AND FEMALE DOUBLE ACT ON BED. "Live show, two quid," she said, collapsing back against the door as they neared.

"What do they do in there?" Tariq asked.

Ramzy looked at the ashen, skinny girl, understood how she had little choice but to be here. He looked at Tariq. "Very little."

At the top of the road, neon lights of the Bikini Bar teased: LIVE BED SHOW. In a kebab kiosk, shawarma rotated on a skewer in front of hot, orange coils. Ramzy stared at the rotating lamb, longed to be among his own people, was too much in the West. He literally dreamed about staying in one place and having the time to write a long, sprawling work, disjoined parts of the story continuing in his sleep.

Ramzy guided Tariq into a dark alley, where cardboard cartons smelling of peaches were piled from the market stalls that pulled in here during the day. Suddenly, Tariq seemed agitated.

"What happened to Saddam?" he said. "Justice was at our doorstep. Why was it stolen from us again? Why?"

Ramzy said nothing, tugged hard on his cigarette, knew from the beginning that the rush to Saddam was a tragic blunder. The American-led coalition, with Saudi Arabia paying half the cost, had expelled Saddam from Kuwait and sent him scurrying back to Baghdad like a cockroach fleeing the light.

"All the talk was finally over," Tariq rushed on. "It was to be the great battle between us and the Israelis. We have to fight them. There is no other way. That is what you believe. That's why I'm here."

Once, long ago, he had believed that. "Our people are helpless," Ramzy said as he brought the cigarette to his lips. "Saddam seemed otherwise to them."

Tariq's voice grew. "When he was losing I was certain the angels of God would intervene to make him victorious against the Zionists. How could it not happen? I don't understand."

Inside Ramzy, love of the innocence of his people mixed with his frustration at their flights of fantasy; after soaring, they could only crash. He dropped his cigarette, ground the glow out and then looked up. "Before Saddam surrendered he had already forgotten Palestine," he said. "We are alone."

Tariq was suddenly silent, as if he had been slapped. His eyes cried that it was not true, that Saddam had sent the Scuds, had wanted to liberate all of Palestine, would have if thirty nations had not stopped him.

Ramzy listened for a long moment for the sounds of approaching footsteps, heard none. Only massive outside pressure would budge the Israelis. He would sneak Khalidi into Israel in seven days. To accomplish it under the immense scrutiny along the borders now that Shai knew about the bomb required a new, more imaginative plan.

"I need someone," Ramzy said slowly. "A man in his twenties who's never been arrested, whose fingerprints the Israelis do not have in their files. I am sorry, but I have to ask you to find me a man who will be killed."

Tariq's eyes widened. "For Ramzy Awwad I can find a hundred, tomorrow. A thousand."

Ramzy leaned back against the cold wall. "No," he said just above a whisper, "only one."

"It's done, easily. What must he do?"

"Come, I'll show you." Ramzy pulled himself from the wall and began walking in the direction of Cambridge Circus, where he had garaged his car. He had maps and much for Tariq to memorize.

Late that night, Ramzy entered Hampstead Heath and walked below where Byron and Shelley had lived, the sound of traffic fading behind him. Ramzy stuffed both hands in his jacket pockets, scared about the risk of a nuclear bomb in Jerusalem. He wondered if he should call the whole thing off. But if he did, what would the fate of the Palestinians be then? An eventual state by political process? Autonomy over collecting their own garbage while Israeli soldiers patrolled their villages? Roadblocks and no vote? Torn, he moved off the dirt road and headed into the tall grass, which soon reached his knees as he eased through the darkness.

An almost full moon bathed the heath. He stopped at the crest of a hill beside a lone tree. His mind still debating whether to abort this operation now, while he still could, he remembered the day he had met Khalidi. After his lecture in the large UCLA auditorium, where he could tell from the questions that aired immutable beliefs rather than searched, Khalidi had introduced himself, urgently insisting Ramzy accompany him to his office.

There, Khalidi had unfolded his plan. Ramzy had stood and stared out the window, knew he would have to think deeply about it. After the American secretary of state's visit to Israel after the Gulf War asking for a freeze on settlements, the Israeli minister of housing, who as defense minister had bombed Beirut to rubble, announced immediate plans for thirteen thousand more apartments in the Territories. At their pain, the Israelis lectured about how dare they throw stones.

To his surprise, Ramzy met Khalidi again that night and agreed to help him. He had wanted to provide a professional for the seduction in Sao Paulo, but Khalidi had insisted on approaching Amal and Ramzy had reluctantly relented. He had decided to initially provide money and see if Khalidi could obtain the plutonium and someone to machine it before he committed further, and to his great surprise Khalidi had succeeded.

A trumpet sounded plaintively in the quiet from somewhere in Hampstead. Two months ago, his ten-year-old nephew, his brother Fawaz's son, had been blinded by a rubber bullet shot into his head during a demonstration in Ramallah. Ramzy felt his throat tighten. He turned and began to walk back.

Even as a child, when he had excitedly set up a stand outside Sidon's Sea Castle to sell kati rolls, the Lebanese youths repeatedly kicked out the legs and called him a Palestinian son-of-a-whore. Like most people, Ramzy had intended a far different life for himself. From university, he had traveled to teach in the Damascus refugee camp with such hope, even though they had only two teachers for twelve hundred children. Undaunted, they split the horde into units of a hundred and each of them took a group for two hours and taught from 7:00 a.m. to 7:00 p.m. six days a week. He had felt certain that eventually his Arab brothers, the world, would come to his people's rescue. Years fell away. Often Ramzy trudged through the desert alone at the end of the day, or lie awake at night asking himself how long this situation would continue.

Gradually they received five additional teachers, and when they made little impact, in despair after the terrible loss of the 1967 War, he discussed the difficult decision with Dalal to leave her for long lengths of time. She agreed and he traveled to the Karameh Camp in Jordan where the Fedayeen had their main base and joined them. Now, for over twenty years he had fought and penned his stories. And though to his people he had fame and renown, as they huddled in the camps he had failed in every major attempt to help them. Even his working with the Israelis and Shai to eliminate the extremist Abu Nidal had been to no avail. He did not regret his choice to take a bleeding and dying Shai to the hospital when he had Abu Nidal trapped in Rome. Shai was a friend; those Israelis in power were not.

Ramzy moved through the grass, wanting to come to a final decision about this operation. He stopped and looked up at the bright, shrinking moon. He had timed the crossing into Israel for less than a half moon. The Palestinians had no other hope for a future.

Ramzy thought about what his mother had taught him in the Ein al-Hilweh Camp after his father's attempt, in his despair, to kill his family. What counted was continued effort into the wind of adversity. It might knock him back but he could never allow it to topple him, no matter how hard it blew. Returning into it with determination, was what mattered. Her words formed the cornerstone of Ramzy's life: personal integrity was achieved by resolutely going on.

He decided with no happiness that the operation would continue into the wind. Khalidi was safely hidden. He had to leave immediately for Lebanon and Syria, had arrangements to complete, changes to make now that the Israelis were onto Khalidi. He had received Shai's message for a meeting. The Israeli's endless enthusiasm brought a smile to his lips, which faded quickly. The friendship meant a considerable amount to him and he knew it was lost now.

Though part of him irrationally wanted to see Shai, he would not meet him.

CHAPTER 10

June 28

In his London shipping line offices, Sabri Barakat slammed down the phone then pounded the intercom button to his secretary. It was a little after 9:00 a.m. and he had not been able to reach his mistress, Christine, since yesterday afternoon. He had no patience for this now. The veins in Barakat's dark-skinned forehead pulsed. Who was it this time? Another young pretty face from a Knightsbridge pub? He would sling her arse out the flat door and down Thurloe Street. Let her try and find some pub crawler to pay for her flat, the closets of clothes and that little Alpha convertible she ran around in.

Maggie came on the intercom. "Yes, Mr. Barakat."

He remembered that silky hair of Christine's playing in his face the week before as she nibbled his neck while he drove the convertible on the M1. Barakat sank deeper in the chair, an acid feeling in his stomach, and reached for the tablets in his top drawer. "I have to go out," he said, his voice beaten quiet. "Keep ringing Christine. Tell her I want to see her. If she could make it lunchtime, in the flat."

The hurt in his voice pained Maggie and she fingered her pince-nez glasses on the chain around her neck. Her hair was held tightly behind her head with two white combs, her face soft and wrinkled. She had been with him for twenty-seven years and cared dutifully for him because it did not occur to her to care for herself.

"I shall find her straightaway," Maggie said.

Barakat chewed the chalky tablets, thought about trying her number one more time, but did not want to hear the phone ringing endlessly. Maybe he should not pay her rent this month and see what she did. He walked into the reception area.

Maggie removed her glasses as he neared. "She's probably having a coffee."

"In whose flat?" he said fiercely.

Maggie spoke soothingly. "She gets restless is all. It's only natural. She's a lovely young thoroughbred and she just needs a bit of pasture to roam about. Keeps her from bolting the fence. Now you shan't pay any mind to it, you hear me. You wouldn't be able to bear her more often anyway with her childishness. Now, you'll have a lovely lunch. I'll see to it that it's all arranged and we'll hear no more about this."

As he looked at her, he felt bucked up. Of course she was right. Why in the world had he gotten himself so worked up? He would want to switch flavors eventually anyway, and there was a delightful blond waitress in the restaurant at the Dorchester he might begin to soften with presents.

"What would I possibly do without you?" Barakat said.

"I shouldn't think you need to worry about that. Old Maggie's always here, just like the weather, now isn't she."

Barakat gave a big smile and headed through his shipping offices for the elevator. She was his anchor. His wife did not understand his business worries and simply expected his wealth to be there each day like the sun when she removed the black eyeshades she slept beneath. Often now, Christine tossed her long hair, frowned and complained he was becoming a frightful bore when he worried in her presence. Angry at both of them, sometimes late in the afternoon over tea he talked to Maggie, who remarkably wanted nothing from him. It never occurred to him to wonder if Maggie was lonely, not having married, or how she filled her evenings.

Downstairs, Barakat moved into the pleasant morning. He wore a gray pinstriped suit with a diamond stud in his red tie. Of average height, with a slight belly of success, he had chipmunk cheeks and full black hair that he had touched up every fortnight before the gray could creep back. He had not had his chauffeur bring up the limousine, as he would enjoy the short walk to St. James's Park. The silly upset about Christine had delayed him. Kenneth Khalidi should already be in the park.

Across the street, a Rover 820 rested at the curb, an Israeli agent named David seated behind the wheel. A second agent, Ronit, stepped from the car and, tourist camera around her neck, shadowed Barakat on the sidewalk. A slim brunette with short slashed hair, chocolate eyes, and thick eyebrows, Ronit passed as Italian, with a flawless accent though her parents' genes had united in Riga not Rome. This was her and David's first field assignment. All the experienced teams had winged to Los Angeles and were rushing back, due this afternoon with Shai Shaham. As she followed Barakat, Ronit thought excitedly that she would finally meet Shai, whose case histories she had studied at the massive Revivim computer.

Meanwhile, she and David would babysit Barakat. It was an easy assignment, and after all her training runs in Tel Aviv and throughout Europe, Ronit felt entirely ready.

On the polar flight to London, while most passengers slept in the dimmed lights Shai sat on an aisle coach seat, a blanket around him. It had been his need, not an operational necessity, to trust Ramzy. If Khalidi somehow got through to Israel it would be his fault. If he had not alerted Ramzy, they would have stopped Khalidi in Los Angeles. Shai felt a despair he had only sank to once before. They had been in Israel on one of his few vacations. Seated on a rock watching Sarit cross the Sinai highway, a futile scream of warning had erupted from his throat as brakes slammed much too late and the soldier's car struck her with that horrible thud that went through him and sent her flying in the air. He ran wildly to where she was crumpled on the asphalt, and with her blood dripping on his hands, he caressed her face. Her eyes were open. She reached up and touched his arm. "You're here," she said, sounding surprised. He bent and kissed her twice on the lips.

As a flight attendant carrying a large trash bag made her final pass through the cabin until the morning, Shai halted her.

"Could I trouble you for some fruit?" he asked. "An apple? Anything, doesn't matter."

"I'm sorry, sir. We have none, I'm afraid. I could probably nick you a bag of crisps."

His dentist, Pia, had sandbagged him in Jerusalem. He recalled how when he had shown up for his evening teeth cleaning Pia's close friend, the renown American immigrant dietician, Julie, had been waiting in Pia's office. Matter-of-factly, Julie told him she was not taking new clients. Furthermore, she said, "If I did take you, there is a six-month wait and there are three Knesset members who have been waiting for months to see me. I take blood tests once a month, can tell what you're eating from them, and if two come back waving red flags, I'm done with you."

Shai had laughed. This was his kind of challenge. She had him describe a typical week's eating, then she had said, "Half the time you're starving your body and the other half binging. I can't have you diet because from the look of you, you're probably 70% muscle and we can't risk that turning to fat. I didn't hear you mention fruit in your week, which I'm sure simply slipped your mind. You'll need five servings a day. Vegetables are free, as much as you want. Chicken's OK, but no chicken wings. Lean beef twice a week. Ice cream once a week, one scoop."

"I haven't had any fruit in five years," he joked, because it was true. "Does a strawberry count as a fruit?"

"Yes, and a bowl of them counts as a serving. I'll want you in a pool. Swimming if you can, walking in the water if you can't. Half an hour a day. No walking for exercise on the streets, too much pressure on those weak feet. With the resistance, thirty minutes walking in the water is equivalent to an hour outside. Pia says a good deal of our fate lies on your shoulders. Too bad you're not a good choice for it."

He smiled. "Agree. I'd never have picked me."

"Pia tells me you're gone much of the time." She handed him a card. "Come see me when you can, but I'll expect you have more than started before you show up, or don't come."

"Thank you for ambushing me. Truly."

"Pia's one of the *Lamed Vavniks.*" A mystical interpretation of Talmudic tradition had it there were thirty-six righteous people in every generation whose presence keeps the world from ending. "There's nobody else I'd drop everything for. Nobody. Now don't think you're getting out of here without her cleaning your teeth. Pia's waiting."

As Shai came up from the memory, he had a sense the flight attendant was watching him, and then she turned around and headed toward the front of the plane. More than any professional therapist could have motivated him, it was the love he felt from Pia and Hirsh that had seeped down deep inside him and led him now to take better care of himself. Shai glanced at Sara and Hirsh ten rows up, heads near, talking despite the hour. He must have been dozing, and he bolted alert as the stewardess lowered his tray table. She slipped a porcelain plate on it with slices of cantaloupe and honeydew melon and a real knife and fork, obviously from first class.

"I'll be back in a few minutes for the plate. Don't want an insurrection back here about special treatment." She smiled. "Mind you, most everybody's asleep."

"You've restored my faith in the world," Shai said, not far from fully meaning it.

Soon both the fruit and the plate had vanished. Shai pulled the flight magazine from the pouch. As Hirsh got up to use the bathroom, Sara looked in Shai's direction, met his gaze, then headed over and bounced down on the seat beside him. She sensed how hard he was taking the Ramzy business.

"You pick your team by how little they sleep?" she said. "Cilia's up pacing the forward cabin."

Shai looked along the aisle, could not see her, thought about how fortunate he was to have all of them. He turned to Sara with a fatherly smile. "You and Hirsh seem to have a lot to talk about."

She looked at him intently, fixed on his expression, and a realization came to her and she laughed. "Now how did I miss that? Only you would send someone out on a date in the middle of a mission. He asks me to take a drive then says nothing. Super fun."

"Everybody warms to him."

"Let's just let nature take its course from this point, shall we."

"Always my intent."

As she returned to her seat, he closed his eyes. We needn't be in competition with love out here, he thought. It should strengthen not distract us.

Standing near the circular Cake House in St. James's Park, Kenneth Khalidi was quietly excited. He had finally received the Dostoevsky novel in his box at the hotel that meant he should meet Sabri Barakat here. The nervous five days waiting had lasted forever. Ahead of him on a wooden bench, a boy of maybe eight poured a cup of seed in his blond hair, and with a flap of wings, pigeons landed on his head and shoulders and pecked. The boy laughed. Khalidi was envious, wished he'd been that free child. He had remained mostly in his room, read and watched television; his habits too as an adult. He wondered if everybody was imprisoned by their past.

"Come, shall we have a coffee?" Sabri Barakat said from beside him.

Khalidi turned, startled. He had not seen Barakat approach.

"Yes, of course."

They moved toward the Cake House. Fountains sprayed into the narrow lake where ducks glided on green water surrounded by weeping willows. Ahead, children threw breadcrumbs and the ducks pecked. In the cafeteria-style line, Barakat shuffled forward with one tray for the both of them, took two small pots of coffee, a porcelain pitcher of cream and paid. As Barakat carried the tray to a table by the glass wall, he thought about how, when Ramzy had approached him with the scheme, he had spent two agitated days deciding, weighing the personal risk against what it could accomplish. What had tipped him was the opportunity to outsmart the Israelis as he had in business dealings with the Kuwaitis and Saudis.

Barakat and Khalidi sat across from each other. The white metal table next to them was empty. Nearby, a group of elderly men were arguing politics.

"There are boxes in the Lancaster Gate post office near your hotel," Barakat said as he poured coffee in both cups. "Before we leave I'm going to shake your hand and pass you a key. Your ticket's in the box along with a new passport. You leave tomorrow. Someone will meet you at the Beirut airport. They'll recognize you."

Khalidi had traveled from California on a forged Canadian passport Ramzy had supplied. "Thank you very much."

Barakat knew that to leave too quickly would appear odd on the very small chance they were being watched. "So, you get yourself any skirt while you've been here?" He grinned, showing perfectly capped teeth. "When I was younger and on the move there was always someone working in the hotel to chat up."

Khalidi's face darkened. He sipped his coffee, set the cup down hard. "I'm not like that. I...am in love."

Barakat waved a spoon in the air. "All love has an expiration date. It's just a question of when." He laughed. "Skirt drives you just as crazy but it's far easier to replace."

"I viewed the William Blake collection at the Tate Gallery."

Barakat allowed himself a small smile. "Yes, excellent. I rather enjoy the Tate myself."

Khalidi talked about his sightseeing, confused that someone as great as Ramzy Awwad would work with this Barakat. In Khalidi's new life the future was all possibility, and he did not yet grasp that, as in his old life, for everyone the road forward was pockmarked with bumpy concession.

Soon, Barakat put his hands on the metal table and pushed himself to his feet, rattling the coffee service. "Well, ciao ciao."

Khalidi rose, picked up his map with his left hand. He gratefully would not have to see Barakat again. "I will accompany you outside."

"Yes, do."

They headed up the grass hill behind the Cake House. "So how are you sneaking yourself into Israel from Lebanon?" Barakat asked when no one was within earshot.

"I do not know. Ramzy and I discussed that he would meet me in Lebanon and we would proceed with the details there."

Barakat felt he deserved to know given the risk he was running, but that tight-lipped Ramzy would not tell him. Barakat reached out his hand to shake Khalidi's. "Safe journey."

As Khalidi grasped his hand, he closed his fingers around a small key.

Behind them, Ronit walked along the walkway arm in arm with David, a camera hanging from her neck. The telephoto lens was in her purse. She had already taken a roll of them in the refreshment stand. Procedure required spotters to run in fours instead of twos, but with no backup they were it. She had been placed in charge, and with only one car, she had to decide whom to follow. They could tail one of them easily and they had been ordered to stick to Barakat. She had seen nothing pass between them. She had to decide, now.

"Take the car and stay with Barakat. I'll take the other one," she said. The young man held a map in his hand, so likely with the extensive London transport system he did not have a vehicle. "He'll be easy to follow, so we'll split up."

David nodded. Ronit kissed him for cover and headed up the embankment.

Khalidi started walking and in his happiness, decided to phone Amal. She should be long since home from the High Sierras. He had left hurriedly after Ramzy's call and had not phoned her since, afraid she was back with Geraldo. As he exited the park, he thought about the way they had made love in his office, how excited she had been at his decisiveness, and suddenly he felt confident. After the state was erected, she would never think of Geraldo. He wanted to hear her voice before he disappeared into the Middle East. He calculated the time. It was late Wednesday night in Los Angeles but she would not mind being woken.

Ronit followed at a discreet distance. The man did not seem to be concerned about surveillance but she would remain vigilant.

Khalidi stared at the willowy clouds overhead as he approached Trafalgar Square. Across the spraying fountains bagpipes mixed with the noise of small cars, vans, double-decker buses and taxis that fought their way forward, the brakes of the black cabs squealing at each stop. He knew their drums overheated in the crowded city. There was no point in boarding the bus just to sit in the traffic as it crawled around the square, so Khalidi consulted his map and strode up Cockspur Street, would catch the bus there.

In the Haymarket, he watched a red double-decker ease from the curb. He had missed it. Then he saw the image of that blond boy in the park pouring the seed in his hair. Surprising himself, he ran for the bus just to do it. It was pulling up the street, but he knew from all his running the UCLA perimeter that he could catch the rear platform. He ran faster.

Ronit swore, memorized the license plate of the bus and started searching for a cab. He must have made her.

Khalidi threw his legs forward, gained, breathed the exhaust, was within reach of the escaping rear. As the bus accelerated noisily, he kicked hard, lunged forward, caught the tall post and hauled himself up with a smile. The uniformed ticket seller angrily strutted toward him.

Ronit tried to flag an empty black cab that raced by her. She looked quickly in the other direction for another bus. The buses would bunch up just ahead in the traffic on Regent and Oxford Streets. She could grab a cab there, weave through the traffic and switch to his bus.

For five minutes, Ronit waited in frantic frustration until the next bus arrived. She rode it along the fancy stores on Regent and Oxford Street, the fingers of her left hand damp against the glass, looking for both his bus and a cab while watching the sidewalks for any sign of him. Only ten short minutes had passed since she lost him and she knew she still had a chance of catching up. She spotted an empty cab before Marble Arch, jumped off the moving bus losing her balance but not falling, and pushed her way into the cab in front of two girls, a flurry of arms, legs and green Marks and Spencer bags.

She slammed the door with the girls' shouting. The driver quickly caught her bus on a residential section of Bayswater Road with monotonous white stucco terraces and dropped her as it stopped across from Kensington Gardens. She jumped aboard. With hope, Ronit searched the lower deck with her eyes, and not seeing him, she climbed the narrow staircase.

An older man and four women sat on the upper deck. A small breath escaped Ronit and she grabbed a pole for support.

In his room in the Andrews Court Hotel, Khalidi sat on the edge of the bed and dialed. It was after midnight there. As the phone rang and rang, he tasted a small fear. She could be at Geraldo's.

The receiver was lifted. "Hello, who is it?" A female voice, rushed, but it was not Amal and it did not seem that he had woken whomever it was.

"It is a friend of Amal's. I would like to speak to her please."

"She's not here."

He said nothing.

"Hello? Hello?" The voice sounded nervous.

"Excuse me, I am here. When will she return?"

"I don't know!" Loud, frightened. "Who is this?"

"Is something the matter?"

"Who is this?"

He hesitated about using his real name, then said, "Shannon, this is Professor Khalidi."

"Dr. Khalidi. Oh, God. Is she with your friends? Some girl called two nights ago and said they had a message from you. She went to meet her and then I don't know what happened. The police called a few hours ago. A bartender told them her car's been in their lot for two days." Panic pushed Shannon's voice. "She hasn't come back. She hasn't called. Geraldo's in Fresno and hasn't heard from her. I'm scared."

His dropped his head into both hands, his voice very quiet. "Who called her and what precisely did they say?"

"I don't know. Some chick. Amal answered. She was wasted

from camping. We were making hot chocolate but she got dressed and went to meet her. She wouldn't say who or where. All she said was that the caller was a friend of yours and that she had some message from you or something."

"You are certain that she said there was a message from me?"

"Yes," she said loudly. "That's the only reason she went."

"Did you tell the police about the message?"

"No." A pause. "I sorta know there's something going on. I didn't want to get anybody messed up."

"Shannon, let me examine this further and see what I can learn."

"All right."

"I'll telephone you in a few days and inform you where she is. Does that make you feel better?"

"Yeah, sure. Then she's okay?"

"Yes. She is with my friends they are on some important business. I did not realize they had left already. I will try and have her phone you directly. Are the police investigating?"

"No, at least I don't think so. They asked me if I wanted to file a report or have them contact her parents and I said no, that she probably just went off with some guy. I made it like she does that, but she doesn't. Not anymore, not in the last year."

"I know," he whispered. Catching himself, he strengthened his voice. "There is absolutely no reason to be alarmed, I assure you."

"Hey, great. Thanks, professor."

He said goodbye, somehow cradled the receiver and sat motionless and terrified. The Israelis had Amal. He had seen pictures of what the Palestinians in the West Bank looked like after questioning: blackened skin, broken bones, swollen faces. He pictured her like that. He closed his eyes.

In his mind's eye he saw Beita, the men being herded down the hill, the houses rising in the air then hitting the ground and falling apart. They had all sat helpless in the soccer field. And now they kidnapped Amal. Fury pulsed through him. The Israelis thought they could do whatever they wanted. They had to be taught a lesson. Maybe he would destroy Jerusalem once the bomb was assembled.

"When were these taken, exactly?" Shai asked as he looked at the rows of enlarged photographs of Barakat and Khalidi on the conference room table at the embassy in Palace Green. He felt no anger, could accept all failure other than his own.

Ronit and David sat sullenly across from him. Shai had faxed photos of Khalidi to the embassy, but the inexperienced team had rushed out to Barakat without heading to the embassy first to view them.

Hirsh, Cilla and Sara formed a semicircle on Shai's side of the table. Hirsh gazed up, caught Sara glancing at him. He did not acknowledge her, looked down, and with hard strokes began to draw a mushroom cloud on a pad. The embassy security officer, Zev Oz, sat at the far end of the table. The polar flight had put them in at lunchtime and they had reached the Embassy at 1:40. Two dozen pavement artists had arrived on various flights.

"They were taken between nine-thirty and ten this morning," Ronit said, digging a chipped red nail into the edge of the conference table.

Shai picked up another photograph and studied it. "Anything handed between them?"

"Not that we could see." Ronit dug the channel deeper. "We didn't know you were after *him*," she said miserably.

Shai neared her. "Of course you didn't. No way to expect it. And how could you possibly be at the embassy and outside Barakat's office at the same time? It was us who failed to provide help. If you had been at the embassy you might have missed the St. James's Park meeting altogether. Now, let's look at the glass as being half full." Shai glanced at Ronit and noted her face had eased and her hands were now on one thigh. Good. Nothing gained in chopping off her head, and she would become a better agent remembering this early failure. Shai went on. "We know he's here and met with Barakat a few hours ago."

"Alert the British and have him picked him up when he tries to leave the country," David said.

Shai suspected Khalidi was already in possession of a false passport or passports. Paul McEnnerney in Washington had run all North American flights everywhere since Khalidi left Los Angeles and not found his name.

"That's an alternative," Shai said. "Now we balance the risks." He lifted his hands in the air, like scales of justice, and tipped one up. "The British pick him up and they or we interrogate him and he relatively quickly spills what he knows. We find out where the plutonium is." He tipped the scales in the other direction. "Or don't, depending on how much he knows about who's handling the plutonium inside Israel. Of course Ramzy would be able to provide us with that information." Shai tipped the scales yet again. "Then maybe by snatching Khalidi prematurely and his not turning up where he's supposed to everybody goes underground." Shai dropped his hands. "Maybe we concentrate on Barakat. Maybe Barakat tells us all kinds of things without Khalidi knowing. Maybe we follow Khalidi in and collect everybody as well as the bomb." He clapped his hands. "Or maybe we try both and see what happens." Shai turned to Hirsh. "That's how we play this one. If they were clever enough to get the plutonium in, Ramzy's thought carefully about how to get Khalidi across the border. I'm going to have a chat with our old mates the British. I want everything you can get on Barakat when I return."

In an uncharacteristic three-piece gray suit and briefcase, Shai approached the annex on Marlborough Street, the smallest of the four buildings that comprised the British internal security service. As he lumbered toward the front door, with a stubby finger he pulled at the back of his shirt collar. He wore a suit awkwardly unless the role required a certain comfort, which he could assume once fully at the task.

Shai's name was on the register as Mr. Gideon Harel and he was given a plastic tag to clip onto his jacket and pointed toward the lift, which creaked to the third floor. After the heavy door reluctantly parted, Shai proceeded through a corridor with worn brown carpet and yellow wood banisters. Fourth door on the left, they had said at reception.

He knocked diffidently on the door; he sometimes lapsed into his childhood shyness, especially in the face of unfamiliar authority. As a boy, he turned his head and looked away when shaking someone's hand, to which his father said, no matter, you'll look them in the eye when you're ready. The door opened, revealing a young man in his twenties with bowtie and tortoise shell glasses, and Shai seemed to rise inside the suit as he stepped in.

"Mr. Shaham, I presume," the young man said, stretching out his hand, his straight black hair flopping over his forehead. It was a conference room and a crystal chandelier hung over a long, oblong table, light reflected in the polish. The room was stark and emotionally, if not physically, cold. Shai bet it was both most of the year.

"Yes," Shai said, grasping his hand and testing the bones as he smiled at him. "A pleasure."

"Wilfred Asprey here. Commander Rutherford shall be with us forthrightly. I rang him as soon as reception notified me of your arrival." He smiled. "Or Gideon Harel's more precisely. You have a safe trip? Come from Jerusalem, just now?"

Shai tried to determine if the man was breezily innocent or the other thing. "Just came from America, actually."

"Ah, yes. Well we all end up in America too much of the time, now don't we. You're into a rough patch with the Palies, I should think. Can I get you a coffee? I'm sure Commander Rutherford will do everything he can to help you. White with sugar is it?"

"No coffee, thank you, Mister Asprey." Shai remained standing, as he had not been invited to sit.

Asprey nodded. He started to speak, stopped, then began again. "While we're waiting, if I may ask, sir. Never been to your country but a friend, well, my lady friend and I were thinking about a holiday, Christmas in Bethlehem sort of thing. But I'm rather concerned. Do you believe it's safe at present, for the lady that is?"

"I think there'll be more soldiers than pilgrims for midnight mass."

Just then the door flew open and Commander Rutherford strode in. He moved with the swagger of aristocracy and the assurance of a soldier who had met the enemy on every front, won most, and came proudly close even when humbled. Regally tall, sporting a sharply tailored suit that unlike Shai he wore like his skin, he had an athlete's body but twenty years past his prime—still slim, but muscles gone unavoidably soft with neglect. Football would have been his passion till his forties, Shai surmised, horses since. He had white hair, an angular nose and thin impatient lips that had been pursed more in anger than for women. A moustache the same color as his full hair added dignity to his visage, and no one on a London street, Rutherford knew with certainty, would mistake him for less than his station. Shai, for his part, had known British con artists on the Cote d'Azur who bore a striking resemblance to Rutherford who specialized in bilking wealthy American widows.

"Is it Mister Harel or Mister Shaham?" Rutherford asked. "Which is the flesh?"

"Shaham," Shai said. "For friends."

"Well that's indeed what we are. Kissed and made up despite the past, now haven't we." Rutherford smiled, too widely. "You and us and even the new Russkies, for the moment, all *de bons amis* in this curious world. Still, your lot hasn't quite forgiven the Nazis for their excesses, have you?"

Shai smiled. "Not like we've forgiven the British."

Rutherford's own grin broadened. "We only hung a handful of you people. A small inconvenience to your considerable determination history has shown." Rutherford sat and stretched his arm out indicating Shaham and Asprey should descend at the near end of the table. Shai lowered himself into a hard chair.

Rutherford placed his palms on the table, his face a glow of satisfaction. "The Palies seem to be doing to you what you did to us. I'd say you're about at 1939, the Peel Commission's met, talked about a state. You've issued your White Paper preventing them from coming in."

His smile gone, Shai said, "The Palestinians rejected partition. They could have had a state forty years ago. They chose the sword and now they're complaining about how sharp ours are."

Rutherford leaned back in his chair, still smiling. "My boy, the world can't get enough Japanese gadgets. We're bedfellows with the Huns, all of 'em now. The world's changed. Who's who they were forty years ago?"

"Maybe everybody is," Shai said, his smile returning. Before Rutherford could respond, Shai snapped open his briefcase, pulled out the dossiers and handed one to Rutherford and one to Asprey, settled a third before himself. Under his hovering eye, the dossiers had been carefully rushed, snipped and pasted together with the designed omissions.

Asprey flipped open the file with a hungry look and stared at the first page as if it were a girlie magazine. Rutherford, who preferred others to do his reading for him, slowly withdrew glasses from his inside jacket pocket but set them on the file.

"So I have it, the Palies are threatening to blow you to kingdom come?" Rutherford said.

"That's the gist of it," Shai agreed.

Asprey turned a page. Rutherford said, "Mind, you can understand their view, I presume."

"The view, yes. The method however has an exaggerated flair we Jews lack. We think on rather a smaller scale." Shai wore an expression of innocence that fit like his suit. He actually meant this. Israeli swagger had put them in the forefront of breakthroughs in drip irrigation, they developed amniocentesis in 1956, and recently the first crib baby monitor, but they had never mastered the large-scale cooperation necessary, like Finland had, to create a Nokia.

"Size never stopped us from grand folly." Rutherford strummed the table and glanced at Asprey. "How's it play, young Wilfred?"

Asprey did not look up. "Very professional, Sir Charles. No major lacunae apparent. I'd like a few more minutes though."

Rutherford swept his hand in the air. "Don't rush yourself, Willy. We have all the time in the world for Mister Harel-Shaham and his compatriots." He pulled his half-moon glasses open with menace, pushed them on the table and the gold frames reflected in the polish.

Shai willed his bustling energy still in the silence, large hands spread on his thighs, damp.

After a moment, Rutherford snatched up his glasses, slipped them on and drew open the dossier. "Why don't you give me the meat of it while young Wilfred labors on. Cut away the gristle if you would."

"Page eleven beginning with the second paragraph," Shai said without opening the file or retrieving his own glasses, which lay in his case.

Rutherford nodded and thumbed through the pages, bending the edges. Shai turned carefully to page eleven—files to him were sacred—more to busy the demons inside him than to ready a response. Rutherford read for a moment then glanced above his small glasses at Asprey. "You with us, Willy boy?"

Asprey rifled ahead. "There, Sir Charles."

Shai waited for them to fleece the file, then said, "We'd like limited distribution on this. Anything leaked to the press might push a panic."

"We are not in the business of bandying about private confidences." Rutherford looked up. When he did read, he read rapidly. "Let's cut to the quick, shall we. What'll you do if they actually put all the pieces together? No notes on that here, I suspect. Wilfred?"

Asprey had stepped up the pace of his reading like a runner kicking toward the finish, was turning pages faster. "Nothing I've seen."

"I'm a foot soldier, not privy to the machinations of the politicians," Shai said, not far from the truth.

"Bullocks. Carmon probably wants to blast everything in range and you people probably have a greater range than even we suspect." He pulled his glasses off. "How do you know this Khalidi's in Great Britain, now?"

"One of our people trailed him to a flight to London yesterday," Shai fabricated. "We don't know what name he's using." Shai reached down, pulled a stack of photographs from his briefcase and handed them to Rutherford. "These were taken in St. James's Park this morning."

As Rutherford pushed his glasses back on and stared at the photograph, Shai studied a copy himself. It was a clear picture of Khalidi and Barakat drinking coffee in the refreshment gazebo, only Barakat had been completely airbrushed out of the photograph. Rutherford looked up and flipped one of the photographs to Asprey, who snatched it like a dog grabbing a ball from the air with his muzzle.

"How did you manage to lose him?" Rutherford inquired, lifting his eyebrows.

"Inadequate surveillance. We weren't prepared. At the last second he bolted for a bus and jumped on. We had people in the street but none in cars."

"So he knows you're onto him."

"That, or he was being cautious."

Rutherford swept his glasses off again. "So I take it we have the honor of your presence here because of a balls-up. Otherwise we'd never have known you were here. Is that the case, Mr. Harel-Shaham?"

"I arrived early this afternoon from Los Angeles. There was no time for liaison."

"No time. Yes, of course. I see." Rutherford tapped the table with the edge of his glasses. "Pity. Think of all the people we had at our disposal, and cars. We positively have a whole fleet of cars for such occasions."

Shai tasted the bile in his stomach. "It is unfortunate."

"So what's this Khalidi doing on Her Majesty's soil?"

"We don't know. "

Rutherford abruptly pushed the dossier aside. "You don't know bugger all, from the looks of this. Or could it possibly be that there are a few chapters missing?"

"We know he's going to try to get into Israel. He left Los Angeles in a hurry. My guess is it's no more complicated than he's on his way. London is in the general direction."

Rutherford laughed. It was the joyless laugh of a man who had parceled out much judgment and little mercy. "On that we're in agreement." He looked at the dossier then up at Shai and his smile was suddenly soft. "I should think we can accommodate you. We can dig up a statute somewhere to hold Khalidi for a few days, yes, Wilfred?"

"The Addicott Act would fit this case."

"Precisely. Nuclear terrorism is not something I'm keen on. We sever the head off this here and now." He gathered the photographs in front of them in a neat stack. "We'll send Khalidi's face out to every border point by electronic wire within the hour. We shan't let him slip through our fingers. Once he's safely tucked away, I think we can work out a mutually satisfactory arrangement for questioning. We have some small expertise in the area from bashing the boyos. I suppose too we can go out for a coffee and let you have a long go yourselves. If he appears drugged on our return, well, who's to say he's not dazed from the bright lights and lack of sleep."

"I appreciate the assistance," Shai said.

Rutherford said nothing for a long moment, then looked at Shai, the hostility gone from his face, replaced by a concern that almost seemed like sadness. He spoke softly. "Tell Carmon something for me. Tell him to learn from us. Tell him once people are willing to die for a cause it can't be crushed unless you're willing to drop the bomb or its equivalent yourselves. Tell him the problem doesn't go away as much as you try and ignore it." He lifted the dossier off the desk. His face abruptly hardened and the warmth fled his tone. He pointed the dossier at Shai. "And you tell Carmon from now on operating on our soil will be managed as it has been today, through channels. Strictly. I want to know everything you're doing here. You have that, do you, Mr. Shaham?"

"Absolutely," Shai said. "Liaison's the ticket. We work together."

Rutherford spun on his heel and marched out.

Shai rose slowly. He felt himself shaking inside from everything he had suppressed and the result was to slacken his motions.

Asprey looked up from where he had returned to plundering the file. "Shall I accompany you out?"

"Why don't you finish reading. I can find the way."

"Very good, sir."

The entire return ride, Shai sat in the back seat of the embassy Volvo, stared out the window and said nothing to the driver. They passed the huge glass-domed Royal Albert Hall then rounded Kensington Gardens and pulled through the large iron gate into Palace Green. A number of embassies, including Moscow's, shared the Green with Princess Margaret's Kensington Palace. The driver stopped in front of the high gate, twenty yards from the three-story, double-fronted house where earlier gentry and stables rather than armed embassies had sat. Shai did not get out of the car. The driver, from Gants Hill in East London hurried around the Volvo and opened the rear door, though he had never seen Shai wait for him to do so. "You all right, are you?"

Shai sat there for a long moment and then nodded. Sometimes every step seemed an impossible struggle. The news media pointed cameras on the West Bank, while the Syrians restricted movement and nobody knew they shot, gassed and bulldozed twenty thousand people in Hama. After regular three year army service, every Israeli male spent at least forty-five days a year in reserve duty until the age of forty, forty-five for officers, and they endured the highest taxation in the world to guard their borders.

Now Ramzy—who symbolized a hope that balanced half his country's zeal to settle deep in the West Bank, no matter who they trampled—was assembling a nuclear bomb on their doorstep. He closed his eyes for a moment, and then afraid he would tumble deeper into himself, he reached for the doorframe and pulled himself from the car.

Shai stood outside the intercom system for a long moment then finally pushed the buzzer and quietly said, "Shaham." A closed-circuit camera was mounted on the top of the high railing. The gate buzzed, and as he pushed through it he heard the Volvo pull away. He slowly crossed the short distance to the front door, rubbed the tightness from his neck and pressed the button on the intercom. At the buzz, he pushed the ornate door handle forward and stepped into the tiny vestibule, a closed door in front of him. As the door behind him shut loudly from its own weight another buzzer released the second door and he plowed through it.

Reaching the lobby, with two plainclothes, armed Israelis flanking the entrance, he pulled in a heavy breath and headed up the carpeted stairs two at a leap, ignoring that his feet hurt more this way. By the time he reached the third floor, he came through the door of the situation room like a bull released into the arena. Zev, Ronit, Sara and Hirsh were waiting. He dropped his briefcase noisily on the floor, did not sit.

"Barakat, tell me."

"The problem is he goes virtually everywhere by his own limousine," Ronit said. She hung her head and her voice lowered. "I should have suspected something when he started out alone in the morning. I'm sorry."

"I have no time for self-pity," Shai said. "Finished? I need all of you."

She looked up at the compassion in his warm, blue eyes. "Okay, finished."

"Good. What else?"

"He lives in Park Crescent," Zev said. "You know the area?"

"Yes." The flats near Regent's Park were equivalent to the posh apartments on Fifth Avenue off Central Park.

"I don't think we can take him there," Zev went on. "He has an art collection with sophisticated alarms, and the streets are busy."

"What about lunch?"

"There's a private dining room on the floor above his offices. His company occupies the whole building." Ronit ran fingers through her short hair. "Seems he has a mistress in Kensington, was there this afternoon. She's young, drives an Alpha Romeo. We're following her."

"But we don't know how often he sees her," Shai said. "The chauffeur armed?"

Hirsh smiled inexplicably.

Zev said, "I can't imagine Barakat would worry about breaking the law."

"Bathurst Mews," Hirsh said.

"What?" Shai stared at him.

"We're in a hurry. It can be done."

A small smile touched Shai's lips. "What can be done?"

"You bloody know what I'm talking about. The chauffeur's family. Name's Fouad Bayaa. Lives in an isolated mews, over the garage. There's a son and two daughters, all under ten. You want their fucking shoe sizes, I'll get that too."

Shai sank into a chair, tugged his tie loose and released the button beneath it. He looked at Hirsh and a grin spread up his face. "That's exactly the way I see it."

"I have a team ready and the flat under surveillance. Ten minutes before you came in the wife and one daughter returned home. The heir to his miserable throne's either out or has been inside the whole time with the other daughter. We have a place to take them in Edgware, a small house where the driveway pulls inside a gate to the garage. An Israeli woman lives there with her husband. A British Jew. He worked for us before he burned out."

Shai turned to Zev. "I need a warehouse or storage area to hold Barakat immediately, in the event we can take him tonight."

"You'll have it within the hour."

Shai spoke to Hirsh. "As soon as you're sure the son's there, take them and get back to me. Get some rings and hair before you go up to Edgware." Shai turned to Zev. "Any response from the call to Ramzy?"

"No."

"And Jerusalem?"

"Nothing on the plutonium."

Shai leaned forward, awkwardly pulled his jacket off and slung it over the next chair. Large rings of sweat spread out from his underarms. He was worried, despite the fact that as of five hours ago Khalidi was here.

"Anything else you need right now?" Zev asked as he stood.

"No. Thanks."

Zev started to walk out with Ronit, leaving Sara alone with him. Shai called after him. "Get me some apples. A few extra for my jacket pockets." Of all fruit, Shai detested apples the most, could not recall in what decade he'd last had one. To prove to himself he could do this, he wanted apples.

"You think we have Khalidi boxed in?" Sara asked.

He looked at her hopeful green eyes. "We have a good chance. Including the small airports, there's not more than two dozen places to jump off this island."

At the post office on Spring Street, Khalidi calmly opened the box and looked inside the envelope. There was a ticket for an 11:00 a.m. flight to Beirut the following day and a Moroccan passport with his picture and a new name. Amal had not known he was headed for Lebanon. He analyzed his alternatives. The Israelis, and maybe even the British, would be searching for him and he needed to arrive in Beirut at roughly 4:00 p.m. tomorrow afternoon, where his unknown contacts would be expecting him.

In the red call box outside the post office, he dialed Barakat's direct line.

"Who is it?" Barakat answered.

"I enjoyed our coffee this morning," Khalidi said. "I need you to phone me back at this number in a few minutes from some number other than your own."

There was a long silence, then Barakat said, "All right. Give it to me."

Khalidi gave him the number then heard an abrupt dial tone. In case anybody appeared and wanted to use the phone, he held the metal arm down and the dead receiver near his mouth. As he waited, hand in his pocket, he fingered the gold pocket watch he had purchased in Los Angeles. The Californium-252 seeds he had lasered into a small BB were secreted in the back. Gold was a superb shield, better than lead, and while an x-ray machine would light up the Californium-252, when he had walked through the metal detector at Los Angeles Airport it had merely beeped at the pocket watch. He had handed it to the security guard and walked through again without any offending sound.

The phone rang and he released the metal arm.

"What's the matter?"

"I need to ask where you are calling from."

"The Israeli embassy," Barakat said sarcastically. "What happened?"

Khalidi told him about Amal and his suspicion they were searching for him in England. Barakat swore an Arabic oath under his breath.

"I want to board the hovercraft to Calais," Khalidi said. "I require someone to drive me who they absolutely will not suspect, who has some reason for going to Paris. I can hide in the trunk behind a lot of luggage."

Barakat was silent for a moment. "It's stupid enough to work. My secretary will take you. There's a primary school on Purchese Street. It's not far from King's Cross Station. She'll meet you there at four-thirty. Can you find it?"

"I have a map."

"You have a map." His tone was sarcastic, his fear apparent. "All right, look. I'll attempt to reach Ramzy. What are you going to do?"

"Fly to Beirut from somewhere on the Continent."

"I'll leave word, but this is the end of my involvement in this. Don't call me again."

"What is your secretary's name?"

"Maggie."

Khalidi heard the dial tone in his ear. He remained in the call box and looked through the glass, saw no one, but knew if the Israelis were there he would not see them. He exited and, clutching only his small carry-on bag, headed down the street. He had several hours to kill.

To his considerable surprise, he found that rather than terrified he accepted the challenge of their chasing him. It would let him prove to himself, and to Amal and Ramzy too, what he could accomplish. He thought of Amal. He was glad she was a prisoner of the Israelis and not, as he had feared, in a mountain cabin with Geraldo. Khalidi did not want her near his Latin charms while he was gone. He picked up his pace. The nervousness was gone and he was beginning to accept that it would reach in then disappear, and he could not hope for it being over as he had so wanted.

He looked in both directions; they might be following him to the plutonium. If Amal had told them about Barakat, they could even have been observing the meeting in St. James's Park. "I have to succeed," he whispered out loud as he crossed the street toward Lancaster Gate Station. He could never return to the pain of his old life. He descended the deep escalator to the trains. Below, in the white tiled tunnel, a longhaired musician with one leg sat on the floor strumming a guitar, his voice echoing through the chamber, his case open beside him with very little change. His suffering reminded Khalidi of his own and he reached in his wallet and threw ten pounds in.

Khalidi emerged into the stale air of the platform, touched with the odor of burnt electricity. A dozen people stood on the platform. More joined them: dark-skinned Indians, a middle-aged British man, a pale British woman with a daughter eating soft ice cream with a chocolate flake, a young man reading a paperback, a brunette in a summer dress that only covered half her thighs. Fear drummed in Khalidi's ears. Any of them could be Israeli spies. The train gratefully sounded in the tunnel then burst through the gaping hole and slowed with a long, high-pitched squeal. The doors parted. Khalidi filed in as people brushed past him.

The motors rumbled, the doors slid shut and the train jerked then eased from the station. Khalidi walked to the rear of the car, reached up to the handle marked EMERGENCY STOP, and yanked. The train jolted to a halt, knocking passengers forward. Voices rose in protest. Khalidi thrust his hand against the rubber edges of the doors and pulled them back. He was enjoying this.

He jumped down into the tunnel and ran the short distance toward the Lancaster Gate Station. He looked back. No one dropped off the train. He would make the last hovercraft at 8:00 p.m. without being followed.

In Bathurst Mews off Sussex Garden—ironically so near to where Khalidi had walked to the post office that if the spotters had been a mere two blocks west they would have seen him—a van pulled into the alley-like street, wheels rattling over the bricks. Living space rose above each ground floor garage. The van stopped in front of a blue door to their right.

Wearing a light windbreaker, Hirsh hopped out with a cardboard box. The lettering on the box promised it contained a four-head Phillips VCR. He rang the bell. Soon he heard heavy steps coming down the stairs.

"Yes?" a woman's voice spoke in English from inside with an Arabic accent. "Who is it?"

"A package from Sabri Barakat for Fouad Bayaa."

The door opened and Hirsh launched a smile. "A new VCR. Four heads." He was covering himself in the unlikely event they already had one. "My boss feels bad that your husband must be away from his family so often in the evenings, so he sent this."

She smiled and gold glittered from her teeth. One lower tooth was completely missing. She was a heavyset woman, wore a long, traditional dress but no head covering.

"Come in, welcome," she said.

Hirsh shifted the supposedly heavy box and entered. As soon as she shut the door, he reached into his pocket and thrust a handkerchief drenched with chloroform around her face and held it tight against her struggling mouth. She sank to the floor. He pulled her heavy body back from the door and opened it. Two agents quickly slipped through.

The agents climbed silently up the narrow stairway, with Hirsh in front. Ten minutes before, the spotters had seen Fouad's son and younger daughter return. The door to the left bedroom was closed and the sounds of television issued from the larger quarters to the right. Hirsh pointed one agent to the left, and with a partner headed for the open living room.

As Hirsh came through the entranceway holding the box, he spoke to the children. "We have a VCR from Mr. Barakat for the family. Your mother told us to connect it."

A boy, maybe five, looked up with large brown eyes from where he drew in a coloring book on the floor in front of the television.

A girl of ten stood at the stove cooking, the smell of lamb and onions rising from the pot. The small boy jumped up excitedly. "We can see films."

Hirsh set the box down on the floor and continued into the small kitchen as the other agent approached the boy.

"Smells good," Hirsh said to the girl.

She looked at him. "Is the VCR really for us, forever?"

He nodded and neared, then his second handkerchief was over her mouth. He was aware of a small scuffle behind him, felt her teeth bite hard into his forefinger and then she folded to the floor. Hirsh spun. The other agent had the unconscious boy in his arms. The third agent came out of the bedroom carrying a two-year-old girl, who had not been drugged but was not crying. Hirsh turned the burners off, silenced the television then removed a large, folded garbage bag from his back pocket. He quickly scooped in toys and stuffed animals for all three kids—it would help them during their captivity.

He picked up the tall, skinny girl from the kitchen floor, lifted her over his shoulder and carried her, the toy bag in his hand. At the base of the stairs, he set her near her mother then opened the door a crack. Beyond the van, flush against the doorway now, he saw a woman walking a small dog. Hirsh waited. He felt no qualms about doing this to children. He felt great sensitivity to children in danger and would see to it that these lovely kids were not hurt.

When the dog walker was gone, he opened the door wide. Two more agents jumped from the rear of the van and Hirsh gently lifted the girl into the windowless vehicle. Hirsh ran back upstairs, grabbed the woman's purse off the kitchen table, did not find her keys, so hurried into the bedroom. The keys were splayed on the bureau. When he came back down, the mother and the other two children were already loaded and the back door of the van shut. Hirsh retrieved the empty VCR box and made sure the front door of the flat was locked. He squeezed past the side of the van, walked casually to the passenger door and climbed in. The van eased from the Mews, David behind the wheel. From parking to pulling away had taken under four minutes.

A little before 5:00 p.m., Fouad Bayaa drove the Mercedes

limousine into Sussex Place and made a wide turn by the Indian Green Grocery into the narrow Bathurst Mews. He was hungry and frustrated. He had just dropped Barakat at home and had to return again in an hour to take him to some do at the Waldorf Hotel. He would barely have time to eat before he had to go out again, and then wait the whole evening by the car in case Barakat and his wife decided to leave the party early. He yawned thinking about it. He stopped and, with the motor running, climbed out and walked to the garage. He unlocked the padlock and swung the right door open first, as he always did for good luck. Fouad believed in superstitions, and though not devout prayed the five required prayers five times daily to be safe. At least he would have time to play with his son. If Barakat had late meetings, sometimes he had to sit around during the day and into the night and Hani was asleep by the time he dragged up the stairs.

As he headed inside, it seemed quiet to him but he supposed Hani and the girls were up to some trick. They liked to hide behind the door and jump on his back and he always fell to the floor so they could climb on him. He hurried up the last stairs, crept to the salon door with its rippled opaque glass center, twisted the handle and burst through.

He stopped, stunned. A large, heavy man with thinning hair was sitting in his chair. Another smaller man with black hair stood at his side.

"Please make yourself at home, Fouad," Shai said in Arabic and pointed toward the sofa across from him. "That is after all what it is—your home, I mean."

Fouad did not move. "Who are you? Where's my family?"

"Well, you're not going to be terribly pleased on either account, I'm afraid. We speak Arabic rather well because we're your cousins. Somewhat distant family though, from Tel Aviv. And we have your family is, unfortunately, the answer to your second question."

Rage hardened Fouad's eyes and he headed toward Shai. Hirsh produced and pointed a rather large Browning Hi Power Standard automatic pistol. Fouad stopped and glared at him. He was a broad man and well muscled, as men like Barakat did not hire chauffeurs merely for driving.

"Now why don't you have a seat on the sofa and we'll put the gun away," Shai said. "Where did you take them?" Fouad said.

Shai spoke as if he had not heard the question. "There are some items on the coffee table I'd like you to look at. If you would be so kind as to have a seat and examine them."

Fouad went to the coffee table. Small plastic bags were laid out across the netting on the Formica surface in front of the brown, vinyl sofa, tape across a tear in its back.

Shai observed Fouad's large shoulders slump. A prayer rug depicting Mecca and Medina adorned the wall behind him. Shai watched him grab a handful of the bags, turn and collapse onto the sofa clutching them. The bags contained his wife's wedding band and earrings, the gold bangles his elder daughter had had on, and locks of the children's hair.

"Your son enjoys coloring," Shai said. "He's fine, by the way. They all are. I absolutely want to assure you of that. When we conclude our business they will be returned to you well fed."

Head down, Fouad sank into himself.

"When do you pick Barakat up next?" Shai asked.

Fouad let the plastic bags drop between his legs onto the sofa, said nothing.

"Is he going out this evening? It really would be far better for everyone if he is. The children might become frightened having to spend the night in a strange place. If you're driving Barakat to an engagement, I would say we could have your family back tonight." He turned to Hirsh. "You think?"

"We could drop them off in the lobby of a comfortable hotel," Hirsh said. "His wife could phone him and he could fetch them himself."

"See? There's always a way to turn a difficult situation around. Now, Fouad, does Barakat have an engagement this evening?"

Fouad laughed, too loud, shook his head. "You know what will happen to me afterward? It doesn't matter that you have the children." His voice rose. "They'll say I should have sacrificed them, that others have sacrificed as much."

Shai removed an envelope from his inside pocket and tossed it on the table, where it landed with a thud. "There's five thousand pounds. Make yourself a new start in Europe somewhere. It's your only alternative and not such a bad one at that. Look around, Fouad. What are you giving up here, really?"

Outside, hungry, Shai pulled a small green apple from his jacket pocket and took a bite. It tasted awful, hard and crisp, and he was in the mood for a juicy lamb shawarma. He chomped the apple down to the core, the taste no better as he devoured it.

At six o'clock, Fouad eased the limousine into the semicircle of elegant flats that faced Park Crescent Gardens. This was his fate, he told himself, so he was powerless to fight it. He pulled to the sidewalk, climbed out and walked up the few stairs to Barakat's door. He wore his work uniform and under his cap his hair was damp. He pulled off his cap and swabbed his head with his arm, afraid the sweat would trickle down his brow. He pushed the intercom button.

Barakat's voice cackled through the small speaker. "We'll be down in a minute, Fouad." A closed-circuit television camera was mounted above the door.

Fouad moved toward the car, his legs weak and almost rubbery as he walked. All the glass except the windshield and front windows were opaque. Fouad stood by the rear passenger door. Sweat beaded under his cap and threatened to drip down his forehead. Barakat came out in his tuxedo. His wife trailed in a green, beaded gown, an emerald and diamond necklace bright around her neck, and emerald earrings surrounded by diamonds at her ears. Fouad opened the rear door. Barakat waited for his wife and she stepped in before him, pulling up her gown as she disappeared inside.

Barakat turned to Fouad. "You all right? You look sick."

"Fine." He coughed. "I'm fine, sir. We had lamb curry for supper. I think I ate too quickly."

"Watch it next time," Barakat said, and stepped into the limousine.

Fouad closed the door, allowing himself for the first time to real feel fury that Barakat always spoke to him like this. He circled the front of the car and slid behind the wheel. The partition behind him remained up as he drove down the broad Portland Place, turned on Oxford Street and soon entered London's second theater district of Aldwych. He wove through side streets and came up the Aldwych Street Crescent from The Strand so he could pull directly up to the Waldorf. Though it was still light out, neon blazed on the theaters. The traffic stalled up ahead as limousines and other expensive cars, stopping to discharge passengers, mixed with theater traffic. The Aldwych Theatre was just the other side of the Waldorf. The traffic was noisy and the area so crowded the black taxis queued single file between yellow lines down the center of the curved street.

Eventually, Fouad pulled up below the red awnings in front of the five-story hotel. Fouad climbed from the car, opened the passenger door and Leila Barakat stepped out. Her husband followed.

"Where will you wait?" Barakat asked. Unlike the Park Lane hotels, there was no space here for limousines to swarm and the drivers to pass the time smoking and talking.

Fouad motioned his head back. "Maybe there'll be room on Catherine Street once the shows start."

"Good. And keep your eyes open." He was beginning to regret he had started with Ramzy and Khalidi. Why should someone of his standing take such risks?

Fouad drove under the towering India House, turned left and immediately pulled to the side. The rear door opened. Hirsh entered, closed the door and Fouad eased back into traffic. From the rear, Hirsh knocked on the opaque partition and Fouad lowered it. Hirsh handed him a pack of Marlboro cigarettes. "Like a smoke?"

Fouad took the cigarettes, forced one out, lit it and inhaled mightily, then pushed the pack back toward the Israeli.

"Keep it." Hirsh's gruffness hid deep warmth for all human beings, and there was nobody, not even Shai, who was more help when friends were in crisis.

Fouad nodded and placed the Marlboros on the seat beside him. He drove through a series of narrow streets toward Catherine Street, smoking silently. Maybe this was all a blessing. He was picturing Spain, somewhere far from the dampness of London. He would find physical work befitting a man, no more of this continuous sitting.

Hirsh watched him, had earlier removed Fouad's pistol from under his seat. Hirsh found himself thinking about Sara, those legs, that quick smile, then he abruptly shut off the image, suddenly furious at Shai for manipulating his personal life.

Fouad spoke without turning back. "How long do we wait?"

"Not long. You're sure she won't want to go home?"

Fouad spun half around. "She loves these fancy dos. Likes to stay."

"Why don't you pull over and we'll make the calls now."

Fouad parked, entered the back seat and dropped beside him. Hirsh smelled the cigarettes on Fouad's breath as he dialed the number on the bulky cellular car phone and handed it to Fouad.

Fouad lifted the receiver to his ear. The machine picked up and Fouad listened to the recorded message from James MacDougal, Barakat's chief of operations. The answering machine beeped. "Mr. MacDougal, this is Fouad Bayaa. Mr. Barakat asked me to ring you. He had to leave London unexpectedly tonight. He would like you to inform his secretary and cancel all his appointments. He said he will get in touch with you when he can." Fouad hung up.

Ten minutes later, Fouad walked past a dark sandwich shop, neared the hotel, saw the light was green at the corner and hurried. If it did not turn red before he reached the entrance it would be a good omen and his family would leave tonight. He ran to the awning and, the light still green, happily ducked inside.

Inside the hotel, he climbed the steps above the open court restaurant with large palms spreading toward the high ceiling, then entered the private dining room, where loud music blared. He looked around the tables with their fine china and tall candles above floral arrangements, felt like smashing something, and then finally found Barakat. Barakat saw him, bounded up and approached.

"Fouad, what is it?"

"Mr. MacDougal just phoned to the car. He said it's an

emergency. Something about a ship sinking. He said he'd meet you in the office straightaway."

"Shit. I'll tell my wife we're going. Someone can take her home. Stop standing there. Bring the car up."

Fouad nodded and left, feeling an unexpected freedom. When he pulled the long Mercedes to the Waldorf entrance, Barakat was smoking a cigar agitatedly on the sidewalk. Fouad hopped out quickly and opened the rear door. Barakat bent, barreled halfway in, and faced someone pointing a pistol with a suppressor at him. He heard Fouad push the door behind him and felt it hit his rear.

"Sit down," Hirsh said.

Barakat's cigar dropped from his mouth and rolled on the seat. He sat and Fouad closed the door. Barakat picked up the cigar, lest it burn the black leather. Fouad was back behind the wheel and the car jerked from the curb.

"What do you want?" Barakat asked with icy fear. "Money?"

"Shut up," Hirsh said.

Barakat ground the cigar into the ashtray. "I would like to know where you are taking me."

Hirsh said nothing.

The car halted around the corner. The front passenger door opened, was closed and they were off again. With a small electric noise, the partition came down to reveal Shai, turned to face Barakat.

"Shalom," Shai said. "You needn't worry about any ship sinking. Put that ruse completely from your mind. See, you actually have a far larger problem to consider. Fouad's left messages for MacDougal and your wife and everybody believes you're off on a long business trip." Shai tilted his head toward Fouad. "With the way you treat him, almost surprised he didn't come to us on his own."

Before Barakat could respond, the partition moved back up.

Maggie drove toward the main entrance of the open-air Dover Hoverport. Behind her the sun had descended halfway to the horizon. It had just gone 7:00 p.m. and they would make the eight o'clock hover flight as planned. The brochure indicated it would only take thirty-five minutes to cross the channel and then maybe another half hour to embark and clear Customs. She estimated they would be driving in France in a little over two hours.

Just before entering Dover, Maggie had pulled off the motorway and the young man had climbed into the boot of the Ford Escort. He had seemed withdrawn to her, not speaking much the entire drive as she chattered away, and she wondered who he was. Barakat had told her only that it was vital the man in her boot arrive safely in France. Occasionally in their long relationship, Barakat had called on her for special duties, but none quite as mysterious and exciting as this. Afterwards, he had always remembered her at Christmastime.

She drove through the main gate and proceeded toward the line of booths on the large, paved tarmac. She was a bit surprised at herself but she was finding this great fun, almost like an Agatha Christie come to life. She had never been on the hovercraft, which flew atop the water. Then up ahead, by the half dozen lanes of parked cars bunched together on the cement, she saw two blue-suited bobbies. They were strolling between the cars. She panicked, thought she should turn and speed away. But they might notice and radio cars to catch her. Not knowing what to do and paralyzed, she stopped at the booth.

The young woman took her ticket, handed her a boarding card and explained that she would be entering from the green lane. Immigration, Customs and Duty Free were in the small terminal to her right and she could clear through after she parked. As she half listened, she remembered something she had read in a Dorothy Sayers novel. The police always had profiles of the criminals' likely accomplices, and she would wager next year's two-week holiday she did not match the profile. She would simply carry on and have a go at being herself.

"Brilliant," Maggie said as the young woman finished. Maggie waved as she pulled away. There were several sets of lanes on the long, concrete tarmac and maybe twenty cars sat in proper rows. Beyond the edge of the tarmac stretched the blue English Channel. The two policemen stood to the side as she edged forward. She felt the fear like a cold hand gripping her stomach. She wished there was another car ahead of her so she could have a look see as to whether they were rummaging in the boot.

She parked behind a black BMW. The two policemen approached. This was it, she told herself, the Tower of London and chuck the key into the Thames. She did not know whether to climb out or stay put, but her legs solved the dilemma because they would not move. One of the bobbies peeked in the passenger window and the other came around to her side. She rolled down the window. He bent and his eyes went to the empty rear seat. Her heart was pounding so hard she was certain he would hear it.

"Good evening, ma'am," he said. "May I see your boarding card and passport?"

"Oh." She rummaged in her purse, grateful for something to do with her hands. "There's nothing wrong, officer, is there? I shouldn't want to board if there was danger." She produced the documents and handed them to him.

"Routine check is all." He thumbed through the passport until he found her picture and looked at it. She knew he was going to ask her to lift the boot now. "Going on holiday?" he inquired.

"Yes. Well, actually no. I have a school friend who lives in Paris. Her husband passed some time ago and she's not doing well. I'm rather worried about her, you see."

He looked straight at Maggie, then handed her back her papers. "Do be careful over there with the right side drive." Then he moved away.

Maggie rolled up the window then got out, and when she turned to lock the door she saw they had both stepped to the next car. Still nervous, she walked quickly toward the terminal. A breeze came off the water. She felt a bit chilly and buttoned her white sweater, which she had crocheted herself last Easter. Two hours was not so long to wait she reassured herself.

Heading north on Edgware Road, beyond the Marylebone flyover Fouad stopped between the entrance to St. Albans Mews and Church Street as the man in the passenger seat instructed. Someone quickly opened the driver's door, Fouad was escorted out, and the same British driver from the embassy who had taken Shai to Marlborough Annex slipped behind the wheel. As the Mercedes pulled back into traffic, Hirsh blindfolded Barakat—too tightly. *Bloody nuclear bomb*, Hirsh thought.

A second team would babysit Fouad Bayaa in his flat, where he could respond to any inquiring phone calls. They would, in time, inform him that they would not be able to return his family to him for somewhat longer than originally expected, but they would let him speak to his wife and children on the phone.

Twenty minutes later, in North London the limousine turned onto an access road before the Cricklewood flyover. In the evening light, they sped in front of a glass-fronted building and entered the Oxgate Centre industrial estate. The massive area stretched for six square blocks and the skeletons of a new industrial and storage area rose across Edgware Road behind them. The area was silent at this hour.

Barakat repeated to himself that later he would have people find all of them and squeeze their balls so hard they would come out their mouths. But a frightened voice deeper inside him yelled at himself for not having more bodyguards. With his prominence in Great Britain, he had believed they would not dare touch him here. As the limousine turned, he shivered behind the darkness of the tight blindfold that reminded him of the shade his wife wore at night. Nobody would realize for days that he was missing; no one would search for him. That twit Christine would be occupying herself with who knew how many in his absence, and putting the meals on his tab at 190 Queen's Gate. When he got out of this, he swore he'd sling her out of the flat straightaway.

The limousine rounded a bend and the driver approached a small building with the sign SAFED TILES, named after the mountain city in Galilee reputed to have been founded by one of Noah's sons after the Flood. A metal grate was shut over a wide delivery door and a small door led to the offices. The grate of the Israeli-owned business clattered up and the limousine drove in. The door crashed down and lights went on. Two armed agents waited inside; one locked the grate.

Shai stepped from the car. Energized with the activity, he forgot that he was ravenous and reminded himself he was supposed to eat full meals, just the right things. He'd send someone to fetch a chicken without skin in pita from all the Jewish restaurants in Golders Green. Hirsh and the driver took Barakat by his upper arms, led him past the stacks of colored and patterned floor tiles and into a back, ground-floor office. All papers, posters and calendars had been pulled from the room. The two additional agents and the driver went through the other door into the reception area to watch the outside.

Barakat felt himself dropping onto a soft sofa and remained silent, muttering that they better not kill him. Someone removed the blindfold. Barakat squinted. The skin beside both eyes hurt.

"Let me explain how this plays," Shai said, hands laced on the desk. "We own Fouad Bayaa. Your housekeeper packed a suitcase for you and Bayaa's picking it up."

Barakat rotated the Rolex watch on his wrist, saw the face. It was eight-twenty. When Barakat spoke his voice came out squeezed. "What do you want? If it's money, I'll pay whatever it is, within reason."

"Money." Shai opened his arms. "Well, Sabri, money we get from rich Jews and the American government. Though I must say that personally I feel it quite unfair we were led to the only sand in the Middle East without a drop of oil under it. How do you suppose that happened? To test us, like at Mount Sinai? You believe in God, Sabri, or you think it's all random rolls of the dice?"

Barakat twisted his watch again, held onto it.

Shai leaned forward. "I often ask myself why a God might intend our way to be so difficult. Can't quite make myself believe it's necessary for salvation. I mean, what kind of a God wants us to suffer first, you see what I'm saying? He has nothing better to do with his millennia?"

"What do you want?" Barakat shouted.

"Where's Kenneth Khalidi?"

"I don't know anyone by that name."

"You had coffee with him in St. James's Park yesterday, a little after 9:00 a.m. Where is Khalidi?"

Barakat was silent.

"Sabri, this is just not going to do." Shai reached into a drawer, pulled out a syringe and set it on the desk. Shai motioned to Hirsh, who exchanged his gun for the needle. "Sabri, take your coat off, please."

Barakat pressed back deeper in the sofa.

Shai picked up the Browning, leveled it at Barakat's face, and said, "Your jacket. Off, now."

Barakat pulled himself out of the tuxedo jacket and threw it on the floor.

"Roll your sleeve up."

Barakat unhooked a gold cufflink and let it clatter to the floor. He pushed up his sleeve. Hirsh neared, slipped the point into Barakat's arm and Barakat winced. Hirsh injected the drug, withdrew the syringe, and Shai gratefully returned the gun to Hirsh, who resumed his position by the door.

After a few seconds, Barakat felt lightheaded and flush. The room seemed to be rotating. Barakat's head pounded. The room was breaking into pieces. His eyes closed.

"Sabri. Sabri."

Barakat's eyes fluttered open.

"Much better. When did you speak to Khalidi last?"

Images washed through Barakat's mind. He saw them in St. James's Park, drinking coffee. Khalidi had called him later. Barakat resisted. He would not tell them, these Jews. They could not make him.

"Your ships transported the plutonium."

"What plutonium?" Barakat said from the daze.

"The plutonium that Khalidi intends to assemble into a bomb in Israel. Where's the plutonium hidden?"

Barakat dropped his head between his knees, tried to heave there but nothing came.

"The drug only offers the illusion of needing to vomit. The sensation will come and go. Where's the plutonium?"

Barakat coughed, still felt like he had to heave.

Just then, they heard the loud sound of cars screeching to a halt.

"What the hell?" Shai said, and stood.

Muffled shooting erupted outside—a quick whoosh from suppressors answered by return fire from the Israelis. Glass crashed. A small explosion. White gas came up under the door, acrid. More shooting on the far side of the door.

Shai had no weapon. "In the warehouse, quick," he shouted. His voice was high, panicked. Hirsh bolted across the tiny office toward Barakat.

The door flew open and three men in black wearing gas masks, pistols raised, burst in. Hirsh spun, fired. The first man dropped. Hirsh was choking. The gas stung his eyes, burned his throat. The second man pumped two bullets into Hirsh's chest; blood sprouted and he fell to the floor. The gun clattered across the linoleum. Shai's eyes streamed from the tear gas. He dove in the direction of the gun, slid across the floor, groped for it.

One of the masked men fired twice at the large, sprawled body. Shai cried out at the second shot. Blood flowed onto the floor beneath him from his side and formed a pool. He groped for the gun, could not reach it. Two more men in dark clothes and gas masks hurried in from the outer office. They grabbed their fallen comrade while the two who had come through first went for Barakat, who was wheezing and coughing.

"Can you walk?" one asked Barakat in Arabic, the words sounding distant from behind the long rubber mask.

Barakat was choking.

"We'll help you."

The Arab took off his own gas mask and placed it around Barakat's face. Two men grabbed him around the waist and lifted him into the front office. Heaving air through the gas mask, Barakat opened his eyes as they carried him, his feet dragging. The front room was a war zone. Bodies of three Israelis sprawled across the furniture and floor. Blood was everywhere, the front window shattered, the blinds half down. The room was cloudy. Barakat felt nauseous and weak.

Then he was outside and the mask was being pulled from him and he was gasping in cold air and they were helping him toward a car and into the back seat. Inside, Barakat fell against the door as the car sped away.

"How much do they know?" Barakat's rescuer asked.

Barakat pulled himself upright. His mouth and throat were raw from the tear gas. "They have this girl, Amal."

"We know. The people watching her were taken by them. We were alerted. We did not make the same mistake. How much do they know? Could you tell from what they asked you?"

He shook his head and the movement made him feel sick.

"Do they know about the plutonium and the yacht?"

The tiredness was terrible. He mumbled, "They know about the plutonium. Not where."

"Good. Did you tell them Khalidi's plans?"

"No. You came..." It was hard to talk. He still wanted to be sick.

"You're sure you didn't talk?"

"Yes. Sure"

"Tell us, it doesn't matter. We can change plans according to what they know."

"Nothing," Barakat said. He coughed hard. "Nothing."

"We lost Khalidi this afternoon. He suddenly started acting to shake surveillance and eluded us. Did he know the Israelis were onto him?"

Barakat nodded. "He tried to phone Amal. That's how he knew they kidnapped her. I left a message for Ramzy in Switzerland."

"We know that. That's why we're here. Where is Khalidi now? We have to protect him."

"Took the last hovercraft to Calais. With Maggie. My secretary. In her boot."

"Where's he going from there? Has he changed plans?"

Barakat coughed hard as the car sped onto a main road and continued at high speed. "Has the ticket and passport Ramzy sent. For Beirut. Going to fly from the Continent."

"Good, then he's staying with the plan and the Israelis don't know. Did the Israelis know he was in London or were they just following you?"

Barakat fell back against the seat. "They knew he was here. Not where."

"So they don't know where he is. That's why they kidnapped you. Amal must have known about you."

Barakat still felt groggy, like he was seeing and hearing everything through a haze. He tried to nod but it made him feel sicker. "Where are you taking me?"

"A safe house until we can get you twenty-four hour protection. You may have to go abroad for a while. We'll discuss it in the morning after you've slept. We'll move your wife and children right away."

He realized now through heavy eyelids that they were on Edgware Road somewhere in North London and gratefully racing back toward the West End.

"Just let me understand a few more things. We'll go over the rest tomorrow. We learn a lot from their questions. Do you think they knew how Khalidi's going into Israel from Lebanon?"

"No. Amal couldn't tell them. Khalidi didn't know. I don't know."

"What name was on Khalidi's passport?"

"I don't know. I didn't pay any attention."

"It was British?"

"Moroccan. Can't you ask Ramzy? He can tell you."

"Ramzy's in Lebanon. He didn't anticipate the Israelis learning about Amal and our losing Khalidi. We have no way to reach him at the moment, all we can do is leave messages. If you know him, you know that's how he operates. How much did the Israelis seem to know about the plutonium?"

"A lot. About my ships."

The man swore, lit a cigarette in frustration, then slowly waved the match out. "You have been through a difficult time," he said. "You'll be able to rest soon. But every minute may matter now. I mean no insult, but it occurs to me now there may be tapes of the questioning somewhere in the warehouse. If you told them where the plutonium's hidden, please tell me now. We know what it's like to be questioned by them. There is no shame in talking. I will send someone back for the tapes."

"I didn't talk. Don't know. I could tell them nothing. I don't know where the plutonium is."

"Fine. I think then we have contained the damage. Thanks to your help, we will have a state soon. Then eventually we will have relations with them. It is the only way for all of us to survive in the region. They are used to being separate, isolated. Even many of their leftists want to give us back land and then set up their army at the borders and never cross it. The Palestinians are, of course, used to crossing into Israel to work. We have no such tradition of isolation and we will have to teach them." He drew on his cigarette again. "May I ask you a personal question?"

"What?"

"How did you meet our valiant leader Ramzy Awwad?"

"His brother and I were friends, in the oil fields."

"Ah, yes, the infamous Kuwaiti fields." He laughed with pleasure. "Before our Iraqi brothers blew them up." He knocked some ash from his cigarette into the small ashtray in the door. "Turn here," he said to the driver.

The car pulled off a side road and then turned and headed back in the direction they had come.

"Where we going?" Barakat asked.

"I needed to be certain we weren't being followed before we headed for the safe house. I just got the all clear sign from that car that flashed its lights behind us."

Barakat sank back in the seat. He felt awful, ached for sleep.

"Try and rest. Khalidi seems safe for the moment. We got you out in time. It could have been far worse."

Barakat tried to remove his bowtie but his fingers kept slipping off.

"Let me." The man unhooked Barakat's bowtie, pulled it away and released the top button. Barakat shut his eyes.

Barakat did not think he actually slept, but he was dimly aware that time had elapsed as the car made rapid turns. He felt even more nauseous from dozing during the movement. His eyelids were heavy and swollen. He had difficulty wresting them open. Finally they flickered.

He tried to sit up but his body felt heavy and he could not. He weakly screamed.

The metal grate clattered up again and the car bounced into the same warehouse beside his limousine. The grate crashed down and Barakat collapsed against the door. The door opened and his head fell and he was leaning into space. He heard an order in Hebrew and then hands pulled him from the car. All the "dead" Israelis were standing there. They held him in front of the fat interrogator, who had a gas mask in his hand.

Shai threw it on the floor at Barakat's feet. "We've had a lot of use for these recently," he said. Shai switched from English to Hebrew and spoke to Hirsh and the other agent holding Barakat. "Take him inside." Then he turned to Yossi. "He talk?"

Yossi nodded.

Shai called after Hirsh. "Get everything on his moving the plutonium. I want to know every person who had anything to do with it." They opened the door to drag the slumped Barakat through and in the sudden quiet Shai heard the sounds of workers replacing the glass window and cleaning up. He turned back to Yossi. "What have we got?"

Yossi told him.

Shai ran for the front office, grabbed the phone and dialed information. "British Rail at Dover," he demanded of the operator, tapping his foot. He wanted to know when the last hovercraft departed. Rutherford could call the French. There was still a chance to catch Khalidi coming off at Calais. He looked at his watch—8:54.

Khalidi drove the Ford Escort, Maggie in the passenger seat, through the dark French countryside between Calais and Hazebrouck. Then, instead of following the motorway south to Paris, he turned left at a sign that read Tourcoing and onto a smaller roadway. He had studied the maps Maggie had purchased in the hover shop.

"Where are we off to?" Maggie asked.

"I don't mean to inconvenience you but I am not entirely certain. Maybe Brussels, Amsterdam, maybe Cologne. Do you need to know?"

"No, just carry on. It shan't make much difference to me."

Comfortable with silence but actually to his surprise enjoying her company, he drove with the speedometer at a steady eighty kilometers per hour.

After a while she asked, "You aren't in any really serious trouble, now are you? You haven't killed someone or any such thing?"

He remained silent.

"My word. Well, let's change the subject, shall we. Tell me about your young lady. You're such a well-mannered gentleman, which I say we don't see nearly enough of these days. I bet she's very pretty. Have a snapshot, do you?"

Khalidi removed his wallet and placed it on his lap as he drove. He slipped his fingers into the corner of the billfold and removed a small color photograph he had taken of Amal in front of the Santa Monica merry-go-round. He proudly handed Maggie the photograph.

"Oh, my. She's smashing. Where is she now?"

Both hands on the wheel trembled and his leg shook on the accelerator, sending the car toward the centerline before he jerked it back into its lane.

"Dear me. Well, you must keep a stiff upper lip, whatever it is. Everything will sort itself out. One mustn't give up hope, I always say. I've gotten through many a dreary day remembering that."

Shai hung up from the British Rail representative and sagged forward in the chair. As the workmen continued their pounding, he was consumed by the urge for a cigarette though he had not smoked in almost two decades. He pulled his last apple out of his jacket pocket.

Yossi looked at him. "Too late?"

"The last cars drove off fifteen minutes ago."

"You going to the French authorities?"

Shai gazed off to where Barakat was being wrung out and did not answer.

"We going to the French?" Yossi repeated louder.

"No," Shai said without turning to him. Then he was up. "Khalidi could veer in too many directions from Calais. Besides, I don't trust the French. Even if they manage to pick him up, I don't know how long they'll hold him or if they'll cooperate."

Shai strode toward one of the cars. He had calls to make from the embassy. Barakat said Khalidi was trying for an alternate flight to Beirut. Khalidi did not know they were onto that and Shai could operate in the Lebanese chaos almost at will. They had people permanently in Beirut and he would have them waiting for Khalidi to land. Lebanon would be the last stop before attempted entry. He was not convinced Khalidi was privy to where the plutonium was hidden anyway.

In the darkness, Shai's hand shook slightly as he opened the car door. Inside, he slammed the door shut with such power that two agents came running out at the noise, guns raised. In the mirror, he saw them lower them as he raced away. Only Ramzy would have the location of the plutonium and he had disappeared into the Middle East. Their reckoning had arrived. Shai demolished the apple in three bites. Shai knew Ramzy, and he knew Ramzy would be meeting Khalidi. Maybe not in Beirut, but somewhere in Lebanon. And Shai would be waiting.

CHAPTER 11

June 29

Ramzy walked through the crowded Souq Al-Hamidiyah in Damascus precisely at 3:00 p.m., following Abdul Jabra's instructions. When last in Abdul's office here years before, the walls were lined with photographs of his commandos setting off in speedboats to attack Israel. Ramzy believed this glorification of very small feats masked a failure to face their real powerlessness. Troubled, his thoughts turned to his wife Dalal in the refugee camp school in the nearby hills. He wanted desperately to talk to her. Simply being with her always made him feel far less fragmented. He would consider the risk of seeing her.

Ramzy picked up his pace, enjoying the giant corridor market, happy to be back in his world. High overhead, the sun beat against the arched corrugated iron roof and slanted through stone and bullet holes; ringlets of light streamed against the windows of the shops. It was hot, but far cooler here than outside. Along the facades of the shops electric bulbs shone.

Ramzy saw a man in a suit without tie separate himself from the crowd, his step too certain for a shopper. Ramzy glanced to his right, to a young man in jeans with a light, unnecessary jacket that would be shielding a gun. Ramzy walked as if he had not spotted them.

He felt them grab him by the upper arms on both sides and guide him down an alley into the narrow shoe sellers' souq. It was very dark, leather redolent. One roughly pushed him face-first against a wall of shoes and probed for the weapon he did not carry. Behind him, Ramzy listened to peddlers' cries reverberating off the high roof, punctuated by the rat-a-tat-tat of the three-wheeled motorized carts that carried goods from shop to shop through the hordes of pedestrians.

"Come with us," the suit said.

Ramzy turned and nodded. They wove quickly down various alleys, past glass blowers in recessed caves, backtracked by a different route, and then a high human whistle sounded behind them, confirming that Ramzy was alone.

Around another corner the two men guided him into a noisy, yellow-tile walled cafe, blue haze filling the room. Waiters in dirty aprons wove among the tables balancing tiny cups of coffee, glasses of sweetened tea with green nana, and tongs holding the heated coals for the water pipes. At a table in the far corner, Abdul Jabra sat alone smoking Gitanes cigarettes, his ashtray messy. His face was ruined and scarred on the left side and that eye had wandered without focus since 1968, his jeep smashed by an Israeli tank shell during the Battle of Karameh in Jordan. His salt and pepper hair was full. As a slim, dark-haired fighter, he had worn it parted down the middle and tied behind his head with a scarf, influenced by the German revolutionaries who had trained in their camps. The small sound of dice clattering on wood game boards rose from nearly every table. As Ramzy approached Abdul, he felt disappointment at one he cared about failing him, not dissimilar from what he felt about Shai and the ironfisted Israelis. The two guards floated toward the entrance, where they remained ready.

Abdul rose with a smile of cheerful insincerity and he and Ramzy hugged and kissed on both cheeks, then sat. Abdul banged on the table and shouted instructions to the waiter, who rushed over, swept away his empty cup and replaced his full ashtray with a fresh one. Abdul ordered them both small, thick coffees.

"I would not kill you before offering you coffee," Abdul said. He smiled, one eye staring aside. The injury had not affected his speech, other than to constantly remind him he was angry.

Ramzy removed his own cigarettes from his shirt pocket and slowly lit one, drew on it, the smoke dropping through his nose. After a long time he said, "When you learn why I've come, I don't think you'll want to kill me."

Abdul snatched his own cigarettes in his hand. "Why should I believe whatever you say? Maybe you're here to trick me into my death? Should I be worried? Are the Zionists coming through the souq now?"

Ramzy pulled hard on his cigarette and the paper cackled.

The waiter rushed near and asked if they wished hookahs.

"Bring the coffee and leave us alone," Abdul said, forcing a bent cigarette from the blue pack. His left hand and arm were rippled and scarred up to his elbow. As the waiter quickly retreated, Abdul unconsciously scratched the top of his hand as Ramzy had seen him do for years. Ramzy felt his physical suffering and softened toward him.

"You're a fool, Ramzy." With yellowed fingers, Abdul lit his unfiltered Gitanes then leaned close. "Why do you bother to talk to them? They'll never give back land to us, even if we would settle for a rump state. They play the charade of talking peace to get American arms. You'll wait two thousand years, like they did."

"I hope to have a state far sooner."

Abdul set his cigarette in the ashtray and scratched the top of his scaly hand hard on the raw spots. He grabbed his cigarette again. "You'd relinquish the fight for all our homes. *You're* a greater enemy than the Zionists. Go get your mini-state. We'll come take if from you, and from there destroy them."

Ramzy wondered how long people could live in self-delusion—a very long time, he concluded.

The waiter arrived with their small cups of Turkish coffee and started to set them before them.

"Hurry," Abdul said.

The waiter finished quickly and bolted back into the kitchen.

"If it wasn't for what your writings do for our people, I *would* kill you," Abdul said, reaching to stub the cigarette into his coffee, then catching himself and grinding it into the ashtray. "Not that they bring us any closer to anything either."

Ramzy lifted the hot cup by thumb and forefinger. "It's something I often think about: doing what I must that will have little effect versus what I despise that will."

Abdul was scratching his hand again. He fiercely forced out another cigarette, struck the paper match hard and bent it. He threw it down, struck another one and it flared. He brought it to the cigarette in his mouth with his good hand, exhaled smoke. "I remember when we were all proud of you, when you killed them."

Ramzy was silent for a long moment, sipped his coffee, surrendering to those memories. Entering the Israeli Embassy in Paraguay, he had released all his anger into an unarmed man and woman. He and his Palestinian fighters had struck in embassies and airports, snatched commercial planes from the skies to give the masses hope after the despair of the loss of the Golan, West Bank, Gaza, Sinai in 1967—to promise them that the struggle continued, to explode their plight onto the world's headlines. Shortly after Paraguay, in the crush of mixed feelings, he had begun to write his stories.

Finally he said, "It had purpose then. We are no longer dependent on the Arab states to act for us. The people have wrested the struggle into their own hands."

"And the world got bored with us. Three years of *intifada*. Now we're dying economically too."

Ramzy looked away. "I had hoped it would succeed."

Abdul laughed derisively. "You have a lot of hope. I have Kalashnikovs."

"And they have tanks and F-16s."

Abdul's face turned into fury; even his dead eye seemed to fill and focus with it. His voice came out with menace. "What do you want?"

"I'm going to strike at them. An army base inside their northern border. I need your assistance."

Abdul lifted his coffee for the first time but did not drink from it. "You? Why now? It's against everything you say."

"It has a larger purpose."

"What?"

"I can only tell you that I'll kill their soldiers. It's what you want. It should be enough."

Abdul bent very near, glared into Ramzy's face, his breath coffee and cigarettes. "What if it's not enough? Without knowing it all."

"Then I will go elsewhere. You will not be part of it." Ramzy lifted his cigarette from the ashtray. "There is one additional point. If you help me, I will be in your debt."

Abdul dropped back. "Kill soldiers. It hurts them more when you murder their children."

Ramzy thought with anger about his blinded nephew, so many of their children dead in Lebanon, in the West Bank. He lifted his cup.

Abdul smoked quietly, the rage leaving his face. He came forward again, lifted his small cup, drained it slowly. When he set it down, there was a vulnerability in his eyes, in the puffiness beneath them. He spoke softly. "Ramzy, you can't imagine what it's like to have never been there. My family. . . I am from the village of Majd al-Krum."

"I know." Abdul had been born in a refugee camp in Damascus in 1948, months after his parents had fled their village near Haifa.

"All I have is a videotape of the village some visitors took for me. You're lucky. You spent your boyhood in Jaffa, can balance between the truth and the dream. To me, it's all a dream. A wonderful, perfect dream of greenery away from the dirt and dust of the camps."

Ramzy exhaled, rubbed his cigarette out. "The truth is, Jaffa is dwarfed by Tel Aviv, Haifa a major Jewish metropolis. They took me to Haifa a few years ago when they had me in Ansar. American technology companies are there now, Intel."

Abdul looked toward the old men rolling their dice. "It doesn't matter what's there now. I live only for my dream. If not my son, the son of my son will return." His good eye came back. "Tell me, Ramzy Awwad, what can I do for you until that day?"

"A single engine plane and pilot. I know you have several Piper

Cubs outside Homs."

"I'll give you one, but their radar will spot it instantly."

"Yes, it would," Ramzy said. "If I flew it into Israel."

In the late afternoon heat, half empty bottle of whiskey between his legs, Ramzy sat along the serpentine Barada River, the hot wind bearing the scent of the apricot trees. He looked at the minarets, mosques and mausoleums of Damascus through the trees that surrounded the oldest continuously inhabited city on earth then angrily brought the bottle to his lips. Abdul and so many like him preferred fantasy. Even West Bank and Gaza Arabs who could travel freely throughout Israel during the day declined to visit their old homes and towns, preferring to envision them unchanged and awaiting their return. They were placing a pistol to their own heads. He would begin a story about a family from Ramallah finally and excitedly driving to the Arab Old Town of Haifa to see their old house, and confronted there by the Jewish city. They would find Holocaust survivors in their home and say to them: the Holocaust was far worse than the catastrophe the Palestinians experienced; you deserve a home, but not my home.

Ramzy drank more. He was terrified about building a detonable bomb inside Jerusalem. Though he would station armed men around it at each moment, what if something happened? He leaned back against a tree. If the Israelis reacted stubbornly, he would use the world pressure of the threat to Jerusalem's Christian and Muslim holy sites to dislodge them.

Ramzy stared to the north at the brown flank of Mount Qasioun and the stone Ottoman homes and gardens where the elite of Damascus eluded the heat. He swigged more of the whiskey, which had no taste now. The UNRWA school where he had taught with his wife Dalal was at the base of the hills, so near he could almost touch them. He ached to feel Dalal's cheek, sleep with her head and small hands on his chest. He tipped the bottle and more harsh whiskey splashed into his mouth.

To the west, the slopes of Lebanon rose in the cloudless sky. The Barada River dropped underground from Lebanese mountain springs and surfaced here, fanning out into the oasis that birthed

Damascus. He tried to think about the early spring months here he so loved, the trees snowy with blossoms, but the image would not stay in his mind. He brought his eyes downriver. Two women lifted their pantaloons and crushed apricots in a stone trough with pumping feet while a small boy pulled the pits from the gruel. Even that sight of the wonderful simplicity of his people brought no smile to his lips.

Ramzy closed his eyes and drank to quiet the fear running through him. He lifted the lip of the bottle to his mouth and his arm shook as he let the liquid slide down his throat, frustrated at not even feeling drunk. He had days like this when he doubted everything, when there seemed no point stepping into a wind that only blew against him. He really did not want to kill those soldiers now, did not want to murder anymore, but killing them was the only safe way to slip Khalidi into Israel. Again he gazed toward the hills where Dalal was, and decided despite the risk he would go there.

He stood abruptly, stumbled, lifted the bottle and turned to smash it against the tree trunk. Instead, Ramzy set the bottle down softly in the dirt and started to walk. In the quiet of the hot wind moving through the leaves, a single howl rose from one of the wild dogs that dozed in the desert heat then stole into the city at night through the Roman Gate to gobble garbage. Ramzy headed toward the hills. Suddenly he laughed out loud. He must be drunk, he told himself, because he was thinking that the bomb threat would succeed.

Cilia sat with Shai in the back seat as the big black cab sped toward Heathrow. It was driven by one of their British Jews, who often queued before incoming Arab flights and rifled briefcases, as all luggage in the London cabs sat in the space beside the driver.

"You think Ramzy will try and see Dalal? Nadjla?" Cilia asked.

Shai turned back from the window, the tiredness veined in his eyes. "He seemed troubled when I saw him in Amsterdam. I thought it was the *intifada's* failure, but he was already well into this. He may be having doubts. If I'm right, there's a good chance he'll want to talk to Dalal or his sister, or have one of them brought to him while he's so near." Shai had masses of men and women watching each. "Likely

Dalal."

"I heard you brought Nadjla down from Sidon to be with Ramzy at your wedding."

He nodded. "Their brother's in East Jerusalem. They hadn't all been together in seventeen years. I should have brought Dalal too, but for some reason didn't think of it."

Cilia was proud of Israel, so many people like Shai. Her voice brimmed with emotion. "I've been trying to tell you but I didn't know exactly what to say. Thanks for all the time with my boys. We had a smashing day and dinner."

A weary smile came to him. "My pleasure. There wasn't anything I needed you for here. Plenty of personnel. And what is there in the end besides those times, really?"

As they continued silently toward Heathrow, maybe because of all this talk of family, looking out the window again Shai's thoughts drifted to his father. On Saturdays, his only day in from the desert fields, the blond-bearded pioneer had worked long hours at his desk. His father had talked readily only when instructing him. As a teenager in pre-state Palestine, Shai had ridden with him in silence deep into the Sinai, where his father had formed an unheard of bond with the nomadic Bedouin, from whom Shai learned respect for the surrounding culture, as well as his Arabic. He had wished his father would speak more. In reaction to him, Shai could be garrulous, but like him stone silent.

As the Middle East Airlines flight from Frankfurt approached Beirut, Khalidi pulled his already snug seatbelt tighter. He did not like flying, would feel better on the ground. He had driven all night through Belgium to Cologne. At the airport, to his embarrassment Maggie had given him a huge hug. Across from the Lufthansa desk, he phoned the emergency number in Zurich for Ramzy and left a message about his change of plans.

Hating to be so sweaty, in the airport bathroom he removed his shirt and tried to wash himself as best he could with wet paper towels then changed clothes. He took the Lufthansa shuttle to Frankfurt, phoned Zurich again, and when the answer was that Jean-Paul had not checked in for messages, bleary eyed and hesitant, he gave the man his Middle East Airlines flight number and arrival time in Beirut. The man responded that he should not worry.

But he was very worried. The Israelis at best were only a step behind him, if not seated in the back of this plane which was bouncing, dropping now through thick clouds, then was through them. Frightened, Khalidi saw the rapidly approaching sea and cliffs and the glittering stone city with the mountains behind it. He wondered if the Israelis were waiting down there for him. He closed his eyes, gripped both arms of the seat. The plane banged down on the tarmac, the engines whined with the reverse thrust, and he was in Lebanon.

Tired, he felt alone in the chaotic terminal. He walked slowly through the people and variously uniformed men, all with weapons, toward immigration, waiting to be met. Someone jostled him and he spun around hopefully. A heavy woman in traditional dress pushed past him. Deflated, he glanced at his watch. It was three hours after he should have arrived from London and he did not dare believe that, if they had not received his message, they would still be waiting. He turned and rejoined the line. Shots or backfires suddenly erupted outside and he jumped. He had seen on television news that the downtown Beirut hotels had degenerated into shooting grounds. He would simply find a hotel somewhere that was safe until he could contact Ramzy through the Zurich number. Suddenly he wondered if you could call Europe from Beirut, if the lines worked. He stepped forward.

Outside, despite the evening hour, the heat rose off the sidewalk. Cab drivers swarmed, offering their services in French and Arabic, and he pushed through them. In a stall, a hunk of meat, the fat visible between the folds, rotated on a skewer before flaming coils. The keffiyehed vendor expertly sliced off shards and caught them in a metal semicircular tray. He had hardly eaten on the plane but he had no appetite. He wondered if he should return to the taxi drivers. They would know the hotels. He turned.

Someone caught his arm and Khalidi spun around. A young

man with a bushy moustache wearing a T-shirt with a strangely out-of-place Snoopy, machine gun slung over his shoulder, gave him a welcome smile and spoke in English. “Mister Khalidi. I have been waiting for you since this afternoon. I am very afraid you are not coming.”

Khalidi wanted to hug him he was so happy but he did not. “I am sorry but I was forced to board a different flight.”

The young man shrugged. “I was told to wait for every flight.”

Khalidi felt the release of relief. “Thank you. Really. Thank you very much.”

He guided Khalidi toward a small battered Toyota in the parking lot. Two other young men lounging against its side wearing the same Western battledress with high-top tennis shoes and accenting machine guns across their chests came to life as they neared. One ran around and opened the rear passenger door.

“We were told you are very important,” the young man said. “I am called Abu Rami. Nickname.” He lowered his gun and pointed it. “It means good like this.”

Khalidi climbed happily into the Toyota. These were his people and he was part of them. The young Arab closed the door for him, ran around the car and got in. A second boy slid behind the wheel. Abu Rami jumped into the front passenger seat and spun around.

Before he could speak, a very pretty girl, maybe sixteen, wearing jeans and a red silk blouse reminiscent of once ubiquitous Lebanese fashion, approached the driver’s window. With the green sheets of the National Lottery in one hand, she bent to reveal small breasts exposed beneath her blouse.

Abu Rami raised his AK-47 and pointed it across the driver at her chest. Anyone might pitch a grenade. “Go,”he said fiercely to the driver, who shot away, and looked back through the rear windshield and watched the girl saunter to the next car. Abu Rami was quickly all smiles again. “You in Beirut before? Yes?”

Khalidi switched from English to Arabic. “No, unfortunately this is my first time. I am sorry that I have not come earlier.”

Abu Rami beamed and slid into the more comfortable

language. "Beirut was the jewel of the Middle East. I don't remember it that way," he added, "but I have many pictures."

The car sped from the airport and Khalidi leaned forward and stared out the window, eager to see everything. Soon they approached a sandbagged emplacement with uniformed soldiers wearing green berets lounging on the sandbags, some smoking. Two soldiers approached.

"Ours? Palestinian soldiers?" Khalidi asked.

The boy next to Khalidi jerked his head back, which was Arabic for no. "Syrians."

Khalidi was nervous. The Syrians in the new alignment against Iraq could be cooperating with the Americans, even the Israelis. The two soldiers, AK-47s off their shoulders and in their hands, neared from both sides. Khalidi realized he was holding his breath and let go.

"Where have you been?" one soldier asked, leaning in the driver's window.

"Nowhere. We're just out riding," Abu Rami said.

The soldier looked directly at each of them then back to Abu Rami. "Go on." He waved them forward with his rifle.

As they drove ahead, Khalidi asked, "What are they doing here?"

Abu Rami shrugged. "Sometimes they kill Christians, sometimes us. Sometimes we kill them. It depends."

Khalidi fell silent as they drove. How could he have wasted so much of his time doing other people's work in the lab? He started to feel depressed, then he shut that memory off and sat up, was here now.

The sun was setting. Silhouettes of tall buildings, their insides hollowed by massive bombs, rose to his right. A human skull was nailed above the entrance to one building. Like the walls in the West Bank, flowing Arabic graffiti covered the structures. Only here, to his horror, instead of announcing strike days and educational symposia they screamed: THE FORCES OF THE NIGHT BEASTS. THE VAMPIRES OF DARKNESS ARE VIGILANT. THE FATHER OF SKULLS WAS HERE. Khalidi stared back and forth out the open windows. Power lines dangled like snakes; burned and rusted car skeletons sprawled in the street. The sounds of bullets rang from some unidentifiable direction. As the sky darkened, black smoke spread into it in the distance.

"What's that?" Khalidi asked, chilled and emotional at this suffering.

Abu Rami looked out indifferently. "Maybe the port, the Syrians and Phalange—the Christian political party, mostly Maronites."

The people on the streets—women in traditional dress, men in business suits, young boys in khaki carrying rifles—seemed to be moving with a special urgency, eager to reach home before darkness. A half moon in the still blue sky kept pace with them through gaping buildings. They passed a building completely crumbled, followed a once-grand avenue, rattling on a street torn from tank treads.

"Israelis." Abu Rami pointed at the broken pavement, then added solemnly, feeling it his sacred duty to be historically accurate, "But the Phalange are the worst." He made a motion across his neck like someone slitting it, then licked with his tongue. "They enjoy it."

Trees were burnt. Fresh vines crawled over the stone facades of buildings toppled in earlier struggles. Piles of garbage dotted the street. An entire quadrant of the city ahead of them was dark, lit only by the bright moon in the deep sky. No one seemed to notice.

They were heading toward the ocean Khalidi thought, or at least he smelled the sea. They turned and high-rises towered to the left, some half finished, their concrete elevator shafts circled by scaffolding, developers optimistically rushing them up in a period of quiet that had neither lasted nor returned. Excited, he craned his head to look. A young boy was driving a few scrawny sheep between the buildings toward a patch of dry grass. Insects swarmed and buzzed in dark clouds around mounds of rubble. A shell suddenly whistled overhead. They turned again and were driving through a narrow lane cleared down the center with rubble rising on either side.

"We try and avoid the Syrians," Abu Rami explained.

Khalidi nodded vigorously. "One day you will leave here for a Palestinian state. In the West Bank and Gaza Strip."

Abu Rami shook his head. "I don't think so."

"Maybe very soon. You will see."

Abu Rami assumed the infinite patience of one explaining matters to a child. "Even if there was a state where you say, there would be no room for us. There are three, four times as many of us in places like this. We could not all return. Many say we must push all the Zionists into the sea. I think we will remain here."

Khalidi was stunned. He fell silent and dropped back in the seat. He had not considered this. What would happen to his people here after his Palestinian state? Suddenly he felt desperate. There had to be a solution to it all, and again he thought about blowing the bomb.

They reached a concrete barrel roadblock. Black smoke billowed beyond it and Khalidi could not see the source. They rolled up the windows and slowed. Young men in bits of khaki with pistols in holsters, grenades hanging on their hips and hoisting machine guns, wore wet red keffiyehs over their faces as the wind blew the smoke here.

"Palestinian fighters," Abu Rami said with a smile. "Not our group but friends."

They stopped, were waved through. The car accelerated, and though they had not rolled down a window, the acrid stench of burning rubber invaded and Khalidi rubbed his watery eyes. Up ahead at the end of the rubble, small boys of no more than eight or nine were running and heaving old tires into the burning pile then dancing back with delight from the orange flames and black smoke. The driver depressed the accelerator in the open space and soon they were winding down the windows and drinking in the warm, humid air that no longer carried the sea's breath.

Abu Rami brightened. "You stay in West Beirut tonight and tomorrow we take you to Ramzy."

Khalidi nodded, his emotions jumbled. The tiredness was returning, slipping back over him after being squashed by the excitement. He leaned against the warm seat.

"I think maybe you're tired after your journey," Abu Rami said.

Khalidi forced his eyes open. "I am sorry. I want to see

everything."

Abu Rami looked at him, genuinely puzzled. "There is nothing to see. Beirut is over."

The driver was slowing at another sandbagged emplacement. A dozen young men and boys in varieties of khaki and jeans burst from behind the bags and ran toward the car, each pointing a machine gun. Khalidi tensed and bolted up but Abu Rami motioned his hand confidently at him.

"Our group," Abu Rami said. "They will accompany us now."

An older fighter, maybe thirty, leaned his keffiyehed head in Abu Rami's open window and they kissed on both cheeks. He gave Abu Rami quiet instructions.

"You see how the Israelis removed us all from Beirut," the young boy beside Khalidi said, tapping his rifle on the seat.

Khalidi looked at him with pride. No matter what the Israelis attempted, the Palestinians would not go away or forget their homeland. He would not go away.

Outside, the man broke from the window, and at his order, his cohorts trotted toward cars parked off the road that Khalidi had not seen in the darkness. Engines roared and lights stabbed the night. Their driver hit the accelerator and swerved around the sandbags, tires whining. One car, a long Mercedes without license plates, burst behind them. Khalidi turned. Two other sedans had pulled across the road and were blocking it.

They joined heavier traffic then made a wild right off a roundabout with a statue toppled on the grass. The street was broad with a grass and palm-lined divider. With a tremendous jolt, they were up over the grass and bouncing for the solid line of palm trees, then swerving in between two with the Mercedes's headlights on their tail. Then they were back on the broad street heading in the opposite direction, Khalidi gripping the armrest hard.

They drove past an entirely flattened block of rubble, turned so suddenly off the broad boulevard with a screech that the car came up on one side then dropped down and they skidded into a warren of streets with every house damaged. Two women flung themselves out of their way as they raced down a narrow alley with room only for their car. They swerved in a variety of directions around corners, and like on the rollercoaster rides Khalidi had hated as a child, he held his breath and looked down.

When his eyes came up, they were on a wider street alongside a huge pine-crowded park. They swerved off the road over the sidewalk, with a smaller bump this time, and drove on the grass. Khalidi thought he saw a large racetrack through the trees and then they were stopped with the lights off in the dark park, Khalidi's heart pounding. Khalidi peered out the rear and the Mercedes pulled up behind them and its lights died too. Two men dropped out of the Mercedes and crawled behind it, machine gun muzzles lifted. Traffic droned in the distance but there were no sounds of engines nearby.

Soon Khalidi saw the two silhouettes return to the Mercedes. Its headlights flashed three times and their car started quickly and sped ahead, frighteningly without lights as the pines loomed directly in front of them. They wove and skidded among them on the somehow wet grass. They rattled down onto a roadway that ran through the park and Khalidi no longer knew if they had their lights on or not. Leaning against the door, he stared down at the floor clutching the armrest with one white knuckled hand, desperate for it to be over, like those rollercoaster rides.

They were swerving and accelerating again, and then they stopped. This time he did not look up. Whether they were at a roadblock, were spying the road behind them or had reached their destination, he did not know or care. Then they were off again.

Sometime later, a hand dropped on his shoulder and he realized they were not moving.

"The Israelis are everywhere. It is difficult to be safe," Abu Rami said. "Come, we will bring you tea, coffee, as you like."

Khalidi looked up and let go of the armrest; his fingers ached. They were in a small parking lot in front of a pockmarked, five-story building. He felt an overpowering warmth for this man his age, who had led such a different life. Khalidi massaged the fingers of his right hand to return the circulation and nodded.

Abu Rami smiled. "We are here. Welcome."

The Mercedes pulled in and more commandos spilled from its doors. Some took up positions in the parking lot while others hurried into the lobby. Khalidi followed Abu Rami and entered the building. The elevator was dead and the stairwell lights a distant memory. Behind two commandos, they climbed to the top-floor apartment. Though not severely damaged, the building was eerily empty.

In the small kitchen, they brewed a large pot of tea, added sprigs of mint, sweetened it with heaps of sugar, and carried the steaming mahogany glasses down to the boys in the landing and parking lot who stood guard. Khalidi remained with Abu Rami and two other men in the kitchen. Khalidi sipped tea, was too stimulated to sleep, wanted to be with these fighters and the sweet tea was reviving him. Their machine guns sat on the narrow kitchen counter. The older of the two new young men was introduced as Hamid. He wore jeans, sandals and a worn, red Ferrari jacket.

Khalidi wanted to know everything about all of them, asked Hamid if he was born in a Lebanese refugee camp. Hamid jerked his head back, explained he been born in Nablus and deported here a little more than a year ago for activity in the *intifada.* Khalidi approached him. He had to know; did he believe two states could live side by side?

Hamid wanted a state so deportation could never happen to anyone there again. The Palestinians would appreciate a state more than the Israelis appreciated theirs because of all the Palestinians had suffered. "I came to this decision years ago, not because of the *intifada.* Living peacefully beside them is the practical, realistic answer and eventually I came to it."

Khalidi felt buoyed.

The other boy, several years younger, took his empty tea glass to the counter and spoke with bitterness. "No. Because of what they did to us, we can never accept them."

A deafening explosion outside rocked the building. The three men moved into a small bedroom, but there was no urgency in their strides and they had not grabbed their machine guns. There were whistles, explosions thundered but the building shook less. Khalidi followed them to the window. In the distance, shells arced through the dark like beautiful shooting stars. Above the skyline, after thuds of explosions, plumes of smoke rose white in the night. He could see no fires because of the nearer buildings.

Khalidi remained transfixed, stared at the firefight, and then it was over and all was quiet again. The stacks of smoke began to spread out and touch each other.

Abu Rami turned to him. "It is our honor that you are here. But now you must sleep. We leave before it is light."

They exited without waiting for a response. Khalidi turned back to the window, opened it, and the warm, moist air hastened in. Oddly, it seemed more unreal that he had spent night after night alone in his small Hollywood apartment writing out lectures than being here. He saw the sprinkling of lights across the city and dark patches where entire buildings were too damaged for habitation. Another cloud of smoke rose from a forest of skyscrapers but he had heard no explosion. Several small fires flickered nearby and he supposed they were bonfires of the militias.

He lay down on the bed in the darkness, still clothed and very happy, and listened to the sounds of Beirut. Arabic music rose from a radio in the main room. He heard a spray of shots somewhere. Nearby? Faraway? The tiredness tugged at him but he did not want to sleep, afraid he would wake and somehow find himself back in Los Angeles. He tried to keep his eyes open. The sounds began to meld together: the slow shriek of a shell, the nearing rise of an ambulance siren, more shots. The music suddenly shut off and excited conversation came from the kitchen. A car screeched around the corner, and in its wake, a long silence like the aftermath of making love, then a sudden, reverberating explosion.

Khalidi snored.

"If I'd kept Ramzy when we had him in Ansar..." Meir Carmon bellowed at Shai as he came through the door. "I don't know how the hell I let that fool Yehuda talk me into releasing him. You two didn't catch Abu Nidal either, as I recall." Carmon brought a fresh Merit to his thin lips and snapped his lighter, the low nicotine cigarettes in recent acquiescence to the service doctor's threat about his blood pressure. His full gray hair was immaculately swept back despite the long day. "Next time you need a friend, find a dog. Or better, go play with a rattlesnake."

Shai did not respond nor did he sit. He had come directly from the airport and was in no mood to discuss Jewish-Palestinian relations of longer than four weeks' duration.

"We have Khalidi in our sights, yes or no?" Shai demanded.

"They ran a circus in Beirut—in and out of alleys, up and down highways. No way to keep up with it. We got a transmitter under their car in the airport. Young female asset placed it while they were gawking at her tits. They're in an empty five-story block south of the Corniche el Mazraa, near the athletic field. They're bedded down, maybe for the night, maybe they'll move him again."

Shai spoke with uncharacteristic quiet. "Is Ramzy there?"

"Hasn't graced us yet with his esteemed presence."

"The teams on his wife and sister?"

"They're drinking a lot of coffee. The wife was out last I heard. We're following her."

"How many bodyguards in Beirut?"

Carmon ground his cigarette into an ebony ashtray with a vengeance, as if maybe it were Shai's neck. "A dozen, in and out, give or take a couple of killers."

"I'd prefer not to move against him just yet."

"We're not going to move," Carmon said. "Not because of what you prefer. And not because a dozen of them pose us much bother. I want him followed to the plutonium."

Shai sat now.

"So, Shaham, how's he coming across? Ramzy going to part the security fence with his magic pen? The standard terrorist route across the Jordan Valley? Where? You're his friend. Tell me how he thinks."

Shai said nothing. Carmon blew cigarette smoke over his head, where it blended with the shimmering colors of the Agam on the wall behind him. Carmon's predecessor and Shai's mentor, The Colonel, had surrounded himself with yellowing newspaper clippings on cork.

"I want to sit on Khalidi," Shai said, "and find out how he's coming in."

"We have so many surveillance teams in Lebanon we may have to annex everything up to Sidon next because of its high Jewish population." He snapped his lighter at another cigarette, maybe aware it was the enemy.

This time Shai read Carmon's bluster as worry. They would switch cars, and they could not hope to keep transmitters under all of them. Even the best surveillance might be shaken on the numerous narrow mountain roads, and they had no idea if or where Ramzy had bases in the Bekaa Valley or south, or if Lebanon was merely a way station en route to an easier crossing from the long Jordan Valley that infiltrators had succeeded in traversing for forty years. Ramzy would anticipate how much force they had along the borders now and would move to counter it. Still, if they took Khalidi, Ramzy might go underground, wait and search for another physicist.

"Any progress on the plutonium?"

"The *plutonium*," Carmon said. He took a paperclip from the small, Polish, engraved wood box before him and savagely unbent it. "What plutonium? There's no talk anywhere, no unusual movement, no excitement. No whisper of it. Our detection equipment can't find a trace from the ground or air." Carmon leaned forward on his elbows. "Yet the plutonium is right under our noses. We see exactly how it was brought in." Carmon lifted the burning cigarette and pulled mightily on it, his cheeks hollowing, then he scowled at the cigarette and smashed it out, reached in a bottom drawer, removed a pack of Swiss Murattis and lit one. He inhaled but seemed no happier. "We wrung out Ramzy's brother. They tell me they don't think he knows anything. His son caught a bullet by the way, while he was pitching rocks at windshields. Blinded him, I believe. I don't buy this bullshit of Golda Meir's that they make us hurt their children, but shooting kids will not protect the state, in the long run."

The news of Ramzy's nephew struck Shai a blow to the

midsection. He wondered if this had influenced Ramzy's decision about the bomb.

"I don't think Ramzy would have told his brother about this."

"Of course he wouldn't. He knows goddamn well we'd tear his brother apart if we got onto him. But what am I supposed to do, *not* question him?" Carmon was back combatively to his cigarette. "The Americans have been breathing down our necks like lovesick schoolboys—too hot and too often. Their ambassador's been in to see the prime minister twice in the last three days. Maybe he just wants to stay out of Tel Aviv. The Americans are strenuously suggesting we kick in Judea and Samaria if we can't find the bomb. Why don't they just send in the Sixth Fleet to evacuate the whole country and give us South Dakota?"

"Do the Syrians know if Ramzy has a base in the Bekaa or south?"

"The Syrians." Carmon laughed. "You'd think we had leveled Baghdad for them. I've never seen such liaison. They're doing everything short of offering us tours of their chemical weapons plants. As for whether Ramzy has people in the Bekaa or south? None to their knowledge. They're investigating." He pushed far back in his chair, carrying the cigarette smoke with him. "They happened to mention that he's been working rather closer with us than with them in recent years. What do you think? Anything to that, really?"

"I was a mistake," Shai said.

It was Carmon's turn to remain silent.

"Maybe we ought to reinforce the instructions to the Syrians again about not picking up Khalidi if they spot him at a roadblock. I'm a little worried on that end. It was one thing requesting assistance and sending them his photograph when we were searching the Arab world for him, but now that we know where he is..."

Carmon nodded. "Agreed. I'll have it hammered in again."

After a moment, Shai said, "I don't think Ramzy would explode the bomb if we refused to capitulate."

Carmon slung the straightened paperclip noisily into the metal trash can at his feet. "Great. I can count on that, since you've proved you know him so well. I'll go to the prime minister with it this very instant. Hand me the phone."

Shai stood. "Meir, I'm sorry. We'll stop it."

Carmon sank back in his chair as if the air had been let out of him. "Who knows, maybe Ramzy's a blessing in disguise. The grown-up in the room with the rest of them." He waved Shai out.

As Shai left, he thought about the picture they had pieced together on Khalidi from mopping up Amal and other sources. It worried him, and Khalidi would ultimately have his finger on the button if they allowed him near it. Shai felt people who leapt too quickly to a cause or from one certainty to another were inherently unstable. Fear hardened in his throat.

Outside the office, Tami was sitting in her alcove and looked up as Shai came through Carmon's door. She had been elsewhere when he arrived but had heard him inside. She moved around her desk, trying to relax the worry from her high cheekbones. His complexion looked pasty to her.

He saw the anxiety on her face, knew it was about him. He wanted to reach out his arms, have Tami fold into them, but instead he said, "The surveillance. I have to go."

Upset and afraid, she said, "You coming home tonight?"

"I don't know," he said, and bustled down the hall to try and outdistance his feelings. He knew she'd be better off not living her life waiting for him. After he turned the corner, he slowed and caught his breadth. He would have to tell her soon about his decision to divorce.

Shai was restless. Surveillance reported that Nadjla was home in Sidon and Dalal not yet returned to the Damascus refugee camp. She was being watched but had made no move toward a rendezvous. Shai had a salad sent up with as much chicken and vegetables as could be piled on, recalling the dietician had wanted him satiated so he didn't graze. Shai encamped himself in his small temporary office and, slipping on his glasses, tried to read reports on the search for the plutonium but could not concentrate. This was the internal service's bailiwick: beating the bushes, pulling people from roadblocks, rousting them from bed. Everything he detested.

When the enormous salad came, with oil and vinegar containers on the side, to Shai's surprise he felt a surge of excitement. Vegetables are free, Julie had said, as much as you like. For the first time, Shai considered that he could do this. He was long on intimate terms with hothouse vegetables, growing up in a Negev desert kibbutz.

With Khalidi apparently bedded down, Shai shoved the files and computer monitor on the floor into a corner and ate with appetite. Then he hauled a small sofa from the coffee room into the cleared space to try and snatch a few hours sleep. He could not live a lie with Tami; if he returned home he would have to tell her, and he just did not have the strength to face that now. With the couch in place, instead he headed again down the hall.

The flocks of courier routes throughout Lebanon were shepherded by a gray-bearded Iraqi Jew named Samuel, who had descended into Tel Aviv in the 1950 airlift via a plane change on Cyprus. The elongated routing for the 100,000 refugees and monstrous extra expense for the fledgling Jewish state were the result of Iraq's insistence that, since Israel did not exist, how could Baghdad allow planes to fly from her soil into the abyss? Women were roughly searched for jewelry before they boarded planes and possessions stolen.

Samuel swore that he would wake Shai the moment Khalidi emerged from the apartment and physically pushed the larger man out of his office. Shai returned to his small sofa, stretched out with exhaustion, and then minutes later was back in Samuel's office clarifying unnecessarily that he wanted to be roused if there was any movement in or out of the building whatsoever. "If the television there goes on or off, I'll get you," Samuel shouted, and Shai retreated with a sheepish smile, but not to his makeshift bed.

He entered the elevator. Khalidi was unlikely to move for hours and an unseen army would be on him if he did. His best guess was that Khalidi would be taken to Ramzy, if not once it was light, in the next few days. He still had hope that Ramzy would seek solace with his sister or wife—he could be waiting for Dalal to return since she was out, or he might attempt to bring her somewhere he felt was safe. The possibility of sweeping Ramzy up from one of the several alternatives was decent.

Shai climbed into his Renault and barreled through the empty streets to make pilgrimage to the Western Wall. He trusted neither in Gods nor Carmon's psychiatrists but the connection to history and tradition calmed him. Much was overflowing in his mind; he had Amal and Barakat and Fouad's family all missing, and people would soon be demanding accountings. More worrisome, Khalidi knew about Amal, which meant Ramzy would soon or already knew about Barakat's abrupt step from his life. Ramzy would realize Shai was raising the guillotine and they all better ride fast in another direction before it fell.

At the thought of Ramzy he gripped the steering wheel. He knew his mixed emotions about Ramzy could affect his judgment. He needed to focus on the operation, not on a personal betrayal. Too much was at stake. He needed to think of Ramzy not as someone he might reach, but an enemy he could order killed without hesitation.

He sped around the curve at the Armenian quarter and plunged down the narrow street, Turkish walls to his right and Arab neighborhoods outside them, and soon reached the plaza before the Temple Mount. Carmon would scream bloody murder at his coming here alone, but Shai could not believe that he would meet his Maker, or alternately secular Zionist pioneers doing a hora around a campfire, from a dagger to the heart while he walked to the Wall.

Shai pulled up outside the barrier to the broad, lit plaza, the gold Dome of the Rock towering magnificently above the Wall on the plateau where the Temple had stood before the Romans razed it. Shai climbed out and talked the soldiers at the low iron fence into allowing him to leave the car there for a few minutes, but was forced first to present a laminated card to override their standing orders. Nightly, Israeli police broke into all cars left in supermarket lots or suspicious locales to check for car bombs, leaving form instructions on the front seats on how to collect for the damage.

In the darkness, Shai shuffled alone with the half moon following him. Sharp stars winked and his shoes sounded softly off the stones. A cold wind came across the plaza, chilling him. He reached the high wall, entirely empty, and patted it with the flat part of his hand as if it were an old friend, though his expeditions here were rare. Shai turned and sank back against the Wall. His hands damp, he pushed away from the stones and started walking toward his car. He did not understand exactly why he had come here, only knew that he was more afraid than he had ever been in his life.

As the city slept, he drove out Jaffa Gate. At the corner of King George and Jaffa Road, he slowed and watched with pleasure as a frail, gray-bearded old scholar in black garb and side curls, maybe unable to sleep too and out walking, prodded the pavement with his cane as he moved slowly up the hill toward Mea Shearim. Something about the old man, the generations of Jerusalemites and what they had endured to be here, struck Shai deeply. He abruptly veered left and headed home.

Though it was after midnight, when he climbed the stairwell he smelled bread baking and he looked down. The neighbors, who were crazy about Tami, liked to joke to him that they were thrilled when he was gone because she was always baking late at night then bringing them breads and pies in the morning.

Inside, when he came into the kitchen Tami was standing kneading dough, flour in her loose hair. She continued working.

"I'm supposed to be the one with insomnia around here," he said quietly.

Still she did not turn, kneaded.

He neared her back, massaged her shoulders with both large hands, felt the hardness. "I have occasional chest pain," he said truthfully while he massaged. "And I'm tired, but I feel all right."

She stopped and turned, tears in her eyes. "I'm trying not to be so frightened."

"I know." Emotion gathered in his throat. "Maybe I'm wrong. Maybe I should come in."

She shook her head. "No, it's where you can give everything you have." She wrapped her arms around him and he felt her tears warm and wet on his neck and he squeezed her against him which felt wonderful. He had been thinking hard on the way back from the Wall, about the future and who the next generation would have to be to manage it smartly. After a moment he released her.

"Tami, would you want a child now, knowing that I might . . ."

She wiped the tears from her cheekbones with the back of one floured hand, leaving white streaks. "I think about it. It would be hard, but it's hard this way too. Shai, whatever happens to you or doesn't, it would be better for me to have a child."

"Tami, I've seen a dietician. She says I can change my life. I can. Let's have a child but not quite yet. I want to get myself in shape and stop this bomb first."

Tears welled in her eyes and she nodded. He brought both hands to her waist. Suddenly, to his amazement, an enormous burden lifted.

Below the star-blanketed sky, Ramzy stood against a tree at the end of the orchards that ran below into the nearby hills and the UNRWA school. High above at the crest of Mount Qasioun rose the steel tower that broadcast Damascus's single television station. The warm wind shifted direction and brushed past him.

He looked at the dark cinderblock house on the lower flank of the mountain, where Dalal was. The lights had just gone on. He remained motionless for another long moment, reliving the touch of her small hands on his waist, her large laugh, the way one foot always wedged around his as he slept. He imagined her face as he slipped in the house, the surprise, her eyes bright.

Then he turned and started back through the orchards. You're "So Near and Yet So Far" Fred Astaire sang to Rita Hayworth in *You'll Never Get Rich*, a silly, slapstick war movie. When he could, to relax Ramzy sought out all things 1940s, the decade of his birth, to see how the rest of the world he was born into looked. It was a respite from the focus on his people.

As his thoughts wandered, to his surprise, rather than frustrating him, being so near Dalal filled him with strength. He would head overland the short distance to the Bekaa Valley in Eastern Lebanon to meet Khalidi. If the Israelis did not kill him, he would lift Dalal in his arms later, when he had time to elude those watching her now.

Khalidi never slept heavily, and in the darkness he heard footfalls outside his door. He bolted up. There was a tapping on the wood, someone entered, and to his relief he recognized Abu Rami.

"You sleep well, yes? There is not so much noise tonight, I think."

Khalidi wondered what time it was. It was quiet outside and he sensed that the city dozed vigilantly, weapons within reach.

"Yes, I slept very well. Thank you."

Abu Raid's boyish grin flashed again. "It will be light soon. We start now."

When Khalidi joined them in the kitchen, they were preparing hummus, olives and pita. One of the young men poured thick coffee and gave the handleless cup to Khalidi. He took the hot edges and sipped.

"It's terrific, and actually I am very hungry," Khalidi said.

The young men smiled their approval and handed him the first plate.

Abu Rami was drinking coffee and smoking a cigarette. Khalidi wondered if he had slept at all. He ate quietly and quickly, did not care anymore that the plates were not perfectly clean. Khalidi was handed mechanic's overalls and had the underside of his fingernails smeared with grease, which to his pleasant surprise did not bother him. Then he was fitted with a false beard and moustache, similar to the one he had tried on in London when Ramzy photographed him there for his Israeli identification papers.

"Ramzy informs us there is a possibility the Syrian roadblocks have your photograph," Abu Rami said.

Khalidi believed he would be safe, that he would succeed, was eager to see Ramzy. "Where is Ramzy?"

"Near. He will meet you soon."

Khalidi's heart leapt. "I want to thank you very much for helping me," he said to Abu Rami, then abruptly grabbed him and kissed him on both cheeks in the fighter's greeting. Abu Rami affectionately held Khalidi's shoulder and smiled.

They clamored past men on the stairs standing beside empty glasses and pistachio nutshells. He was led to a small, battered Fiat. A driver jumped behind the wheel, carrying only a pistol in his waistband in this machine gun universe. He zipped his jacket over his overalls as he sat. Abu Rami pushed his machine gun under the seat of a small Toyota truck, a blanket of straw and two goats in the flatbed, the cabin and body of the Toyota remarkably untouched by anything other than Beirut's dirt. Two young men jumped in the back and also covered their machine guns.

With the small truck trailing as they drove off, Khalidi felt excitement, the nagging nervousness gratefully mostly gone since London. He wondered if the Israelis could be following him here but believed it impossible. By the second checkpoint—one Lebanese, one Syrian—Khalidi knew his disguise would work. The sandbagged emplacements felt almost routine to him now.

The sun peeked over tree-crested mountains to his left, which meant they were traveling south. On a broad, four-lane highway with car skeletons periodically lining its banks as if washed up by a river, a dense refugee camp became visible beside the roadway. As they raced alongside it, the destruction inside was horrific even for Beirut. Block after block of the one- and two-story cinderblock huts were smashed into entire rows of rubble. Those that stood all had gaping shell holes. Twisted corrugated roofs dangled down buildings. A table was visible on an open second-floor hut with its roof swatted away. Behind a downed chain-link fence, a few goats drank from a muddy shell crater. Women in long dresses balanced water jugs on their heads as they walked down a dirt lane. Nobody he asked could differentiate between the destruction the 1982 Israeli invasion and more than year-long occupation had caused, and the casualty of the now fifteen-year-old civil war between Christians and Muslims that had left over 100,000 dead. Abu Rami had explained that the previous year the Arab League had brought together both sides in Taif in Saudi Arabia, a treaty was signed and things had been better since, though Syria was supposed to withdraw but had not yet.

Khalidi glared at the destruction, the breath leaving him. Not able to bear it any longer, he looked away. The Palestinians had to have a homeland, for *all* their people.

They drove along a silent, bombed-out amusement park, all the rides rusted. The two crossed landing strips of the airport were visible. Beyond stretched the flat ocean and the coastal road south. The Fiat turned into the mountains.

They climbed and wound through forests with magnificent vistas below. From a distance, Beirut was a diamond perched on a headland jutting into the blue sea. They drove through stone towns with red-tile roofs, passed opulent villas and resort hotels, many pitted by shrapnel. A wide truck with live chickens bearing right at them almost pushed them off the road and the small Toyota truck behind them honked violently and almost ran the large truck into the ditch in retaliation, the eventual dinners squawking. The air cooled and the scent of pines rose. Beyond a bullet-riddled monument of Saladin on a horse, they slowed before another sandbagged emplacement. The soldiers wore black berets and hoisted M16s instead of AK-47s.

"Lebanese?" Khalidi asked.

The driver nodded.

They were waved through and Khalidi looked back as the Toyota truck followed. Attractive open shops selling clothing, shoes and pastries appeared on both sides. Khalidi absorbed everything, thought about how wonderfully alive he felt. He realized suddenly that he had not thought about Amal since landing in Beirut and strangely he felt guilty, as if that was a betrayal.

The road steepened, grew more lush and the air crisper. A full taxi wove past them. Gorgeous villas with red roofs peeked through the trees. In the hills, Khalidi saw a huge villa with three identical smaller ones to the side between the pines. Empty military jeeps and army trucks rested outside them.

"A Saudi sheik's once, the smaller ones for his wives," the driver explained.

"Lebanese or Syrians?"

"Syrians, the rest of the way now."

Khalidi closed his eyes, as the Syrians probably had his photograph. They drove through a beautiful stone town shaded by pines, apparently a summer resort in headier days, its shops open but with Syrian military vehicles everywhere.

Soldiers sat on low stone walls, at sidewalk cafes, smoked, drank sodas, some played cards. Posters of Hafez Assad gazed down from buildings. He wondered why Arab leaders always put their faces on buildings. He suddenly wondered if he wanted fame for this, his photo everywhere. He was not doing this for personal glory, but he did want the professors who had treated him as a serf, and of course Amal, to be impressed. Khalidi was proud at how little fear he felt. On the far side of the town, they approached a Syrian checkpoint and were waved through.

The road narrowed through thick trees. They climbed, crossed a rushing torrent, another checkpoint, sped through the towering narrow pass between the mountains, then descended. They wound down through birch forests, leaves rustling in the wind, and then abruptly a wide, long plain opened below with a spectacular mountain range rising from its far side. The early morning sun glanced down on green fields and orchards on the three thousand foot high plateau floor, streams and pools of water glistening among them. Villages were scattered between the green.

"The Bekaa, Shiites." The driver motioned, then sucked in air and smirked. "Hashish."

Khalidi nodded. Had never touched drugs, but decided he would if they were offered.

The road wound and plunged. At the base of the mountains they entered the town of Chtaura, swarming with Syrian soldiers and Syrian-plated passenger cars whose owners it seemed shopped here for Lebanese produce and goods. More posters of Assad stared from buildings. Khalidi was not sure if they were intended to create adoration, fear or both, but he saw it as more play-acting rather than accomplishment. At twin taxi stands beside a dry fountain, passengers piled out of a Syrian taxi and into a Lebanese one, then each headed toward its respective capital. White sheep carcasses hung by the hind feet outside a butcher's shop, herbs growing from their rears. Khalidi sat fascinated. The driver explained the wider road to the right continued to Damascus and that before the roadblocks it took an hour and twenty minutes to drive from Damascus to Beirut.

They sped north along the base of a mountain. Just beyond the town, they slowed at yet another Syrian emplacement with thick apple orchards running to the edge of the dusty road that hardly had room for traffic in both directions. Ahead, the valley broadened, seemingly pushing back the hills and mountains.

Khalidi checked again for the small Toyota truck, which he spotted at their tail. He was almost in Israel, was on the side of justice. A hundred yards behind the truck, he saw a battered Lebanese taxi.

Inside the taxi, the Israelis behind the wheel and in the passenger seat, having taken over at Chtaura, waited to clear the roadblock and continue following Khalidi. They had been unable to slip a transmitter under the Fiat, but a dozen Israeli teams sat in vehicles nearby and should have no trouble staying with the target.

Three soldiers stood lazily around the sandbags. Instead of the Fiat being waved through with the flick of a rifle muzzle, a young Syrian soldier with dark glasses came around the driver's side, AK-47 held across his chest, finger on the trigger. The Toyota truck with the goats pulled up close behind them. The Syrian drew off his glasses, lowered his head and asked where they were going, but all the time his eyes were on Khalidi. This was the first checkpoint from the Bekaa that led back through the mountains to the population centers along the coast. The driver told the soldier they were headed to Rayak, a nearby city on the road to the gigantic Roman ruins of Baalbek up the long valley. The Syrian folded his glasses, seeming nervous. He told them to wait. As he headed back to confer with the other two soldiers, the driver reached over and flashed the parking lights once. Off to the side, the soldier who had approached them removed something from his shirt pocket and showed it to the other two.

Khalidi looked back and saw Hamid and another young Palestinian shifting slowly in the back of the small truck.

The driver spoke to Khalidi. "When I say so, head down. It will be soon." He flashed his parking lights.

One of the soldiers saw the flashing lights and abruptly headed toward them, pulling his weapon from his shoulder.

"Now," the driver said.

Mouth dry, Khalidi ducked, and tires squealing, the Fiat burst ahead. The soldier who had lowered his weapon fired from right to left and the bullets peppered loudly into the side and rear of the speeding Fiat. A roar of shots from the truck slammed into the soldier and he slumped to the ground. Hamid, crouched, fired from the flatbed as it raced toward the Fiat beyond the roadblock.

The other two soldiers shot at the truck. A goat cried and went down, blood pouring through its white hair. The two Palestinians noisily emptied their clips as the truck raced forward. A bullet slammed into a soldier's forehead and he fell back against the sandbags and crumpled. The third soldier's firing hit the truck's windshield, shattering it, and the truck veered out of control, skidded and crashed loudly into a tree, blocking the entire narrow road in both directions. A Palestinian and the live goat were thrown from the rear. The goat scampered to its feet and ran between the trees. The Palestinian splayed on the road did not move.

The Lebanese taxi stopped, unable to circle the truck. The apple groves ran right to the road and there was no way through them. They watched the Fiat with Khalidi speed away and the Israeli in the passenger seat grabbed his walkie-talkie.

Dazed, Hamid remained on his back in the straw on the truck floor, could see Abu Rami's blood all over the rear cabin glass. The last soldier behind the sandbagged emplacement shot at the inert body on the road with short bursts, hit it, and the body flinched then was still again. He sprayed the side of the stopped truck. In the distance, the soldier could hear Syrian jeeps and cars from Chtaura racing to them. He stayed down, protected by the sandbags, and waited.

Hamid heard the approaching vehicles. In minutes, the remaining soldier would alert them about the Fiat and they would either overtake it or order the soldiers to form a cordon to the north and surround Khalidi. He had to kill the third soldier, make it look like only the truck had been stopped. Had to prevent them from learning about Khalidi.

Clutching his machine gun, he climbed over the bloody goat and slipped out the back of the Toyota. Shots rang over his head and he dropped to the road as one ricocheted noisily off the metal cabin. He crawled to the driver's door, pulled it open, tugged at Abu Rami and saw he was dead; shards of glass dug into his face and deep in his neck. He let go, shuffled low toward the rear panel of the truck, unscrewed the gas tank and struggled out of his jacket and then shirt. He ripped the shirt down the back and then tore a long, wide length from it. He slung his machine gun over his chest, stuffed one end of the cloth deep into the gas tank, and lit the length of shirt.

With the truck blocking the lone soldier's view, he scampered low as fast as he could up the road. Hamid heard the deafening explosion, flattened, and the heat blasted over him, blistering his bare back and neck, singeing his hair. He rose to a crouch and turned, ignored the pain of the burns. Flames, heavy with the smell of gas, leapt from the fireball. Still low, he ran back toward the blazing truck, the heat pushing at him. He could hear the Syrian trucks and jeeps approaching. He would kill himself rather than be captured, but he had to eliminate the soldier. Hamid came around the side of the flaming truck, weapon leveled.

The Syrian soldier was cautiously approaching the explosion as jeeps and trucks screeched forward behind him, storming around the Lebanese taxi. The soldier saw him and flexed to fire but Hamid had already squeezed the trigger, charging forward yelling *Allahu Akbar,* and a burst of bullets caught the soldier in the stomach and chest and he spun in a pirouette of death.

A half dozen Syrian soldiers fired from the jeeps and Hamid was kicked backward with the force of so many bullets slamming into him, his gun dropping soundlessly from his hands in the roar of continued firing.

The taxi with the Israeli agents, seeing there would be no way around, reversed and maneuvered through the Syrian army vehicles and raced back. They could speed east out of Chtaura on the Beirut-

Damascus highway, then beyond the town cut back north and join the road to Baalbek, some three or four kilometers beyond the burning truck. They had already radioed up ahead to the teams stationed in the Maronite and Greek Orthodox town of Zahle, some seven or eight kilometers past the shootings, who at this moment were speeding to intercept the Fiat with Khalidi.

The Fiat barreled up the road. The driver had been chosen for this assignment as he knew the terrain of the Bekaa from the time he lived in a nearby Muslim village. Khalidi was staring at the dark smoke rising from the explosion. He dropped back into the seat, trembling. They had died for him.

"Is there a possibility to escape?"

"The Syrians will come any second," the driver said.

They came to a paved road that headed southeast through a small village and then back to the Damascus road. Despite the screaming urgency to bolt off this road, the driver forced himself to continue, fearing the main highway. He had originally planned to turn southeast at the secondary road from the Zahle crossroads, but he dared not stay on the road to Zahle now. The unpaved mountain roads would probably be the safest, but they would take him far in the wrong direction and he would still have to descend to the valley again and attempt to cross it unnoticed. He passed a paved road, then immediately afterward a dirt road, both climbing to the left through hills strung with vineyards of the nearby Jesuit winery at Ksara. There was no traffic on the main road heading toward them.

Three minutes longer, the driver told himself. If no one spotted them it would be hard to determine which way he had turned. Time seemed frozen. He glanced at the speedometer needle wavering above 120, then in the mirror. Still no cars ahead or behind. He prayed, and then he saw the right turnoff to the village of Saadnayel.

He slammed the brakes and pulled slowly onto the dirt road with railroad tracks of the old Beirut-Damascus line, weeds rising through them, running alongside it. Though the road was relatively smooth from the summer heat, the Fiat crawled at twenty kilometers per hour. The flat ground beside the road was untilled, the view back to the paved road open.

Khalidi's hands were squeezed together in his lap, his face white. "Hurry," he shouted. "Hurry. " He could not be stopped with all he would achieve.

"I must go slow," the driver said. "Dust can be seen for great distances."

Khalidi pulled in a breath and nodded, stared back toward the roadway, ashamed at his outburst. They rattled on wood planks over a trickle of a stream, then wound through flat fields burnt yellow-brown with thistles, dry grasses and the indomitable wild hollyhocks. The air was hot, but unlike the coast, dry, the Bekaa watered by springs and the tributaries that flowed down the mountains that framed in on either length. But unlike the dramatic gorges and pine-crested peaks of the Mediterranean side, the mountains across the valley ahead of them were lower and softer. They picked up speed and dust spun from the wheels now in a small cloud. Nervous, Khalidi looked behind them. The driver tensed as the curving road straightened and neared the paved road that ran from Zahle southeast to the Damascus highway. There was no way to avoid the intersection and anyone who might be waiting there, having anticipated their route. He drove faster.

To his enormous relief, the intersection was empty. They crossed it and were now back on their original route. The narrow roadway was paved, and soon led to the Roman ruins of Baalbek, an ancient Canaanite city named for Baal, christened Heliopolis by the Romans. Beyond pieces of Roman columns strewn through the trees rose the columned temple to Bacchus, remarkably still intact. Khalidi stared at it, felt it was a sign, that he was the continuation of history. After the ruins, the road turned to dirt again. Khalidi looked behind them.

"We'll be there soon," the driver said. "Our men will be waiting."

Khalidi turned to him, feeling rage and not knowing at what or whom. "They are dead, back there, Abu Rami and the others."

"We do not fear death," the driver said, but his eyes were glassy with pain. After a moment, he said, "Only Abu Rami and myself knew our destination. He would not let himself be taken alive."

Khalidi felt his own eyes go warm and moist and he nodded. He had never imagined such sacrifice existed, and he could hardly contain his pride.

The road climbed to a rise surrounded by tall weeds with a view in every direction. As they reached the summit, the Fiat stopped. Cars emerged from the weeds on either side of the road. The driver got out, conferred with another man. Khalidi saw a tree beside the road with a man high in it with binoculars. Quickly, the driver came back to the Fiat and they drove off.

The driver said, "They were told that the Israelis were probably following you but they see no one."

Khalidi brought his fingers to his mouth and nodded. The Fiat headed through lush orchards and irrigated fields near the picturesque village of Bar Elias with its houses of compressed clay walls and flat roofs. They crossed more small streams, then cultivation was replaced again by bare, sun-beaten earth as they neared the mountains.

Their destination at the end of a dirt road was yet new terrain, a small circular stone building with pink granite columns, with neither base nor capital, erected by the Arabs from Roman ruins but then ruined itself. Green marshes, flooded by underground springs, spread in all directions. At the sound of the car, a flock of white birds lifted against the barren flank of the Anti-Lebanon chain. Around the building of indeterminate use in this isolated marsh stood half a dozen cars and jeeps, a trailer, and more than a dozen armed guards. Frightened, Khalidi hoped that Ramzy would be there. He was desperate to know how he was crossing into Israel.

Shai stood in the corner of Samuel's office and absorbed the blow with a silent grimace, like an old prizefighter. He said nothing for a long time. He did not move and his eyes seemed distant.

"Where?" Shai said finally, the distance in his face gone.

Samuel bent his small, bearded face over the large topographical map of Lebanon and Shai hunkered down over the long green finger of the Bekaa between the mountain ranges. Samuel pointed to the Syrian checkpoint where the shooting had erupted.

"But they headed north at the Chtaura crossroads," Shai said, more to himself than Samuel, Israel obviously the other way. He stubbed his finger into the map before Chtaura. "They could have turned south here. They could have continued on the Damascus road and turned south at half a dozen places, paved and unpaved." He pushed his finger into the map there. "So where were they going?"

"Not to the border."

Shai said nothing. The Lebanese border was their most heavily fortified; first the security zone inside Lebanon, then the mine fields and the electrified fence, with soft sand after it to reveal footprints. They should be heading into Jordan. Israel patrolled that border but could not cover every kilometer of the long length. What the hell was Ramzy planning? Israel had lost 2,656 dead and 9,000 wounded in the 1973 Yom Kippur War—greatly due to those in power's condescending view of the enemy's capability after the easy six-day victory in 1967—and now the brilliantly orchestrated *intifada* had cost them over one hundred military and civilian deaths.

"Concentrate on the Bekaa," Shai said. "No reason for them to have gone back into the mountains other than to temporarily avoid the Syrians."

"We're doing that already but we're talking about an enormous area. Who's to stay they weren't circling north before they headed here?"

"Beirut. Let's send commandoes to the apartment, bring everybody back for questioning."

Samuel scratched his beard. "I had that idea. The place's abandoned. They must have gotten word about the attack outside Chtaura. Probably worried the Syrians captured someone alive and would move in on them."

Or Ramzy was being cautious, Shai thought. That's what he would do himself—empty the place immediately afterward and disperse. Hands in both his pants pockets, he stared out the window. *So how are you bringing him in, Ramzy?* He clenched his fists in his pockets.

Then Shai sat in front of the map and began to patiently study the terrain north and east of Chtaura for a way to locate them.

After midnight, the manager of The Jerusalem Pool on Emek Refaim Street, one of the few public pools in the city, bent at the shallow end and removed the lane guards one by one from the six lanes, tossing each toward the center of the still pool.

The manager had somehow unearthed a bathing suit lost long ago that fit Shai perfectly. Shai could neither swim the long length nor walk very far before it became too deep, so the manager had suggested he try the width. Shai looked up at the huge clear sky, stars everywhere, and approached the pool.

He had a lot of people to be doing this for, he thought, but knew he was here for himself. From the top step, he plunged forward and hit the cool water. As a boy, he had swum with his father often in the magnificent and varied blues off of Taba in the Gulf of Aqaba, where the Sinai Mountains came down to the water's edge. Shai's muscles seemed to have memory and he swam stronger than he imagined he could. After four fast width laps he was breathing hard and began to walk in the water, thinking warmly of the breadth of experience his father had shown him as a boy.

Sometime later, Shai was lost in thought, pushing forward and unaware of how long he'd been in the water, when the manager said, "It's an hour; you said thirty minutes."

Shai smiled and headed for the steps, panting. He knew he had a tendency to push too hard with exercise, which could lead to his soon giving up. "Right," he said. "Next time stop me at half an hour. For now."

CHAPTER 12

June 30

In the passenger seat of a wounded Mercedes, Ramzy rode into the marsh where Khalidi was hidden. He had spent the night in Damascus with acquaintances the Israelis could not know, then had been driven by supporters to where he crossed the border and the low Anti-Lebanon range by horse to avoid observation on the roads. The Mercedes had met him at the base of the hills.

High grasses and tall, reedy plants with long, flat leaves rose around the muddy water. Ramzy watched a guard following where Khalidi walked along the edge of the marsh. Ramzy felt admiration for this young man, so safe in his cocoon in Los Angeles, who now risked everything.

A mosquito buzzing by his ear, Khalidi turned at the sound of the heavy car. When Ramzy stepped from the Mercedes, Khalidi jogged eagerly toward him.

Ramzy extended a hand as Khalidi neared but Khalidi bypassed it and kissed him on both cheeks. Then, head down, Khalidi explained about Amal's disappearance, adding quickly that he had told her about the yacht and Barakat. His face flushed with shame because Ramzy had instructed him not to tell anyone. "I am sorry. It was stupid. But she still thinks the bomb's going to Tel Aviv."

Ramzy was counting on that. "I received your message about Amal. I tried to reach Barakat but he's out of town unexpectedly."

Khalidi's head came up. "The Israelis have him."

Ramzy gave a tight nod, as if to indicate the Israelis seemed to be holding everybody these days, including some fifteen thousand Palestinian residents of the Territories. Ramzy had greatly hoped for more empathy from a people who had been hated throughout history. Khalidi had managed miracles so far, and Ramzy could feel no disappointment at his boasting. As they walked along the edge of the marsh, four armed men trailed a short distance behind. Khalidi was amazed that when Ramzy walked he made less sounds than the mosquitoes.

Ramzy said, "Barakat does not know where you are in Lebanon, so he cannot tell them. As soon as you enter Israel, you'll receive authentic West Bank papers. You'll take the place of Marwan Rida, a real person. You live in the Dheisheh refugee camp outside Bethlehem and work illegally in Tel Aviv in the Yemenite Quarter. You assemble sofas. The workers there are brought in by the Arab overseer. The Jewish owner does not know his employees. We have chosen Rida carefully."

"Where will Rida be?"

Ramzy stopped walking, watched and listened, then relaxed. The speck in the sky toward the south was a bird flapping toward them and not a distant, yet unheard helicopter. He followed the flight of the bird, riding on warm currents now without moving its wings. Ramzy's throat was raw and dry from all the cigarettes, his stomach sour.

"What about Rida?" Khalidi repeated in the silence. "Where will he be? They can find him."

Ramzy's eyes remained on the bird, whose light color blended with the whiteness of the Anti-Lebanon Mountains as it glided up them, the emotional anguish and physical pain sharp in him. He suspected ulcers, and forgave himself for drinking in the Damascus orchards when he knew he must not. "He won't be hiding. They'll know exactly where he is."

"I don't understand."

Ramzy's eyes came back. "We have much to discuss, some changes since the Israelis know about you. But it makes no difference. They will not find you. You go into Israel tomorrow night. I met with your Hal Bundy in Copenhagen three days ago. I have the laser from him."

Khalidi stopped. "I would like to know how I am to cross into Israel."

"Of course. They'll be watching the Jordan Valley too closely now. Please, come with me."

They walked back toward the building. The sun was reaching its zenith, the air hot, the mosquitoes pestering with quick dives. They reached the trees, where men with machine guns stood in the shade of the many cars and a trailer, fingers curled around their triggers. As they neared, the men crowded excitedly around Ramzy. Some reached out to touch him as they pledged their honor at working for him.

Ramzy stopped to hug each, to offer a few words of encouragement. He bore their adulation of him uneasily, believed he did not deserve it as he had achieved so little for them. Ramzy moved to the rear of the trailer and, without enthusiasm, unlatched the doors and drew them open.

Khalidi came around. With excitement, he leapt up into the trailer, eyes wide at what he saw there.

Below the Roman amphitheater at Caesarea, Shai trudged toward the sea along a sloping path beside banana fields. Ahead of him, small waves broke softly and reached up the sand. He felt emotionally invigorated, but physically tired from his swim. Established eight years before the Jewish state, this kibbutz had taken the name Sdot Yam, 'Fields of the Sea,' intending to develop both in agriculture and fishing. Though with not atypical Israeli alternations to an original, the huge stone tile factory at the kibbutz entrance now generated the bulk of Sdot Yam's income.

Worry, though familiar, was not an emotion Shai was on comfortable terms with. The plutonium was inside Israel, Ramzy had placed it there, and at the moment he could not locate either. Shai passed the large greenhouse, where the bright sun opened winter roses for Europe. The greenhouse was The Colonel's domain now, as the service had once been. With nothing to do but watch the Lebanese roads and wait for Ramzy's attempt to slip Khalidi across one of their borders, without knowing exactly why, Shai had phoned The Colonel to tell him he was coming. The Colonel had recruited Shai, who had been floundering during regular army service in a combat unit, and Shai supposed he was seeking a father's knee.

On a small hill overlooking the scrub brush-covered sand dunes, Shai approached the lone bungalow the kibbutz had built for their famous member should be choose to retire there, though none had expected his homecoming as early as eleven years ago, when he drove his aging Morris there seeking asylum from the Jerusalem wars he had lost to Meir Carmon.

Shai saw The Colonel sitting on his porch in a sweater despite the humid heat. The hedge of white hair surrounding his baldpate had grown long, lifted in the breeze, and he was staring out at the sea through round, silver, wire-rimmed spectacles. Apparently The Colonel did not notice his arrival, as he did not turn his head as Shai neared.

Shai slowly mounted the steps and still did not draw attention. A large glass jar of sun tea with a screw cap sat on the weathered wood table beside two glasses. More bottles of the tea he had brewed rested in the dirt beside the porch, the bags floating in them.

"Colonel," Shai said.

The Colonel jumped in the chair, turned, and then the deep crevices in his face seemed to fill in as he brightened.

"Shai, yes, well. Good to see you. Come sit. You must try some of my tea. You want ice? I have it just inside. No problem to bring some. Really, no problem at all."

Shai dropped into the chair. "Tea's fine, no ice."

The Colonel reached forward, pulled the jar near, and with arthritic fingers struggled with the metal screw top, unable to twist it.

Shai reached over. "Let me do it. It's probably damp from the ocean."

"Yes, yes the dampness." He speared both tall glasses in front of him between stiff thumbs and forefingers, pushed them toward Shai.

Shai easily slipped the screw top off, splashed the dark tea into both glasses. He felt bad he had not come here for so long. Shai set a glass before The Colonel. "I think about you more often than anyone knows, wonder how you are."

"I'm fine, absolutely fine." He smiled. "No need to worry yourself. I have my roses, my tea. Quiet. This magnificent view. Couldn't do it now if I wanted. I see that. Simply couldn't." With both hands stiff like claws, he circled his glass and dragged it nearer. "How is she by the way? I mean your wife, Sarit."

"Sarit was killed in a car accident. I'm married to Tami now."

The Colonel drank some tea, held the glass on the table with both hands. "Yes, I knew that. Of course. Tami. I was at the wedding, wasn't I? Yes, I'm sure I was."

"You were. On Tami's parents' balcony in Ramat Eshkol."

The Colonel stared at the sea and listened for a long moment.

Shai wondered if he was trying to recall or was lost tracking some other memory.

"Colonel."

He continued to gaze out at the ocean.

Louder. "Colonel."

He turned back slowly. "Shai, yes. You were saying—Sarit's fine?"

His deterioration sank Shai deeper into the chair. He closed his eyes for a moment then fought his way up, like a diver pulling through water toward air. He sipped some tea. "You remember that Ramzy Awwad was at my wedding?"

The Colonel's entire countenance lifted. "Yes, yes most certainly. I worked very hard to have Yehuda Shamir release him from Megiddo prison without Carmon suspecting why. Yehuda and I, we had you two go after Abu Nidal together. Yehuda died, you know."

Shai nodded, feeling his own mortality. Yehuda's heart had failed. "Yes, several years ago."

"Fine man. More than a fine man, a fine friend. I planted a rose bush on his plot myself. I think he would have liked that, me digging into him even when dead." He laughed and then lifted his tea with both stiff hands, sipped some noisily. "I told you the whole purpose of it all, didn't I? With Ramzy, I mean, trying to push your friendship."

Shai thought uncomfortably about how The Colonel had handled him the way he did his people. The apple fell a little too close to the tree. "You told me much later."

"Yes, good. I remembered I'd told you. Do have some more tea; I have quite a lot. No one really to drink it with, actually. Everybody's so busy. This generation's glued to the television at night. Sometimes the volunteers come to talk. The Swedes seem to particularly like my tea." He turned back toward the ocean.

Shai knew now why he had come, what he wanted. "Why?" he asked. "Why did you feel it so important to create such an intricate operation for me to meet Ramzy, to bring us together?"

The Colonel yawned, rubbed his eyes with the backs of his hands, the rigid fingers covering his face like someone shielding himself from a frightening movie or a bright blast. He swung toward Shai with energy Shai did not think he possessed.

"Why was it so important? Shai, they're here, the Palestinians. No choice about that. We're both wounded peoples, you see. Have to learn to trust." He drew his glass closer. "In my small way, you see, I thought you and Ramzy might, well, lead the way."

"It hasn't worked out."

"Yes, so I suspected from the way you asked." His face sagged and there was fragility in his eyes. "Much that I'd planned hasn't worked out. Carmon, for one. I tell you, there are far more disappointments along the way than you expect when you're young. Well, let's at least have some more tea. Take a jar home to Tami, if you like." He brought his glass to his lips and sipped the dark brew. "Nothing wrong with being dependent on a woman either. One has to be strong enough for that too. Though being dependent's not quite the fashion these days, is it?"

Pounding up the walkway, Shai left Sdot Yam with his spirits lifted. He and Tami would have The Colonel over for dinner after he found the bomb. He would drive down and pick him up himself. Pasta with vegetables. Pasta, like fruit, a food with which he'd been previously unacquainted, was now mandated to replace beef. Shai climbed into his car and just sat. The whole rapprochement with Ramzy had been for nothing, but beneath his hurt and the fear he recognized and felt now for the first time why Ramzy was doing this, how long this occupation ground on. As much as Shai wanted to stop Ramzy, he longed to talk to him. For a long time, Shai did not move. Finally, he twisted the ignition and sped away. Lebanon was not that large. There had to be a way to find them.

At Ben Gurion Airport, Hal M. Bundy stepped from the terminal into the heavy heat. On the far side of low iron gates, a crush of people waited for arriving passengers. Happy to be active and back here, Bundy wheeled his rattling luggage cart alongside them.

At the curb, a beige Subaru 1600 with the logo of a smiling camel and the words ELDAN RENT-A-CAR on the passenger door was waiting. As Bundy identified himself, the driver hurried out and helped Bundy load his luggage. They drove a short distance, then through a gate in a chain-link fence to the lot where fleets of small cars waited. Inside the trailer that served as Eldan's office, the pretty, dark-haired woman behind the desk offered him a white Subaru 1600 and confirmed the cellular car phone he had ordered, explaining that all their phones were transportable and could be moved from vehicle to vehicle. Ramzy had checked with their New York office to determine exactly that, wanting a phone Bundy could pull from the car and whose whereabouts would be unknown to any potential listeners snatching Bundy's conversations with him from the air.

She filled out forms and explained the cellular phone would be simpler to use than in America. There was a separate area code, 050, for all cellular phones. Unlike America, there was no need to call a carrier when he drove into a new service area because the small country's entire transmitter system was one company. Bundy feigned interest, as Ramzy had explained the Israeli cellular system in

Copenhagen.

Bundy drove out of the rental lot, and at the military checkpoint at the airport entrance he was waved through without stopping. He was Caucasian and his license plates yellow, denoting Israeli, with a green checked border announcing it to the police and military as a rental car. At the crossroads immediately outside the airport, his map spread on the seat beside him, Bundy turned right. Humming as he drove, at Neve Yarak he followed a fork toward the ocean and continued north up the broad, four-lane coast highway. He looked at the water—beautiful light blues and greens near the shore, deep blue farther out. This was one of the most beautiful spots on earth. Low, green cotton fields gave way to banana fields, and then more cotton, and he smelled the fertilizer. Soon, large fishponds spread back from Zichron Ya'akov. They had really made something of this country, no denying that. At Atlit, a beautiful Crusader castle jutted into the sea. Across the highway, pines covered the growing mountains.

As Bundy neared the southern outskirts of Haifa, he turned off and approached the MTM Scientific Industries Center located by the sea. The enclosed area of a few square blocks, with two-to-four-story buildings, reminded him of similar high tech R&D sites in America. At the gated entrance, he explained that he had ordered something by mail from Fibronics and the gate rolled open. He drove in. Freshly painted parking lines ran diagonally from the buildings. Inside the four-story, glass Fibronics building, Bundy had no trouble purchasing the ten kilometers of plastic optical fiber, and the four hundred micron diameter fiber fit easily on a single spool. Though nobody asked, he volunteered that he was doing R&D on interfacing between computers and telephone lines. Several people nodded their approval and he paid in cash. The optical fibers glued to the high explosive around the plutonium, along with the laser, would establish a live bomb.

Bundy drove back toward Jerusalem, where he would check into the Jerusalem Plaza Hotel. He would pick up Khalidi tomorrow night. That Ramzy was one smart fellow, and the drive from Jerusalem to the northern border was only a few hours.

Late the following afternoon—Sunday, and a full work day in Israel—Tariq, who had met Ramzy in the London theater, and Marwan Rida, the sofa factory laborer whose life Khalidi would step into, drove a yellow license plated Citroen from the Arab village of Beit Jann in the Galilee north toward the border with Lebanon. Israeli Arabs inside the Green Line were full citizens and their cars bore the same yellow plates as the Jews everywhere, including the West Bank. The tension was so tight inside Rida as he sat in the passenger seat, afraid he might snap, he drummed along fiercely on the dashboard to Jimmy Hendrix's "All Along the Watchtower," beamed from Abie Nathan's peace ship in the Mediterranean. The sun glinted through the windshield, but his face was burning up beyond the heat. Suddenly he noticed that he had been pushing his right foot against the floor hard and he stopped.

Tariq had borrowed the small Citroen BX 16 from a cousin for the afternoon, explaining that they were going swimming. They were dressed in bathing suits with striped T-shirts and American sneakers, and towels lay across the back seat. They carried no other clothes or any weapons. They should be taken for dark-skinned Sephardic Jews heading for one of the many springs, nature reserves or waterfalls in the lush region between Kiryat Shmona and Banias at the base of the Golan Heights. If stopped, they had their authentic West Bank identification cards and there was no legal reason for them not to be here as long as they returned to the West Bank by sunset.

As they approached Kiryat Shmona, large apartment blocks jutted from the hills. Rida looked out at them. He had a large forehead, a deep, intense gaze, thin moustache and beard. Rida thought about his two martyred older brothers, in whose memory he was doing this. The eldest, then fifteen, was shot in 1981 by soldiers, and his next older brother died in the Dahariya prison near Hebron after he killed a soldier by dropping a concrete block on his head in Nablus. Rida pounded the dashboard harder.

Uniformed soldiers, their forefingers down in hitchhiking stance, crowded the intersection where the road branched east to the Golan Heights. Rida looked away, slapped both his knees now. His job working illegally in the sofa factory was humiliating. Some soldiers were continuing straight on through to what in more hopeful times they called The Good Fence, and into the strip they had seized in Lebanon. Others headed to the bases that dotted this side of the border. To the near west and north stretched the low, brown, dry, shrub-covered hills of Lebanon in this finger of Israel pushing into her flank. There were no roadblocks here like in the West Bank and no one stopped them.

Worried about Rida but saying nothing, Tariq turned on the road that headed east, a few kilometers from the border and paralleling it. All the settlements here—Ma'ayan Baruch; HaGoshrim, where Tariq knew they made a fortune manufacturing the Epilady products for the West's spoiled women; Dafna; Dan—were surrounded by high fences with huge bales of barbed wire wound around their tops. Heavy, iron, electric gates blocked entrance to each kibbutz and armed soldiers sat in guardhouses behind them. Apple, plum, and corn fields, as well as orange groves surrounded by tall Cypresses to protect them from the wind, stretched outside the fences. Tariq found no pleasure that the Israelis had to barricade themselves here; he knew what it meant to live in fear of their soldiers storming into Ramallah.

A large walled and barbed wire surrounded army base sprawled next to HaGoshrim, with a lowered blue and white boom across its entrance. The buildings inside were concrete. A short distance down the road to Kfar Szold, a small, temporary, tent army base surrounded only by barbed wire had risen from the weeds. Beyond it stretched the flat Hula Valley, once a massive swamp, now lush with fields and fishponds.

Rida felt deflated at seeing the army bases. Expecting to feel eagerness for revenge for his brothers, instead he missed them so deeply he wanted to cry. Hot and somewhat dizzy, he stuck his head far out the window and the warm breeze struck his face as the car raced forward.

Tariq continued east, the high Golan Heights rising ahead. A few minutes beyond Kibbutz Dan, he turned left down a narrow one-lane road, following the signs to the nature reserve of Tel Dan beside the border. Tall eucalyptuses lined an enormous field to their right of small green plants grown for animal feed. With no other cars on the road, crickets chirped in the quiet. Tariq glanced at Rida, who had his head back now and was looking wide-eyed at the car roof.

"We're almost there," Tariq said.

Rida closed his eyes.

A kilometer down the eucalyptus-lined field, they stopped at a gate, paid and were given a map of the reserve in the shadow of Lebanon. Inside, the rush of a river could be heard above the picnicking Israelis, who were barbecuing between the trees and eating at the white tables of an outdoor fish restaurant. The Dan springs was the oldest and most important source of the Jordan River. They walked along narrow dirt paths into the reserve, with laurel and oak trees so large their crowns intertwined blocking the sky. Long vines dropped everywhere. The air was damp and sweet, the path snaking around pools with myrtle bushes, then parts of the river with water rushing over rocks. Israelis wandered through the reserve, many with children, studying the flora and fauna, calling out loudly to each other. "Hey, Moisheleh, hurry, a salamander."

Despite the shade, Rida was so hot he felt the skin was going to separate on his face and everything burst out. It seemed like he had been waiting a year, though it had been a little over a week, and now finally it was tonight. They reached a quiet pool surrounded by trees and low bushes. Rida left his flip-flops on the path and stormed in, kicking the icy water. He dropped down on his back, not minding the freezing temperature, sank his burning face under the surface and drank. The tall, thin Tariq bounded in after him. When Rida sat up, Tariq splashed him.

As Tariq laughed, Rida stood and retaliated with fierce and wild splashing. Rida continuing to propel the water, faster and faster, coming closer and closer to Tariq until Tariq was almost knocked over and, frightened, he ran out of the pond. Rida stopped, stood there for a moment feeling much better. He stepped from the water, slipped his arm around Tariq and they continued down the path, their shirts soaked and their flip-flops squishing.

At 6:00 p.m., a loud horn sounded through the reserve. Those Israelis still in Tel Dan began to filter down the paths toward the entrance, uncharacteristically obeying because of the proximity to the border. Tariq and Rida stood in a grove of Syrian Ash trees with thick knotty trunks. They hugged, then Tariq moved alone toward the entrance to drive the small Citroen back to his cousin. Rida headed deeper into the trees, shivering from fear.

A little after seven that evening, still light out, two American volunteers at Kibbutz Dan, Elana Nelson and Robbie Cohen, students at Boston University and Oberlin College respectively, walked up the long eucalyptus-lined road toward Tel Dan. Both wore shorts and tennis shoes, and Robbie had a sleeping bag over his shoulder. Crickets thundered in the quiet, not even the rustle of a breeze through the tall trees. With four people to a room in the volunteers' quarters, privacy was nonexistent.

Robbie longed to be a writer and had hoped for some time on the kibbutz to put down stories, but between Elana and the work schedule he was having trouble penning a letter a week to his parents. He told himself that he was young and there would be time to write later, after he gathered more experience, though deep down he knew this was an excuse. For the last month, he and Elana had exchanged head colds from both the late outings in Tel Dan and the screaming alarm clocks in the dark mornings that insisted they rise to work, alternately in the barn, fields or kitchen.

At the entrance to Tel Dan, Elana immediately tackled the locked six-foot-high gate, her long, fine, platinum hair swaying. She hauled herself up the iron bars, slung one tanned leg over, grabbed onto the top with both hands, extended herself down the other side and dropped softly to the ground, her chiseled features imploring him to follow. Impressed yet again with her multitude of talents, the wavy, dark-haired Robbie threw the sleeping bag over and climbed the gate himself. She was an army brat, her stiff, WASP father hauling her and her mother around the globe until the divorce. Whether Elana had decided to convert to Judaism from conviction or rebellion, Robbie was not sure. With the way she made love it did not matter, but as a writer he felt he should know.

The only sounds were small, dark birds flapping between the

branches and the rushing water. After moving through dark trails below the canopy of trees and plunging vines, Robbie spread the sleeping bag out in an open area beside a place in the river where torrents dropped and surged white over rocks. Elana was out of her clothes and tennis shoes, which she pulled directly off her feet, before he had finished unlacing and removing his shoes and socks. Legs slightly parted, she stood pouting playfully above where he sat on the rocks, and he hurried.

As a lover, she was diametrically different than everywhere else in her life—soundless, like a fragile bird, as she descended and dropped softly on him. Silent, she hardly stirred, and she was so vulnerable, at times he wanted to stop and simply hold her. Sometimes he did midway, which unfortunately he could tell she took as lack of passion.

For a long time they rested entwined on the soft sleeping bag in the warm air, and as usual he felt there should be something profound he should say, though he could think of nothing besides that she felt good, so he remained silent.

As the sky began to darken, she waded alone a little way into the churning, icy stream and he watched her. She bent to cup some water in her hands and her hair dropped toward the river, the ends bouncing in it. She had a beautiful body: silky skin, with goose bumps now, taut but not large breasts, a slightly rounded buttocks, terrific legs. Though he knew she was trouble, he was falling in love with her.

Then, in the last light, he clearly saw a man with dark features crouched between low green bushes across the narrow river watching Elana, a crazed look on his face.

"Elana," he said, trying to sound calm. "Come here, sweetie."

She let the water trickle through her fingers. "No."

His legs were weak. He wondered if the man was alone. He reached for a sharp rock and secreted it in his hand. "Elana, *please*."

She looked at him with displeasure, then walked back through the water. When she came up on the bank, he circled his arms around her waist and hugged her. He looked over her shoulder and saw that the man was gone, which frightened him more.

He whispered in her ear. "There was an Arab across the river staring at you. Get dressed casually and let's go."

She nodded nervously, then after a moment said loudly with feigned exasperation, "Okay, okay. If you want to write then go write. Jesus."

They climbed quickly into their clothes, and when she bent to slip on her shoes she picked up a rock like he held.

"I don't think we should run," he whispered.

"Okay."

He lifted the dusty sleeping bag and they started to walk quickly out of the reserve. Listening, he heard no sounds above the river. As they ducked under the now dark covering of trees there was a rustle in the bushes ahead of them. They stopped and she grabbed his arm with sharp nails. Very frightened, he tightened his fingers around the rock.

"Who's there?" he asked.

Silence.

"Who's there?"

Nothing.

Abruptly, a small animal darted across the pathway and into the underbrush.

"Come on," Robbie said.

He grabbed her hand and they ran. Minutes later, they came out at the picnic area near the closed restaurant, both breathing hard, and kept running. They hit the gate together, clamored over it, and raced toward the kibbutz.

"We have to tell somebody," Robbie said as they ran.

"No," she said. "What's to tell? Some pervert was watching me. It's not the first time. Nobody needs to know we were out here."

"All right," he conceded.

CHAPTER 13

July 2

"Okay, I'll have dinner with you," Sara said to Hirsh as they walked in the dark just outside the office. "But it's not a date. Pizza. Someplace completely tacky."

Hirsh showed an uncharacteristically large smile. "You want to drive your own car?"

"No. I've been in a car with you before. I survived. Though you drive a little slow, which I get, you're old."

"I'd guess the young guys follow you like puppy dogs," Hirsh said.

"More like they're in heat."

"How do you choose?"

"Very carefully. Usually by intelligence, and with a reference from someone who knows him. And in case you're curious, I grew up lunatic religious. So I kiss somewhere between the twentieth and thirtieth date. Guys hear this and they want to go out with me every night for three weeks. Stupid line. I don't know how they get any girls."

"No need to start counting," Hirsh said. "Since this isn't a date."

She slid into his car beside him and looked away so he wouldn't see her smile. "Exactly."

At a wood table in the loud restaurant, he asked what she wanted on the pizza.

She frowned. "Everything. Is there any other way?"

"In Johannesburg they serve what's called meaty grill. Spare ribs, bacon, barbecue sauce and parsley."

"I'd skip the pizza part and just have the rest."

Hirsh watched her unkempt red hair dance as she studied the menu. He was accustomed to arousal but it had been a long time since he was excited. The restaurant was kosher, as almost all Jerusalem restaurants were, so no cheese and meat together. "Rather lighter fare here," he said.

"Not the way I order. It's a two-week deal if I ever cook dinner. I have to have a recipe with a picture, and go to the market with that picture."

"Why a picture?"

"I have to know, well, did it turn out or not." Her eyes remained on his. She looked down at the menu again. "Since you won't last the thirty dates, this other woman that you're going to marry, how many little brats you thinking?"

"Zero or four."

Her head came up but the sass had left her face. "The army? You want spares in case any are killed?"

"No. I'm just not one for half measures."

"Good. We're getting double the hottest peppers, eggplant, avocado, pomegranate…"

Both arms wrapped around Tami, Shai woke with a start in the darkness and lifted his head. The clock read 3:50 a.m. He sank down against the pillow, arms still around her then nuzzled his head against her hair, knowing she never stirred when he did. He released her, climbed out of bed and padded barefoot toward the dark living room.

The summer mountain nights were cold and the stone floor tiles colder. In his underwear, he went to the window and stared out at the unlit street of small stone apartment buildings. In the last day and a half

Lebanon had swallowed Khalidi, and presumably Ramzy as well. Suddenly, Shai sensed a dream about Ramzy had woken him.

He roamed to the bookshelf, lined with row after row of Tami's literary and film works in English and Hebrew. He searched on the bottom shelf in the lack of light and pulled out a slim volume in English, Ramzy's *Men in the Darkness* and other short stories. All of Ramzy's writings were banned in the West Bank and little had appeared in Hebrew.

Haaretz had translated the short, autobiographical "Land of Shriveled Oranges" from this volume. Shai gazed out the window again and thought about the story of the young boy first person narrator, pulled by his father from his sleep deep in the night, climbing with one suitcase into their truck to flee the 1948 fighting. The narrator sits in the back on his knees silently watching everything as the family drives from Jaffa to Lebanon to await the Arab victory. Eventually, in the refugee camp in Sidon, they learn that the communiqués had lied, that Tel Aviv and Haifa are not burning and they are not returning home.

Shai looked at the slim book, suddenly felt uncontrollable rage that they would imprison someone a few kilometers from here for holding this volume as he did. People long powerless often tried futilely to control everything in their reach. Over the last two decades, Ramzy had made his own certainly hellish journey and come to stand beside them, delivering promise that there was a place to end all this, that the Palestinian people could, if not embrace the new political reality, at least accept it. That Israel could make peace, if not with the Palestinian heart, with the Palestinian mind. Again, Shai longed to talk to him.

Shai moved to the kitchen table, turned on the light and plummeted down into the seat, his feet icy. Ramzy's file lay closed on the table but he made no move for it, most of the recent entries of his own manufacture. Shai had signed it out in frustration, had mined it backward and forward and, as expected, found not a speck of gold. His memory was as deep as ever and he knew what was there.

A short time later, he heard Tami rising from the bed and heading barefoot toward him. She came into the kitchen in a long cotton nightgown, lowered herself into the chair next to him and brushed her heavy hair back.

"You want some hot cocoa? The warm milk will help you sleep."

"No."

She laughed. "No you don't want the cocoa, or no you don't want to sleep?"

"No, I don't want you to move. I want to look at you."

She patted her thigh. "Come on, give me those feet."

He hoisted his legs across her thighs, felt her fingers massaging his cold toes. Some of their best times were sitting opposite each other on the sofa, legs extended and touching while they talked.

"Did it occur to you, mister master spy, that you could look at me just as easily if I was over there?" She motioned her head toward the range.

He dropped his feet to the floor, reached over and pulled her chair near him. "No." He kissed her.

The phone sounded.

Shai was across the living room before the second ring. He recognized the voice first, Carmon, then absorbed the clipped message. Shai's mind riveted on the method of entry, but he asked instead how many soldiers had been killed at the Nahal base. The answer, seven, lanced into him like that many bullets. A *glider*. Almost an hour ago.

"Maybe it's a diversion. Maybe it's unrelated. It's shit anyway you smell it," Carmon hissed. He had already pressed the Northern Command to return and scour the rest of the border, worrying about how many units had been transferred toward the Nahal base.

Already thinking in that direction, Shai requested a helicopter and Carmon informed him that one was bearing down this moment on the rooftop above his office, and why didn't he go check it out himself since he was driving everyone crazy as it was by prowling around the corridors like a bear who had lost his way to the honey.

Shai hung up and dialed Hirsh's number but there was no answer. Without missing a beat, he dialed Sara, who answered sleepily after half a ring. He asked for Hirsh and a second later Hirsh was on the line fully alert. "Meet me on the helicopter pad," was all Shai said, then hung up.

Shai hurried into the bedroom to dress. Tami trailed after him. After he told her what happened, she sank on the edge of the bed. As he pulled yesterday's clothes from the chair, Tami went into the living room and returned with the car keys and wallet he always left on the coffee table. He forced his feet into his shoes, didn't tie them, and grabbed the keys and wallet from her hands.

The Bell helicopter was waiting atop the tall building like a chicken squatting on a nest. As he pulled himself into the cavernous rear beside a uniformed lieutenant, Hirsh was already sitting against the wall, his face sullen. The helicopter rose into the darkness and Shai quickly sat.

"This is what we have," the lieutenant said.

Shai could barely hear him above the pounding rotors as the helicopter lifted and shuffled nearer.

"A single, motorless glider, composite and resin construction, no steel. Tandem seating. Pulled into the air by a small plane. We did not spot the glider until it nearly landed. The entire border area went on alert."

"The infiltrators, any alive?" Shai asked. He disliked the word "terrorist," which was becoming a receptacle for all radical belief in the neighborhood.

"No. They both proceeded on foot to the Nahal base, penetrated the defenses. Three units were dispatched to the scene. The army's been returned to the border. If it was a diversion, there's no sign so far of another penetration of the security zone or fence. We think it's related to another incursion but we can't see how."

"They'll bloody fall all over each other to take credit for it," Hirsh burst up from his quiet.

As the helicopter plunged north through the night sky, Shai clenched his fists. Nahal was the acronym for *Noar Halutzi Lohem*, Pioneer Fighting Youth, a world from the elite combat units. Nahal members joined together from a youth group, spent the first six months in agricultural training on an established kibbutz, and then divided the remainder of their service between military maneuvers and assisting a new agricultural outpost. Outside, the end of the sky began to lighten. The lieutenant dozed.

Hirsh rose, sat beside Shai and leaned back against the reverberating hull. "Sara. You concerned I'll be worrying about her when we're working together?"

"No. You already worry about everybody so nothing's changed."

"What about her being distracted?"

"Possible. But she's focused and still proving herself. Not to me but to herself. She gives all of her. If anything, there's a little danger the other way, that she'll behave like it doesn't matter that you're in danger. It's a risk, but if there were a rule book I'd throw it away this time."

The helicopter hovered and descended toward the base. Shai stood impatiently, turned to Hirsh. "What you said at dinner in Sao Paulo. It helped. A lot. Thank you."

The skis touched earth and Shai was down. They walked quickly through the cool twilight beyond the slowing rotors to where an army captain waited. The base was too quiet, the young soldiers moving in a daze or standing in shock. Electric lights shone everywhere from the tents and along the perimeter strands of barbed wire wound through the tall weeds. Several of the tents were toppled and shredded. Near the large mess tent, the seven corpses were laid out, covered by khaki blankets. Shai could not look at them and instead lifted his eyes beyond, toward the green Hula Valley. When he turned back, he saw Hirsh's lips were trembling and his eyes were near tears.

"How did they get on base?" Hirsh asked the captain, not terribly older than his raw recruits.

"They fired at the single guard at the gate. From two angles. He panicked, fled. He can't give a coherent statement now."

"Any word from Northern Command about other incursions?" Shai asked.

"No breaks in the fence. Nothing spotted on the ground," the captain said in clipped monotone. "We had the entire border lit with flares as soon as it happened." His face was tight and ashen. "The glider's beyond Kibbutz Dan."

Shai pushed his damp hands in his jacket pockets. "Let's see the infiltrators' bodies."

The captain bobbed his head sharply and led them to one of the smashed tents. On the far side of it a corpse lay in the dirt, covered with a blanket. A smashed guitar, apparently blown from the tent, had landed near the feet. On the far side, an AK-47 lay where it had toppled from the terrorist's grip.

"May I?" Shai asked the captain, nodding toward the body.

"Of course."

Shai pulled off the blanket and stared without emotion at the bloodied corpse but did not recognize the face from any of their files. He bent and checked each pocket, starting with the jacket, then moved to the shirt and then pants but found nothing. Hands bloody now, he examined the shirt and jacket labels, which were of standard Lebanese manufacture. He loosened the belt and fly and heaved the evidence on its stomach.

"You want help?" the captain asked.

Shai did not answer. He pulled back the rear of the pants, brushing against the still-warm flesh. Lebanese manufacture on the pants and underwear labels too. A trickle of blood rolled down the dark buttocks. Shai moved to the feet, unlaced the right combat boot all the way, then pulled it off and inside found Syrian marking, which he expected from the horizontal sole lines.

Shai stood. "Anybody touch him, take anything from his pockets?"

"No one," the captain said.

Hirsh approached the young soldiers watching from a distance, saw how shaken they were, knew exactly how they felt. "Can you get him something to wipe his hands on," he said quietly.

A young recruit bolted from the circle and ran toward the mess tent.

"The other body?" Shai asked.

"Here." The captain strode toward a tent that appeared undamaged, Shai and Hirsh a step behind. The body lay covered in the entrance. Inside the tent, belongings were strewn everywhere, blood pooled in two places. Shai observed the wavering line of bullet holes in the rear canvas and his breath caught in his throat as he wondered if they had passed through or around their boys. Two flew in, two dead, Shai thought. With Ramzy in Lebanon, too damn neat.

Shai bent and eased away the blanket, again not recognizing the face. As he began his examination of the second bullet-riddled corpse, the soldier who had dashed to the mess tent entered with a white towel. Hirsh took it from him, giving the boy a warm smile. Hirsh turned to the captain. “How many wounded?”

The captain’s ramrod posture slumped and his voice broke. “Twenty-two. Five seriously.”

Hirsh closed his eyes.

Shai rolled the heavy, dark Palestinian over, his AK-47 under him, pushed it to the side and continued his pillaging. He found no papers and this clothing was purchased at different stores than the first body’s, but still Lebanese. He wore the same Syrian boots. Shai rose and took the proffered towel from Hirsh and scrubbed his hands on it, the blood bright as it came off on the white. “Let’s see the glider.”

“I’ll have someone drive you,” the captain said.

“Have a radio with them, please.”

“Two minutes. On the road.” The captain headed off.

Shai turned to Hirsh. “Stay here in case anything comes in from Northern Command. Find me.”

Hirsh began to walk with him toward the jeep. “Gliders are obviously Abdul Jabra’s tradecraft. He trains the pilots outside Homs. I read the transcript of the interrogation of the pilot of that motorized one that made it to Nahariya.”

“Yes, this has Jabra’s signature all over it,” Shai said. “Gliders. AK-47s. Syrian military boots. Just couldn’t be clearer.”

Hirsh stopped, a head below Shai’s round height. “When it’s this tidy, it isn’t.”

Shai gave him a small smile, then strode off to the jeep already waiting on the road, an antenna rising from the rear.

A lieutenant approached from the jeep. “We found the glider

on our second sweep. Four kilometers from here. I'll show you."

They drove toward the brown slopes of Mount Hermon, the sun brightening behind it, and then turned left on the narrow road toward Tel Dan. The low curves of Lebanon's body beckoned ahead, once so seductive, now only a memory of a promising courtship disintegrated into a tragic, violent divorce that those who were not blinded by belief saw coming.

"Were there roadblocks?" Shai asked.

"Initially, yes. Until the terrorists were killed and we determined there was only one glider. Units were ordered back to the border. Northern Command was worried about a diversion and an attempt to break through the fence."

Shai was worried about the coincidence of an attack from Lebanon at the moment they were waiting for Khalidi to infiltrate. They bounced off the road to the right at an opening in the line of towering eucalyptus trees with their peeling barks and sweet scent. Shai jumped out, though crazily for a moment that he felt lighter, and headed into the enormous field of tiny alfalfa plants. Perfectly intact, the sleek black glider stood in the middle of the field like a prehistoric bird with an enormous wingspan. The wings could be folded up and the glider easily transported in a trailer. Two soldiers waited beside it clutching Galil assault rifles.

Impressive landing, Shai thought in the shrinking moon, *and excellent choice of a site*. The long, wide field stretched below a barren hillside to the east and the tall eucalyptuses blocked all view to Kibbutz Dan to the west. To the north lay only the Tel Dan Nature Reserve and the border, to the south more trees and fields. The glider interested Shai less than the surroundings. From a distance, he slowly circled the plane. He picked up two pairs of tracks with the distinctive horizontal grooves of the Syrian boots as expected, which headed through the alfalfa toward the main road. With the two large kibbutzim on this side, they would have crossed the road and continued through the fields there to the Nahal base. He wondered if he was wasting time as Khalidi moved across the Jordan Valley.

He approached the plane, studied the tandem seats. There were no navigational charts. The pilot had apparently memorized the terrain, or else he dumped them on the way. The lieutenant, at the edge of the field near the jeep, said loudly, "Anything I can do to help you?"

Without looking up, Shai continued his meanderings. He searched the ground in the direction they had come, from the Tel Dan road. The dirt between the alfalfa was trampled with the diamond shaped prints of Israeli paratrooper boots; the flags outside the Nahal base were paratrooper. He continued with his head bent forward over his girth and searched carefully between the footprints, his breathing a bit heavy. On a small space on the carpet of alfalfa he saw half a footprint of an open-toed flip-flop that appeared fresh, partially crushed by diamond paratrooper prints. He followed back through the alfalfa toward the jeep, and between the paratrooper feet saw a full flip-flop print and then several others. Shai straightened, motioned toward the soldiers, and both of them trotted near.

"Any civilians here since you found the glider?"

"No," they echoed.

The paratrooper tracks ran on top of the flip-flop prints everywhere he found them. "Is there any report of anyone being here before you arrived? From the kibbutzim?"

"I don't know," one answered. The other remained silent.

"Find out for me, please." Shai headed toward the lieutenant waiting in the opening between the trees.

"You find anything?" the lieutenant asked.

Shai said nothing and continued past him, staring at the ground. For a moment, the lieutenant wondered if he had heard him. He headed out to the road and watched the heavy man in civilian clothes.

Shai turned back and looked through the eucalyptuses at the glider. The other prints were probably irrelevant, made before the glider landed. But who would be walking through a field that led nowhere with those kind of shoes? The prints beside the road showed they had come from the direction of Tel Dan and the border, but a short way up they disappeared on the asphalt. Still, anybody from Dan might walk up to the nature reserve and back in these kind of shoes. He strode quickly to the jeep, where the lieutenant now stood.

"Get me your captain and let's get back to the base."

Seconds after they sped onto the main road, the captain came over the radio.

"Please have the secretaries of every settlement in the area at your base in ten minutes," Shai said. "No excuses, no delays. If the secretaries can't be found, bring someone of similar authority." A dozen kibbutzim dotted the border area.

"Done," the captain said over the static.

Back at the base, waiting for the secretaries to arrive, Shai stood unmoving beside flapping, torn canvas, his eyes on the bloodstains on the tent floor. A short distance behind him, Hirsh was talking to the captain. Shai brought his eyes up and, without turning, began to listen.

". . . commanded the assault on Ma'alot," Hirsh said, his voice soft. "God, I know how you're feeling right now. A lot of us know. It's terrible but you're not alone. I'm going to leave a way to find me. I need you to find me, for me."

Hirsh saw Shai, approached and said, "The border's quiet. No breaks. No tracks. No bloody anything."

Shai nodded and said nothing, nor did he offer any explanation of what he had found. He looked at the bloodstains then back to Hirsh. His voice rose. "What's to investigate here? Why bother to dig deeper…from their view? Okay, maybe to determine exactly who did it. But what difference does that make? We retaliate against a couple of Jabra's bases or maybe we use the opportunity to hit a few of his hard-line buddies in the Bekaa too." He was almost shouting now. "Few will argue they don't deserve it, and we show them collectively there's a hard price for all of them to pay for this. So what's to delve into here, *really?"*

Now Hirsh was sure he was onto something. "How long you going to keep what you found to yourself?"

Shai spun and hurried toward the sound of a kibbutz truck speeding toward the base. Hirsh moved off to check the route from the glider—with this bomb, happy that it was Shai and not one of the less thorough officers heading the hunt. More important than Hirsh knowing, he was calmed that Shai knew.

Shai did not wait for all the men and women to assemble. On the road at the entrance to the base he spoke to the first three—a woman from Dan, a man from Dafna, and a woman from Kibbutz Snir, south of the border road and east of Tel Dan. The alfalfa field, he quickly learned, belonged to Snir.

"I need you to go back to your kibbutzim and pull every person into the main dining room, immediately," Shai said, addressing them all. "I mean exactly everyone. From every barn, every field, every factory. All the children, everybody watching them. I want not a single person left anywhere. No exceptions under any circumstances. Not one. Understand?"

"Is there still danger?" the longtime pioneer from Dan asked. "Why the dining room and not immediately into the shelters?"

"There's no longer danger here, but there's grave danger elsewhere in the country." A small truck sped toward the base from the main road. "I need to know if anyone saw anything or anyone unusual, any Arabs, anyone out of place, yesterday or last night. Particularly in the area of the alfalfa field east of Tel Dan and the border. If anyone's seen anything, no matter how trivial it seems, I want them brought here immediately. In addition, I want to know if anyone was in the alfalfa field in the last week wearing flip-flops."

"Okay," the man said for them all and they strode for their vehicles.

The secretary of Kibbutz HaGoshrim arrived, stopped his truck with a high-pitched squeal of brakes, and jumped out.

"Anything else?" the captain asked.

"Yes. With all these fields, can you get me some apples? A lot of them."

Kenneth Khalidi sat confidently in the passenger seat of the Subaru as Bundy sped down the coast highway toward Tel Aviv. Small waves on the flat surface of the ocean reflected the early morning light. Soaring through the darkness in the silent glider had been an exciting experience for Khalidi and he felt powerful, knew he would succeed.

He looked out the window. The area was barren, undeveloped.

Strands of rusted and broken barbed wire ran periodically between the highway and the sea, and he wondered which war they were from. "We are near now?" he asked.

"Oh, I'd say we don't have too much farther." Bundy felt little fear, though it still paid to be vigilant. "Can't give you the exact time. But we should be at the junction to Tulkarm mighty soon."

"Good. Thank you."

The Netanya junction loomed before them. A large gas station sat off to the right and new houses with red tile roofs dotted the left. "What do you know, here we are." Bundy came off the highway and stopped at the intersection. The sign read Netanya to the right and Kfar Yona to the left. He turned toward Kfar Yona and the West Bank, only sixteen kilometers from the coast here. Bundy understood why the Jews were squirrely about borders, their country only eleven miles wide here. *Should have taught them to be more neighborly*, Bundy thought.

Soon, Bundy saw the large civilian prison Tariq had alerted him to watch for. They had met for the first time the previous evening in a fish restaurant in Haifa, before Bundy drove to the border to fetch Khalidi. Tariq had told him the *intifada* leaders liked to meet in restaurants in Tel Aviv and Haifa where they were far less likely to be disrupted than in the West Bank.

Orange groves filled the flatlands to his left. Khalidi thought with pain how this had once *all* been his people's homeland. As the road climbed toward several Jewish farming kibbutzim and moshavim and the hills of the West Bank, it narrowed to one lane.

Bundy saw Tariq, dressed in working clothes and a keffiyeh, standing at a bus stop and he pulled the car over onto the dirt bank of the road just beyond.

Carrying workers clothes, a keffiyeh, and a lunchbox for Khalidi, Tariq leaned into the driver's window. "I see you have arrived safely," he said. He looked at Khalidi. "Welcome. Everything is on schedule. The workers' bus will arrive in twenty minutes. You will be in Tel Aviv within the hour."

At 7:05 a.m., the secretary of Kibbutz Dan, thin gray hair pinned behind her head, arrived at the Nahal base with the young American volunteer Robbie Cohen. Two soldiers escorted them toward the communications tent. Shai sat stooped forward just inside on a low, straw stool, devouring his fourth apple. Again, he worried that he was chasing a paper dragon here while Ramzy's men delivered Khalidi into the Jordan Valley for the more likely crossing across the muddy stream into the friendly West Bank.

"Excuse me, sir," one of the young soldiers said from outside the flap.

Shai's head came up. He saw the group waiting for him. In seconds he was up and outside, shaking hands with the young American, thanking the soldiers for their help and insisting they return to their duties. The American had not made eye contact when he shook hands and his grip had been weak.

The tall weeds bending in the warm breeze, Shai walked Robbie toward the periphery of the Nahal base, asking him what college he was from, if he was on the Kibbutz Ulpan studying Hebrew or primarily working.

"Oberlin. Ulpan," Robbie answered.

The green fields and fishponds of the Hula Valley sparkled before them.

"You know what happened here, I take it," Shai said. "You saw something that might help us?"

"I don't know if it'll help." The American looked at him and his face had gone even whiter and his voice shook as he spoke. "I should have told somebody, but Elana she's my girlfriend, sort of my girlfriend—anyway, she's into being private and she doesn't like anybody to know we're out together. It's a bit painful for me." He stopped, took a breath. "We were at Tel Dan. Elana was naked, standing in one of the streams, and I saw someone in the bushes watching her. I think he was an Arab."

"What time did you see him?"

"I'm not sure. About eight. It was just before sunset. I could still see him in the light. He looked wild. It freaked us and we left."

"Would you recognize this man if you saw him again?"

"I think so."

"This is a big help. Really. And very important. Come."

As Shai had hoped, the American's stride strengthened. The base was beginning to move at a faster clip. Torn tents were being taken down and replacements hammered into the hard earth, the sound of mallets against metal stakes rhythmic. Shai asked, "Did you see what kind of shoes he was wearing?"

"No. I'm really sorry, I didn't." As Shai led him across the small base to a tent, Robbie asked, "Do you think the man I saw killed the soldiers?"

"I think he did something. Let's see if we can figure out what."

Two soldiers stood guard outside. Shai lifted the tent flap. Robbie stepped in and Shai followed. The smell was already rough and Shai knew he would have to move the bodies soon. Shai went to one corpse and drew the blanket completely off him. The dead man lay on his back.

Robbie stared. The lines of his face and mouth tightened and he looked away quickly and staggered slightly. Then he came nearer, bent and looked again. He straightened. "It's him. He was wearing a T-shirt and shorts but I'm sure." He cried out miserably. "I'm sorry. God, I'm sorry."

"It would not have saved anyone here if you'd reported it," Shai said. "An Arab in a T-shirt inside Israel looking at a naked woman wouldn't have registered even a blip on the radar of what we're looking for." Shai put a hand on the American's shoulder. "But now that you've come forward and recognized him, you've lit up the whole screen for us."

As Robbie watched the man run awkwardly towards a tent with antennas around it, he thought, that he'd humiliated himself about enough with the blonde beauty. He'd end it tonight and then figure out whether he wanted to start writing or not, and get that book on urban planning he'd seen in the kibbutz library that greatly interested him.

Shai ordered Carmon called. The border patrol had spotted the glider descending around 3:30 a.m. and the entire area had gone on alert. Robbie had seen the dead terrorist before sunset, seven hours *before* the glider landed. It was a perfect smokescreen—two attack the base and two dead. Only the two who struck here were not the same two who flew into the country. Khalidi had come in on the glider, then the Palestinian already here, likely from the West Bank, had taken his place and, with the pilot, attacked the base. That's why only one set of flip-flop prints heading toward the glider. *Should have seen it earlier*, Shai thought angrily.

As he waited for the call to go through, he raced over the calculations. It should take a little under three hours from here to Tel Aviv if they drove directly. He had gotten the report almost an hour after the incident. From then until now maybe an hour and fifteen minutes had elapsed. It might have taken the two killers another twenty minutes to a half hour from the landing to walk to the Nahal Base—while Khalidi sped toward Jerusalem.

There were cursory road checks around Tel Aviv since the threat of the plutonium. Such checks were not unusual, and existed permanently at the western entrance to Jerusalem. They had already established roadblocks at the entrances from the West Bank. Less than three hours had elapsed since the glider touched down. They had a chance.

When Carmon came on the line, Shai said, "Khalidi's here. I'll explain later. He may have genuine West Bank papers. Stop all Arabs going into Tel Aviv. Get photographs circulated." He broke the connection before Carmon could demand answers. Ramzy would have Khalidi step into the dead man's life. Shai knew because that's how he would do it. Now he had to find out where this corpse had walked when upright.

With a keffiyeh covering most of his bearded face, a day laborer's lunch basket at his feet with a box of Farid cigarettes and crumpled East Jerusalem newspaper in it, Khalidi sat in the back of the Leyland diesel bus bound for Tel Aviv. Tariq was several rows in front of him. A tall, narrow building shot up facing the ocean from the desolate dunes, the descending letters MANDARIN HOTEL on its spine. Arab men in work clothes and keffiyehs half filled the torn, dirty seats. The muffler sputtered, and from the driver's radio came the voice of the famous Lebanese singer Fairuz, accompanying herself on the oud. The overhead racks brimmed with plastic baskets of onions, tomatoes and potatoes. Tulkarm and its surrounding villages were close enough to Tel Aviv that these men commuted to their jobs.

Tariq willed himself not to look at Khalidi. There was no telling who was on this bus and what they were watching for. He glanced at his watch. They would be safe inside Tel Aviv in another twenty minutes.

Khalidi leaned back, surprised at how comfortable he felt in this squalor. He and Ramzy had outwitted them. It was all perfect finally, everything. Except for Amal. He pictured that afternoon in his office when he made love to her standing, smashing his books, and felt exhilarated.

As the Arab bus neared Tel Aviv, the highway broadened into three lanes in each direction. Khalidi gazed at the ocean. It was such beautiful country, and in a few days his people would have a state, a start.

Tall, dirty, stucco apartment buildings with antennas loomed ahead on both sides of the highway. This must be the outskirts of Tel Aviv, he thought, and leaned forward. The traffic was bunching. A sign with an arrow to the left read Tel Aviv University and beyond it they were slowing, being motioned over by blue uniformed police officers at an Israeli roadblock. Yellow-plated cars continued unimpeded.

The bus pulled over and stopped, the old hydraulic doors front and back sighing open. The men were quiet, most looking away. Fear touched every part of him. Two Israeli policemen stepped into the bus from the front clutching small machine guns. Khalidi had the overwhelming urge to bolt for the back door as they walked through the bus toward him. Halfway down they stopped. Khalidi could not understand the conversation, as they spoke to the man in Hebrew. The young man beneath their gaze took out his orange-cased identification card. The policeman studied it for a long moment then handed it back. They continued questioning him. Khalidi looked down. The policemen continued down the aisle, nearing.

Fear was the only emotion he had ever known now. He could not remember back even five minutes ago to his total confidence. His mouth was dry, his legs trembling. He glanced quickly at Tariq, tried to decide if it was better to gaze down or if that would invite their attention.

The officers approached, stood over him, spoke to him in a Hebrew he did not understand. He quickly removed his identification and thrust it at them. Ramzy had arranged to have his head attached to Rida's genuine papers. One opened them, studied the photograph then his face. The other spoke in Hebrew again.

"I don't understand Hebrew," he said in Arabic.

The man switched easily into Arabic. "Where do you work?"

"A sofa factory."

"What are you doing on this bus if you live in the Dheisheh Camp?"

"By time I go from Dheisheh to Jerusalem to Tel Aviv I'm very late for work. I stay with cousins in Tulkarm."

The man handed him back his identification card. "Don't be so nervous. You come and work and nobody will bother you."

Khalidi took his papers and stared down. To his relief, he heard their footsteps exiting the back of the bus. He brought his head up. The doors banged closed, and with the grind of gears, the vehicle nosed back into traffic. They crossed a bridge over a river and suddenly were in the city, teeming already this early with cars and sleek, modern Mercedes buses. Large stuccoed apartment blocks were everywhere.

Khalidi leaned back, his shirt damp against the vinyl seat and sticking to it. Khalidi did not know it, but he had passed through the roadblock ten minutes before his description reached the checkpoint.

Concerned they would be too late at the roadblocks, Shai sat in the Nahal base communications tent, an idea working through his mind. The army officer was on the radio to Northern Command summoning a military investigating team now that Jerusalem seemed finished here.

"I would like the press brought in immediately," Shai said to the captain when he was off the radio.

The captain rose from his stool. "We've kept them away."

"Give them total access. Full photographs of the bodies. Is there someone who can take fingerprints right away?"

"The police in Kiryat Shmona would be the fastest."

"Have that done first. Then the press. When they're finished, have the bodies refrigerated and quietly brought to Jerusalem, Hadassah Ein Kerem. I'll arrange for them to be received. For the press, no mention of anyone from Jerusalem being here. This was a normal terrorist attack, the speculation Abdul Jabra's people because of the glider. Nothing out of the ordinary, just like it's happened a hundred times."

"All right."

Shai started to leave then turned. "What's the report on the wounded?"

"One died. It looks like the rest are going to make it."

"Good."

Shai went to call Carmon and brief him on his plan in the event Khalidi was already in Tel Aviv. He wanted no tightening of the roadblocks, no prohibition on workers leaving the Territories, no sign that they knew Khalidi had dropped in on the glider that would push them into changing plans. He sensed how he could find Khalidi.

"So your Ramzy figures we're going to shoot the terrorists' mouths shut," Carmon said to Shai as they waited in Carmon's office for a return call from the *Haaretz* editor. They had already secured cooperation from *Maariv, Yedioth Ahronot,* the *Jerusalem Post* and Israeli television. Carmon pulled on his cigarette. "I mean, they're sauntering right up to a heavily armed base. Who's going to survive that? And even if they're killed at the gate, so what? To us, it's just another bungled Palestinian operation, of which there's certainly no shortage of precedent."

Shai sat across from Carmon on the soft sofa. "The likelihood is that anyone attacking an army base and wanting to get killed could manage it."

"So who took his place? Given, there are probably thousands

in Judea and Samaria willing to die for the cause, not to mention the rabble in Gaza."

"In other words, a lot of Palestinians have lost hope."

Carmon drew hard and the Muratti burned bright. "Time. How much do we have?"

"I don't know," Shai said. "Not long. It depends on whether they have everything ready to assemble it. The physicists tell me Khalidi would not put the high explosive around the plutonium before they brought it here. Too dangerous. Unfortunately, high explosives are easy to obtain in the Middle East. He'll have to cast a precise mold for the HE, wait for it to harden, assemble the triggering device, whatever that is. It's not easy to do right, but he's eminently up to the task. We're talking maybe two days. Presumably we'll receive an ultimatum about withdrawal soon."

"I'm seeing the prime minister and inner cabinet in an hour." Carmon mashed his cigarette out. "They want to play rough, I'll show them rough. We evacuate Tel Aviv and bus in Palestinians from the Territories immediately."

Shai was silent for a long time, then he stood, went to the window and looked down at President's Park, where children were running through the pines. One might soon be his. He spoke without turning back. "It would take a day to evacuate the city. Look at the bottleneck we had with only a portion trying to flee the Scuds." He faced Carmon. "Even if we tried it in dead of night, they would see it, hear it. I don't know Khalidi would react. Don't know how much control Ramzy has from wherever he is. I'm afraid of what Khalidi might do if he woke up and found the city a quarter evacuated and cars moving. I'm worried about the same thing if we bring the army in, seal the city and start searching house to house."

"You said they need time to assemble it," Carmon bellowed.

Shai's voice rose like a trumpet challenging Carmon's percussion. "What if I'm wrong and it's assembled already? Or he can assemble it readily when he sees the evacuation? Amal told us he wants to trade for a state. I believe that's why Ramzy's backing this. That means negotiations. Time. I want to run it that way. Delay and find them."

"And give them a state if that's the only way? That it?" Carmon's voice had dropped into an icy monotone, which meant he was beyond routine fury.

"I want to find the bomb before it comes to that."

Carmon rose behind his desk. "Let me tell you this, Shai. Your Ramzy thinks we're controlled by the Americans, lots of them do, but we'll tell the Americans to go to hell too. Let's say we withdraw at this blackmail, temporarily. What's your Ramzy counting on, that once there's a Palestinian state we won't go back in? Because of the loss of lives, American pressure? I'll tell you what we do. As soon as we have the bomb, whether it's in two days or two months, we roll in with tanks. If they think they saw an iron-fisted policy before, they're going to think that was a birthday party in comparison."

Shai came back across the room and sank onto the sofa. In the uncomfortable silence, he said nothing.

"Say it," Carmon spit out. "What?"

"Ramzy would anticipate that response. He would not go to such great lengths without having a counter threat ready."

"So what's he going to do? Tell me."

The worry had been gnawing at Shai all along, under the surface like an underwater volcano. "There's the matter of their having enough plutonium for a second bomb."

"What's he going to do with it? Threaten to blow up Beverly Hills, Golders Green?"

"It's more than possible."

"Where's your Ramzy anyway? You're supposed to have him under a microscope, along with our new buddies in Damascus."

"He's not going to fly out of the airport."

The phone rang, loud in the gulf between them. Carmon snatched the receiver and dropped into his seat. From the conversation, Shai could tell it was *Haaretz*. What they had on their side was that Israeli newspapers always printed pictures of slain killers and television always broadcast shots of the event; to do so would not seem unusual. The editor was asking why they wanted him to run the close shots rather than a long view of their bullet-torn corpses. Carmon said the answer had to be held from the story. The editor agreed. Carmon told him they needed to identify the terrorists without it appearing so. The editor immediately agreed. Only the close up photographs had been released to the Arab press.

Every West Bank and Gaza informant, every soldier there, was being instructed to watch the cities, towns, villages and camps for signs of mourning, celebration of martyrdom, agitated talk—anything that might identify the dead man. When his picture was spread in newspapers and on both the Hebrew and Arabic nightly news programs, people where he lived, his family, would react. Normally the Israelis would not notice or pay attention to such mourning with the almost daily death toll among the Palestinians. Still, Shai knew in 1.7 million people the mourning would be difficult to spot.

Carmon hung up and reached for his cigarettes. The phone suddenly rang again. He grabbed it and waved Shai out of the office.

Shai began the next wait with his normal impatience. The fingerprint report came in and matched no arrest records. To everyone's surprise except Hirsh, who was equally elated, the news bolstered Shai and he clapped his hands loudly, handed hope that he was on the right track. He explained to perplexed colleagues that a sizable percentage of young male Palestinians between the ages of sixteen and thirty-five had been picked up at some time in the more than two decades of occupation, and someone so committed that he would volunteer to die *should* have a record. The fact he did not led Shai to believe Ramzy had purposely chosen him in order to put Khalidi in his place.

With rampaging energy, he arranged for the BBC to obtain video footage of the attack and sell it to Jordanian television to broadcast on their English and Arabic news broadcasts that evening, though he knew even without his intervention they probably would have received the tape almost as quickly. The West Bank and Jerusalem were well in reach of the nearby signal from Amman and all the cinderblock refugee camp huts sprouted television antennas.

Until after the evening news broadcasts, unless he got silly lucky it was too soon for there to be any word on the identity of the dead Palestinian. So, more than a few times Shai appeared at the door where Samuel monitored movement in Lebanon and liaised with the Syrians.

"Nothing new on Ramzy's whereabouts, now please get out," Samuel said when Shai ducked his head in again.

Shai smiled, and soon was as at the pool in Emek Refaim open to the public. He had not told Tami about the swimming, fearing that, like his walking, he could become busy and stop. He laughed at himself, not sure how he could be busier than he was now. He eased feet first into the deep end, not wanting to draw attention to himself with a mammoth splash. He started to butterfly across the cool water, choosing the tougher and more exhausting stroke. By time he grabbed onto the far edge he was panting so hard that a lifeguard came rushing over. Shai waved him away before he arrived. When his breathing finally slowed, standing in water that bobbed at his waist, Shai began to walk in his lane toward the deep end. When the water reached his neck, he turned and trudged back. To relax, he played a Keith Jarrett jazz piece in his head as if he was listening to it walking on the sidewalk. After his sixth makeshift lap, his breathing labored again, he climbed out of the pool by the steps and, shaking, grabbed onto the railing so he would not fall.

Back in his office, he acquiesced to the tiredness rolling over him and curled on the small couch. He fell asleep, jammed in the sofa, while he waited for word from the informants, the soldiers, from Samuel… from anyone.

In the Yemenite Quarter of south Tel Aviv, Khalidi meticulously washed the men's tin dishes and silverware in the stained sink that delivered only cold water. In the corner, a small black and white television the workers had purchased by pooling funds blared the last minutes of an Arabic-language melodrama before the Israeli programming returned to Hebrew and the news.

In the hall on the second floor of former living quarters turned into this manufacturing factory, the remaining seven men stretched out or sat on narrow cots topped with thin mattresses. The hall was divided by sheets of plywood scrawled over with obscene drawings, and the colorful call of the *intifada*. A single neon bulb dangling from the ceiling by a long cord pushed a ring of light out from the center of the room covering a small portion of its space before the darkness. The smells of sweat and the sea mixed with the odors of the onions and potatoes the men had cooked in a corner kitchen containing a single, rusted gas burner. Above the partitions, a long clothesline ran the length of the hall, with towels and torn underwear moving in the breeze that entered through the ocean facing windows.

Khalidi finished washing the dishes and, frustrated that he had no towel to dry them, wrung his hands on the floor. He stacked each wet dish in an exact pile by the utensils he had already lined up, forks together, then knives then spoons. Upset by the way they worked and lived here, they had not seemed to react or care when he volunteered to clean the kitchen. He turned. Cigarette butts glowed from the beds of most of the men. He stepped around empty soda bottles and other litter, too tired to pick them up now, and sat on his bed, the cot squeaking. Dust rose from the blanket and Khalidi stood up quickly to escape it. How could they make anyone live like this?

When Khalidi had arrived that morning—it was hours before the owner would turn up in his fancy car—the young, mustached Palestinian overseer who brought the workers from the Territories announced loudly that Khalidi was now to be known as the absent Marwan Rida and that their silence was as important as the stones of the uprising. Smiles had brightened faces.

Before dinner, in the midst of his numerous questions about their lives, an older man had kicked at his bed. "I go home to my village and my neighbor's son, a young hothead of eighteen, comes over and demands to know how long I'm going to keep working for the Jews. This kid dares say such things. If I don't work here, who's going to feed my children? This thug? I'll tell you what's happening here. I'm afraid of this kid because he may bring his friends, then they'll burn my house because I'm making these lousy sofas."

Khalidi looked at this man lying on his cot and emotion again choked his throat. A voice shouted out suddenly for everyone to watch the news, that it was important. Beds creaked as Khalidi joined the shuffle to the small set. The close shot showed two dead Palestinians lying face up inside a tent. Then the camera panned to dirt stained with the Israelis' blood and the announcer gave the names of the seven dead soldiers, showing small pictures of each in the right hand corner as the main picture panned the base.

Excitement leapt through Khalidi at this victory; the pilot had confessed his fear that he would die without killing any of the enemy. Then sadness flooded through him for the fighter who had died for him. Talking loudly, the men read the Arabic subtitles as the newscaster continued that the two terrorists, whose faces loomed large on the screen again, had flown into the country and landed in a glider. Khalidi relaxed with the report that they had descended from Lebanon. They would have no reason to search the West Bank for Marwan Rida's identity.

The report shifted to stone throwing and tear gas grenades launched by soldiers at boys in Hebron, causing their retreat. The men were excitedly discussing what to do to honor the martyr Rida's death when the overseer stood on the end of a bed and ordered the sound turned down on the television. When the men quieted, he told them there was nothing to honor, no memory. Marwan Rida was sitting among them this very moment. Two martyrs had flown down from Lebanon and had been killed by Israeli soldiers. Whether they understood or not, they nodded.

"We rise early," the overseer said, and stepped down from the iron frame.

The men dispersed and someone switched off the bulb. In the darkness, Khalidi picked his way between the bales of cloth and skeletal frames. As he moved toward the window, he heard the scurrying of rats' feet and his heart raced.

Through the dirty glass glittered the lights of Tel Aviv, where the Jews ate large meals and watched television on the sofas Palestinians made. Out of the darkness, steps approached. He turned and saw the overseer.

"You are safe," the overseer said. "The owner rarely comes up here, pays no attention to the workers, and would not recognize Rida."

A snore echoed through the room. "How many work, live like this?" he asked. He hurt everywhere in his body over this degradation, so familiar to him.

"Illegally and unregistered, inside the Green Line maybe a hundred thousand. It would take much time to search everywhere, even for them. And if they do, we will move you to a place already searched."

Khalidi turned back to the view. If they did not withdraw from the West Bank, he might just as well blow the bomb. The Palestinians would have no future and he would have no life. In a book on Jerusalem, he had read how in 1969 there had been a fire in the al-Aqsa Mosque, set by some deranged Australian. Arabs and Muslims all over the world immediately accused Israel. Wild crowds from Morocco to Pakistan marched and roared for *jihad.* And only the smaller of the two great mosques had been partially damaged. With Jerusalem and the Muslim holy sites turned into glass, the Muslims would overrun Israel and create a Palestinian state for those in the Beirut camps too.

In Independence Park in downtown Jerusalem, Tariq and Omar sent shovels silently through the soft dirt where Omar had buried the plutonium sphere five days earlier. In the quarter moon, they used no flashlights and dug quickly, the view to Agron Street blocked by the rose garden and trees. They could see the bell-crowned, square tower of the YMCA above the dark branches.

The tall, broad Omar lowered himself into the deep hole, dirt piled on one side. He reached through the cool earth with both hands, felt the lead dental aprons, and quickly began pushing the dirt away. He reached down again around the sides, grasped the bottom of the sphere, and with great effort lifted. First he felt resistance, then the sphere broke loose, dirt sliding into the impression and partially covering a dental apron that had fallen. Omar turned and handed the sphere up to Tariq, who carefully set it on the grass. Omar hoisted himself up from the hole like someone pushing out of a swimming pool. To his surprise, he felt sadness that it had come to this, all the attempts by both sides to forge a solution always ending in heart breaking disappointment, maybe for them too.

Suddenly, they saw a sweeping flashlight in the distance among the trees. Tariq lifted the sphere and shields and whispered to Omar to grab the shovels. They walked as quickly as Tariq could manage across the grass. Tariq looked back as he walked; the light still bobbed through the faraway trees.

Omar saw the American waiting beside a white Subaru, which was parked on Agron Street beside a small Citroen. Omar hurried ahead and set the shovels down quietly beside the Citroen. The American opened the trunk and Tariq lowered the sphere and lead aprons into the slatted wood crate in Bundy's Subaru. Without speaking, Bundy helped wedge the aprons around the sphere.

Bundy hopped in the car, his engine sounded in the quiet, and he drove away.

Sara and Hirsh sat in Sara's favorite spot in Jerusalem, the very small Uganda Bar in a quiet alleyway a few blocks off the downtown center. She was testing Hirsh, certain the venue was too avant-garde for him. A live performance of loud electronic music blared from the stage. Early on, she'd had enough of archaeological digs, excursions through the underground water tunnels, and other Biblical sites that had drawn her father to move them here. With the fountain pen he always carried, Hirsh drew a cartoon caricature on a napkin of Sara with large exaggerated eyes watching everything.

"Seems like the place to hang it," Hirsh said. "I can ask them."

"If we're going to do that, I'd like bigger breasts."

He began to draw them, and then said, "Prefer you the way you are."

"Bullshit." She grabbed the drawing and crumpled it but she mostly believed him.

In a city that both folded up and woke early, the Uganda opened at noon and closed at 3:00 a.m. The white wall behind the stage was covered with comic book figures in black line drawings and swatches of yellow. Coffee shop by day, bar by night, the two electronic music owners sold indie CDs and obscure comic books to Israeli hipsters. It was ironically named for the 1903 British proposal to set up the Jewish state in Uganda rather than here. Comics filled the shelves on one length; CDs sat on the opposite shelves.

One of the owners, Udi, came over balancing two beers, pita, a plate of hummus, and a comic book, the latter of which he set down beside Sara.

"The new *Wonder Woman* just came in for you," he said over the music. "Hide it before it ruins my reputation."

Sara laughed and looked at the cover. Wonder Woman was captured by a tree hovering in the night sky, its roots and bark binding her, and the title of the episode read: THE ROOT OF ALL EVIL. Sara loved the comic's long distance from reality and it disappeared in her purse. She turned to Hirsh. "I'm just your average girl dreaming of being a superhero. The hummus here is the best in the city, from a little restaurant across from Damascus Gate."

"We're the only Israelis who dare go there these days," Udi said. "I leave CDs as a tip."

"His car has comics inked all over it," Sara said. "All the young people in East Jerusalem know it. They adore him."

Hirsh laughed. "Fabulous." He had come to Israel alone from South Africa at seventeen and loved rebellion and ingenuity. After Udi ducked away, Hirsh said, "This place is great."

"Shit." Her elbows on the table, Sara rested her head in her hands. "I was hoping you'd hate it. I was going to send you home alone as punishment."

"Maybe next time you can come up with something better."

His confidence was making her silly crazy for him. "Don't think I can't," she said.

In the late-night darkness, led by Bedouin hashish smugglers, Ramzy rode a horse through the low Lebanese mountains into Syria. He would head overland to Turkey, where he had friends, and from there to Paris.

Ramzy turned in the saddle and stared south toward Israel, wondered where Shai was now, what he felt. Shai believed eventually there would be a solution, but Ramzy knew though the Israelis might even conceivably return the sparsely populated Golan Heights to Syria, which would only be a trade to hold onto the West Bank, the Syrians would drop the Palestinian cause like a hot ember as soon as they had their mountains back. Then, with peace made with Egypt and Syria and Iraq reduced to rubble, the Israelis would offer some local autonomy in the West Bank.

A horse snorted ahead of him and Ramzy shook himself from these thoughts. He wondered what Shai believed now, if he would come after him to try and kill him or send someone else. He hoped it would not be Shai but of course it would be.

Ramzy turned back in the saddle, kicked lightly at the flank and the horse cantered to catch up to the two Bedouin. If he failed, Ramzy worried about the future his people faced. He reached restlessly in his shirt for his cigarettes. He dropped the reins around the horn, cupped the flame with his hands and lit the cigarette. He inhaled the dry smoke.

Ramzy took up the reins and turned his thoughts to Khalidi in the sofa factory. He would convince Shai that the bomb was in Tel Aviv and divert him into expending their energies there, while Khalidi assembled the weapon in Jerusalem, where the threat to Israel was greatest. He galloped down a hill, the wind in his hair, loved riding had ironically learned it from a British girlfriend while at university in Manchester. Tearing through the countryside then and now at full gallop made him feel free, which his other mind knew was an utter illusion.

CHAPTER 14

July 3

The phone sounded in Shai's office and he snatched the receiver before the ring expired.

"Shai Shaham?" the voice asked in English with a heavy Arabic accent.

"Who is this?"

"In the park in Old Jaffa above St. Peter's Church there is a very large palm tree. Please dig at its base. It is in connection to the man you are searching for." The line went dead.

The small park on the hill overlooking the Jaffa harbor was quiet as Shai headed to the summit. There were too many pines and palms and the hill too sloping for the helicopter to land here, so they had set down on the beach nearby and an army jeep had whisked him to Old Jaffa. Shai hurried up the stone path to the small plaza atop the hill, sweating in the already hot, heavy morning, his feet hurting with each step. Rain Birds rotated over the grass, and above their sound rose a small tapping of chisel against stone from some unseen workman. A group of soldiers stood around the tall, aging palm ahead of him, their shovels relaxing on the white stone.

Shai arrived panting, identified himself, and a puzzled

lieutenant handed him a small segment of heavy greenish metal rounded like a piece of a globe. It had been surrounded by a leads surgical apron. That was all they had found. The earth around the palm was entirely torn up and the officer asked if they should widen the circumference or dig deeper. Shai whispered no, that they could go. The officer asked if he was certain and Shai nodded.

As they began to fill in their excavations, Shai looked at the view. To the north stretched the entire Tel Aviv coastline, a slight haze hanging over it. In his hand he held a segment of machined plutonium. Safe to handle, but with similar parts of the sphere in place it could destroy all this.

Shai sank down on a bench. Ramzy had sent him proof and a warning: the plutonium was in Tel Aviv, and all of this could be destroyed.

In the southern Jerusalem suburbs, Hal M. Bundy knocked on Reverend Wayne Littell's door. Littell quickly ushered Bundy inside and slammed the door, the sound echoing down the stone hallway.

"You weren't followed?" Littell said, his tongue anxiously sweeping his lips. He waddled into the living room with Bundy taking one stride to his every two. "I can't believe I'm doing this. Do you appreciate the risk, Hal? Do you? Do you know what I've done? Put Sally in danger, that's what. Sold my soul for thirty pieces of silver. I have half a mind to tell you to go away and then just tear your check into shreds, scatter it to the four winds."

"Let's have a cup of coffee," Bundy said, sitting on the sofa. Sun poured through the closed balcony door from the open hills stretching toward Bethlehem. "No sugar. Wouldn't mind some fresh fruit either. A plum, apple, whatever's handy."

Littell stared like someone about to stamp his foot, then turned and retreated into the kitchen. He came out shortly with a glass plate and two plums, the plate wet where the water dropped from the fruit.

"Good," Bundy said.

Littell banged the plate down on the coffee table and sank into the chair opposite Bundy. "The water's on."

Bundy lifted a plum and took a bite of the soft fruit. After a moment of chewing he asked, "Where's Sally?"

"I sent her away. Shopping, for what may be my last meal as a free man. I didn't want her to be a party to any of this. She doesn't know a thing about it, you hear me. She's put up with a lot being here all these years—ridicule, even threats. You think it's easy being at this outpost? To the television preachers in their three thousand seat cathedrals it's the Holy Land. Here, it's Israel. You try and bring in a tape recorder and you have to deal with their insane tax laws, not God's glory." He opened his mouth to continue but the kettle shrieked and he stood.

When Littell returned with a tray bearing two milky coffees in glass mugs and a plate of long butter cookies and napkins, Bundy was contentedly finishing the plum. Littell set the tray down on the small table in front of the sofa without his usual agility and the coffee sloshed into the saucers.

"Damn, just damn," Littell said. He collapsed into the seat, leaned forward and lifted the coffee with deft, fat fingers and set a napkin between each mug and flooded saucer. He took his own cup without the saucer. "What do you want the gun for anyway? Tell me that. I believe I have a right to know."

"It's to help the Palestinians gain a state. Is the gun here?"

"I said so on the phone that I have it, didn't I? What do you think I did, buried it under some rocks outside?" He sipped the hot coffee. "I don't know what I could possibly have been thinking when I agreed to this. I haven't slept a night through since it's been in this house. Every sound seems like footsteps on the landing. It's been a nightmare, I tell you." He put his coffee down, lifted a cookie and waved it in the air as he talked. "I'm too old for this kind of thing. Just because you don't show your age. Try living in this climate for seven years. See what that does to you." The long cookie disappeared into the tunnel of his mouth like a train, silencing it for the moment.

"How about if I just take the weapon off your hands."

Littell chewed quickly and swept his tongue across his lips to clean them. "No matter what, I'm going to know you have it. I'll know it."

Bundy was about at the end of his patience and his voice came out with quiet menace. "Forget I was here."

Littell bounded to his short height. "Don't say another syllable. Nothing, I tell you. This is my little patch. All I want is to farm it in peace. That's not too much to ask, is it? I think not."

He stormed toward the bedroom and came back with a gun wrapped in a plastic Hamashbir department store bag. While he was gone, Bundy had been writing another check. Littell thrust the gun out by the fingertips, as if it contaminated him less. Bundy offered the check as he took the gun. Littell released the weapon but did not take the oblation.

"This is not about money," Littell thundered.

Bundy set the gun down and, with a small smile, held the check as if to tear it.

"Don't." Littell dropped back into the chair and his hands flew into the air. "Leave it, on the coffee table. Just leave it. There are too many projects. Vital work."

Bundy set the check down, unwrapped the gun and great pleasure eased through him replacing the anger. It was a small Walther PPK/S with two magazines and a suppressor. He removed it from the plastic with reverence, the way others slid diamonds from velvet.

Bundy removed the magazine and tried the slide's action. It snapped back. "A lovely piece of weaponry. Where'd you lay your hands on it?"

Littell's cup was back in the saucer and another cookie dangled from his fingers. "I know people. They're grateful for the moments of peace I offer. There are rewards here. Great rewards." He dipped the cookie in the coffee, held it there.

Bundy replaced the gun in the plastic bag and rose. "Maybe it would be better if I left, before Sally returns."

Littell removed the cookie from the coffee and it fell apart beside the saucer. As he stood, he glanced over and tried to see the figure on the check on the table. He swallowed and walked Bundy to the door.

"My best regards to Sally," Bundy said.

"Yes, yes, of course. I'll tell her we had a wonderful chat. Look, Hal, I'm sorry if I'm a little nervous. It's just, well, you took me totally by surprise with all this. I want you to know I fully trust whatever it is you're doing has an important purpose. I know that in my heart."

Bundy extended his hand.

"Excuse me," Littell muttered and quickly brushed the cookie remains from his fingers off on his pants and shook Bundy's firm grip.

Outside, Bundy walked intently toward his car. *You fraud, Littell.* He hated Christians who could not make it in the world, who earned their salary off Christ's body. He drove down the broad, steep highway toward the main city. In the rocky, open field to his right children were flying remote airplanes. Farther on rose a small Arab village with a single stone minaret. Everybody was close together here in this small land, Bundy thought. On his side of the road, a boy and a girl were heading up the hill, the boy bouncing a ball.

Bundy watched two remote planes chasing each other, guided by this country's future pilots. A yellow plane looped around then burst up the side of the mountain, chased by a camouflaged painted fighter. As it should be, here soldiers were hailed as heroes. As a World War II hero, doors had flung open everywhere for his father's real estate business. He'd had to pull himself up by his bootstraps, hide his service in Vietnam, as people viewed those soldiers as incompetent and cruel. Anger rose through him and he squeezed his eyes shut for a moment to calm himself. That did not matter. He had proved how strong he was by defying the bottle and prospering. His father unfortunately had not lived to see what a success he'd become, but Bundy believed he was watching him now.

The boy alongside the road bounced his ball into a rock and it careened into the street. He dashed after it.

Bundy followed the dogfight up into the blue sky and then down perilously close over the field's boulders. He returned his eyes to the road and, horrified, saw the small boy running in front of his car. Bundy slammed the brakes, but he struck the boy with a loud thump and the car bounced as the front then rear tires ran over the body. Bundy slowed, glanced in the rearview mirror and saw the older girl bending toward the boy in the street. Farther down, a car was coming up the hill.

Bundy pressed on the gas and the Subaru sped ahead. If he remained, he would be detained and delayed. Who knew how far the inquiry might go. Bundy raced down the road. He had to hide the car, could not leave it at his hotel or abandon it on the street, as he had rented it in his own name.

Fortunately, he already had the perfect place to stash the Subaru. At the bottom of the road he turned left and, following the map on his seat, continued toward the western suburb of Ein Kerem, the birthplace of St. John the Baptist. Though the girl would be able to identify the make of car, it was virtually impossible that in her shock she had memorized the long license plate number. Even if she or the car coming down the roadway had noticed the green rental car border, there were hundreds, if not thousands, of white rental Subarus in the country. Because the major Japanese car manufacturers had buckled to the Arab boycott until very recently, every rental agency in every city had fleets of Subarus, for years the only Japanese car Israelis could purchase.

The road wound down into a beautiful terraced valley brimming with olive trees and vineyards. To the side ran the Ein Kerem spring. The turning to the left lead to the two-story Church of the Visitation, its belfry and colorful façade mosaic depicting St. Mary's visit from Nazareth to Ein Kerem. With great emotion, Bundy had already visited the grotto below the Franciscan Church, where John had been born.

He continued to a quiet street of individual old stone houses. Bundy pulled up in front of number 42. He stepped out, unlocked the two-car garage, opened it, then pulled the car in and closed the aluminum garage door behind him. He turned on the light and inspected the front of the Subaru. There was a dent and chipped paint where he had struck the boy. For a long moment he remained still to honor the boy's sacrifice for the cause.

He retrieved the gun from under the seat and climbed the stairs that led to the kitchen. Two days before, he had entered the Anglo-

Saxon Realty company, not far from the Jerusalem Plaza Hotel where he had been staying, and at Ramzy's instructions had rented this furnished house for six months.

He would shower, eat something, then take the bus to the center of the city and rent another car with the passport Ramzy had given him.

Shai stood in his office staring out the window, the tension so tight inside him he had fallen quiet and stopped roving the building. The plutonium was inside Tel Aviv, Khalidi hidden in the city, and Ramzy certainly out of Lebanon by now, if he had ever been there. He had made no movement toward his sister or wife. Nobody had yet identified the dead terrorist and he was beginning to fear he would not. Shai heard the small sounds of female steps coming through his open door and turned.

Sara's hair was pulled back in a ponytail, revealing more of her creamy-skinned, lightly freckled face. She was carrying a tray with a salad and a tall plastic bottle of water.

Shai tried unsuccessfully to suppress a smile. "What's that?" he asked, as she removed some empty coffee cups from his battlefield of a desk and set the tray down.

"It's a salad. I'm sure you've heard of it. It goes by another name too; it's called lunch."

"You must be mistaken. Lunch is meat, gravy, potatoes. Unless of course you're in America, when it's a hamburger, fries and a coke."

"You may recall that this is what you asked me to get you."

The smile still on his lips, he dropped into the chair.

"No progress on Khalidi or Ramzy?"

He shook his head.

She sat on the edge of the desk, tapped the floor repeatedly with her foot. "You going to ask about me and Hirsh?"

"No."

"Good." She started toward the door then turned back, ponytail flying. "Good as in, we're good. Thanks." And she was gone.

In police headquarters in the Russian compound, investigator Giora

Weizmann went to the door and took the chocolate bar with strawberry filling from the officer who had run down to the kiosk for it. Weizmann wore a small, knitted, black skullcap. The ten-year-old girl, Tali, sat across from his desk. The window was open and a fan turned overhead pushing the warm air at them. The walls were whitewashed and bare except for the Society for the Protection of Nature poster, still turned to February, and the large photograph of yellow broomrape plants.

Weizmann was methodical and behind in everything. It drove his wife mad that he carefully read his junk mail, especially since he always had so little time. Tali's cousin had been killed by a hit-and-run driver on the Gilo road and the policeman had asked her parents to let him talk to the girl while her memories were freshest. Tali had told Weizmann that her favorite candy was strawberry-filled chocolate.

Weizmann came across the room and handed the bar toward the girl. Weizmann had a slim featured face, a small body and a quiet, deliberate voice that rarely rose in pitch.

"I don't want it. I have too many butterflies in my stomach." She had stopped crying but her eyes were puffy and moist. "I'm so sad that my cousin died."

Weizmann sat across from the girl and placed the chocolate on the desk. Despite nearly three decades on the force, the hit-and-run of a seven-year-old still shook him.

After a moment he said, "Your parents are on their way. They said I could talk to you before they arrived, if that's all right with you. If you want we can wait."

"I saw everything that happened to Dov. His ball hit a rock. He ran after it in front of a car. The car killed him. I know what death is. My older brother was killed in Lebanon when I was five. I think of him when the ark's opened in synagogue."

The investigator nodded. "Did you by chance see what kind of car it was?"

"A Subaru 1600. It was white. It was a rented car."

"How do you know it was rented?"

Tali gave him a look. "It had green stripes around the yellow plate," she said impatiently.

"Was there the name of any rental company? On the back glass, the bumper, maybe the side doors?"

"No."

"Any logo? A smiling camel, an orange sun—"

"I said there was no name of the company," Tali interrupted.

Weizmann waited for a long moment. "Did you notice if the driver was a man or woman?"

"Man."

"Would you say it was a young or an older man?"

"I didn't see."

"Did you by chance notice his hair color?"

"I didn't see."

"Did you see if he had hair or was he bald?"

The girl shrugged.

Weizmann waited patiently and then asked, "Did he wear glasses?"

The girl tapped her foot against the desk.

The inspector gave a slow smile. "I gather you didn't see."

"I feel that God's my brother's friend and now he's going to be Dov's friend too," Tali said.

"I'm certain he will."

"Are you going to ask me about the license number?"

"Did you see the number?"

"I looked at the car as it drove away. One of the first numbers was seven. I'm sure. It's my favorite number."

"Did you see any more of the number?"

Tali shook her head no.

"Was it the first spot? Second? Or would you say it was the third?"

"Second or third. Not first but near the front. For sure."

Weizmann edged the chair back, rose and approached the girl. "May I ask if you're positive you saw it? It's your favorite number. Maybe you see it in a lot of places? Do you like to look at sevens?"

"I like to look at song contests on TV. I saw a seven."

The inspector filled with hope. This might considerably narrow the search. “Did you see anything else that I neglected in my ignorance to ask?”

“No, I would have told you.”

The inspector smiled. “Tali, thank you. I’ll check if your parents have arrived yet. Will you be all right here alone for a few moments?”

She bobbed her head in a nod. “Of course.”

Just then there was a knock at the door and Weizmann crossed the room and opened it to the parents. As they called out to Tali, the girl bolted off the chair, ran to them crying and wrapped her arms around her mother, who had tears in her eyes.

The inspector told the parents they could take Tali home and he headed into the corridor, puzzled about the hit-and-run. The boy chased the ball into the road in front of the car. The skid marks had showed the Subaru had not been speeding. It had clearly not been the driver’s fault. So why not stop? People who did not want to be questioned about one matter usually were evading another. He would put extra officers on this, start checking the car rental agencies in Jerusalem. If that did not pan out, he would broaden the search. He wanted to know who had bolted from the scene and why.

A possible lead to the identification of the terrorist killed at the Nahal base reached Shai a little after 9:00 p.m. An hour and a half later, in the small Ammunition Hill park in the north of Jerusalem, Shai waited with several armed soldiers and a man named Bishara Hazouri, released recently from Jneid Prison and still in inmates garb. Under the cover of darkness, a man from Nablus with a copy of *Al Fajr* under his arm with the front page photos of those slain in the north, had furtively approached a patrolling soldier. He identified himself as Mohammad Hazouri and claimed to have information about one of the men pictured in the newspaper that would certainly interest the security services. He wanted his brother, Bishara, released in exchange. Bishara Hazouri, Shai quickly learned, was serving the first of three years for stringing nylon wire across the alleys of the Balata Refugee Camp near Nablus at the neck height of soldiers speeding in open jeeps. Shai empathized with the despair of living in those camps, and in their shoes he too would take extreme measures. They waited now for Mohammad, who had refused to talk further until he saw his brother. sss

As the half dozen soldiers guarded the unshackled Bishara, Shai paced alone through the darkness of the former main Jordanian outpost on the Jerusalem front. Shai had chosen Ammunition Hill, a short walk from where the Nablus Road entered Jerusalem, as it was located so close to East Jerusalem. He gazed down the hill. Tall Israeli apartment buildings lined the far side of the broad, grass-divided Eshkol Boulevard. It was hard to remember that this had all been an uninhabited part of Jordan before 1967, and that for nineteen years their only access to the cut off Hadassah hospital and the Hebrew University just up the hill on Mount Scopus was a UN convoy every two weeks.

In the cool, moonlit darkness, Shai walked along the concrete trenches still preserved in the grass. He felt the deaths of Jordan's boys here almost as deeply as the loss of theirs. A soldier trotted near and told him that Mohammad had arrived on foot. When Shai returned to where the small group was clustered in the dark under the trees, the two brothers were hugging, the recent arrival in work clothes with a Detroit Tigers baseball cap. Shai waited a moment then interrupted in Arabic.

"Mohammad, you have something for us?"

The brothers broke the embrace and the baseball cap turned toward him. "How do I know that if I tell you what I know you won't take Bishara back to prison and maybe throw me in too?"

"Both of you will be free to go as soon as I have the information. If what you say proves true, the current conviction against Bishara will be misplaced. If the information is a trick, the security services will come after both of you. You will be arrested." He looked at Bishara. "This is a one-time pass. You string fish wire again or anything like it, we arrest you and the old conviction reappears too."

"I had a girlfriend once in the Dheisheh Camp," Mohammad said. "Her brother had a friend in the camp who sometimes visited after the meal. I no longer go there, have not seen or heard of him for almost six months. Until today. He is the one in the photographs who attacked your base and killed the soldiers. He is not part of Abdul Jabra's group.

I know him."

"His name?"

"Marwan Rida."

"And he lives in Dheisheh?"

"Yes."

"Does he work in Tel Aviv?"

"I think so. He only came home occasionally. I don't know anything. No one talks now about those who work in Tel Aviv."

Shai removed a newspaper clipping from his front pocket, unfolded it in front of Mohammad. Once of the soldiers lit a match and held it near the paper for the Palestinian.

"Which is Rida?" Shai asked.

The circle of light danced across the pictures. Mohammad immediately pointed to the photograph of the man Robbie Cohen had seen in Tel Dan. A quiet excitement spread through Shai.

"Let them go."

Mohammad moved quickly toward Shai. The soldiers tensed their grips on their weapons, lifted them. Mohammad said, "The fish wire, you have to understand what's it like in the camps, we feel so abandoned. Helpless."

Shai did something then that surprised the soldiers. He reached out his hand, clasped Mohammad's in a handshake. "You are safe," he said.

The Palestinian grabbed his brother's arm and both ran down the grass toward the brightly lit boulevard as a large red and yellow bus labored up the hill toward Mount Scopus. By foot, the brothers could be in the West Bank in ten minutes.

Shai almost allowed himself some excitement that he was closing in.

In the sofa factor, Khalidi lay exhausted in Marwan Rida's cot after the long day cutting fabric. The television was off. Men smoked tiredly in their beds while others already snored. He had learned that the men made the journey to their faraway villages and refugee camps about once every two weeks. His eyes closed and he felt himself almost melting into the mattress. Rats scraped in the corner. His eyes flew open. It was just until tomorrow. He would be in Jerusalem tomorrow afternoon. He thought with pleasure at the brilliance of Ramzy's move bringing him here first, which would never have occurred to him.

Despite the warmth, for protection against the rats Khalidi drew the thin blanket over himself, cringing as dust lifted into the air. He had lain awake far into the night last night. The exhaustion, the anticipation of tomorrow sapped him. Finally, he fell asleep.

Shai stood in the cold, damp night along the main highway just beyond Bethlehem. Across the road stretched the Dheisheh Refugee Camp. A tent encampment erected in 1949 to temporarily house three thousand Palestinians who had fled villages around Jerusalem and Hebron during the 1948 War, with natural population growth Deheisheh's population had swollen to fourteen thousand. The one-story cinderblock houses, topped by corrugated iron roofs, sprouted concrete growths of kitchens, outhouses, niches, all with rusty iron beams and pipes visible. Since the last time Shai had traveled this main road, a twenty-foot-high chain-link fence had been thrown up around the camp to prevent the rock, bottle and Molotov cocktail toting children from hurling their rebellion at passing cars. This late, only a few lights shined from the low windows.

A dozen soldiers carrying a combination of M16s and Uzis, some with radio sets strapped to their backs, gathered on this side of the empty highway. Shai knew how most of them felt; this was distasteful work and all they wanted was to burst in and clear out without incident. Most spoke little about their service here to family or friends. The price on the psyches of their boys was high and Shai knew this needed to be discussed.

A young helmeted lieutenant separated himself from his men and approached Shai. "Whenever you're ready."

"Let's go," Shai said.

The army had long ago sealed the entrance to the camp with tall concrete-filled barrels. More chain-link fence, set in the concrete, towered from their tops. Single file they squeezed through the space between the end barrel and the stone building, where additional soldiers squatted permanently on the roof.

Inside, on the relatively wide main road, they walked through the dirt and immediately separated into two columns, one heading up each side of the road. Steps sounded in the quiet. A cold slice of moon shone on the camp. Everywhere Arabic protest had risen in large colored letters across the buildings, then was painted over.

The lieutenant walked beside Shai in the center of a column. The silent men were tense. A flaming bottle might fly at them from any corner. Dirt lanes wove between the houses in all directions off the wider, hilly road they followed. The men knew their way from a myriad of patrols. Everywhere they passed doors and window frames on the low cinderblock houses painted blue to scare off the "evil eye." Houses were crammed one against the other, one atop of the next, sharing walls. Shai had never been to Dheisheh before. Shai knew that few Israelis saw these places, the news never broadcast them—for his people, out of sight, out of mind.

As they approached a concrete wall to their left whose center has been smashed down as if by a giant karate chop, the lieutenant spoke a quick order to his men and they merged into a single line and ducked through the wall. Shai surmised it had been opened by soldiers for general access. Shai stepped over the chunks of cinderblock into a small garden with a low concrete block fence, his feet hurting less he thought. Soldiers' flashlights danced through the dark. Several huts faced the garden. Clotheslines ran from a tall tree to the house; a large aluminum jar filled with well water stood atop a rusting steel table; a blanket hung over an opening to the toilet.

The soldiers stepped between mud puddles and concrete blocks. The lieutenant touched Shai's shoulder and pointed with his rifle toward a stucco hut jutting like a tumor from a larger, concrete-block house. He whispered, "There."

The lieutenant called out an order. Four men quickly surrounded the house. Three others, including the lieutenant, burst through the unlocked door, Uzis extended, and shouted orders. Two soldiers pulled themselves onto the roof, banging the corrugated iron noisily with their boots. Alone in the garden, his mouth dry, through the window Shai watched the darting flashlights. He went to the door and looked in.

A middle-aged man and woman and about eight or nine children all sat up and squinted in the bright beams, the younger children wailing. Several pulled scratchy, wool blankets around themselves in the damp cold. The thin mattresses completely filled the floor of the single room and the soldiers had nowhere to walk except on the blankets and mattresses, the mud coming off everywhere. Flashlight beams swung as they moved. Shai saw the typical 2x2 inch pictures of dead or imprisoned sons or relatives nailed to the wall in frames fashioned from red-tipped matches. Above the photos on the peeling wall defiantly hung a basket woven from the red, green, black and white colors of the outlawed Palestinian flag. The soldiers on the roof suddenly stopped pounding and the children's crying reverberated in the small space. In the middle of the wall, Shai saw what he was looking for—a mother-of-pearl picture frame with a photo surrounded by fresh flowers.

Shai wiped his feet as best he could on the edges of a concrete block and walked into the odor of so many people in such close quarters. He took a flashlight from a soldier, went to the flower-surrounded picture frame and examined the photo of Marwan Rida.

"Take the parents," Shai told the lieutenant.

The lieutenant gave the order in Hebrew, and in Arabic another soldier told the couple standing in the corner to step outside. Shai watched them. The woman, who had been sleeping in long underclothes, glared at Shai with a cold hatred that penetrated. She reached toward a nail on the wall for a long, black Arab dress, and as she pulled it on with one hand he realized her other hand was paralyzed. He hoped it had not been from a soldier's baton. She then drew a large black scarf from an unseen pocket and secured it around her hair and chin.

The man had been sleeping in his work clothes, as if ready to rise at any time and go wherever he was told. He slipped on sandals and shuffled silently toward the door. In Palestinian culture, only the women and girls donned mourning clothes, and they would wear black for the initial forty-day mourning period, or an entire year depending on the intensity of their grief. His wife ignored the soldiers, stepped across the room to the eldest daughter, maybe seventeen, seated cross-legged and comforting a screaming boy in her arms, and loudly told her to watch over the family until victory came. What saddened Shai was that she believed it would come. He was aware of his self-delusions which included a good deal of self-righteousness.

As they exited the hut, Palestinians peered from the windows of adjoining houses. Single file again, with the couple at the point, the soldiers started on a different and apparently longer route that curved down toward the highway instead of back up through the garden. Soon, the children's crying grew fainter behind them, replaced by the sounds of boots. None of the young soldiers spoke; fingers on triggers, eyes pierced the night.

They turned left into a wider road and the soldiers automatically separated into two columns and continued up both sides. Fresh, unpainted concrete block construction rose everywhere here.

As they squeezed through the space between the barrels and the house at the blocked entrance, Shai looked back at Dheisheh with heaviness, then walked slowly toward the soldier who was ordering the Palestinian couple into the first of their three jeeps.

"Have them driven to Hadassah Hospital, Ein Kerem," Shai said. "I'll meet them there."

Approaching the large hospital, which rose from a mountain height in the valley below the chimney-like sculpture of the Holocaust Memorial, Shai instructed his jeep driver down a one-lane incline to the left of the main hospital. The jeep with Rida's parents followed. A corridor entrance stood at the end of the basement-level parking lot and cars could drive in here to retrieve bodies for burial. Shai instructed his driver to park there, where a night shift maintenance man was already waiting for them. Shai went to talk to him as the soldiers brought Rida's parents.

Shai stepped into a corridor with large pipes running the length of the open ceiling. Generators reverberated nearby and an antiseptic smell struck him. The dairy cafeteria up ahead doubled as a massive bomb shelter, with huge rubber-edged metal doors. Shai followed the maintenance man a short distance along cracked and broken floor stones to the morgue. He opened the door and Shai stepped into a small vestibule with drains in the red tile floor. Two large, silver refrigerators hummed. The maintenance man opened the left one. Shai entered the cold walk-in refrigerator. Metal shelves lined the walls, the smell damp decay. One side was empty, the other contained only two bodies.

Shai came back to the tile vestibule, closed the refrigerator door behind him and told the maintenance man to go, that he would lock up when he was finished. Outside, Shai motioned the Arab couple into the vestibule. He offered no explanation and they came forward without one. Shai could see in the woman's narrowed eyes beneath her black scarf that she knew. The woman stood in the middle of the tile floor directly over a drain. A half step behind her, her husband fingered a strand of green worry beads that clicked softly at his flip. His eyes bore a tired blankness.

Shai opened the refrigerator door wide. Cold poured out. The lower corpse's skin was ashen gray, the edges of the bullet holes across the body black-purple, the lips white. A tag hung from his wrist.

"Please look at the body," Shai said.

The woman came near while the man held his place, eyes down. As the woman entered, the man's head rose from the floor.

Shai watched the expression on the woman's face, saw the slackening of the strength, the flash of pain in the brown eyes before they hardened again. Shai saw the tears roll down the man's face and an animal wail tore from his mouth, even louder in the small room. "Marwan." He ran into the large refrigerator, grabbed the cold body and held it to his.

Shai pictured the covered bodies of the Israeli dead in the Nahal camp and everybody's pain entered him and he felt like he was swelling. So much stupidity and stubbornness everywhere here. He went into the corridor and told the soldiers to take the woman, hold her outside. As one of the soldiers put a hand on the woman's arm, she drew it away. She offered no resistance or words as they lead her out. The soldiers closed the door behind them.

Inside the refrigerator, the man fell to his knees beside the open shelf, tears streaming down his face. He touched the cold face of his son with an outstretched hand, then ran a finger along the many bullet holes, sobbing louder.

"How long since you saw him?" Shai asked.

The man said nothing.

"How long?" Shai said, approaching him.

"Ten days," the man whispered.

"He worked in Tel Aviv?"

His worry beads clattered to the ground and he gave a quick nod.

Shai stood over him. "Where did he work?"

"You killed his two older brothers. Now you've killed him," he said. "Who is next? Which of my children is next?"

"Where in Tel Aviv did he work?" Shai asked.

The man bent over the body, kissed his dead son on the lips.

Shai squatted in the cold, the smell of the unwashed father mixing with the chemical preservative on the corpse. "Where in Tel Aviv did your son work?"

The father was arranging the son's hair. "In a factory."

Gently. "Do you know where in Tel Aviv it is?"

The man wiped the tears from his face with the back on his sleeve, shook his head no.

"Do you know what kind of factory it is?"

"He made sofas."

"What kind of building did he work in?"

"I don't know. We never went there. It was a building."

"Did he work in the basement? High up?"

"Up. He talked of a view of the ocean."

"Did he make anything besides sofas?"

"I don't know. He made sofas."

"Did you have a way to reach him there?"

"No. He came home, to the family. He was a wonderful boy.

He brought money. He came home, always."

"He must have said something about the area where he worked."

The man reached down, retrieved his strand of beads, stared at them.

"I'd like to release your son to you, let you bury him with honor in your family plot. But first I have to know the area where Marwan worked and then I must confirm the information. Then you will have the body. Until then, Marwan will remain here, naked, as the doctors, the female medical students, come in and out of this room. After what he's done, I will have to ask for special permission to return Marwan to you. Without your help, I'm not sure I will be allowed to let you have the body at all."

The man buried his head in his dead son's cold flesh and wept. "The Yemenite Quarter," he said between gasps. "He said the Sephardis were the worst bosses. He worked there. For the Yemenites."

Shai rose, softly helped the father up with vast compassion for his loss, and led him toward the corridor. The Yemenite Quarter had three to four thousand people. It would not be difficult; he would have the address within the hour.

Waiting for the anti-terror unit van a little after 3:00 a.m., Shai sat in an unmarked police Opel Kadett at the corner of Hakovshim Street two blocks from the ocean. Tired, he leaned his head back against the seat. A half block ahead of him, the narrow Yishkon Street ran in one direction inland. The internal service had quickly learned the only sofa factory in the Yemenite Quarter was situated in a rundown two-story building with an inside courtyard. The owner, woken by phone, admitted that he housed illegal Arab workers, but he did not know if he employed a Marwan Rida. He paid them cash and kept no records. He had been there earlier in the day, seen all eight workers, but could not identify a photograph of Khalidi. The overseer brought different workers and how did they expect him to possibly know them all? He sketched a floor plan for them.

Shai saw a closed van with the gas company logo pulling up

behind him. The army van passed him and quietly turned into Yishkon Street. A second team in the back would be waiting to bound up neighboring roofs should sharpshooters be required to fire through the windows. They were not yet in place for fear of being seen.

Shai stepped out of the car and walked slowly toward the corner. Hunks of stucco had fallen from the building, revealing the stone blocks beneath. Window shutters were faded and peeling and there was the scent of raw meat from some unseen butcher shop. The Yemenite Quarter was a square mile of crushed, narrow, one-way lanes with two- and three-story buildings. Cafes, restaurants and stores often occupied ground floors, with residences and the ubiquitous laundry hanging from balconies. Power lines were bootlegged from poles and crisscrossed everywhere.

Shai stopped at the corner and, hiding his bulk against the stone, peered around it. In front of the building someone had cut metal solar canisters lengthwise, set them along the slim sidewalk and planted flowers in them. He watched the assault unit of six men spray oil onto the door's hinges, silently open it with the key the owner provided and enter the courtyard, followed by a second unit to cover the lower floor. Shai followed them.

He eased through the open door into the courtyard. Soldiers were just reaching the top of the stairs. The second team waited silently by a door to the lower floor below the outside stone steps. A cat hissed. The lower team would go at the sound of the upper team's assault. At the top door, a soldier carried a sledgehammer in case a new lock had been installed that the owner had missed.

Shai remained still, not trusting that he could mount the stairs quietly. An acid taste came up from his stomach. Then the team burst in, the second team was through the lower door, and Shai was racing up the stone steps with all his strength, panting, his chest tight, waiting for the sound of shooting, waiting for a much more massive sound and flash.

He heard the Israelis shouting in Arabic. Shai pulled himself up by the broken railing and burst inside the top floor.

Soldiers stood throughout the sleeping quarters, rifles

extended, a single bulb hanging from the ceiling lit, as the Arabs sat in their beds, hands atop their heads. With beams of light, several soldiers searched through a corner shower as well as a kitchen at the opposite end of the large room. Two swept their lights under each cot, while others shoved aside sofa skeletons. Shai approached and scanned the room with his eyes, and then with fear he saw it—one of the beds was empty.

"Line them up against the wall," Shai said, a rivulet of sweat dropping down his back in the humid night.

The officer shouted the order in Arabic and the men climbed off the squeaking cots. The officer ordered them to keep their hands on their heads and several jerked them back there.

The men moved to the far wall and Shai counted them—seven. He walked to a young soldier, took the flashlight from his hand, approached the line of men and studied each face, disappointment dropping through him like a physical despair. The officer spoke in his walkie-talkie to confirm the lower floor had been secured. The men blinked and turned their gaze as Shai beamed the flashlight in face after face.

"We'll search the rest of the area," the captain said to Shai. "What do you want done with these?"

"Hold them here for the moment."

Shai watched the soldiers search but he knew he was too late. He headed down the stairs, the tiredness going through him with each step. Shai knew Khalidi was not in the building and the search downstairs and through the courtyard confirmed his suspicions. Shai ordered the Palestinians driven to the nearby Defense Ministry compound for questioning and fiercely kicked at a soda can in the courtyard, sending it clattering against the stone. It was almost like Ramzy was toying with him.

Shai left the Defense Ministry to helicopter back to Jerusalem like an aging athlete—shuffling tired feet, his lower back in pain, and remembering when he could run forever without feeling an ache. A team of army interrogators had hammered at each of the men individually and produced the same story, with enough variations to suggest it was not rehearsed. A little over an hour before the soldiers had arrived, a young boy none of them had seen before had hammered at the downstairs door, shouted up and finally succeeded in rousing them. He asked for Marwan Rida and the "new Marwan" followed him downstairs and did not return. They heard a car engine start up around the corner, and from their descriptions the location seemed very close to where Shai himself had waited for the army assault. Everyone in the neighborhood had been woken by the police and questioned and there had been one suspicious sighting: a fat man hiding around the corner of Hakovshim and Yishkon Streets. The concerned citizen even produced the full license plate number of the Opel Kadett police vehicle Shai had been in.

Shai had questioned the Arab overseer personally and eventually rung from him that late one night when home in el-Bireh—essentially a suburb of Ramallah some fifteen kilometers north of Jerusalem—two young men with red keffiyehs wrapped around their faces approached him "in the name of the people" and said that someone important was coming to replace Marwan Rida early in July and the switch had to be kept secret. He had no idea who they were.

Some sixth sense told Shai the overseer was telling the truth, but he still ordered a sodium pentothal derivative. This was no time to trust instincts, despite his superlative track record in that area—until recently. If they could learn who had approached the overseer they would be at the end of another branch of the trail.

Shai suspected now that somebody had been watching Rida's hut in the Dheisheh camp, observed the army burst in, and alerted confederates in Tel Aviv. That's why the escape a mere hour before. No coincidences. Khalidi probably had been taken now to wherever in Tel Aviv they would assemble the bomb. *Stupid. How stupid can I get?* Shai berated himself as he climbed into the helicopter exhausted and mumbling. For about the hundredth time since Khalidi had escaped the sofa factory, he wondered why he had not considered something that obvious. He should have seen it right there in front of his nose. He could have lured Rida's father somewhere out of the camp without suspicion with about a thousand excuses. Maybe. For the father leaving in the dead of night would have been suspicious despite the reason. Still, Shai felt he should have managed it.

So why had Ramzy put Khalidi in a sofa factory in the first place? Shai wondered as he closed the helicopter door. He wouldn't assemble the bomb there with so many people around. What was Ramzy up to? Why not just take him directly to where he would build it? This didn't make sense. Come on, come on. This was Ramzy. There had to be a reason.

Maybe the place they were to assemble it was not ready yet. But why would the place they were to assemble the bomb not be ready?

The helicopter lifted into the darkness and cleared the satellite dish-crowned Defense Ministry in the center of Tel Aviv, with its silly signs in Hebrew, English and French prohibiting photography all over the fences. Might as well hang out banners and invite people to take pictures.

He had no leads, nothing.

His eyes closed and the tiredness slid over him, squashing him. He forced his eyes open, could not allow himself to sleep now. A yellow-white dawn was beginning to brighten the sky beyond the pine-dotted mountains. He had to figure out what to do, where to search, what Ramzy was up to with the sofa factory. *Ramzy, why this bomb?* he implored silently across the abyss between them. He began to drift. With the beating of the rotors, Shai slumped forward against the shoulder belt and his snore was like a scream.

Earlier that night, after receiving the call from Dheisheh about the soldiers bursting in, exactly as Shai had surmised, Tariq had summoned a young boy and sent him for Khalidi. Then they had driven from the Yemenite Quarter and out of Tel Aviv entirely. As had been anticipated and then confirmed, the roadblocks were examining cars entering but not exiting the city.

In Tulkarm, some thirty kilometers north and slightly east of Tel Aviv in the low foothills of the West Bank, Khalidi worked with Tariq's uncle, Abu Faris, in his auto mechanic's garage. The weak bulbs illuminated the interior in small patches of light. They were constructing the lead neutron "gun" to aim the Californium-252 into the plutonium. The muscular, round faced Omar sat on a pile of worn tires in the dark corner, fear running through him at the enormity of all this. Tools were scattered on a wood shelf that ran the length of the garage. Tariq had taken the Chevrolet Impala with yellow plates Abu Faris had borrowed from a friend just across the Green Line in Taybeh and gone to meet Bundy on the main road to Netanya. Bundy would never find his way through the maze of streets.

Unlike the inland nationalist hotbed of Nablus, at the outbreak of the *intifada* the Israelis had expected Tulkarm to be a "cool" area. Its residents had regularly descended to the beach at Netanya and worked the short distance inside the Green Line, and Israelis had crowded the Tulkarm marketplace on the Jewish Sabbath. Both camp and town had wrested themselves free from more than twenty years of the status quo and erupted.

Khalidi stood with Abu Faris over the tool bench working with two blocks of lead. In his fifties, Abu Faris's eyes were closely set together and seemed small through heavy rimmed, thick glasses. They drilled a hole in a block of lead to fit a cartridge and screwed another block of lead behind it to prevent the cartridge from accelerating backward. With a whirring drill, Abu Faris pushed a thin hole in the rear block for the optical fiber to pass through. The Californium-252 would fit easily into the ordinary 9 mm cartridge Abu Faris had provided. Khalidi was proud of the simplicity and ingenuity of his design. The lead would serve also to shield the Californium-252 buried in it and keep the neutrons from floating around and hitting the plutonium before the cartridge was fired. To create the nuclear explosion, the neutron-loaded cartridge had to be triggered and the Californium-252 "bullet" smashed into the plutonium exactly ten microseconds after the plutonium imploded.

The sound of a car approaching was loud in the quiet. It stopped outside. Abu Faris walked toward the grate. He pulled a rope cord hand over hand and with the scraping of metal the door lifted. Headlights glared through the opening, blinding them, and when the door was high enough a car drove in then cut its lights. Abu Faris lowered the door.

Hal Bundy stepped out of the Impala's passenger seat as Tariq exited the driver's side.

Bundy was smiling. "Clean as a baby's bottom around the Jerusalem house. Should be smooth sailing."

"Then let's go," Khalidi said. He picked up the lead block "gun" and headed toward the car.

"Let me just have a stretch here." Bundy raised both hands high over his head and then arced fluidly forward until his fingertips touched the ground before his toes. He rose up again and repeated the motion. Khalidi was standing by the Impala, hand tightly gripping the door. Bundy approached. "Come, let's have a look at the work. The roads will be just as clear in five minutes."

Khalidi reluctantly thrust the heavy lead blocks at him.

Bundy took them and gave a low whistle. "A beaut." He inspected the drilling, tested where the cartridge sat snugly in the front block. He looked at Abu Faris and pointed a finger. "You come America, work for me. Excellent job."

Tariq translated and a grin came over Abu Faris's face.

"I suggest that we go," Khalidi said.

"Sure." But instead of heading for the Impala, Bundy brought the lead blocks to the work shelf, found pliers and carefully edged the cartridge out. Then he headed back to the Impala with the "gun" and handed the cartridge to Khalidi. "Just in case I'm stopped. I can talk my way out of quite a lot, but that would be a might much."

Khalidi saw that he was right and nodded. Tariq opened the trunk and Bundy set the blocks inside. Khalidi climbed into the front seat. Across the garage, Omar was reaching between the tires and pulling out two AK-47s smuggled in eons ago from Jordan. As they all climbed into the Impala, Omar secreted the weapons under the front seat. If they were stopped, they would open fire.

The Impala headed out. Tariq knew the location of the Jerusalem house, had already delivered to Bundy the sacks of explosive and the steel molds Bundy had machined in San Francisco and transferred to Ramzy in Copenhagen. The molds looked like two bowls and had been smuggled in with the explosive from Jordan across the Allenby Bridge with a shipment of kitchenware. Sugar had been mixed with the powdered high explosive, which actually would enhance the explosion, and the sacks labeled as CONFECTIONER'S SUGAR. The explosive would be sweet to any potential taste at the bridge.

Outside Netanya, they pulled over beside Bundy's burgundy Peugeot 505 and transferred the lead blocks to it, along with Bundy and Khalidi. There were never any checkpoints on the highway to Jerusalem, and as they drove through the night none had been erected in the emergency, believed to threaten Tel Aviv. Before the last climb to the crest of the city, where the police permanently sat, both cars pulled off the road. Omar hid the guns beneath pine needles in the forest of young trees where the weapons could be retrieved if needed. While Bundy and Tariq drove on at a distance from each other, Omar led Khalidi by foot over the hills toward the city.

A little over an hour later, Tariq retrieved Omar and Khalidi, who were waiting among the trees of the cemetery on Mount HaMenuchot inside Jerusalem's western suburbs. Omar was surprised but pleased at what good shape Khalidi was in and they had arrived earlier than expected. In the darkness, they drove to the rented two-story house in Ein Kerem. The yellow-plated Impala would cause no notice overnight and Tariq would return it in the morning.

Khalidi, Omar and Tariq approached the front door and Khalidi knocked. Bundy let them in and clapped Khalidi on the back. Inside, Khalidi smiled. Finally here, he was eager to begin assembling the bomb.

In Paris, from a cellular car phone driving through the fourteenth arrondissement so the location of the call could not be directionally traced to where he was staying, Ramzy listened to his contact speaking from another cellular phone in a moving car in Jerusalem. Still, they spoke elliptically in English as Ramzy drove through a soft rain, the wipers swiping the glass. The contact told him he had withdrawn funds from his bank early as another creditor had demanded immediate payment and he had sent the funds on. The other creditor had been most insistent.

Ramzy understood that they'd had to take Khalid out of the sofa factory early as the Israelis had been closing in.

"They knew where your funds were?" Ramzy asked.

"I'm afraid so."

"Then there's no need to go ahead with tomorrow's transaction."

"Of course, no point now."

"Well, thank you very much," Ramzy said, "for all your assistance."

Ramzy hung up relieved. Ramzy was afraid Shai would know he would not detonate the bomb and, as time ticked down, would call his bluff and have the city hermetically sealed and searched house to house. They would find it. Now, he was confident that Shai believed the bomb was in Tel Aviv. He had arranged for an East Jerusalemite to approach the Israeli security services tomorrow—*after* he had moved Khalidi to Jerusalem—and for money offer to identify the dead terrorist in the newspaper as Marwan Rida from Dheisheh. He had people watching the Rida family in Dheisheh around the clock. When the Israelis went to Dheisheh to investigate, or if either of Marwan's parents had been summoned from the refugee camp, his instructions had called for them to move Khalidi instantly, which was clearly what happened. If his plan had not been disrupted, when the Israelis found the sofa factory tomorrow they would have discovered Khalidi had just left. The Israelis should continue to search Tel Aviv, believing they were very close and had just missed him.

The rain stopped and Ramzy turned the wipers off and drove, the tires making sounds on the wet street. A peculiar notion struck him. What if somehow he succeeded and the Palestinians had a state? What would he do with the remainder of his life? Fight the hard-liners who would want to take over that state and from it all of Israel? Devote himself to writing that vast novel for which he never had time? Excitement rose in him at the prospect of changing to a life away from the constant moving. Abruptly, he hammered that hope down, fearing disappointment again. He lifted the receiver. He had another call to make—to Shai.

A little after 1:00 a.m., Cilla sat in her small Jerusalem apartment playing Solitaire on the kitchen table, nearing the bottom of a huge container of fresh orange juice she'd started two hours before. Back in Israel, there was little for her and Sara to do, as Shai had vast resources at his fingertips inside the country while their talents were best plied around the globe. She looked at the clock for maybe the hundredth time. It was two hours earlier in England, and if she was going to try Cyril it had to be now, before it became too late. She took one last swig, and though she needed the loo, she dialed.

Her ex-husband answered. He was not surprised to hear from her as periodically she rang late at night to ask about the boys. They made small talk, which was part of her tradecraft and came easily. She asked all the usual questions, school and sport, to delay.

"I'm going to move back to London," she said finally. "Not sure when exactly, but I should think soon. The time with the boys when I was there was wonderful."

"It was good for them too," Cyril said. "They're still talking about how the wind outside at Windsor Castle held them up when they leaned forward. If you can manage it, I think it's a smashing idea."

She sank back on her couch, tears in her eyes but not in her voice. She had expected protest, but he was a good man, which was why she had married him. She was the loon. She had felt smothered by him because she'd never done anything that much mattered, her father had always said she'd not amount to anything, and trapped in the house she yearned for something more that had to be out there. There was, and she was grateful for these years in the field. "No solicitors. I'll see them as much as you think best."

"Thank you. Let's just see how it goes, shall we? What will you do?"

"I don't know. I don't care just now. Sell clothes in a shop to start."

"You'll be okay in dreary old London?"

"I think so. In comparison to what I've seen, London's not half bad. Please don't tell the boys. I want to ring them myself once things are sorted out."

"Sleep well, Cill. It's late there."

She wiped tears from below her eyes. "I shall try my best to. Thank you, Cyril." Afraid she would burst into hard tears of gratitude, she hung up.

Tami sat on the bed in their apartment writing on a pad of paper. The end table clock read 5:50 a.m. Her one fear in eventually becoming a mother was that she would be overprotective and pass a sense of panic and mistrust of the world as a dangerous place to her child—as her Holocaust survivor parents had to her.

Tami had decided to pen letters to her child that she would present to him or her much later in life, sharing how she felt and what occurred throughout their lives. After much soul searching, she had decided to write about her fears and later discuss what she wrote. Maybe if the child understood her fears, which she knew she would transmit no matter how hard she tried not to, it might help her offspring overcome their own.

She wrote rapidly about exactly that, how we all make mistakes and Shai had taught her to admit and laugh at her foibles rather than defend or deny them. Her hair fell in a single braid down her front over an old, large sweatshirt of Shai's, THE COYOTE printed above an American Indian geometric design. She liked wearing his clothes when he was gone.

She heard Shai's key in the lock, ran and opened the door before he could. When he entered, his eyes were bloodshot. He looked very weary.

"I was in the office. I couldn't come up with anything," he said.

She held her voice firm. "What happened in Tel Aviv?"

He dropped heavily on the sofa and told her. Then, as if on cue, the phone rang.

"Probably Carmon." Shai struggled up and lifted the receiver. "Hello?"

"Shai?"

"Yes." The voice sounded familiar but he could not place it.

There was a pause. "This is Ramzy Awwad. I hoped you might be home at this hour."

Shai felt a kaleidoscope of emotions, none separating themselves out into a single color. He sank down on the arm of the sofa. "Ramzy, why this?"

"If you don't know why, I suggest you talk to Carmon and the rest of those in power about their plans for the future. I'll be at the Jardin du Luxembourg at 8:00 a.m., Paris time. By the large fountain. Have someone of authority meet me there." The line broke for a moment with static then was back. "Alone."

"Ramzy, *you* have to think about the future, what this will do."

Shai heard the pain in the Palestinian's voice as Ramzy said, "Shai, please don't. Please. It's too late for that now."

There was a burst of static and the line went dead. Shai gripped the receiver for a long time.

Tami came near, holding her braid with both hands.

Shai turned to her, shaken, wanted desperately to be in Paris. Maybe if he was there he could reason with him. But there was no possible way to arrive in time, which was what Ramzy intended.

"For a moment, I thought I could reach him," Shai said.

CHAPTER 15

July 4

In one of the upstairs bedrooms in the Ein Kerem house, Khalidi began the final stage of fitting together the bomb, the coincidence of the date of America's freedom coursing emotionally through him. While they slept, the epoxy added to the high explosive had dried solidly around the sphere. Khalidi kneeled beside a rectangle of plywood, measuring strips of the plastic optical fiber with a tape measure and cutting each to an identical length on the board with an X-ACTO knife. A buffing wheel sat beside him to polish the ends of the fibers. The tedious task at hand was to glue a hundred fibers individually and symmetrically around the sphere. The laser-triggered high explosive had to achieve a precise implosion. Bundy had purchased the standard equipment he needed in several stores in downtown Jerusalem.

With no nervousness as he measured and cut the fibers, Khalidi thought about Amal. He felt painfully embarrassed that he had put the operation at risk by bragging to her. Gradually, and he was not sure when it began, but sometime after he had landed in Beirut, he had been asking himself who was the woman Amal? If she cared about him or more about what he was doing? She had never let go of Geraldo. He did not want the Israelis to harm her, but he would not see her again.

He sharply cut a length of optical fiber, and in his mind cut the cord to Amal too. He felt a little self-conscious at the grandiosity of the thought, but everybody would have freedom today. He set the knife down, felt stronger and happier than he ever had in his life.

He saw Bundy approach with two mugs of coffee. Khalidi was working in a girl's room, with decorative dolls from around the world along a high shelf and a desk at the far wall with thin books above it. Bundy looked at the plutonium sphere on the plywood, still wrapped in the lead dental aprons, and took a satisfied sip of his coffee. Their troops would not have failed in Vietnam if they had not had one hand held behind them by the meek politicians.

The plutonium would have to be uncovered for the better part of a day while they glued the fibers to it, but the Israeli ionization equipment, which would have to get fairly close, should present little danger of detection since it was searching Tel Aviv—or even if they had some small presence searching here.

Bundy set Khalidi's coffee on the small desk. "How you comin'?"

"The silicon bathtub sealant you purchased will perfectly provide the cushioned tie-down to the sphere. It will be ready in a few hours."

"I'll phone Ramzy and give him the big news." Bundy headed for the door and then turned. "Some job we did, all of us." He gave Khalidi a reassuring expression. "Don't worry, the Israelis won't find us. And they'll concede. The withdrawal will be complete in a few days."

"It is not enough," Khalidi said, hanging his head.

"I don't follow you, son. You'll have your state."

"There's five million Palestinians. This mini-state won't be enough."

"The rest is in God's hands. In the end, the temple will be rebuilt in Jerusalem as is prophesized. Then there'll be complete peace and harmony between you and the Israelis, between all men. We all must be patient until that day. Rejoice in the erection of your state until then."

Khalidi looked at him and felt better. He did not believe in the coming of any Messiah, in easy answers, but Bundy was right. He should celebrate in the creation of the state. Let Ramzy and those like him worry about the next step. "Thank you, that helps."

Bundy gave him a broad smile. "Good. I'll go make that call to Ramzy. Now don't you fret. They'll skedaddle out of there. No question. "

In the adjacent bedroom, Bundy picked up the transportable cellular phone with the long cord that fitted into a car cigarette lighter. As he came down the tile stairs, across the open salon Tariq sat on the white leather sofa, with Omar in an oversized, soft, white armchair. Both held their AK-47s across their laps. A low, black cadenza ran the length of the wall. The stone house was pleasantly cool in the morning.

"I'm going out," Bundy said. "The phone battery needs to be charged every day anyway."

Omar nodded and Tariq gave him a huge smile.

In the rented Peugeot, the phone plugged in and charging, Bundy drove up the road out of Ein Kerem, the sprawling Jerusalem Forest to his left. Sometime eventually, he reminded himself, he had to head to the Plaza Hotel, gather his things and check out. He had kept the hotel room as a backup, part of his training as an intelligence officer with Marine Aircraft Group 13 at Chu Lai.

Nearing the military cemetery at Mount Herzl, he picked up the phone and dialed the number in Paris. Both he and Khalidi agreed it would be nearly impossible for the Israelis to eavesdrop on a call from a moving cellular phone. The difficulty was honing on the frequency, which in a moving car switched in the midst of a conversation. The danger was that the technology to pinpoint a frequency was essentially the same as Israel's highly developed missile technology, where the army raced rapidly for frequencies. Still, his call, for all intents and purposes, was safe.

"Hi, this is Ralph," Bundy said when Ramzy answered.

"How's everything?" Ramzy asked.

"Just fine. We're about ready." He spoke loudly over the noisy, thickening traffic.

“There are no problems?”

“Not a one.”

“Good. Thank you.”

“Give a holler whenever you want,” Bundy said and hung up.

Bundy wondered what Ramzy would do if the Israelis did not acquiesce. His sense was Ramzy would not destroy such holy sites of Islam. Still, it hardly mattered, as Bundy felt certain the Jews could not take the risk.

“So what if we take Ramzy in Paris?” Carmon said as Shai came through the door. Smoke snaked from a cigarette in Carmon’s ashtray.

Shai did not sit. “He may have left orders for them to detonate if he doesn’t phone at a given time.”

“You’re the one who assures me he won’t blow us all up to see if Allah *is* up there with a harem of virgins to hand out.”

Shai was starting to think he, not Carmon, should be relegated to running poodles around a ring. He spoke quietly. “I still believe he will not blow it.”

“But he’s in Paris, not here.”

Shai said nothing because it was true, and it plenty worried him that Khalidi had his finger on the trigger.

“So what the hell do we do now?”

“I don’t know,” Shai said. “Maybe we start pulling our soldiers out of places they shouldn’t be in the first place.”

Before Carmon could erupt, Shai was gone.

On his desk, Giora Weizmann patiently spread out the separate sheets that contained the particulars of the eight white Subarus that had a 7 in the second or third place on the license plate. He had a second folder with fourteen cars with a 7 in the first, fourth and fifth digits, but he was ignoring them for now and trusting the girl.

Outside, Arab women’s high-pitched ululating rose. The main prison for Arabs in the Jerusalem region, Moscobiyya, jutted from the police headquarters building in the compound purchased from the Russian Church. Weizmann stood and looked out. On the far end of the blacktop rose the beautiful green-domed Cathedral. Near, as usual, women in long dresses, their heads covered with white scarves, stood outside the prison entrance with large plastic bags of fruits and vegetables, crying out with clicking tongues. They knew the Israelis fed their men well, but helpless and needing to do something, they brought food.

Weizmann came back from the window and did something his colleagues found peculiar. Standing, he looked at the sheets upside down from a 45-degree angle. He had been the youngest of eight sons and two daughters. Early each morning his father had gathered the boys around the Talmud on the kitchen table, and at the age of four he joined them. Relegated to a rear corner, he first learned to read by staring at a page upside down from that position, and he still felt more comfortable studying a perplexing report this way. You could tell the male birth order in a Yemenite family by their position at the table. Weizmann found great solace in God, and when humanity behaved despicably, about which he had daily reminders, his belief lent him hope that this was not all there was, that something higher existed that you could trust.

Four of the cars had been rented by Israelis and four by foreigners. He had placed the Israelis on the bottom row and the foreigners on top. He knew it was ethnocentric, but he believed an Israeli would not leave a child bleeding on the road.

Weizmann leaned both hands on the desk and studied the information for a long time, letting each name penetrate. Hugo Grynstein, from London, had rented a car in Tel Aviv and had checked in at the Hilton there. Next, Joseph Telushkin, from Manhattan, was staying with Rabbi Levi Weiman-Kelman and his wife here in Bekaa. The third car had been hired from Europcar in Haifa by Pierre Trigano of Paris, whose local address was the Yaarot Hacarmel Health Resort. The last, Hal M. Bundy from Millbrae, California, rented at the airport and was staying at The Moriah Hotel in Tel Aviv. Then he went over the Israelis: one car rented in Eilat, two in Tel Aviv, and one in Tiberius.

Weizmann came around the desk and carefully gathered the

papers together and replaced them in his folder. He would call the police in each city and have officers inspect the eight cars for dents and determine if there were corroborative reports on their locations at the time of the accident. Then he would drive to see Rabbi Weiman-Kelman himself. He'd heard about the American-born Reform rabbi and would enjoy meeting him. A few years ago, a nearby Orthodox rabbi had burst into the Reform congregation, shouted it was a house of prostitution, and tried to make off with the Torah scrolls because women were handling them. The traditional Sephardic Jews had come to Israel from millennia in the Arab countries and had a lot in common with the Reform Americans. Both went to synagogue on Shabbat morning and then in the afternoon drove to soccer games, though the Sephardi could not countenance women reading from the Torah. Giora loved his culture's juggling of tradition and modernity.

As he left the building, he was confident he would find the culprit soon.

In the gray morning, Ramzy walked through the Jardin du Luxembourg. The unseasonably cold wind slapped his cheeks, but his mind elsewhere, he did not feel its sting. Rain had pelted Paris for a brief burst only an hour before and puddles dotted the walkway, the downpour unleashing the scent of the greenery. Ramzy held a pack of cigarettes tightly in his pocket with his right hand but did not remove them. He was glad Shai did not have time to dash here, and then he worried irrationally that maybe Shai had found a way to manage it.

The walkway led into an open space before the fountain. A tall, slim man in his late sixties was waiting, hands inside the pockets of an elegant raincoat. He boasted a full head of wavy white hair, a white moustache and glasses. As Ramzy approached, the man walked toward him with loud steps. A single, elderly Frenchman sat on a bench on the periphery bundled in a coat, scarf and beret reading *Le Monde,* his cane leaned against the wet bench. He had placed a section of the newspaper under him. Ramzy wondered if he was Israeli intelligence.

Ramzy's coal eyes remained on the nearing man who stretched out a hand. "Mister Awwad, I'm Eliezer Tsur. I'm the Israeli ambassador here. I've come alone."

Ramzy took his grip, which was firm and dry. "Thank you for meeting me."

Tsur nodded. "I want you to know from the outset I'm here only to listen. I have no authority beyond that. I do have a general knowledge of what has transpired."

"I have a message for your prime minister and cabinet," Ramzy said. "Once we have a state, your people will see in the time they always speak of that we are developing ourselves and not dreaming of destroying you. You will come to accept us. You will withdraw now from the West Bank and East Jerusalem, or Tel Aviv will be destroyed."

Tsur's voice was quiet. "And what will that do for any hope for your people's future?"

Ramzy looked at the spray of the fountain. "Under your settlement policy we are increasingly left with less and less." A patch of blue sky opened brightly between the clouds. "You have until Friday at sundown to complete your withdrawal. Two days. Total withdrawal or I will order Tel Aviv razed."

The ambassador's voice rose slightly. "We won't give in. Don't be mistaken."

"You will capitulate. You have no choice. Tell your leaders I'm saying to them what Moses said to Pharaoh: 'Let my people go.' I have only one plague. Do not make me strike you with it."

Tsur's blue-gray eyes were soft and he nodded. "I will transmit your message."

"I have one further message for your prime minister, who calls us cockroaches," Ramzy said. "Please inform him that we have enough plutonium for two weapons. When they consider the plan that they will withdraw now then march back in when the bomb's discovered, tell them if they do we will bring the second bomb into Israel. But this time, there will be no negotiations. We will destroy Tel Aviv before you know there's a bomb to hunt."

Just then, the old man on the bench, both hands atop his cane, pushed his way to his feet and, tucking the newspaper under one arm, began to cross the plaza toward them, thrusting the stick in front of him before each step. The old man seemed to take forever to pass.

Ramzy reached into his coat pocket and gave Tsur a piece of paper. "This is a number where you may reach me. At sunset on Friday it will be too late. No excuses. No extensions. If you attempt to stall or evacuate the city we will immediately destroy it."

Ramzy turned and walked toward the street, his clothes beneath his light raincoat soaked with sweat, the dampness in the hair cold at the back of his neck.

"'*Let my people go.*' He actually said that?" Carmon said across his office at Shai. "Well, let them go wherever they want. Jordan would be nice. Let them go there. *Gezunterhait.* Go."

Shai sank slowly onto Carmon's deep sofa. "What was the result of the inner cabinet meeting?"

"The result of the meeting?" Carmon withdrew a Muratti, lit it furiously, snapped the lighter closed. "We're cordoning off Tel Aviv this moment, searching house to house toward the sea."

Fear charged through Shai.

"We'll show them." Carmon stubbed the partially smoked cigarette out. "A call's going now to your Ramzy informing him that planes armed with nuclear weapons are staying aloft and that all the Arab capitals and refugee camps will go if Tel Aviv is touched. The Cabinet's in absolute agreement, if Tel Aviv goes, the Arab world goes with it."

Shai said nothing.

"They want my assessment of Awwad." Carmon's voice quivered with restrained fury. "And they want *your* official assessment. Want to know if they refuse to withdraw, if such a literate, educated gentlemen like your Ramzy would actually turn the lights out on the Middle East and deny us all the privilege of reading his past and future works."

Shai looked directly at him. "I think he's convinced we'll withdraw."

"Terrific. Hell, why bother and look for the thing then? We can just pull out." Carmon threw himself back in his chair and the springs sang. "Awwad's social calendar is just full up. He's seen his friends the Russians in Paris. Just couldn't see himself not inviting them to his little party. Not wanting to come without an escort, they hopped right on the phone and rang up Washington." Carmon came forward in the chair, menace in the motion. "The pressure's so fierce you don't even have to pick up the phone to hear it coming over the wire."

"What's the prime minister saying to them?"

"I don't know. Probably that he listens to God, not Washington, bless him."

Shai stood.

"Where you going?" Carmon asked.

Shai did not answer because he didn't know. He walked out. In the vestibule, he came up behind Tami, who swiveled in her chair toward him. He stood quietly opposite her for a long moment. She reached up and took his hand.

"I'm scared," he said.

There was strength in her eyes. "You think Khalidi might do it on his own if we don't capitulate?"

"I'm worried about it."

She held his hand warmly in both of hers. "Maybe you weren't so wrong about Ramzy. Maybe the forces out there were just too strong for him to resist. What would you do if the Soviets had killed a thousand Russian Jews for protesting?"

Shai knew that though she constantly worried about small things, she was a rock in a real emergency, hated in the American TV shows when someone was shot and the wife was kneeling by the body crying and not calling for an ambulance.

He looked at her, squeezed her hands, then moved down the corridor with renewed vigor. But as he walked, he was still bothered by why Ramzy had put Khalidi in the sofa factory.

Late that afternoon in downtown Jerusalem, seventy-five-year-old Eiran Avihai strolled through Independence Park as he'd done daily since he retired from his supervisor's job with the telephone company.

His wife had died the year before of cancer. He carried a copy of *Haaretz* and a small plastic sack with slices of bread for the birds. He had already glanced through the newspaper but there was no mention of the strong military presence in Tel Aviv. Rumors abounded that terrorists had infiltrated but there was no panic. He sighed. They lived with these threats and worse.

In 1973, he had lost his older son, Tsvi, on the Golan Heights—where rockets had slammed down at the Galilee settlements between 1948 and 1967 until their boys stopped it—and his younger son, Danny, was a colonel in the army. Avihai continued toward his favorite spot near the rose bushes. He knew from Danny what few others in the country did, that the threat to Tel Aviv was nuclear. Avihai had been planning to spend a few weeks with Danny and the children in Tel Aviv now that the kids were on summer vacation, but Danny had insisted he not come. When he had started crying over being denied the visit, in desperation Danny had confided the truth. And Danny refused to send the children to Jerusalem, would not use privilege to protect his family. Though Avihai was terrified for them, he understood. Besides, he had every confidence in the army, led by fine officers like his son.

Avihai continued through the grass. He could hear children shouting far off in the thick trees in the direction of the foreign journalists' building. They raised good kids here—a little irreverent, a little cocky—and he secretly loved watching them on the beach, the young women and men with such healthy bodies.

To the right of the roses a mound of dirt stood at the edge of a hole, still there since yesterday. He was certain it had not been dug Monday afternoon. For safety, he wished they would finish whatever work it was and close opening. He sat down on his wooden bench in front of the flowers, set the newspaper beside him and removed some bread. In this blasting dry heat, it felt good to rest after his walk from the bus. He tossed bits on the grass and soon small black birds descended, snared the morsels and flew off with them.

Avihai read and, after a few minutes, dozed in the sun's warmth. A jet fighter bursting the sound barrier woke him and he jerked his head up. Frightened for an instant, he stood. Already on his feet and a little stiff, he wandered over to the hole to see if there was an irrigation break. He looked down from the edge and to his surprise could not imagine what anyone had been working on. There was no water, no pipes, only some gray plastic stuck between the soil. He lay flat on his stomach, reached down and caught an edge between his fingers. It was stiff, though malleable.

He pulled, and though it was heavy, it came away from the loose dirt. He set it on the side of the hole and then pushed himself into a sitting position. He studied the oddly shaped whatever it was. Puzzled, he searched the seams that ran around it and found a small place where the threads were worn away. With his keys, he worked at the seam until it opened and then pulled the plastic cover from the edge with a ripping sound, revealing meshed silvery metal.

He realized that it was one of those lead aprons dentists used. There was no possible explanation for why it was here. And then it struck him slowly, too unbelievably, that radioactive material might have been buried here and the lead used to conceal it. He read a lot now, and he had seen something somewhere about this. He stood, holding the dental shield. He had to take the bus home and call Danny.

Hurrying, he tripped, pitched forward and the newspaper and plastic bag flew. Searing pain bit through his left ankle. "Help!" he called hoarsely, but nobody heard. He pushed both hands on the dry grass, got to his knees, stood with all his weight on his good foot and toppled to the side, his elbow striking the ground hard. He lay there unmoving and remembered reading about an Italian woman who, with superhuman strength, lifted a car to free her trapped daughter. "Tsvi!" he called, "Not yet. Not coming yet." He rolled onto and up on his knees, and then stood. The pain was so great, he decided with utter clarity that he simply would not feel it.

Sometime later, he did not know how long, he pitched forward on the empty bus bench. Because this was Israel, a half dozen cars pulled over illegally and the drivers and passengers ran to him.

On the phone, stunned, Shai listened to the report about the lead dental apron found in Jerusalem. They had confirmed radioactive traces on it and in the hole. Shai requested the dental apron be driven to him and the officer promised it on his desk within the half hour.

Shai saw it now with the clarity brought after a city's haze had been banished by a downpour—Ramzy had intended he find Khalidi in the sofa factory. That was also why the plutonium segment in Jaffa. Either Amal had lied to him or Khalidi had lied to her. All to convince them the bomb was in Tel Aviv. If they refused to capitulate, at the eleventh hour Ramzy would alert them, the Christian world, the Muslim world and the Americans there was a bomb in Jerusalem that could vaporize all the holy sites. A fierce fear shook him. He envisioned what the Muslims would do if the bomb destroyed the holy mosques. And Khalidi had his finger on it.

Shai attacked the phone, the first call to the Hebrew University physicist he had consulted throughout this ordeal, who confirmed Shai's intuition that Khalidi would need a large number of the thin dental shields to completely mask the plutonium. He then called Pia, his dentist, thanked her for the introduction to the dietician, who was amazing, and asked how many supply companies in the country handled dental aprons. There was only one, in Tel Aviv. Shai got the name, phoned, charged through layers of bureaucracy and, tapping the floor, waited for a response to his request for information about any Arab or other dentists who had ordered an unusually large number of cling shields in the last year. Still waiting, he switched to another line and asked Tami to hurry in.

He was still on hold when she came through the open door. "Doctor Hanoch Armon, director at Shaare Zedek," he said, the receiver held against his ear by his shoulder. "Either get him here or I'll go to the hospital or his home. Whichever's fastest."

She disappeared into the corridor.

Someone finally came on the line and informed Shai there had been no large purchases of cling shields from Jew or Arab. Good, he thought.

Soon, Tami informed Shai that Dr. Armon was waiting at his home on Ben Maimon Street. Shai drove the short distance through the early evening to the fashionable suburb of Rehavia. Ben Maimon was a narrow, quiet street of three-story stone apartment buildings flanked by leafy trees. As in all of Jerusalem, every inch along the sidewalk was filled with small cars.

Shai had not met Dr. Armon before, but in recent months the director of Shaare Zedek Hospital had been in all the papers battling with the West Bank's military-dominated Civil Administration over the treatment of critically ill Palestinians in Israeli hospitals. A pillar of the *intifada* was the Palestinian refusal to pay taxes. They had cut their payments by 50%, and contributed that only to keep their starving economy alive. In retaliation, the Civil Administration had cut by 50% to 75% paying for the treatment of grave diseases in Israel that West Bank hospitals were unequipped to handle.

Armon treated Palestinians under the names of Jewish patients who had just died. He took in a burn victim who required skin grafts, guaranteed most of the $50,000 fee himself, and then telephoned the Civil Administration and demanded the money. The government paid. When he had serious cases and the Civil Administration did not want to cough up, he and colleagues threatened to talk to foreign journalists. With doctors from Shaare Zedek and Hadassah Hospital, they supplied sophisticated medicines to West Bank hospitals so that treatment could be performed there. Armon was quoted as saying no Palestinian should die because of government cutbacks.

As Shai parked illegally, sticking into the intersection, birds chirped in the trees. The dry heat was breaking for the day and a scraggy cat dozed under a car. In front of the building shaded by massive pines, flowers of a dozen shapes and colors pushed up through the red-brown soil. On the second floor, pots with sprawling red, pink and white geraniums ran along the length of the balcony.

Dr. Hanoch Armon, a man of average height and a slight build, ushered Shai into his living room. "We need your assistance," Shai said as they sat.

"Ask, and if I can help, I'll help."

Shai rapidly unraveled the truth of the nuclear threat. In the Israeli gesture, Armon clicked his tongue as he shook his head. "There are no dental clinics to my knowledge in the Territories," Armon said.

"Only individual offices. There isn't even an office I know of that has more than two dentists."

Shai did not show his disappointment. "Then I'm guessing that someone or several people went around and collected a dozen or more aprons. Is there someone you know who can ask who was approached? It might be enough if we could even find one dentist who donated his shields or was asked."

"How much can I tell them?"

"At this point, as much as you need to."

"I have friends. Who do I phone if I find anything?"

Shai wrote down Tami's and his office numbers, and their home number.

Armon stood and spoke as he walked Shai to the door. "There was a cancer patient, a young man from Hebron. He had been traveling to Hadassah for chemotherapy, throwing up the whole way from the anxiety, then the same at home from the medication. Dr. Lina Qadir at Makassed Hospital called me. I arranged for the young man to receive chemotherapy in a Hebron hospital, as well as injections for the nausea, prevailed upon the Civil Administration to fund it. I've helped her on a number of cases. I believe she'll assist me." They reached the door. "I will try my best, but you understand this will be difficult."

"Doctor, push to the limit. I don't care who's woken, at what hour. If they have to, call every dentist in the West Bank. We're running out of time and we have no other leads."

"Go," Armon said.

Back in his office, as the sun set through the window Shai waited, neck aching, hoping Armon would unearth a trail through the bushes. A three-quarters finished Styrofoam cup of now cold coffee sat before him. He had started as of now to drink it black, which tasted terrible. The army was beginning to quietly search the Arab quarters of Jerusalem. Shai had prevailed upon the military to continue to go house to house through Tel Aviv, to lull Ramzy into believing the bomb in Jerusalem was safe.

Giora Weizmann entered the tall Jerusalem Plaza Hotel. He had heard that the army was swarming through Tel Aviv. Something was going on. Still, whatever it was, others were attending to it, while his task remained the hit-and-run driver. He believed he had identified him.

At the house phone, Giora asked for Hal Bundy's room and waited as it rang. He had checked out a revolver and wore it comfortably in a shoulder holster beneath the sports coat he had donned to conceal it. The Tel Aviv police reported that Bundy had never showed up at the Moriah Hotel in Tel Aviv that he had given as his address at the airport car rental desk. Weizmann had begun by checking all five-star hotels in Jerusalem and had hit Bundy on the fourth try.

He hung up, went to the desk and quietly told the registration clerk that he would like to speak to the manager. The manager had gone home but the assistant manager was in her office. The clerk entered a door behind the registration desk, then came out and bid Weizmann enter.

Weizmann showed the middle-aged woman his identification and asked to be shown Hal Bundy's room. She immediately went to the front desk, returned with a key and escorted him up to room 1012. After she opened the door, he thanked her and said he would rather have a look around himself and would return the key to her personally.

The drapes were open and there was a lovely view of Independence Park, and beyond it the Old City. The bed was made and the room exceptionally neat. Weizmann checked the closets first; the quality and cut suggested financial comfort. In the end table drawers, he found some Danish coins. The bureaus yielded that Bundy unpacked his socks and underwear neatly. Weizmann spent another forty-five minutes meticulously going through the room, and what struck him was the absence of a single sheet of paper. He found no airline tickets, receipts for tours, business memos, letters—no indication of Bundy's movements. Virtually no finding could have made Weizmann as suspicious.

Weizmann examined the room to make certain he had left no signs of his search and went to the bed and pulled the spread tight from where he had wrinkled it when slipping his hands under the mattress. Satisfied, he walked into the bathroom, looked around one final time, then left.

Outside, he searched the hotel parking lot for the white Subaru. There was a beige one, and he checked both the license plate and scratched the paint with his key near the bumper but no white appeared beneath it.

Back in the assistant manager's office, Weizmann learned that Bundy had taken out a safe deposit box, and a check of the index cards indicated that he had not cleared the box. The hotel's safe deposit boxes, housed in a small room behind the desk, needed two keys to free the lock. Weizmann knew that he had insufficient evidence to gain a judge's order to open it. A check of the minibar receipts disclosed that Bundy had removed two bottles of orange juice but no alcohol. So, he didn't drink and he had no documents.

Weizmann asked the assistant manager to phone the maid who worked that floor. Fortunately, she was home and said there was something strange about that room. Nobody had slept in it or, as far as she could tell, even been in it in the last two days. She had not seen the guest at all, so could not give Weizmann a description. No one at the busy airport car rental agency had remembered what he looked like either. A desk clerk did recall giving Bundy his key several days earlier. He described him as fifties, short blond hair with a blond moustache, but had not noticed anything unusual about him or his being with anyone.

Weizmann would send the complete license number out nationwide and begin to check hotels for Hal Bundy elsewhere in Jerusalem and throughout the country. He would contact the FBI for a report on Bundy from that end. Though he knew he would have to be patiently insistent with his commanding officer and quietly hold firm, he wanted twenty-four-hour surveillance inside the hotel. If Bundy had his clothes and his safe deposit box here, he would return. It was all too odd to ignore.

Giora walked outside. He had pieces of the puzzle of Hal Bundy, but needed more for the picture to become clear.

In the Ein Kerem house, a twenty-minute drive from where Giora

Weizmann exited the Plaza Hotel, Khalidi and Bundy surveyed their work. The slatted wood box with the high explosive-surrounded plutonium sphere inside had been bolted to the plywood. A hundred plastic optical fibers were glued uniformly around the sphere and bunched at one side. In seconds they could be inserted into the end of the small artillery range-finder laser they had brought in the glider. The remainder of spool of optical fiber sat in the corner. Beside it, Khalidi had placed the loaded neutron "gun."

Earlier, in the downstairs kitchen, Khalidi had removed the Californium-252 from the gold pocket watch. He then took the 9 mm cartridge, removed the bullet and the powder, then drilled a hole in the base of the cartridge. The neutron-loaded bullet had to be fired into the plutonium exactly ten microseconds after the plutonium imploded. When light raced through a fiber, it slowed to .7 feet per nanosecond, or seven kilometers in ten microseconds. The same single triggering of the laser that imploded the plutonium would run another pulse through seven kilometers of fiber, delaying the firing of the bullet by the required ten microseconds. He had inserted the length of fiber from the spool through the hole in the cartridge and cemented it with a drop of the silicon sealant. He had put the new primed charge in contact with the fiber, then refilled it with powder and pressed the lead slug with the Californium-252 in. The last step was to insert the cartridge back in its niche in the front lead block.

Upstairs, Tariq stood in the doorway holding his AK-47. Omar remained downstairs. Bundy and Khalidi had layered the dental aprons around the box.

"It's ready now," Khalidi said to Tariq.

Khalidi sat down on the bed, quieted and shaken by the enormity of what he had accomplished. He was so grateful to have left that old horribly painful and lonely life. Tariq held his machine gun tightly as he stood over the bomb. Omar climbed the stairs and joined them, weapon in hand. Ramzy had instructed that they remain with the bomb at all times now and to shoot anyone who attempted to insert the fibers in the laser. What they were doing scared and worried Omar and he would be vigilant.

Bundy gazed at the Palestinians and went over in his mind how he would kill all three of them.

CHAPTER 16

July 5

A little after midnight, Shai walked into Carmon's office, which smelled of cigarettes and aftershave. In his chair, back to Shai, Carmon faced the window smoking. When Carmon came around, his visage was ashen, his eyes deepened, his mouth loose. His face looked quite naked.

"I just spoke to the prime minister. With the bomb in Jerusalem, we're capitulating. We're beginning the pullout at 7:00 a.m. unless we can stall Ramzy."

Shai dropped in the chair, shaken, wanting an exchange of land for a solution but not like this.

"The Americans will make financial restitution to the settlers. The prime minister's going to play it as a humanitarian gesture. We're keeping the big settlements just over the Green Line. We're going to hold on to the Old City and put troops along the Jordan River to guarantee their so-called state is demilitarized. We won't budge on either. The cabinet's unanimous. They can put their flags on the mosques or whatever the hell they want. If that's not enough, if Ramzy still wants to blow up the Middle East, let him. Our planes are armed and remain in the air. Call him. Try to extend the deadline so we can find this thing." Carmon picked up the phone receiver and held it in the air.

Shai felt his heart beating hard and gave a small nod, was terrified what Khalidi might do if he discovered them closing in on the bomb.

Carmon dialed a single digit then spoke into the phone. "Put it through."

At Shai's request, the Paris police had already determined that Ramzy's number was a transportable cellular phone. Shai had not asked them to take any action, feeling safer with Ramzy in at least some control of the threat. With both hands, he slowly pushed himself up from the chair and headed toward the outstretched receiver. When he took the phone it was ringing, and then the receiver was lifted on the other end and there was no static. Despite his better judgment, he felt hope.

"Hello?"

"It's Shai. I have an official message for you."

"I'm listening, Shai."

"We can't make the deadline. It's impossible to pull the settlers out in that short a time. Also, most won't travel on Shabbat. We need until sundown Sunday."

"You have enough buses and trucks to take them out before darkness on Friday."

"It can't be done. Ramzy, don't risk everything over two days."

"The deadline stands. If you persist I'll hang up."

Shai knew it could be accomplished Thursday and Friday and he had not expected to succeed in stalling. He sank down on the edge of the desk. "All right. Friday sunset. We'll begin the pullout tomorrow morning but here are the conditions." He gave them and then went on. "If this is unacceptable and you are prepared to follow through with your threat, we will launch all our planes with their nuclear payloads toward their targets."

Pain in his chest, fear deeper in his heart, Shai waited for a long time.

"It's acceptable," Ramzy said finally over the line. "Tell them if they ask again for even one hour more, Tel Aviv will go up in that hour. I know how they work. Tell them I am not a frightened teenager on my first mission. Tell them."

"All right."

"Thank you." Ramzy broke the connection.

Shai cradled the receiver hard.

"What did he say?" Carmon asked, holding his cigarette down.

"Friday sundown. He agrees to our conditions."

Carmon looked away. "Please find it," he said softly, and for the first time in memory he was pleading.

As Shai walked out, he felt icy fear. His job was to locate the bomb. That his only lead was finding the source of the dental aprons scared him to his core.

Wearing a light jacket despite the warmth, Hal Bundy left the Ein Kerem house and drove to The Jerusalem Plaza Hotel. The traffic was light at this late hour, bunching only when he reached the city center.

Across the street from the hotel, he drove for a long time through the maze of side streets until he found a spot to park. For general precautions, he did not want to drive up into the hotel parking. It should only take a few minutes to retrieve his belongings. He had not been in his room for too long which could create suspicion.

Bundy entered the hotel at a stiff, fast clip. The lobby was quiet, the grand piano closed in the bar where several people sat at small tables. Bundy went to the desk and asked for the key to room 1012. Yael, the young woman there, reached behind her to the slots and retrieved a key. She looked around casually for the night manager, was supposed to alert him immediately if someone asked for that key. Two policemen were in the bar.

"I have something in the safe deposit box," Bundy said.

"May I see your key, sir?"

Bundy removed the long key from his pocket. It had a number 34 on the head. Yael pulled an index file from under the desk, flipped through it and drew out the card for box 34. With another card she covered the signature on the first line of the card with his signature. "Would you sign, please."

Bundy quickly did so. Yael removed the index card; the signatures matched. As Bundy came around the desk, she drew up the ring of keys that were fastened to one of her belt loops. She unlocked a drawer and pulled out a master key for the safe deposit boxes then met Bundy at the door behind the desk. Yael unlocked it and they stepped in. She would not be able to alert the manager until she opened the box for him.

She went to the wall of boxes, inserted her key in his box, twisted it, and he wiggled his in the second lock. "Tell me when you're finished," she said and headed to find the night manager.

"Wait." He pulled the airplane tickets and passport from the box. "That's all I need," he said and handed her back the key. He headed outside and across the lobby to the elevators.

In the bar sipping sodas, police officers Yohanan Bar-Yehuda and Rachel Goodman had the 11:00 p.m. to 4:00 a.m. shift waiting for Bundy. Bar-Yehuda was large and stocky with thick eyebrows and a nose that had been broken and not reset properly. Rachel was slender in all aspects, her thin brown hair held in a headband. Dressed casually, he in jeans, she in black cotton pants and a beige blouse, her gun in her purse, his in a waist holster, they were talking quietly when the young night manager hurried over.

"He's here. Bundy's here."

"Where?" Bar-Yehuda asked.

"He took something out of the safe deposit box and got in the elevator."

Rachael grabbed her small black purse, with Bar-Yehuda a half step behind. Before she could push the elevator button, the doors of the right elevator parted. Rachael tensed. A young American in his thirties, bald, short, with glasses and a red beard, stepped out. Rachael and Bar-Yehuda hustled in and she pushed the plastic 10, which lit at the touch of her clear nail. The doors closed before anyone else entered. Their orders were to bring Bundy in for questioning and then call Giora Weizmann. Weizmann had no indication that Bundy was dangerous, but they had been told to proceed cautiously.

They followed the corridor signs to 1012. They listened but heard no sounds within. The corridor was empty. Bar-Yehuda eased the pistol from his holster and Rachael removed the Browning automatic from her purse.

Bar-Yehuda knocked on the door and they both stepped away from it, covered by the wall. They heard footsteps approaching and a man called impatiently from inside. "Who is it?"

Rachael spoke far better English and said, "The police. We would like to talk to you."

Silence. Then after a moment, "Certainly. Just one second. I need to get my pants on, especially if it's a lady."

Bar-Yehuda quietly tried the knob, which was locked. From the tenth floor there was no place Bundy could escape. They waited, Bar-Yehuda thinking that in exactly two minutes he would kick the door in. They heard footsteps on the carpet, then the door was opened a short distance.

"Please come in," Bundy said. "I hope nothing's the matter, you coming this late."

Bar-Yehuda pushed in first and Rachael followed and shut the door behind her. Bundy had stepped back, had both hands in the pockets of his blue windbreaker.

"Hands, out," Bar-Yehuda said.

"Of course, sorry."

Bundy removed his left hand and, in the same motion, fired the PPK/S twice quickly from inside his pocket. The suppressor did its job, and the first bullet quietly whooshed into Bar-Yehuda's stomach and he fell forward, surprise on his face. The second hit Rachel in the chest and she clamored back against the door. With lightning motion, Bundy pumped a second muffled bullet into each of their slumped bodies before checking to see if the guns had dropped from their grasps. Bundy saw that the pistol was still entwined in the large man's fingers, and the PPK/S out of his pocket now, he fired another shot into his skull. The head jumped. The woman's gun had fallen far out of her reach in front of her.

Bundy looked at his half-packed suitcase on the bed, left it there, walked around the large man and pulled the woman away from the door so he could open it. He took off his jacket, wrapped the light blue nylon around his gun and, with his finger on the trigger, drew the door open. No one was in the corridor. He stepped out, closed the door behind him and headed for the elevator.

Downstairs, he walked across the empty lobby, fairly certain that the desk clerk who had opened the safety deposit box for him was staring at him, but she did not move toward him. He hurried out the glass doors past the doormen, and once he was out of sight on the sidewalk darted across the street through the traffic toward his car.

As he pulled the Peugeot away from the curb, he saw no one who might identify the car. His pulse calm, he consulted his map. There were many one-way streets in Jerusalem but they were indicated with small arrows. As he turned right and drove down a hill that led to the Valley of the Cross, he thought about the crucial last passages from the Book of Daniel: *Go now Daniel, for what I have said is not to be understood until the time of the End. Daniel cried, How long will it be until the time of these wonders? The answer came to him: From the time the daily sacrifice is taken away and the Horrible Thing is set up to be worshipped, until the end there will be 1,290 days.*

The Horrible Thing was the Antichrist. From the Antichrist's masking himself as a man of peace, it would be a mere 1,290 days before Jesus returned to usher in the glorious new world.

Bundy headed for the house in Ein Kerem.

At 4:00 a.m., Shai was curled on the small sofa in his office half-asleep, a blanket pulled partially over him. The light glared overhead. A little after two he had lain down intending only to rest for an hour and had drifted in and out of sleep, too exhausted to force himself up to kill the brightness. So far the searches in East Jerusalem had unearthed nothing. Though Shai knew that he and so much of what he loved might imminently be vaporized and the landscape forever altered, he had no inclination to take stock, to mentally traverse roads or tributaries he might have tread. Shai inhabited the present.

The phone rang and he flailed at the blanket slapping it to the floor, and in his socks, he finally was at the desk and had the receiver.

Dr. Armon spoke calmly. Maybe he was used to 4:00 a.m. hospital emergencies, Shai thought as his other mind grabbed the news. Armon's friend, Dr. Lina Qadir, had spoken to a dentist in East Jerusalem who had given lead aprons to a young man named Samir Aeid of the *intifada* public health committee. Dr. Qadir knew Samir and had driven to where he lives with his parents in Nablus. Samir had known nothing of a nuclear bomb and had simply delivered the lead shields without understanding why. Both Dr. Qadir and Samir were presently sitting across from Armon in his living room if Shai cared to speak to them.

Shai grabbed his shoes and bolted for the corridor, only taking time to shove his feet into them as he waited for the elevator. Outside, the Jerusalem streets were dark and quiet, though as he drove in the open valley around the trees of Sachar Park and climbed the hill into the dense stone buildings of Rehavia he saw rising smoke and a fire engine spraying water through the driver's window into a parked car with no sign of an accident. In the last two weeks, more than twenty cars had been set alight in West Jerusalem by Palestinians sneaking over from the eastern sector. He thought about Dheisheh and understood. Shai barreled around the fire engine without slowing.

In his apartment entranceway, Armon whispered to Shai that he had played it that the Palestinians were going to explode the bomb rather than mention their demands for a state. In the living room, introductions were made. Dr. Qadir was a diminutive woman, maybe fifty, short dark hair and porcelain-blue eyes that followed Shai's every movement as he filled the room, pumped hands and said his hellos as if this was a party with old friends and not a pre-dawn council to avoid a war, or worse.

Samir sat forward on the edge of the couch, his eyes on his hands. Armon and Shai dropped into armchairs across from the sofa, where Qadir edged closer to Samir.

"I am asking that you do not arrest him," Qadir said to Shai. "It is not a condition. He will tell you everything he knows regardless, and as you see he has come here on his own. He does not want to be responsible for a nuclear explosion. Also, since he is from Nablus, I strenuously ask that no word of his being here reach there."

In Nablus, the hotbed of the West Bank, local youths ran rampant building the *intifada*. "No jail, no loose talk," Shai said, looking at the young man, whose head remained hung. "My word."

Qadir went on. "Also, I must tell you that he does not know very much and I am not sure that he can help you at all."

Shai addressed Samir. "How many dental aprons did you collect?"

His head came up slowly. "I think fifteen."

"Were you the only one collecting them?"

"I don't know. I'm the only one I knew. Nobody told me that anyone else came to them."

Fifteen would be enough. "Who told you to get them?"

Samir was rubbing one hand back and forth nervously over his thigh. "I don't know. A teenager runner with his face covered came with written instructions from the Voice of the People. I don't know who sent him. You don't ask questions."

"Where did you take the aprons?"

"Tulkarm." His voice rose with fear. "I don't know to who. It was night. I drove to the empty lot near the Arab Orphan's Committee. Someone came. He had a keffiyeh over his face. I didn't see him. His car was around the corner."

"When?"

Samir looked down at his hands again, now dangling between his legs. "Two weeks ago, a little more maybe."

A week to ten days before they buried the plutonium in Independence Park. Tulkarm was only forty kilometers from Tel Aviv and there were no roadblocks between the town and the coast highway. Likely this was more ruse. Ramzy's tradecraft. All roads, should Shai successfully find them, lead to Tel Aviv. Still, people in Tulkarm knew something or had helped. Otherwise, they could have brought the aprons directly to Jerusalem.

Shai leaned forward. "Have you had further contact with these people?"

Head down again, he shook it.

"With anyone in Tulkarm about this after that night?"

Samir shook his head again, and then he took an audible breath that was like a rasp. Without looking up, he asked, "Are you going to arrest me now?"

"Look at me," Shai said.

His head came up, terror in his eyes.

"You speak to no one about this, or I'll personally ensure that everyone in Nablus knows you cooperated here."

He gave a small nod.

Shai pushed himself to his feet, approached Qadir. "Thank you very much. Please take him home. Sometime soon, will you be my guest for dinner with Dr. Armon? I'd like to hear about the difficulties you're facing at Makassed."

"We'll have much to talk about then."

He smiled at her. "I suspect we'd have a lot to talk about whatever the subject."

He turned to Armon. "I need the phone. Private."

The withdrawal was due to begin in two hours, and with who knew whose finger on the bomb's trigger, he had to get to Tulkarm.

Bundy rested on his bed in the darkness fully clothed, unable to sleep, sweat coating his face. Tariq and Omar had remained together throughout the night in the next room with the bomb, alternating between one sleeping and the other alert with his machine gun. He had counted on being able to take them individually. Confident that with the morning and the necessity to eat and use the facilities they would at some point separate, he waited.

A strange vision rose in his mind. He saw himself conversing in the clouds with Judas Iscariot. Judas was explaining that though he tumbled through history as a traitor for betraying Jesus, his crucial role had been preordained by Him. There would have been no salvation unless he sold Jesus for that silver. Judas told Bundy that he too would go down in history as a monster, but his role was vital.

Frightened rather than comforted by the vision, Bundy sat up abruptly and switched on the lamp. He pictured what would happen after he flattened Jerusalem and Ramzy and Khalidi were blamed. The Israelis would rain nuclear retaliation on the Arab world, triggering Russia's descent on the region as God had foretold in Ezekiel 38. He pulled his Bible from the end table, turned to that passage for comfort:

Son of dust, face northward toward the land of Magog and prophesy against Gog king of Meshech and Tubal. … In distant years you will swoop down onto the land of Israel that will be lying in peace after the return of its people from many lands. … You will come from all over the north with your vast horde of cavalry and cover the land, and my holiness will be vindicated in your terrible destruction before their eyes, so that all the nations will know that I am God.

The accepted interpretation was that the land to the north was Russia. With the help of the United States, Israel would obliterate the Soviet invaders. Ezekiel foretold that the 1948 restoration of Israel "from many lands" signaled the beginning of the everlasting kingdom. They were already living in the End Time; all believing Christians knew that.

Jerusalem would be habitable again in twenty years—a blink of an eye after two thousand years of waiting for Him. With Russia destroyed, the Jews would return and accomplish the vital rebuilding of the Temple. Then a man of mesmerizing authority and power will rise, the most revered leader in the history of the world—the Antichrist. Believing him a man of peace, the Jews will be fooled into making a Covenant with the Antichrist. Frightened, Bundy replayed the promise of 2 Thessalonians 3-4 in his head: *The man of rebellion will come—the son of hell. ... He will go in and sit as God in the temple of God, claiming that he himself is God.*

He would unleash his wrath on earth. As the Battle of Armageddon churned toward its cataclysmic climax and it seemed all life would be sucked into the vortex, at that very moment Christ would return and defeat the Antichrist with a word from his mouth. Greed, hatred, bigotry, war would be replaced by the new world order. The End of Days would be a time of no sorrow, no tears and peace on earth.

Bundy sat back against the wall with the Bible on his lap and trembled. He had sensed, maybe always, that he was destined for something far greater than machining metals. The tension tightening in him now, the way it had before when he used to drink to snap it, he raced to the Book of Revelations, read fiercely but could not concentrate. He pulled the pillow hard over his face, clutched it there. After Khalidi first approached him, he had prayed for weeks for guidance, not daring to believe his calling could be this important. But it became clear over time that all the signs were there. He took the pillow and squeezed it hard to his chest with both arms. The Lord had brought Khalidi to him with the plutonium for a reason, and it was not for a few Palestinians to have a state that would not matter in The End.

Why was he shaking? Why now? He wanted to scream, rip apart this room. But more, he ached with everything inside him for a drink. He could easily make some excuse to go out. He would have a few glasses, just to stop the terrible pressure. It would not matter after tomorrow. He jumped off the bed. The tension was so taut he wanted to slam himself into a wall to break it. He *had* to have a drink. He dropped to the floor and began doing push-ups.

He shoved up and dropped down again and again and again, his arms wavering from the exertion, his breath rasps. He could not start drinking now, he repeated to himself, could not fail Him now. This was His final test.

After exactly fifty, Bundy collapsed onto his stomach sweating hard, muscles aching, his face wet against his forearm. Feeling better, he turned onto his back on the stone floor and saw himself floating in the clouds with Him. The conversation with Judas Iscariot had been a vision sent by Him to comfort him in this hour of need. The police had been intended to discover his name so he would not use the remote control timer and live. It had been ordained that he would meet Him in the clouds now.

Bundy rose, sweat dripping down his back, went to the dresser drawer and searched under the shirts to confirm the hunting knife was there. It was, and he ran his finger gently along the edge of the sharp blade, imagining Khalidi's neck. He waited for dawn.

Shai's helicopter descended in the dark field in front of Moshav Nitzanei Oz just inside the Green Line. From here, the three-kilometer ascent to Tulkarm had been a desolate, mined, no-man's-land before 1967. Shai bounded from the helicopter, Hirsh beside him. A blue license-plated Ascona waited on the side road to Nitzanei Oz, with a plainclothes Sephardi behind the wheel who passed easily as an Arab. Tall cornfields stretched on this side of the narrow roadway. Shai and Hirsh walked past the single pillar of the monument to the area men who had fallen in the Yom Kippur War.

Shai looked at the pillar then turned to Hirsh. "If we live through this, I better get an invitation to a wedding."

Hirsh smiled. "I figure I better ask quick, before she informs me of the date and place."

Shai laughed, enjoying the release. They entered the car, Hirsh in the back, and dust lifted as the Ascona immediately moved.

"I'm Eli," the driver said. He was full-bred sabra: handsome, dark wavy hair, dark eyes, alluring smile. Shai had told the internal service he wanted an expert on Tulkarm to accompany him to the man in the large town with the greatest influence.

"How many main *hamulas* in Tulkarm?" Shai asked, referring to clans/family groups.

"Four. Jalad, Awwad, Karameh, Jayousi. It's a conservative town. Family influence is substantial, in elections too."

"The Awwad family any relation to Ramzy Awwad?"

"No. I'd have heard about it. I'm taking you to Dr. Souheil Jalad. His is the dominant family. He's from the older generation but has excellent relationships with the new young leaders. I phoned him."

Shai settled back in the seat, looked at the stone town sloping up the hills in front of him with minarets rising above the low buildings. Rather than entering the main town, the driver followed a secondary road that skirted it to the left and continued in the direction of the Tulkarm refugee camp, and eventually Nablus.

"Tell me about Dr. Jalad," Shai said.

"One of the leaders of the Arab Nationalist Party in the early

'60s with George Habash before Habash went radical. Member of the Jordanian Parliament in 1962 when they opened it to West Bankers. Lasted about six months. Then an anti-Palestinian prime minister took power over there. I can't remember his name."

"Al-Rifai," Shai said.

"Right. Al-Rifai. Under Jalad's lead, Tulkarm refuses to acknowledge Al-Rifai. The Jordanians march in, break up a big demonstration, execute two dozen, toss Jalad in prison where they break both his arms. Later they jail him again for refusing to take a post in the Jordanian government. Actually, we put him in Sarafand Prison ourselves after the Six-Day War for four months until everything cooled down in the town."

Shai was beginning to have a feel for the man's strength and dignity. "Family?"

"Born in Tulkarm. A number of his brothers and sisters are doctors, some engineers. One brother's a tumor surgeon in Kuwait, went through hell during the Iraqi occupation, beaten pretty brutally." Eli lifted his eyebrows. "I guess the Iraqis temporarily forgot that they had invaded Kuwait to free their Palestinian brothers."

"The rest of the family?"

"There's a sister who's a dentist in London. Our Doctor Jalad went from Cairo University to medical school in the American mid-West somewhere. Kansas, I think. Has three children. None of the family's living here. The brothers and sisters are all over the Arab countries, Europe and the US. His children are in Cleveland and London."

The Palestinian exile, Shai thought, while Israelis were fleeing the turmoil for Los Angeles. The two peoples had great similarities yet understood each other less because of it, could not see the resemblance.

Eli turned right up a side road into the town. Beautiful two- and three-story stone homes surrounded by flowers sat on a bluff overlooking the ocean.

"He's tough," Eli said, "but he's been a moderating force with the young. When someone's killed there's a three-day period of offering condolences and people choose one day to visit."

Shai nodded that he knew.

"He goes all three. Uses it to speak to the young hotheads. He tells them to choose small stones, not to injure but to make our life hell. Urges them to control themselves from revenge, to stick to the philosophy of the stones. I think he genuinely wants to keep them out of the hands of Jihad Islam and Hamas. Is concerned how powerful the fundamentalists are becoming. This is a tough town. The boys go through the stores to make sure there's no Israeli products on the shelves. If they see them a second time, they burn the place."

The car stopped in front of a three-story house surrounded by a high wall that enclosed the inner courtyard. When Eli turned off the motor there was silence, and no lights anywhere in the street except for the bright middle floor of Jalad's home.

Hirsh leaned forward from the back seat, his pistol jutting under his jacket. "I'll watch from here."

Shai nodded.

The outer door in the cement wall was ajar and it squeaked as Shai pushed it open. Eli followed. Inside, Shai caught the small scent of lemons. Tall rose bushes illuminated by the light from the windows rose in front of trees dripping yellow.

They climbed the stone stairs along the side of the home to the middle floor. "What's below?" Shai asked.

"A small medical office. His main office is in town. We let patients come here during curfews."

Dr. Jalad opened the door before they could knock. His face was tanned red behind black-framed glasses, his hair close cropped and gray. He wore a short sleeve, creamed colored shirt that bulged over a slight belly, gray slacks and loafers, and a gold watch.

"Please come in," he said as he turned and walked through the atypically open Arab house with walls knocked down between the lounge, dining room and kitchen in the Western style. He led them to a lounge with two inexpensive brown sofas in an L-shape, a television, and a magnificent view through the open window of fields below, then Netanya, and the ocean flat in the dark beyond the few lights of the city. A grand piano sat in the living room. A copy of *Psychology Today* lay closed on a coffee table crowded with small metal and turquoise turtles. Shai and Eli sat down amidst embroidered pillows.

Jalad sat on the other extension of the couch and waited. Innumerable times he had been summoned to the military governor's office—a sandbag, cement wall, and barbed wire surrounded fortress since the *intifada,* he thought with pleasure. He had been questioned often at home too.

"Dr. Jalad, my name is Shai Shaham."

Jalad shifted in place. The interrogators always called themselves by Arabic names: Major Yusef or Captain Ibrahim.

"I come here at a time of grave emergency for both our peoples. At this moment in Jerusalem, Palestinians have assembled a nuclear bomb. I tell you quite directly that we do not know where they are. They're threatening to destroy the city if we don't withdraw from the West Bank."

Jalad picked up a small turquoise turtle and held it in his hand.

"If they blow up Jerusalem, we have planes armed with nuclear weapons already in the air. We will take out every Arab capital, destroy every refugee camp that is not too close to us. What we will do to the refugee camps that are close I do not want to imagine. As is, we will begin at 7:00 a.m. to withdraw from the Territories." Within hours Jalad would hear of the pullout and he could not lie about it. Shai leaned forward. "This is not the way. I want a state for your people. But there is great danger with this bomb, to your people too, and the mosques."

"If you withdraw, maybe then the danger will be passed," Jalad said, closing his hand over the turtle.

"First, this is not the way to gain your independence. As you people say to us, we must both live in the region together." Shai now played the best hand he had, though it was essentially a bluff. "Second, and far more importantly, we have indications that the man controlling the bomb is, unknown to those helping him, quite unstable. He's a Palestinian-American physicist at UCLA. We've delved into his background and the people who know him there. The bomb was his idea, not that of someone from here. Dr. Jalad, we believe he's planning to detonate the bomb in Jerusalem regardless of whether we withdraw or not."

Shai noticed that as Jalad set the turtle down on the edge of the table his hand shook slightly. Shai was not convinced Khalidi, seeking self-aggrandizement, would *not* detonate.

"Why do you tell this to me?" Jalad asked after a moment.

"The trail to the bomb leads through Tulkarm. We have very little time now. A little over two weeks ago a young Palestinian, Samir Aeid from the health committee, brought fifteen dental x-ray aprons to someone late at night in Tulkarm." Shai removed a dozen small photographs of Khalidi from his front shirt pocket, handed one to Jalad and set the rest on the table. "This is the man we're looking for, the physicist Kenneth Khalidi. I don't know if he's been in your town or not. But someone here knows about the dental shields. They probably know a lot more too. They may have seen Khalidi somewhere else, near the Lebanese border, in Tel Aviv."

Jalad set the picture down on the table, made no move toward the others. He pulled off his glasses, began carefully cleaning the lenses with a handkerchief from his pocket.

"We can help each other," Shai said. "I need your help to prevent Jerusalem from going up. Tulkarm can benefit from our assistance. You need manufacturing to supplement the agriculture that's traditionally sustained you."

"Like your kibbutzim," Jalad said.

"Exactly. We need the microchip alongside the orange tree. You no longer import our pickled products—olives, eggplant, cucumbers, carrots—that we both know are tremendously popular in all the West Bank. There's not a single factory for producing those products in the Territories."

"I am obviously aware of this."

"I'll get you half of what you need—two hundred and fifty thousand dollars." Shai did not know if he could pry the money through Carmon. If not, he would go to Sam Wolf and his friends in Los Angeles. "We'll make it look like the money came through the Spanish government. Your people are out of work because they don't want to work for us anymore. I'll help you start them working here in Tulkarm, for Tulkarm and for all the West Bank."

Jalad slowly returned his handkerchief to his pocket. He retrieved the small photograph of Khalidi again. "He has the bomb been assembled?"

"Yes."

Jalad was silent for a long moment. He could not fathom Jerusalem destroyed. He believed in the revolution of the stones, not in jihad or nuclear weapons that could obliterate everything here for them too.

"I promise nothing but I'll see what I can learn. How may I reach you?"

Shai gave him Tami's work number. He would have her rush to the office and not budge from her desk. He would wait at Nitzanei Oz. "I'll remain nearby," Shai said.

Jalad nodded.

As Shai left with Eli, the first morning light was a pale streak on the horizon.

In an ornate, book-lined study in Paris's sixteenth arrondissement, Ramzy hung up the phone, the report that convoys of empty Israeli military vehicles and buses were streaming into the West Bank reverberating through him. The curling yellow sheets of his hand-penned story on the desk before him, Ramzy initially did not stir from the chair in the apartment of the oil-elevated couple from Dubai. Slowly he rose, not allowing himself any excitement. Yet.

He went to the window and looked at the swollen gray clouds. He feared that somehow at the last moment this too would be snatched from him. He asked himself if he would be able to continue into the wind like before if it was. He was not certain he would. He pressed his face to the cold window, watched rain begin to dot the dry sidewalk, and held on to the fact the Israelis were withdrawing. When he came away, his face left a print of forehead nose and lips on the glass. He drew a smile on the window over the frowned lips and smiled himself. Ramzy returned to the desk. Though the hours flew now, the seconds crawled.

When the withdrawal was complete he would tell them where to locate the bomb. It appeared, as he had hoped, that he would not need to alert the world publicly to the danger of the nuclear weapon in the holy city.

Still, the thought of the bomb in Jerusalem unnerved him, and he would rest far easier once it was disassembled. He had needed a live bomb to make his threat of the second bomb credible.

Ramzy looked at the sheets of his story then lifted his fountain pen, wanted to finish "Return to Jaffa" this morning, about a family's visit to pre-1948 home and then a return to Ramallah, and mail it to the Cairo newspaper that printed his stories. Whatever happened in the next twenty-four hours, it was imperative that all his people, in and outside the Territories, faced that there was no permanent return to Haifa and Jaffa. He wanted this story printed, not knowing how long he would remain alive now.

Giora Weizmann stood inside room 1012 in the Plaza Hotel with a bevy of uniformed and plainclothes police officers as the two covered bodies were slowly wheeled down the hall. An occasional camera still flashed as the room was being ransacked for clues Weizmann did not expect them to find. He walked slowly out into the hallway, looked down at the bloodstains and, a quiet anger running through him, leaned against the wall. None of this made sense.

He had every available police officer in the city in search of the white Subaru. Weizmann also had the border patrol, airport and ports alerted.

Finding himself at the elevators, Weizmann pushed the button. He did not know what he had here, but the trail had gone cold.

Shai waited impatiently in the small office in Moshav Nitzanei Oz. He checked his watch again and it had managed to move ahead by three minutes. A plate of demolished grapes sat in front of him that had done nothing to abate his craving for actual food. Dr. Jalad had phoned Tami, then Shai had quickly phoned Jalad's house. Jalad had discovered something and was coming to see him.

Finally, Shai heard a car on the road and he hustled outside. A warm ocean breeze carried the scent of manure and he could hear the rumble of a tractor somewhere. Jalad and Eli climbed from Jalad's Daihatsu sedan. Hirsh stood beneath a tree, gun in easy reach. Eli remained outside as Jalad joined Shai in the small office. Neither sat.

"This man you seek, Khalidi. He was in Tulkarm two nights ago," Jalad said. "Very late at night."

The same night they assaulted the sofa factory. At least that confirmed he was not in Tel Aviv but in Jerusalem.

"I will not tell you how I learned this," Jalad said. "I do not know where they went and I am convinced I have all the information the man knows. Khalidi was in his establishment. They assembled something from two lead blocks back-to-back, the front one with a hole. Clearly, it was part of the bomb."

"Who was Khalidi with?"

"An American. He did not speak Arabic. He is in his late forties to mid-fifties, tall, strong body, blond hair, blond moustache."

"His name?"

"He was not called any name that anyone heard. He was only here for a short while, some minutes. I asked this question several times. It was obvious that you would need to know. I was quite specific."

"Did he have a car?"

"No, he was brought here by Palestinians."

An American could move easily anywhere. He needed a name, the car, something to trace him from. Shai felt calmer occupied with the search.

"Is there anyone from Tulkarm with them?"

"From Tulkarm, no."

"Other Palestinians?" Shai knew Ramzy would have Arabs he could trust with them.

"There are two others we know of. I will not tell you who, but I can assure you that no one in their families or cities knows where they are. I have already checked this myself. If they did, I would tell you. The families will call me if there is any news and I will alert you. They have also never seen the American or his car."

"The car the Palestinians drove?" He could have the police and army out on the streets searching for it.

"It has been brought to me. I do not know where it was. I have returned it to friends in Taybeh."

Shai believed him. He would not have told him all this and withheld information about a vehicle.

"Dr. Jalad, I must identify these two men. If this bomb's exploded…"

"I cannot tell you. I swore on my honor to obtain the information I give you. You may take me in and use your drugs and clubs, but then you will inflame an already tense situation in Tulkarm, maybe in all the West Bank. Though I am old, I can assure you that I'm still quite stubborn. The information, by the time you have it, will in all likelihood be too late. Again, I tell you these men's identities will not lead you where you need to go. I am convinced the families do not know. If I was assembling a nuclear bomb, I would not tell my parents where I was doing it. Nor my friends."

Jalad removed his glasses and held them in his hand, his eyes soft, seeming vulnerable without the glasses, but his voice was firm. "I do this not for your factory, which we need and will take in exchange for my assistance. I do this because it is right."

"Is there anything else?"

"About this incident, no. About the will of the Palestinian people to have a homeland, I think you and the Americans have much to learn."

Shai reached out his hand. "Dr. Jalad, thank you. You will be hearing from me."

Jalad slipped his glasses back on and took the Israeli's outstretched hand. "You are welcome in my home at any time."

As Jalad left, Shai called Tami to tell her he was helicoptering home. The American was their best lead, but how could they possibly identify him. There were over two hundred thousand Americans in the country—immigrants, tourists, press. He started to tell her about the American.

She interrupted. "In his fifties, blond, blond moustache?"

"How do you know that?"

"Shai, we just got a report from Giora Weizmann with the Jerusalem police. An American named Hal Bundy fled a car accident then killed two police officers in the Plaza Hotel who went to question him. He's disappeared."

"Weizmann's number."

She gave it to him.

The army's Special Unit for the Fighting of Terror had moved into the police compound in the heart of Jerusalem and was ready to move in an instant. "Alert the anti-terror unit. Check all the rental agencies to see if Bundy's rented an apartment or house. Check the back newspaper ads too. If you can't match the name, give them the description. He'd probably want a house but don't overlook apartments. I'll call back." There were relatively few detached houses in the city.

Shai paced with the phone at his ear.

Bundy had been using his real name all along. Hiding in plain sight. After waiting for several maddening minutes while they searched police headquarters for Weizmann, during which time Shai considered hanging up and recalling from the helicopter, he finally got Weizmann on the line. Shai explained quickly who he was.

"He hit the boy Tuesday afternoon near Gilo." He gave Shai the Subaru's license number.

Shai thanked him, ran outside, his feet for some unexpected reason not hurting, and waved to Hirsh. From the helicopter, he called Tami and gave her the Subaru's license and instructions to flood the city and find it, break into garages if necessary.

Downstairs in the Ein Kerem house, Khalidi, Bundy and Omar sipped coffee at the kitchen table, Omar's AK-47 across his legs. Plates with the remains of food sat before them.

Bundy had finally slept for a few hours and woke feeling better, having overcome the urge for alcohol. He hoped it had been his last temptation. He watched Khalidi, considered shooting both him and

Omar in the kitchen, but even with the muffled bullets Tariq might hear upstairs. He would take Tariq first, now, quietly with the knife.

"Gotta use the bathroom," Bundy said.

Omar lifted his cup, was starting to have second thoughts about this bomb, wished the revered Ramzy Awwad was here and he could discuss his doubts with him.

Bundy strode out the kitchen and up the stone tile steps. Inside his room, he closed the door and pulled the Walther PPK/S from the closet. He went to the dresser, opened the top drawer and placed the gun there in the event he needed it. He covered it with a single shirt and pushed the drawer partially closed with his thigh. Birds sang in the pines outside, and Bundy believed these particular birds would be singing in the clouds with Him soon.

He opened the second drawer, checked under the top sweater and felt the large knife. Then he picked up the car cellular phone on top of the dresser and took it into the bathroom with him. He ran the sink water and dialed the country code for the United States, the code for San Diego and his home number. He waited as the call went through. After two rings, he heard a fumbling with the receiver. Mary would be asleep at this hour.

"Hello," she said groggily. The connection was clear.

"It's me, dear."

"Hal. Hello. How are you?"

He had told her he was returning to the Holy Land to resume bringing the Gospel to the Jews. "Fine. Look, I can hardly hear you," he lied.

"I hear you perfectly, Hal."

"Maybe the problem's on this end. I'll give you a number. Splash some water on your face, take a moment to wake up, then call me back."

"All right. Can you hear that?"

"Yes, dear, but not well."

"Let me just find a pen," she said, yawning. "Okay, I've got it. Go ahead."

He gave her the number.

"I'll call you back in two minutes."

"Good."

He hung up, turned off the water, crossed to the room and placed the phone on the bureau. Then he opened the door to the hallway and stepped across it.

At the foot of the stairs, Bundy saw Omar coming out of the kitchen with a cup of coffee in one hand and his assault rifle in the other and suddenly Bundy worried that he was bringing the coffee up to Tariq and they would both be back in the room. But Omar eased down on the soft living room chair. Bundy heard Khalidi in the kitchen washing the dishes.

The cellular phone rang.

Bundy hurried to it, released the receiver and said hello.

"That better?" Mary asked.

"Hold on for a moment," he said and put the receiver down.

Bundy hurried into the hallway and, from the entrance to the bedroom with the bomb, spoke to Tariq, who was already moving toward him having heard the phone. "It's Ramzy. He wants to talk to you."

Bundy turned and walked quickly back into the bedroom as Tariq followed. Bundy went to the open dresser drawer and let Tariq, AK-47 in his left hand, move for the phone on top of it. As he had hoped, Omar had remained downstairs. Even if he had come up the stairs, he would have had time to take Tariq silently first.

Bundy stood by Tariq. As Tariq lifted the receiver, his back to him, Bundy reached for the knife. He grasped the handle and fiercely swung toward Tariq's throat.

Feeling the American too close as he brought the receiver to his ear, Tariq abruptly turned. Terrified, he saw the knife coming at him. "Omar," he shouted, his voice muffled with a gurgle as the blade thrust in. He felt searing pain. Everything slipped from his fingers, the machine gun and phone clattering against the dresser. Unable to talk, he felt the blade come out and immediately slam back in.

Bundy released the knife, let the dead body drop to the floor. Omar was pounding up the stairs. Bundy quickly swiped his bloodied hand against his shirt, yanked the other drawer open, pulled out the pistol and dropped prone behind Tariq's leaking body, the nose of the suppressor on the dead man's rear.

Omar approached the doorway cautiously, leaned partially in, gun leveled. A bullet whooshed at him, exploded into his shoulder, and he fired at the motion behind Tariq's body, the bullets jerked too high. In pain, Omar dropped back from the doorway and leaned against the wall breathing hard, his vision cloudy with agony as blood flowed from the wound.

Bundy stretched an arm cautiously out to Tariq's AK-47 on the floor, grabbed the handle and drew the weapon to him. He had hit Omar. He had the advantage and Khalidi was unarmed and inexperienced. Bundy lifted the AK-47. He had handled a lot of these Russian rifles in Nam. He did not know how seriously he had wounded the Arab but could hear him breathing hard in the hallway. Still shielded by Tariq, Bundy pulled the magazine from the PPK/S. He tossed it through the entranceway into the hall, where the metal clattered noisily on the tiles.

Shots burst in the direction of the magazine and Bundy saw Omar's AK-47 extended in the doorway. Bundy fired a burst at the assault rifle, hit it, and the AK-47 flew from Omar's grasp. Bundy was up and running as Omar dove on the stone tiles for the rifle. Bundy fired into Omar's large body, hit him as he groped on the ground and his hands fell still. Bundy approached, heaved him over with a foot, bent and felt for his pulse. None.

He came down the stairs in search of Khalidi, the assault rifle raised. The kitchen water was off. He moved slowly, heard no sounds anywhere.

"Kenneth, these two were not with us," Bundy called out. "Everything's okay."

No response.

Bundy entered the living room and surveyed it. Khalidi could have taken a knife from the kitchen. No movement. "Kenneth."

Silence. If the amateur somehow managed to kill or disable him, the Palestinian plot, ironically, would still be operational. Bundy gave the couch a wide berth and peered behind it but Khalidi was not there. He could be in a closet or waiting behind a corner with a makeshift weapon. Bundy moved to the kitchen, peered in from the entrance. Silence. He entered, caution in his steps. Khalidi was strong from his jogging, could leap quickly with those muscled legs. The refrigerator suddenly hummed and he spun but it was only the motor.

"Kenneth, we're friends, not like the others. I won't hurt you. You have my word."

Bundy stepped toward the hallway, would spray each of the closets. There were no sounds and the silence was beginning to unnerve him. Where was this stupid kid? Bundy removed his damp hand from the rifle and quickly wiped it on his pants. He darted around the corner of the stairs, rifle pointed. No one. Bundy looked up the stairs. He had left the other assault rifle there. He better go pull the magazine. Frustrated, he turned and fired a horizontal burst into the hall closet, the shots ripping through the wood in an erratic line. He moved to the closet door and yanked it open. A single jacket hung on a hanger there, swaying.

Bundy decided he would hear Khalidi heading for the stairs and would be able to cut him down before he was halfway up. He walked back into the kitchen. There was a closet tall enough for someone to hide in across from the refrigerator, and a rear bedroom through there. Where was the jerk? He would not ruin everything. Bundy slowly reached for the pantry door, twisted the knob, and quickly pulled it open. Cleaning implements.

Moistening his lips, Bundy continued into the back bedroom. He had to be there. From a distance, Bundy crouched, AK-47 extended, and peered under the bed. Empty. He did not think even Khalidi was stupid enough to hide under the bed. He circled around an armchair, giving it wide berth, but Khalidi was not there. A smile came to his lips as he looked at the closed closet. He raised the rifle, aimed low at the door expecting Khalidi would be crouching. He fired a quick burst into the wood, heard something fall with a thud inside against the door. Bundy moved forward cautiously. The closet might be too wide for him to have hit Khalidi and he might be clever enough to fake the sound.

He sprayed another burst high in the door in case there was a shelf.

Then, through the kitchen, he heard a sound—the garage door lifting downstairs. Panic went through him. Bundy bolted into the kitchen, raced down the inside stairs, darted between the Subaru and the Peugeot, and burst outside through the raised door. Across the street, he saw Khalidi running. Bundy raised his rifle, finger on the trigger.

Khalidi disappeared down the steps toward the house there. Bundy ran after him. Reaching the sidewalk, he stopped. Neighbors may have heard the shots or might see him with the weapon. Khalidi would continue into the olive forest and might hide behind a tree there and jump him. Khalidi did not matter anyway. The bomb was inside the house.

Bundy hurried back into the garage, purposely left the aluminum door open, and then hustled up the stairs. He went directly to the bedroom with the weapon. It would take him less than a minute to place the fibers inside the laser and flip the switch. He could destroy all of Jerusalem from here.

But there was one problem. He was in a valley and was worried that the hills might cushion and absorb the blast. There were not many private houses in this city of apartment blocks, and this was the most private one he had found available for rental. It would have been too dangerous to have Arabs coming in and out of an apartment building. Bundy set the AK-47 down, retrieved the pistol and snapped the magazine in. Back in the bedroom, first he picked up the neutron gun, whose single optical fiber running through the large spool, had not yet been slipped into the laser. He placed the cement block gun on the spool and PPK/S in his back pocket and carried them both down to the Peugeot. He had left the garage door open because he wanted a full view of the street and surrounding area each time he came down. He was not concerned neighbors might see him placing boxes into his car.

After three trips to the garage and his shirt changed, Bundy had the bomb completely assembled in the rear seat. The bunched strands of fibers from the back, including the single strand from the neutron gun, were neatly inserted into the laser in easy reach beside him in the passenger seat. Bundy backed the Peugeot into the street, stopped, climbed quickly out of the car and closed the garage door so the Subaru would not be visible. Probably an unnecessary precaution, he thought.

Bundy drove toward the center of the city. The two mosques atop the Temple Mount had to be razed for the Temple to be rebuilt.

Across the street, his shirt sticking to his stomach from the heat and the nervous fear, Khalidi waited behind a bush. He had just watched Bundy pull away.

Khalidi ran hard, yanked open the light garage door. He had seen the Subaru keys on a dresser in Bundy's room. He ran upstairs, trying hard not to look at the dead Palestinians. The keys in his hand he picked up the car phone from the floor, felt the nausea rising inside him, ran, and in the hall skidded on Omar's blood.

He jumped in the Subaru, backed out with a screech, and roared up the hill. He knew what Bundy intended, had to stop him. He fumbled with the phone nervously against the wheel as he dialed Ramzy. Then he saw Bundy's burgundy Peugeot at the top of the hill.

As the helicopter descended in Jerusalem, Shai's fear was like the ache of an injury that disappeared with motion but throbbed through him now as he sat. As the skids touched down on the grass area beside the ministry, Tami pulled the helicopter door open. Shai and Hirsh hurried down.

"We located the house," Tami said loudly over the slowing rotors. "In Ein Kerem, rented under Bundy's name."

Shai spoke under the pounding rotors. "When will they get there?"

"Two minutes. The anti-terror unit."

"They know to stay well back?" With the withdrawal begun, they did not want to scare a nervous finger into detonating.

Tami nodded. "They're taking thermal imaging." To locate those inside she did not need to add. "We still have every police officer in Jerusalem on the street looking for the Subaru. In case it's not there."

Shai nodded.

Bundy felt a surprise jolt as a car smashed into him from behind. His seatbelt snug, his chest hurt but he was fine. He glanced in the mirror and saw Khalidi in his Subaru. Bundy smiled. Didn't think the kid had it in him. Bundy cursed that he had not brought a gun with him; with God's guidance, had not thought he would need one. He punched the gas and raced toward the top of the rise, looked in the mirror. The Subaru, its front smashed, was speeding after him.

Hands gripped tight on the steering wheel, Khalidi was crazed, had to stop Bundy from triggering the bomb and destroying everything, both his dreams and this city.

Shai sat alone in his car outside the ministry. He had just learned of the two dead in the Ein Kerem house and that the bomb, Khalidi and Bundy were gone, as was the Subaru. When the thermal imaging had shown two likely dead, the ionization equipment reading almost no signal of plutonium, no other occupants, and the garage open, Shai had agreed with Carmon that they send in a lone nineteen-year-old female soldier in civilian clothes, who was with them for just such a contingency, to pose as the owner's daughter's friend. When nobody answered the doorbell, she took the garage stairs inside.

Shai worked his way through the options of what had happened. The bomb was now in the Subaru. The FBI had Bundy as a former army officer with drinking problems and a hardcore Evangelical. Khalidi wanted a state, not devastation, and would not likely have killed Ramzy's men even if he had the prowess, which he did not. Shai felt it before the thoughts coalesced into clarity—the stone mountains of Ein Kerem would muffle the blast.

From Ein Kerem, there were two routes toward the Temple Mount: straight along the congested Jaffa Road to the Old City, or climb through Ramat Eshkol to Mount Scopus and the Mount of Olives. Shai picked up his car phone and had Carmon disseminate what Bundy was doing. He expected that Bundy had killed Khalidi too and they were searching Ein Kerem for his body. They had roadblocks, and teams of sharpshooters hidden all over the city.

"Get rid of all the roadblocks, leave the sharpshooters hidden,"

Shai said, explaining that if threatened with being stopped Bundy would detonate on the spot. Once out of the Ein Kerem valley, anywhere was high enough to destroy Jerusalem. Shai sped toward the climb to Ramat Eshkol and the unobstructed views of the Temple Mount.

Just past the circular tower of The Hilton Hotel, Shai's phone rang. They'd spotted the Subaru only five minutes ahead of where Shai was now. Sharpshooters were in place a few minutes ahead of the car. Shai drove maniacally, hand nonstop on his horn. And then he spotted the Subaru halfway up the hill ahead of him.

A small wisp of steam rose from Khalidi's engine. Inside, he collapsed in depression, as on the rise he had fallen back two car lengths behind Bundy. Khalidi pushed the accelerator to the floor, but not only was he not catching up, he was slowing.

Shai was right behind the Subaru when he saw the front windshield and all the side windows shatter as sharpshooters hit the driver's head simultaneously from five directions. The car started to roll backward downhill. Just as Shai's car phone rang, Shai halted the rolling car with his own's front bumper. Shai ignored the phone, was the first on the scene. He yanked open the driver's door, saw the mess of a dark-skinned man slumped on the wheel, and felt the loneliest terror of his life—neither the bomb nor Bundy was in the car. Vaguely aware his car phone continued to ring, Shai grabbed the keys from the Subaru's ignition and ran to the trunk. He put the key in and opened it, but it too was empty.

His phone was insistent and Shai lumbered to it. He leaned in and grabbed the receiver.

"It's Ramzy. A burgundy Peugeot 505. Bundy has the bomb in it. I don't know his route."

Shai said nothing and hung up. Climbing into the car, he simultaneously called Carmon, rolled down his passenger window, and took the PPK from his glove compartment. He backed up, jerked around the Subaru and raced toward Mount Scopus and the road up ahead that forked to the Mount of Olives. Just then, Shai spotted Bundy's car and moderated his speed so he would both close the gap but not appear to be barreling at him.

Bundy looked in the rearview mirror and saw a car nearing but it was not Khalidi, which did not surprise him since he had noticed the steam rising from his engine. Khalidi had not been able to follow him further. As the road climbed, he saw a park up ahead and looked down at the map again. The greenery was Ammunition Hill. Beyond it, Bundy could see the tall buildings of the university that covered Mount Scopus.

At the next intersection, he would turn right along Wadi al-Joz, which would take him directly into East Jerusalem and the Mount of Olives. In minutes, the New Age would be accomplished. *Thou shall not depart from Jerusalem,* Luke said in Acts. To Bundy's surprise, he thought about Mary. He had never told anyone—except for a Vietnamese prostitute he visited in Little Saigon in Orange County whenever he had to drive up to Los Angeles—but Mary was a bore. He was rather happy not to spend any more time with her.

Bundy placed the map on his lap and returned his hand to the bomb trigger. In the sweetness of His presence, joy gathered in his throat. A wide grass divider separated the two directions of the roadway. Seven- and eight-story stone apartment buildings lined both sides of the street, low stone walls in front of them. Bundy approached the intersection that would lead him to the Mount of Olives. He drove now with a more complete peace than he had ever known.

Shai gained on the Peugeot, eased alongside as if to pass it, as Israelis did wantonly. Bundy's window was rolled up. Shai held his gun low in the passenger seat, knew it would be too risky to sight on him with the bomb trigger certainly in the American's fingers, if not easy reach. And though Shai hated guns, there was something only Hirsh knew about his relationship with them.

Bundy simultaneously heard the shattering of glass and felt unimaginable pain in his head, but he did not hear the second and third bullets, as he was already dead when they crashed through the window and tore off the left side of his skull. Bundy's body dropped forward against the steering wheel. Shai continued past the Peugeot whose forward momentum luckily slowed on the rise. As it slowed even further, Shai maneuvered in front of the car and the Peugeot hit his softly and stopped.

What only Hirsh knew was that Shai practiced obsessively at a public firing range as a challenge to keep up with Hirsh's score.

Shai did not move as police and army vehicles screamed to the scene. Giora Weizmann checked for a pulse on Bundy's neck. Confirming he was dead, he pulled Bundy to the street, got in, shut off the motor and gently put the car in park. Police vehicles blocked off the roadway in both directions. Police in the street ordered people back into their cars until the street was clear. A woman in her late thirties carrying a small toolbox walked calmly from a police car toward the Peugeot. She was not in uniform, her hair in a chestnut ponytail.

Shai slowly approached the Peugeot, his legs weak and shaking, as if now that the danger was over he could allow himself to feel it.

The ponytailed physicist from The Hebrew University climbed inside the car and began removing the optical fibers from the laser.

Shai stood by the window and said nothing.

Soon, she climbed out. "Shai, I'll take the neutron source then you can move it. It won't detonate, but gently is still encouraged."

Shai managed a small smile. He adored his people.

The physicist came around to the rear door, opened it, and snipped the optical fiber that led to the large spool. Then she began carefully removing the lead shields from around the crate. She retrieved something that looked like two lead blocks face-to-face then replaced the shields. As she stepped out of the car with the twin blocks, she pointed toward a cartridge imbedded in the front block. "The Californium's here."

A silver Audi was allowed through the lower police roadblock and Shai saw Carmon speeding toward them. Shai needed to leave. Not that he was avoiding Carmon personally, he was simply exhausted and did not want to talk at all. An army vehicle pulled up. An officer stepped out, slipped behind the wheel of the Peugeot and started the engine. Shai was quickly in his own car. The Peugeot moved up the hill with police cars front and back, sirens on, blue and white lights rotating. Shai drove ahead, and as they turned back toward the city, he continued to Mount Scopus.

Atop the mountain, he sat on a low stone wall and stared out at the desert, thought about his time there with his father, whom he so loved and feeling a little guilty about it, hoped he would have a son.

EPILOGUE

July 22

Shai sat on a bench in the Santa Monica Palisades Park that overlooked the blue-gray ocean and waited for Ramzy. Shai had been swimming so much he'd lost twelve pounds the first two weeks and his dietician ordered him to slow down. The sea breeze brushed through the palm and eucalyptus trees on the narrow, mile-long green park. From below the cliff, car noise rose from the Pacific Coast Highway. Across the highway was a row of small houses, then a wide beach, empty at nine in the morning, with a concrete bicycle path snaking alongside the clean sand. An occasional roller skater glided along the path. A few birds flapped low over the water.

To the north, haze half covered the Malibu Mountains. In front of him, an older couple had brought chairs and a folding table and played checkers. A black-bearded artist with a paisley cap and plastic containers of paint had set a white T-shirt on an easel and was boldly stroking an ocean scene on it. Shai loved Los Angeles.

He saw the curly haired Ramzy walking across Ocean Avenue toward him, his step even. Ramzy had phoned him at home and asked to meet him here alone. Shai had agreed and not told Carmon, who would have stationed an assassin behind each of the numerous palms.

As he watched Ramzy near, Shai was like someone bucked up by hatred for a betraying lover, but who felt that rage slipping once he saw the person. What remained was vulnerability.

Ramzy reached him. "Hello, Shai."

"Come, sit," Shai said. For Shai, friendship was an emotion that moved naturally to the surface like a submerged diver needing air.

As Ramzy sat, he reached in his pocket, removed a key and held it toward Shai, who made no move for it.

"About two miles from here on Wilshire Boulevard," Ramzy said. "Bekins Storage. Number sixty-eight on the third floor. Use the name Vincent Thomas. I took the liberty." Ramzy produced a California driver's license with Shai's photo on it.

Shai smiled.

"The plutonium's there in a lead box."

Shai took the key and license and remained silent.

"I'm not here to apologize."

"I don't think we'd have stopped Bundy in time without your and Khalidi's help." Shai stood. "You wouldn't have blown it, would you?"

"I would not have. But if this situation continues next time someone else will. If your hearts are closed, open your eyes."

A truck rumbled past on the street. They started to walk toward the pier without speaking.

Finally Shai said, "Have you thought about writing that big novel?"

"Yes, often."

"If you wait for the conflict to end, I fear you may never write it."

Ramzy laughed. "You have a point."

AUTHOR' S NOTE

Events in the Palestinian village of Beita occurred as described in the novel. Subsequently a group of Israelis formed The Beita Committee and raised money to rebuild demolished homes, replant olive groves and provide legal representation for the imprisoned villagers.

The writings of Ramzy Awwad are loosely based on the work of the Palestinian writer Ghassan Kanafani (1936 - 1972.)

The first Palestinian *intifada* lasted from December 1987 until 1993 when the Oslo Peace Accords were signed. Twelve hundred Palestinians were killed and tens of thousands of Palestinian children injured by Israeli soldiers. Sixty Israeli soldiers and a hundred Jewish civilians lost their lives.

The second *intifada* began in September 2000 when Ariel Sharon, the leader of the Likud party, visited the Temple Mount with a vast complement of Israeli police officers. Stone throwing protesters were met with tear gas and rubber bullets. The violence escalated. On the Palestinian side it was marked by suicide bombers and shootings; on the Israeli, by aerial bombardments, tank fire and targeted assassinations. In early 2005, Palestinian and Israeli leaders committed to a roadmap for peace that mostly ended the turmoil. The toll was three thousand Palestinians and a thousand Israelis dead.

Increased tensions in 2016-2017, often marked by Palestinian stabbings of Israeli checkpoint officers, many of these assailants shot dead, is sometimes called The Knives Intifada. It did not develop into a national uprising.

Made in the USA
Middletown, DE
19 February 2019